T0147194

THE SEATTLE CHANGES

A
Ray Neslowe
Mystery

Also by Eric B. Olsen

Fiction

Death In The Dentist's Chair

Dark Imaginings

Proximal to Murder

Death's Head

If I Should Wake Before I Die

Non-Fiction

Ethan Frome: Analysis in Context

The Intellectual American: Essays

The Films of Jon Garcia: 2009-2013

The Death of Education

THE SEATTLE CHANGES

A Ray Neslowe Mystery

ERIC B. OLSEN

authorHOUSE®

AuthorHouse™
1663 Liberty Drive
Bloomington, IN 47403
www.authorhouse.com
Phone: 1 (800) 839-8640

Published by AuthorHouse 05/21/2019

ISBN: 978-1-7283-0992-7 (sc)
ISBN: 978-1-7283-0991-0 (e)

Print information available on the last page.

This book is printed on acid-free paper.

for Laura

INTRODUCTION

While *The Seattle Changes* was the last novel I ever wrote, it easily had the longest gestation period of any of them. In 1991, sometime after I had finished writing my first novel, *Death's Head*, I read a story in the Seattle paper about a small Portland publisher called DimeNovels! that intended on putting out twelve short novels every month in a variety of genres. The stories were each about a hundred pages and came in cardboard displays that were intended for the check out counters at grocery stores, gas stations, drug stores and the like. The first thing I thought of writing for them was a detective story, and so I sat down and tried to write the most intriguing first chapter I could think of. But since I had no plot in mind and had written no outline, I soon bogged down without any real idea of where the story was going. Then it occurred to me that simply expanding something I had already written would be a much easier and far quicker task, so that's what I did. I took a story called "2:00 a.m. Feeding," fleshed it out to a hundred pages, and changed the title to *Blood Feast*. But DimeNovels! went out of business the following year and it would be two more decades before I included the novella and its sequel in my collection of short horror fiction, *If I Should Wake Before I Die*.

The first chapter of that untitled mystery, however, went into a file, then migrated to a cardboard box in the garage for the next fifteen years while I pursued a career in teaching. But I continued to read detective fiction at the time, and even managed to find a literary agent who wanted to represent me and try to sell my two dental mysteries. Since I had never sent out my horror novel, *Dark Imaginings*, to anyone I also decided to give it a polish and see if she might want to try selling that as well, but she disliked it and said she was only interested in the two mystery stories. The reason this is important is that at the end of *Dark Imaginings* the main character begins writing his novels on a manual typewriter, and so it wasn't long before I became intrigued with the idea of writing a novel like that myself. When my wife Laura bought me an old Underwood typewriter for our anniversary, I immediately thought that the opening chapter of my detective novel would be a great way to start a new book. So I painstakingly retyped that first chapter, giving it a good edit, thinking I would work on it in a slow and methodical way and in a year or two have another mystery novel to my credit. But I found I had the same problem that I did the first time—with no plot in mind, nothing came of that revised first chapter either.

Several things happened over the course of the next few years that account for the present story. The first was that my agent had been unable to sell my dental mystery series, and so that led me to go the self-publishing route and put them out myself. One of the things she said to me at the time, however, was that perhaps I should try a different protagonist, a regular private eye instead of a dentist. That was all well and good, but with teaching full time and becoming more interested in writing non-fiction I didn't think too much more about it. Another thing that happened, at the very beginning of my teaching career, is that I had to stop drinking coffee. One day at school my heart began to race so fast that I thought I might have to call an ambulance to take me to the hospital. Fortunately, my prep period started just a few minutes later and after my heart rate returned to something approximating normal I made the decision not to drink anything with caffeine in it again, especially coffee. It wasn't until after we had moved down to San Jose in 2003 that I thought about taking a crack at another novel, a true detective novel as my agent had suggested. Once again that opening chapter I had written became the starting point . . . and once again I floundered. There was a difference, though. This time I did have a story idea and had outlined several chapters, but I just couldn't seem to get anything on the page when I sat down to write.

During our stay in California, Laura had enrolled in a hypnotherapy school in Marin County and occasionally she would practice the things she learned on me. One day I told her that I was stuck in my attempt to write a new novel and she said I should try hypnosis to see if it might make a difference. What came out of that session—something I had completely forgotten about—was that when I had been writing fiction in the past I would always drink coffee while I was working. But since giving up coffee because of my heart I hadn't touched it. Laura suggested that I get some decaf, make my coffee just as I had before, and see if it made a difference. Did it ever. Instead of diving into the novel, though, I thought about seeing if I could complete a short story first. Well, with my cup of decaf at my elbow, I was able to churn out the thirty-page Steve Raymond, D.D.S. short story, "Lying Through Your Teeth," in a week's time. I polished it as best I could, then sent it out to *Alfred Hitchcock's Mystery Magazine*, and was delighted when a few weeks later I received an email from the editor saying that she wanted it for a future issue. But for some reason I still didn't go back to the novel right away, and decided to exercise my rediscovered writing powers even further by attempting another lengthy short story featuring the detective from my new novel: Ray Neslowe. The result was "The Olympia Riff." With two stories now under my belt—one of them sold to a national magazine—I finally turned my attention to what I had decided to call *The Seattle Changes*.

What I love about the title is the same thing that struck me the first time I heard the name of Kevin Costner's film *Dances With Wolves*. Without any other context the word "dances" initially seems as if it's the noun, that there were some kind of dances taking place associated with wolves. It's only after watching the movie that it becomes clear "dances" is a present tense verb, something that the main character is actually doing. With my title the opposite happens. Out of context, the first thing that comes to mind is that the word "changes" is a present-tense verb, that the city somehow undergoes a transformation. But as the first epigram preceding the novel makes clear, the word is actually a noun that jazz musicians use when referring to the chord progression of a song. Initially, the whole point of writing the novel was to take my Steve Raymond character from the dental mysteries and simply convert him to a private eye. Since my dentist was a lover of jazz, I did the same for my new protagonist. I also used my dad's name again, this time for the detective's first name instead of his last. The idea for his last name came from an old girlfriend of mine who liked to spell people's names backwards to see what they sounded like. Mine was Neslo, but that didn't look like a real name, so then I had the idea to add a "we" to the end so that it would look more like Marlowe, Raymond Chandler's quintessential California private eye. And thus the name Ray Neslowe was born.

One of the challenges associated with publishing my other fiction had been the question of whether or not to update the stories, which ultimately I decided not to do. This, however, is the first of my novels that actually could have been updated, as it is the first that contains cell phones and the Internet, but in the end the story simply wouldn't allow for it. The idea for that story also came out of my time in California. Laura was working for eBay at the time, in their corporate offices in San Jose, and computer fraud was just beginning to become a major issue, especially phishing and identity theft. Today, however, these are fairly well known cons, and so even had I updated everything else I still would have been left with a subplot that was dated, and no real desire to create something entirely new to take it's place. So, as with the other novels, I made the decision to leave everything as it was, complete with flip phones, Gateway computers, AOL discs, dial up Internet, and brand new innovations like thumb drives and a search engine called Google. The novel also makes mention in a few places of recent airline restrictions that had been implemented in the wake of the 9-11 attacks, along with a bunch of obscure references to some of my favorite movies—though this may be the first novel I ever wrote that doesn't have a reference to *Jaws* in it.

Something else that struck me as I was editing the book was how much of my fictional world I had brought back in order to connect the story to the rest of my works, especially my horror writings. Carl Serafin, who only had a cameo in *Dark Imaginings*, is my protagonist's lawyer. And from that same novel came Stanford Dalton and John Haggerty, who were first created by my friend Patrick for the unfinished horror novel *Blood Hunt* that he and I had started writing together, as well as my own creation, Kevin Adamson, the City Attorney. Continuing in the horror vein I also revived Jim Razor, as well as Jack and Marian Ransom, from the *Blood Feast* novellas, the couple now with a son who was to have played a major role in the unwritten *Son of Blood Feast*. Gary Vaughan and his group from *Death in the Dentist's Chair* put in an appearance at a downtown music spot, and in an unnamed cameo sitting in with the band is none other than Steve Raymond, D.D.S., on saxophone. The one character who is conspicuous in his absence, however, is Daniel Lasky, who had appeared in all four of my previous novels.

Since I was between teaching jobs back then, and had plenty of time to devote to writing, I was able to finish the novel in a mere six months. Laura's father, who had written detective novels in his youth, had given me a piece of criticism about my previous novels that I tried to incorporate into this book. He said that those works didn't really evoke the sense of place in which they were set, and while I purposely made the attempt to do that in this novel I don't think I succeeded. There's a lot of emphasis on the weather throughout, and I tried to bring Seattle as I had known it to life, but it's clear in reading the story nearly fifteen years later that I was far more interested in character than setting. I think I always have been. And speaking of characters, as I had done in my previous novels, many of them bear the names of friends and co-workers I've had over the years. One of the most shocking to discover, however, was that of Rob Dodson, because a few years ago I learned that he had died of cancer. I had worked with Rob at the University Book Store in Bellevue in the early nineties, and the two of us had become good friends as co-workers. I can't think of anyone who was more of a pleasure to work with than Rob. He was energetic and friendly and completely selfless. We had something of a falling out before I left the store—due entirely to my own immaturity—and I still regret that I wasn't able to touch base with him later. While I never had conscious role models in my life, if I had, he would certainly have been at the top of the list. Rob Dodson was, quite simply, one of the best people I have ever known, and like Gary Vaughn from *Death in the Dentist's Chair*, I'm glad that I will always be able to remember him as part of this work.

I'm fairly positive that I sent the manuscript to my agent, and whatever flaws there are in my fiction that kept my previous works from being published were apparently still in evidence in this novel as she had no better luck. But just as I had done with the dental mystery series, I immediately began planning the next book for Ray Neslowe. Since my first short story about the character had been set in Olympia, and the first novel in Seattle, I made the decision to have him be a sort of travelling detective. I would put the name of the city where he was working in the title of the books, and combine it with a jazz term. I don't do a lot of traveling myself, but I did enough that I thought I could make the series work. We had lived in California for a couple of years, so I was planning on setting one of the books in San Jose. Laura and I had also been to New Orleans once when she was working for eBay, but then we took another trip there a few years later so that she could enjoy it this time without working. Just before we left I realized that there was no better place in which to set a novel about a character who plays jazz, so while we were there I did a bunch of research for the setting. The sequel to this book was called *The New Orleans Blues*—not a clever title, but perfectly descriptive of the story—and I completed about forty pages of the manuscript before I simply lost interest in writing fiction altogether.

While I may go back and complete that novel at some point, I have no plans to do so at present. What's clear from looking at those few pages, however, is that my main character had already undergone a very discernable transformation. Rather than simply being another version of my amateur sleuth, Steve Raymond, my character was beginning to take on the more confident attributes of the classic private investigator. He could still wisecrack with the cops and make false assumptions, but underneath it all was an incredibly serious attitude that had been missing from my other books. And that's probably a good thing. The real problem with my other mystery novels, I only discovered years later, was something I had actually done on purpose and may have resulted in inadvertently sabotaging my attempts to get published. Recently, I considered trying to see if I could write the third story in my dental series, *Brush with Death*, and so I thought I would take a look at a few new books on writing mysteries to get some inspiration. One of those, *Mastering Suspense, Structure, & Plot* by Jane K. Cleland, begins with an anecdote by the author that completely took me by surprise.

> Shortly after I submitted the manuscript for *Antiques to Die For*, the third entry in my Josie Prescott Antiques Mystery series, my St. Martin's Minotaur editor took me to lunch. She'd barely sat down before she said, "I realized overnight what the problem is—you don't know you're writing cozies." I was, needless to say, shocked, chagrined, and appalled, but only with myself. I never thought of myself as a cozy writer before that seminal lunch. I was going through a hard time, and I had allowed my emotional turmoil to infiltrate my novel. Instead of writing sweet, I wrote dark. By adding elements more appropriate to a noir novel, like angry confrontations between my protagonist and her boyfriend, I risked alienating my readers. I didn't know my genre and I didn't know my readers. (Cleland 8-9)

I was more than a little shocked to read that myself, but for very different reasons. One of the things that absolutely stunned me when I first received the letter from my agent saying she would represent me, is when she called my mystery novels "cozies." I hated cozies, and I certainly never would have been caught dead trying to write one. As a result, one of the things I went out of my way to do in those novels was to mix Steve Raymond's amateur bumbling with a healthy dose of serious suspense and danger. After receiving her letter, I completely dismissed my agent's categorization of my novels and did my best to forget about it. Cleland's story, however, made me reassess my agent's words in a new light. In her book, Cleland goes on to talk about the dangers of defying reader expectations, but in my case I think it was going against editor expectations that accounts for why I was never picked up. Sure, I mixed genres, but that was the whole point, so sue me. Whatever it's failings in the marketplace, I think the combination works, and it seems to me that the few people who have actually read the novels tend to agree. Nevertheless, while Ray Neslowe has the same goofy enthusiasm in *The Seattle Changes* that Steve Raymond did, the shift in his character that was beginning to happen with *The New Orleans Blues* was probably a step in the right direction, and makes me feel as if my growth as a writer may have resulted in a publishing deal somewhere down the line. For now, that's good enough for me.

Today, I'm happy writing non-fiction. I think what happened at the end of my experience writing fiction is that my intense desire to see myself published sort of killed the joy of writing for me, and that's probably why I simply abandoned it. So this time I made the conscious decision when I began writing non-fiction that I would purposely refuse to let myself become obsessed in the same way. Now I submit proposals to a few university presses, just to make sure that the consensus on my writing is still the same, and then I go ahead and publish them myself. Publishing all of my fictional works in the same way has also given me a new sense of pleasure in what I accomplished all those years ago, and for that I'm also thankful. It's one thing for a person to say they've written ten books, as I have, and quite another for those books to actually be available as concrete objects on Amazon and Barnes & Noble, or to be able to give them to family and friends. Sure, I paid for them, but now they actually exist, in a way that a manuscript in a box buried somewhere in the garage doesn't quite. I may go back and take another crack at fiction at some point, but when I do it will be a very different experience than it was before, and because of that *The Seattle Changes* really does signal the end of the first chapter of my writing career. Fortunately, there have been further chapters since then, and with any luck, many more chapters in the future.

Eric B. Olsen
April 6, 2019

Changes: Chord progressions. The harmonic progression
of an existing theme on which a jazz performance is based.

—New Grove Dictionary of Jazz

When you have to explore every night, even the most
beautiful things you find can be the most painful.

—Dexter Gordon
'Round Midnight, 1986

CHAPTER ONE

I had just run into the alley, out of breath and sucking wind, so when I saw the headlights turn in at the other end ahead of me I did the only sensible thing I could think of: I stopped and raised my hands. Twin beams of blinding white light rumbled down the alley and screeched to a halt about twenty yards in front of me, pinning me where I stood. But as soon as I heard the doors to the van slide open I did the only other sensible thing I could think of: I started running again.

The second I cleared the alley and turned the corner, I heard the squeal of rubber on cement. They thought I would give up quietly, but they were wrong. They also weren't going to be quite so friendly next time.

I didn't think they had planned on gunning me down or they would have done it in the alley. But being run over didn't seem like much of an alternative. Though I was on the sidewalk, it was nice and wide and not the sort of thing to dissuade a potential *Death Race* driver. Ducking into a doorway offered about as much cover as the pitcher's mound at Safeco Field during a Mariners' game, so I did my last sensible thing that night: I dove head first to the cement and rolled under a parked car.

The van exploded from the alley in a cloud of exhaust and burning rubber, fishtailed in the middle of the street and roared by me. When the brake lights came on at the end of the block the vehicle hesitated only a moment before turning to the right.

Instantly, I was up and on my feet running as fast as I could . . .

in the same direction the van had gone. I wanted to make sure they didn't double back and catch me in the open. I reached the end of the block just in time to see them make another right—they were circling the block. Once the van was out of sight I continued running toward the darkness of the waterfront, hoping to lose them in the maze of industrial buildings south of town.

I turned into the next alley to my left, trying to put as much distance between myself and my pursuers as I could manage, and after taking a right out the other side I figured I was at least two or three blocks away as I continued running west. A block north and another west and I was nearly out of breath. I stopped in the shadow of a broken streetlight and leaned in the doorway of a gray brick building to rest.

The adrenaline that had carried me this far had just about dissipated and I felt my knees beginning to give. With my back against the cool brick I took long deep breaths and felt my whole body shaking. But headlights two blocks away snapped me back to attention. The building I was against was too long to get around in time and I couldn't risk exposing myself by going across the street. As the lights continued to approach all I could do was go to the ground alongside the building and lie still behind the skinny shrubs that passed for landscaping.

When the lights were closer I could see it was a cop car. Jesus, that was all I needed. The blue-and-white moved agonizingly slow as it passed by. I hadn't even realized I'd been holding my breath until the taillights turned the corner. My heart pounding and my breathing labored, I rolled on my back to think and considered the empty sky while my body tried to settle down. It was a clear night but the urban glow from the city's lights had washed away most of the stars. I had to get someplace safe.

Once I could walk again, I pushed myself up and headed back east as fast as I could. There was only one place I could think of to go, and as I headed in that direction I tried hard not to think about what I was going to do when I arrived. Meanwhile, I took inventory.

I brushed dirt and beauty bark from my Levi's and took off

my black sport coat to check for damage. The back came clean easy enough, but the elbows were another matter. I did my best to rub out the dirt and then slipped the jacket back on over my forest green T-shirt—my working clothes. Any dark colored clothing will keep you hidden when there is little light, but colors like dark greens and blues look a lot less suspicious than all black if you happen to get lit up by headlights or a flashlight.

As I made my way up Holgate toward Beacon Hill, there were enough cars and errant pedestrians to make me feel relatively safe. And that was dangerous. I couldn't afford to stay out in the open much longer. Even though I was several blocks north of where the van had caught me, it wasn't nearly far enough away to relax.

It was a warm night in early September, and I broke into a light sweat as I pushed myself up the Beacon Avenue overpass across I-5. After four more blocks of looking over my shoulder I was finally able to cut through a footpath to College, and a couple blocks later I slid behind a car in the driveway of a darkened house. Across the street was an old brick apartment building. I could see the front door of the building from my vantage point. There were lights on in two of the apartments, including the one on the third floor, upper right.

My watch said it was just after three in the morning. Why was the light still on? Was someone else there? Would I be walking in on something I didn't want to know about? Without any answers I took a seat on the cement and waited. Waiting for what, though, was another question I didn't have an answer to.

Five minutes later I heard police sirens and I stood up and crossed the street. I didn't need to be caught by the cops skulking in someone's driveway. I only hesitated a moment before using my key to let myself in the front door. The familiar smell of old carpet and that evening's cooking calmed me considerably, and after a deep breath I ascended the stairs.

As I reached the third floor the apartment was the first one on the right, number 302. Before I could give myself a chance to get nervous, I knocked. I heard something fall inside the apartment and tensed, then I took a step back and waited for an answer. Finally I heard the chain slide back and saw the knob turn.

"Hello, Sta—"

A second after she'd opened the door, Stacy Lambert slammed it in my face. That was a relief. I was afraid she was still mad at me.

Before I could knock on the door again I saw a strobe of red and blue lights coming in through the windows in the stairwell. I ran over quickly and looked down to see two Seattle blue-and-whites disgorging their black-clad riders. At the other end of the building was another stairway that let out onto the alley, and I ran the length of the hallway and down the stairs as fast as I could. One of the banisters nearly gave way rounding a corner, but I managed to make it down to the back door in seconds. I whipped it open and was instantly blinded by spotlights.

"Freeze, motherfucker!"

Now, I have a difficult enough time keeping my heart rate steady when I hear, *Do you know how fast you were going, sir?* But, *Freeze, motherfucker*, put me into a vapor lock. I froze. A burst of garbled voice from a police radio was followed by someone grabbing me around the upper arm and pushing me face-first against the side of the building.

Cops moved past me through the door as the one behind me cuffed my wrists. But instead of being ushered into one of the patrol cars, they hauled me back inside the apartment building. I didn't ask what I was being arrested for, partly because I was curious as to where they were taking me, but mostly because I was still too scared to talk.

After being escorted back up to the third floor I immediately registered that most of the cops who had come up the other stairwell were standing outside Stacy's open door. If I hadn't just seen her a minute earlier I would have feared for Stacy's life, but I couldn't imagine what the hell was going on now.

As it turned out, I didn't have long to wait. With all eyes on me I was guided into the apartment. The first thing I saw was Stacy sitting on the couch crying, two cops standing over her.

Then I looked down and the second thing I saw was the man on the floor. He was in bad shape but no one was attending to him. You didn't have to be a doctor to figure out that, with half his face missing, he was dead.

CHAPTER TWO

What had once been the man's face was now a pool of blood, and when it finally hit me what I was looking at I broke away from the cops and ran—to the bathroom. My mouth suddenly tasted salty and I began sweating. I could feel the bile in my throat just as I reached the doorway, but even with the light out I could see the lid to the toilet was down. And with my hands cuffed behind my back it wasn't about to come up. But my dinner did, right into the sink.

Afterward, I stood up and was glad I couldn't see myself in the mirror. By turning around I was able to reach the tap and rinsed my mouth out. The sink didn't drain very well but before I could do anything about it a cop stuck his head in the doorway. "Let's go."

I did, and when I returned to the front room a familiar voice boomed out. "You gotta be kidding me. Hey, Haggerty. It's the peeper."

Stanford Dalton and John Haggerty, homicide detectives from Seattle's major case squad, were both looking at me now. Dalton stood an inch taller than me at six-two, and went about two hundred and ten pounds. He was wearing a dark blue suit, probably Armani, gleaming oxfords, probably Gucci, Rolex watch, pinkie ring . . . you get the picture. Haggerty, on the other hand, had a build more similar to mine—slender, one seventy-five or so but only stood about five-ten or -eleven. He was into tweed and corduroy and elbow patches, and continually talked around an unlit pipe he kept clenched between his teeth.

It was going to be a long night.

Haggerty mumbled something around his pipe but Dalton talked over him. "I didn't think you carried a gun, peeper. I didn't think murder was your style."

It was going to be a *very* long night.

"I didn't kill anyone, Stan."

He was on me before I could take another breath. "You listen to me, peeper." His finger poked me in the chest, hard enough to bruise it felt like. "When you talk to me it's *Lieutenant*, you got it?"

Never mind that I hated his calling me *peeper* with a passion.

"Dalton," Haggerty interrupted, "the M.E.'s here."

One of the uniforms started to take me out but Dalton said, "The peeper stays."

Stacy must have been in the kitchen because the couch was vacant, but the victim was right where I'd last seen him. Then a plainclothes detective who was dusting for prints opened the door and Emily Richards, one of the assistant medical examiners, made her way right to the body, set down her black bag and went to work. I didn't want to watch and tried to back out of the living room.

"Where do you think you're going, peeper?"

Emily looked up, our eyes met, and then she shook her head and went back to work. Dalton, however, wasn't through with me yet. He charged over to me so fast that even the uniform standing next to me flinched. "You want to tell me who that is on the floor?"

He stood inches from me, his nostrils flared, his face blue from the thick, black whiskers I knew he shaved twice a day, and even this close the normally pungent smells of coffee and cologne emanating from him could barely overlay that of blood and vomit.

"I don't know who it is."

"Then what were you running for?"

"I wasn't running. I was just leaving the building."

"Which brings up another interesting question. What were you doing in this building in the first place? I know for a fact you don't live here."

"I was visiting a friend."

"Miss Lambert?"

"If you must know."

"Oh, I'm gonna know, peeper. Before I'm done with you I'm gonna know everything."

"Very recent," Emily said, and stood up. "He's been dead an hour, tops."

Dalton didn't look away, didn't even blink. His eyes narrowed and he said to the uniform, "Take him downtown and book him. Breaking and entering, criminal trespass, resisting arrest, harassment . . ." Then he smiled. "Murder, conspiracy to commit murder, obstruction of justice—"

"All right, Dalton." Haggerty took him by the arm and began leading him away from me.

Without looking back, Dalton said, "Get him outta here."

*   *   *

"Goddamn it, Ray. Don't you have a watch?"

In point of fact, my watch was now residing in a large manila envelope that was probably still with the desk sergeant in booking. Or maybe it had been filed by now in a wire basket labeled "Prisoner Property." In addition to my watch the envelope also contained my wallet, eighteen dollars in cash, thirty-seven cents in coin, a cell phone, lip balm—

"You couldn't have waited a couple of hours until I was at the office?"

"I'm in jail, Carl."

"Oh, that's just great. What case did you screw up this time? You know, my clients can't afford to have you blowing investigations. Hell, *I* can't—"

"It's murder, Carl."

The silence on the other end was exactly what I'd hoped for,

8

though I was careful not to say that *I'd* been arrested for murder, because I hadn't.

"*You* were arrested for murder?"

Great.

"Look, Carl. The police found a body and I just happened to be in the area—"

"In the *area*?"

"I happened to be running—having nothing to do with the murder—and they thought that I was running from the scene."

After a beat he said, "You can't arrest someone for running."

"Come on, Carl. When can you get me out?"

After another silence and a heavy sigh he said, "Court doesn't start until nine. I'll try to be there before then but I can't promise anything."

"I'm not going anywhere. Just do what you can."

"All right. I'm sorry. I'll be there before you're arraigned. Are you in County?"

"No, just a holding cell downtown. They're expecting you."

"Okay. Don't worry. I'll get you out today. Now, I gotta get back to sleep."

Carl and I said our good-byes, and he went to bed while I was taken back to my cell.

At least I was just in a holding cell. Despite Dalton acting as if he hated my guts, I knew he must have arranged it. I had been booked for fleeing the scene of a crime, but that was a nuisance charge. It wouldn't take five minutes before a judge to clear it up. Even so, Dalton could have had me booked into the King County Jail, a maximum-security facility if ever there was one. Instead, I was in the cage at police headquarters with two other men who looked decidedly non-threatening. People didn't spend the night in the cage. I was the exception and I knew I had Dalton to thank for it.

I had first met Dalton on a case a few years ago. A man had been charged with killing his wife but the police couldn't find any evidence against him. A few months earlier the woman had filed for divorce, and I had been hired to make a case against the husband. Technically, Washington is a no-fault state, so it wasn't a question of *getting* the divorce. My work had more to do with negotiating how much the husband was going to be on the hook for when the dust had settled.

Two weeks before the murder I had taken some pretty spectacular color shots of the husband and his girlfriend at their love nest on Bainbridge Island, one of which showed the husband cutting his lover's skin with a knife as part of the sadomasochistic rituals that were part of their routine. The knife in the photo turned out to be the murder weapon. Once they knew what they were looking for, Dalton and his partner eventually found it and the guy is now doing life in Walla Walla.

But that's not why Dalton hates me.

That was another case. Another divorce case. This time it was the man filing against the woman who, unbeknownst to me, just happened to be Dalton's daughter. To make a long story painfully short, because of my expert detective work she not only lost custody of her two-year old daughter—Dalton's granddaughter—but was also screwed in the divorce settlement.

Never mind that she had been practically hooking for cocaine, or that her husband had spent nearly two hundred thousand dollars on treatment for her and none of it had apparently taken, or that Carl never told me her maiden name, or that I never would have taken the case had I known she was Dalton's daughter—all of which Dalton knew. But since I was the one who dug up the dirt on her, in his mind I was the one responsible for everything.

So now he hated me . . . but not really. If tonight proved anything, maybe it was that Dalton had finally begun to realize his daughter's problems had nothing to do with me.

I rolled up my jacket into something resembling a pillow and laid back on one of the wooden benches in the cage. I was exhausted. Just as the sounds of the precinct house were beginning to coalesce and lull me to sleep, I heard my name pierce the white noise and jar me back to consciousness.

". . . Neslowe."

I sat up, barely able to keep my eyes open. "Yeah?"

"Let's go. You're being transferred."

"Transferred?" I grabbed my jacket and walked over to the door of the cage as the uniform unlocked it. "Where the hell am I being transferred to?"

"County."

"Why?"

He pulled me out and handed me off to another uniform. Between them we walked toward the elevator that would take me up to the ninth floor of the Criminal Justice building and across an enclosed sky bridge to the King County Jail.

"We just got a call from Lieutenant Dalton. His orders."

"Orders for what?"

"You're being charged with murder."

CHAPTER THREE

"What the hell's going on, Ray? A few hours ago they were holding you for fleeing the scene, and now it's murder?"

Camilo Carlos Serafin—Carl to everyone except his wife— was a damn fine lawyer and one of the few friends I'd stayed in touch with from high school. He'd probably even called to find out the actual charge against me before he went back to sleep. But at that moment I wouldn't have cared if he were the shittiest ambulance chaser in Seattle. I was out of lockup and into an interview room.

Carl was heavy-set, in a doughy sort of way, with a slight paunch that he kept held in nicely by the vest of his three-piece suit. His short, black hair framed his dark features and was just going gray at the temples. He set his briefcase on the small wooden table and immediately loosened his tie. It was eight-thirty in the morning.

"What do they have on me?" I asked him.

His eyebrows raised. "You don't know?"

I sighed. "Dalton and Haggerty are the arresting officers."

"Oh, that's just beautiful. No wonder it's been like pulling teeth to get any information around here."

"Do you know what they have?"

"They have a gun they think is the murder weapon."

I held out my hands. "That's great. My .38's still in the car. There's no way it could have been—"

"It's not a .38. It's a .44 Magnum."

"So what? I don't even own—"

Carl put his hand up and stopped me. "It's registered to you, June of 1989."

I sat back for a moment, numb, and ran my hands through my hair. Then I closed my eyes and said, "Shit."

"Yeah?"

"My dad." I shook my head. "When he found out I was going to be a P.I., he bought me the .44. Probably because he saw it on a Dirty Harry movie. No way was I going to carry around a cannon like that, so I put it in the closet and forgot about it."

"So, someone broke into your apartment?"

I smiled grimly. "Unless, of course, I killed the guy."

Carl had been reaching to open his briefcase and stopped. "Something you want to tell me?"

"Sorry."

"Okay." Carl took out a legal pad and had me go over my story. He said he would try to get me out on bail, and would post the bond for me if that happened. I didn't need to ask what would happen if he didn't.

By nine we were done, and I was taken back across the sky bridge that connected to the courthouse to be put in a holding cell to await my arraignment. I was still wearing the canvas jump suit that all prisoners in County were given. Mine was red to designate that I'd been charged with murder. Thankfully, most of the other murderers in my tank had been asleep when I arrived the night before, though I still spent my few hours there with one eye open. Once I was put in the cage, however, I couldn't even remember falling asleep and I came to in a fog hearing my name again. This time I was taken by special elevator directly to another holding cell just outside the courtroom.

Carl was waiting for me at the defendant's table when I was ushered in. Just seeing him there helped me relax. A court officer took me from the prison guards and stood me next to him.

The judge had been reading from a clipboard and looked over her glasses at me. "In the manner of the People vs. Neslowe, how does the defendant plead?"

"Not guilty, Your Honor," Carl said without looking up from his legal pad.

"Your Honor, the People would like to request that the prisoner be held without bail."

I looked over to the plaintiff's table and couldn't believe what I was seeing, an intense black man in charcoal gray pinstripes and gold, wire-frame glasses. It was Kevin Adamson, the City Attorney himself, prosecuting the case. I'd only ever seen him on TV before, usually behind a bank of microphones talking about high profile cases. This was not a good sign.

Carl looked up and whispered, "Je-sus Christ."

Suddenly I wasn't so relaxed anymore.

"Your Honor," said Carl, standing up. "Mr. Neslowe has an exemplary record as a contract private detective in Seattle, the sole proprietor of his own business, and is no threat to flee. He has held a license to carry a firearm for fifteen years and has no previous record of violence, despite his dangerous profession. With all due respect to Mr. Adamson, the defense would request that Mr. Neslowe be released on his own recognizance."

That one surprised even me.

"Your Honor," Adamson shouted indignantly.

I looked at the judge and I swear she was trying to keep from smiling. She raised her eyebrows at Carl and said, "For murder?"

"May we approach, Your Honor?" said Carl, and then I knew what he was up to. He had wanted to argue in private all along, and making an outrageous request was the easiest way to get to the bench.

I took the opportunity to look around the room and couldn't see Dalton or Haggerty. I didn't know whether that was good or bad. Maybe they didn't really believe I was guilty and so they hadn't bothered showing up. Or maybe they did, and didn't want to risk the humiliation of seeing me released. Either way, Dalton had certainly made his presence felt. He had fed me into the system and it was churning me out like raw meat through a sausage grinder.

Speaking of which, I hadn't eaten since the day before, opting to skip the prison breakfast, and my stomach had been in a knot all morning from wondering what was going to happen to me. I also had a three-day growth of beard and was starting to smell a little ripe. Then there was sleep, or the lack thereof. I felt completely drained in a way that my brief nap had only intensified. In short, I was a complete wreck.

That Carl came back from the bench frowning didn't help matters either. He shook his head as he stood next to me and I said, "What?"

"Listen."

The judge pushed her glasses back up on her nose and frowned, too. "While I agree with Mr. Adamson that this is a serious crime, I also have to take into account Mr. Neslowe's past actions as well as the evidence at hand. I'm not convinced that Mr. Neslowe is a threat to the citizenry, or that he would flee the jurisdiction. But this is a capital offense, and such charges we take seriously. Therefore the court orders bail set at the amount of five-hundred thousand dollars, and a trial date set for October twenty-first."

She rapped her gavel a couple of times, a court officer stood me up, and I thought for sure I was headed back to County. Then I looked behind me and saw that Carl was following us. He talked to the bailiff and I was taken instead to one of the jury rooms off the back hallway.

"Are you going to be able to swing fifty-thousand?" I said when the door had closed behind him. Ten percent was the standard amount needed to get a bail bond.

"I'm still trying to think." He threw his briefcase on the table. "If it was just a matter of getting it from the firm it wouldn't be a problem. Hell, we've probably got a hundred thousand in petty cash."

"Yeah, well . . ."

Carl rubbed the back of his neck with one hand and looked at his watch on the other. "The thing is, they're not any happier with you than Dalton is. And when they find out I'm representing you, they're going to be just as unhappy with me."

I said nothing. I appreciated Carl's help more than I could

say. He'd even continued to hire me when the firm had wanted my license revoked. But at the moment I didn't really give a shit how his partners were going to feel. I just wanted to know if I would be spending the next two months in jail.

Finally, he sighed. "Yeah, I guess can swing it. I'll have to cash out some of my investments. Jesus, Marita's going to have a fit, but I suppose if you can handle everyone being pissed off at you, so can I. I'll make the arrangements now so that you won't have to go back to lockup."

Carl pulled out his cell phone and began making calls while I sat down at the table, too numb to think, too tired to sleep. When Carl was finished he picked up his briefcase and started for the door.

"Well, that's it," he said. "They'll start processing your release as soon as you get back." He stopped and turned to me after he touched the doorknob. "And don't call me at the firm, okay? Get ahold of me tonight at home and we'll talk about what to do next."

I didn't say anything again.

"And you might want to think about getting some sleep."

"Thanks, Carl. I mean it. I really appreciate this."

He nodded. "Yeah, I gotta go."

As he opened the door to leave, two corrections officers entered to take me back to the holding cell. They were both young, in their early thirties, and gave off the aura of enjoying their work perhaps a bit too much.

"Got a message for you," the one behind me said as we walked down the hall. "Came for you while you were on your way to court."

"Yeah?" I turned to look at him.

His face immediately clouded over. "Eyes front." I did as I was told and we walked the rest of the way in silence. Then, as we waited for the elevator to return from holding upstairs, he said, "It's from someone named Stacy Lambert. She said it's urgent." He and his partner were now grinning at each other, but I didn't get the joke.

"She said she needs to meet with you," he said, still smiling. Then he delivered the punch line. "Today."

CHAPTER FOUR

But the joke was on the corrections officers. I was out a few hours later. As I stood in the doorway of the Criminal Justice Building, trying not to fall asleep on my feet, I watched the rain beat on the pavement and attempted to gauge which of my miseries was the worst. Since I didn't have my car I was going to have to walk no matter where I went, and finally hunger won out. I turned up my collar and headed toward Pioneer Square. Stacy could wait.

At least it wasn't freezing cold. Water plastered my hair to my head and began running down my back before I had gone a block. By the time I had covered the three blocks to 1st Avenue, I was soaked to the skin. Another thing to add to my list of woes.

I turned south and just off of Washington Street, nestled in between a Thai restaurant and an Oriental Rug place that was forever going out of business, was a single glass door, blacked out from the inside. Blue neon above it read, The Low Note.

Pulling open the door I could see light and hear the soft buzz of jazz at the end of the long dark hallway. The music coming out of the stereo rose to a comfortable level as I reached the main room. I entered just as a bari sax solo was ending and a piano solo began.

At the far end of the club was a bar, square and projecting out into the room like the horseshoe counter at a diner. Above the bar was a large, square rack that hung down from the ceiling and held glasses. Below that was another that held what looked like a thousand homemade cassette tapes—all of them jazz—and most of them, I knew from experience, with a baritone saxophone in the group.

I didn't have an office, couldn't afford one. But if I needed a place for people to leave messages, or somewhere to meet a client, or just a place to rest up after a hard day, it was the Low Note. Wiping down the bar was a large black man with nearly white hair and a smile that a politician would envy. Dewey Beckley nodded to me as I walked up and took a stool.

"I take it you neglected to bring an umbrella with you this morning."

I peeled off my jacket, resisting the urge to wring it out, and hung it over the stool next to me.

"Please," said Dewey, holding out his hand. "Let me hang it up in the kitchen so it can dry."

"Thanks, Dew. Could I get maybe a couple of eggs and a stack of pancakes while you're back there?"

"Certainly," he said, taking my jacket. "Sour cream and Tabasco?"

"Yeah, and a bottomless cup of coffee."

While Dewey was gone I turned around, thankful to be back in the comfort of familiar surroundings. In the far corner of the room, opposite the door, was a small bandstand set up with a Hammond B-3, a drum kit, and a small Fender Reverb guitar amp. Dewey's house band was made up of kids, mostly, from junior colleges in the area.

Dewey had begun playing the baritone sax professionally in Los Angeles right out of high school, about the time the Central Avenue district was dying in the late fifties. I even had one of his first dates—an early session for Les Koenig on Contemporary—at home on vinyl. Now he sat in with the band when he felt the urge, and tended bar the rest of the time.

Dewey had owned the place for as long as I could remember. He was in his mid-sixties, but if it hadn't been for the white hair you wouldn't have known it. He was well muscled, probably from hoisting the huge saxophone onstage for so many years, and well known in the music education community—he was a favorite at high school and junior college workshops. And he would look at you askance if you referred to him as African-American. I have no idea what that's all about.

The Low Note was dark, which I liked, and served breakfast all day, which was a godsend. It also smelled of stale beer, but was smokeless so at least it didn't feel like you were eating out of an ashtray. There were three other people in the place with me, a couple who looked as if they were tourists, and an old guy sitting at the bar reading a paper.

Dewey brought my coffee right away, and the food came a few minutes later, Tabasco going on the eggs and sour cream on the pancakes. I took my time eating, letting Dewey refill my cup and listening to the music. It was an older recording I wasn't familiar with, probably cut in the sixties. A baritone sax quartet, of course.

"From appearances, I'd say you had a rough morning." Dewey was drying glasses that had come out of the dishwasher and hanging them up.

"That's one way to put it. I just got out of jail."

He stopped with the glasses for a second, waiting for me to continue, and then I gave him the short version while he finished drying. Being arrested for murder had impressed him, but that was before I came to the part about the fifty thousand-dollar bail bond.

"And he had it?" Dewey said, wide-eyed.

"Well . . . not on him, but yeah, after he cashed out some investments."

Dewey shook his head. "Must be nice."

"Come on, Dew. You've had offers four times that high for this place."

"Absolutely," he said, giving me that vote-getting smile. "But that's not quite the same as being fifty-thousand liquid, is it?"

I drank some more coffee while he went back for another tray of glasses. When he returned I asked him if anyone had been in the day before looking for me. Dewey smiled again and motioned his head toward one of the speakers, "Who is it?"

"Aw, come on, Dewey. Not today."

But he had already grabbed the coffee urn and headed out to refill cups. There were probably a dozen people in the place by now.

Dewey liked to play a little game with me. Most times it was innocuous enough, but in situations like this it became damned irritating. Before he would tell me if I had any messages or give me any information, I had to guess who was playing baritone sax on whatever tape he had going at the moment. And what really got to me was that he never made me guess unless he actually had something to give me.

So I listened. I'd spent enough time in the Low Note that I'd heard a good share of Dewey's collection, enough so that I could distinguish most of the major bari players anyway. But that was it. I couldn't tell you what album the song was from, or when it was recorded, or who the rhythm section consisted of. Dewey could probably tell you what the guys had been wearing the day they made the recording. Thankfully, all I had to do was name the sax player.

Whoever it was knew his way around the horn. He had great bebop chops, but that was about as far as it went. There was nothing else really distinctive about his playing, not that *I* could hear, anyway. Dewey came back just as the song was ending.

"Well?"

"Just a second."

The next song began, and when I heard the flute I smiled.

"No fair," Dewey said.

"Jerome Richardson." He was the only guy I knew from the sixties who played both bari and flute.

"All right," he said. "There were two gentlemen in here last night around closing. They had a picture of you. It looked like a surveillance shot."

I nodded. "It was. Were they big guys?"

"That's right, very large, black suits and sunglasses."

"Looked like middle linebackers?"

His brow furrowed. "More like pro wrestlers."

I didn't take the time to ponder *that* distinction. "What did you tell them?"

"That I hadn't had the pleasure of your acquaintance."

"They believe you?"

He shrugged. "Difficult to tell. They didn't seem the type to care one way or the other. They left right after that."

Dewey's wife Jeannine called him away to the kitchen just then and I used the opportunity to walk back to the payphone by the restrooms, as the battery in my cell phone was dead. Stacy answered on the second ring.

"I'm so sorry about last night, Ray. But I was expecting the police, and then you showed up, and with Pete . . ."

Had I heard that right? "That was Pete? What the hell happened, Stacy?"

She didn't say anything for a long time. "I can't do this on the phone, Ray. Can you come over?"

"You working tonight?"

"Not until two."

"Okay. I'm walking, but it shouldn't take me too long."

"You at the Low Note?"

"Yeah."

"Hurry, Ray." Then she hung up.

Dewey was still in the kitchen when I returned to the bar, so I called back and asked him to bring up my jacket. It was nearly dry and I put it on over my damp shirt and settled up for the meal. I told Dewey I'd see him later that night and headed out into the weather.

After walking down the dim hallway I was more than a little surprised to find the sun had broken through the clouds when I opened the door and it stopped me in my tracks. If I hadn't been squinting I might have seen it first. Then again, I might have begun walking down the street and it would have been too late.

As it was, I stood there for a moment letting my eyes adjust to the light and that's when I heard it: the side door of a van sliding open. It was directly in front of me, and I could get my eyes open just far enough to see two pro wrestlers in black suits climbing out.

CHAPTER FIVE

I scrabbled backwards, clawed open the door, and bolted back down the hallway with my heart in my throat. I didn't see Dewey as I passed through the bar, but then I hadn't really taken the time for a good look. My eyes were trained on the restrooms.

I flew into the men's room and locked the door. Just as I remembered, there was a window against the back wall. Immediately I began working on getting it open, knowing it let out on the alley in back. It wouldn't budge.

Sweat began to ooze from my pores, and a high, keening noise began to emerge from my throat as I struggled with the frame. The lock was open, it hadn't been painted shut and the frame even felt a little loose, and still the damn thing wouldn't go anywhere. I would have broken the glass out but the wire mesh running though it rendered that option useless.

Then the door to the restroom exploded inward with a loud boom.

I turned, my back against the wall, and froze. They entered the tiny space single file and I felt my bowels liquefy and my sweat turn oily. The one with the crew cut and sunglasses checked the single stall to make sure it was empty while the one closest to me with a flat face and red ears reached into his coat. There was nothing I could do now. It was all over.

But then he turned his head. Both of them had. I'd been so intent on the two goons that I hadn't heard what they apparently had. When I looked past them I saw the most beautiful sight imaginable: Dewey, standing in the doorway with a sawed-off shotgun in his hands.

"All right, boys. As the owner of this establishment I'm going to have to ask you to leave. So let's get those hands where I can see them and get you the fuck out of here. We'll discuss financial compensation for the door when we get outside."

The one closest turned back to me, glared, and then marched out after his partner. I sagged against the wall and slid to the floor. Dewey didn't risk a look back as he followed them out. But before I could even lower my head and breathe a sigh of relief Jeannine stuck her head in the door.

"Come on, Ray. Dewey says you should slip out through the kitchen while he's got them two up front."

She ran in and helped me to my feet, and then guided me through the kitchen and pushed me out the back door. I tried to thank her but she cut me off.

"Dewey says until you get rid of those guys you should come in through this door. Just knock and I'll let you in. Now, get out of here."

It was advice that was easy to follow. I ran west to Alaskan Way before I turned south, and then I made my way down to Occidental alongside Safeco Field to give myself a little more cover. Once past the stadium I was in the same industrial area I'd been in the night before. Nearly five hundred yards of naked sidewalk loomed ahead of me before I could safely turn onto Holgate. I jogged most of it, then turned north and walked, catching my breath and keeping an eye peeled for the black van.

Clouds had once again blanketed the sky overhead, holding on to the rain instead of soaking me this time. The breeze coming in off Puget Sound wasn't that cold but it chilled me in my damp clothes and made my eyes feel as if they were full of grit. Several times as I was heading up to Beacon Hill I found myself staring dumbly at my shoes, only to snap my head up and make sure I hadn't been spotted. It was a *long* walk, and nearly an hour had passed from leaving the Low Note to the time I finally ground to a halt at the door of Stacy's building.

I hadn't told the cops anything the night before. They knew I wouldn't, because of Carl, and so they didn't know I had a key. Though it wouldn't let me into her apartment it would get me into the warmth of the building, but I was too tired to even dig it out of my pants pocket. I rang her bell, told Stacy who it was, and pushed through the door when I was buzzed in. She was waiting for me at the top of the stairs.

I stopped at the landing just below her and looked. She was thin anyway, but the worry on her face seemed to accentuate it. Her dark hair was mussed and fell limply around dark eyes, thin lips, slightly crooked teeth, and eyebrows that were a little bushy. It was a beautiful face, one I had obsessed over for the last six months.

"Ray? Are you all right?"

I knew I must have looked as lousy as I felt. I nodded anyway. "I spent the night in jail."

"Oh, my God." She put her arms around me as I reached the upper landing. "Was it about last night . . . Pete?"

"Yeah."

"They don't think you killed him, do they?"

"No. At least I don't think so. But I have the feeling they want me to think they do."

She had tears in her eyes. I didn't know what else to say. I stood there looking at her and then, quite unexpectedly, she raised up on her toes and kissed me.

It wasn't a peck. My arms found their way around her and pulled her against me tightly. It was probably the wrong thing to do, but I couldn't help myself. And though I would have thought my body had nothing left to run on, it evidently had other ideas.

"I need a shower, Stace," I whispered, trembling in her arms. "I'm disgusting."

She led me inside and helped me undress. Originally I'd been thinking a shower of the cold variety might be in order, but when she began undressing herself I couldn't hold back any longer. I kissed her again for a long time, my hands exploring her familiar flesh until she broke away and pulled me toward the bathroom.

Once she had the steam billowing over the shower curtain we both stepped inside and lost ourselves in the mist.

First she pushed me to my knees and lathered my head with shampoo and rinsed me off. When I stood back up she soaped my body while I returned the favor. Then, with the water cascading between us, she pulled me close, wrapped a leg around me and leaned us back against the wall.

We stayed in the shower until the water began to get cold. After Stacy had toweled me off, she put me into bed and climbed in beside me. We made love again and sometime after that I began to drift off.

Of course I still had a murder charge hanging over my head, as well as my friends in the black suits to deal with, but that could wait. Fuck it, everything could wait. And I sunk into a deep, peaceful sleep, the most peaceful one I'd had since Stacy broke up with me nearly six months before.

CHAPTER SIX

Soft light filtered in through the curtains in the bedroom as I finally woke up. The clock next to the bed said it was ten after seven, and the only reason I knew it wasn't morning was that Stacy was gone. There was a note next to the clock with a key holding it down. It was a single key, the one to her apartment door, which meant she must have known how I'd let myself into the building the night before. I closed my eyes as I fell back on the bed and groaned. I shouldn't be here. It was stupid. But even as I was thinking that, I knew I was going to stay. The worst thing about it was that I didn't even know why.

It would be too easy to say it was just the sex. She had gotten under my skin in a big way six months ago, and though I had dealt with our separation intellectually there was something about her that bypassed my intellect and went right to the animal part of my brain. We hadn't even been together very long—a few weeks—but the craving was still just as strong as the day she left. Like an addict, I found myself rationalizing all of the reasons why I should stay, at the same time knowing that the decision had already been made. I took a look at the note again. It said she would be home around three in the morning and that she hoped I'd be there—preferably in bed—when she arrived. I groaned again.

Eventually I tired of examining my weakness for Stacy and managed to find my way out of bed. I walked out to the kitchen and made some coffee, then I dressed. On the way back to the kitchen I looked through Stacy's music collection, but other than a disc of Mozart piano quartets there was little there that interested me, so I decided to do my thinking in silence as I poured a cup and sat on the couch. In the daylight it seemed impossible that it had only been the night before that the police had been here. My eyes were drawn to the place on the floor where Pete Willis had laid dead last night and, in terms of problems I needed to deal with, Stacy receded well into the background. Someone had blown Pete's head off with my .44, and I didn't like what that implied— the killer was someone I knew.

I hadn't been to my apartment in a couple of days so the possibility existed that the place had been ransacked, but I didn't think so. I was willing to bet that it looked untouched. And if that were the case, then whoever had stolen the gun knew what they were looking for. But who could it be? Hell, *I* hadn't even remembered the thing was there, and I certainly couldn't remember telling anyone else about it.

And now, by staying here with Stacy, I was going to look even more guilty to the cops because they would have a motive. The reason Stacy had broken up with me in the first place was to go back to Pete Willis. I say "go back" because Stacy had only recently broken up with him when we began seeing each other.

She'd worked at the Low Note as a waitress for about a year, and in that time we'd become friendly but nothing more. For one thing she was a lot younger than I was and I knew she was already dating Pete. For another, I had no occasion to meet her outside the confines of her work. But in the course of our conversations I discovered that she and Pete had been having troubles for a while. Then one day she showed up for work in tears. It turned out that she'd told him it was over after he'd confessed to being with another woman. To be fair, Stacy had gone out of her way to make it clear to him she didn't want a serious relationship, that they should be able to see other people. Still, in her mind that wasn't necessarily a green light for sex.

It was complicated to be sure, but then Stacy was a complicated woman. That was part of her charm. Initially I'd simply taken her out to console her, but it turned serious quickly and my complete willingness to indulge in passions of the flesh with a younger woman had left me totally unprepared for what happened next. Pete came crawling back, and she decided she had to give him another chance.

To say I was devastated is only a slight exaggeration, which was the strangest thing of all. It wasn't like I was in love with her, but I quickly realized that going cold turkey with anything was a new experience for me. And, like a fool, I'd unwittingly set myself up by not hating her for her decision. Somewhere in the back of my mind I guess I figured the thing with Pete would eventually play itself out and we would get back together.

Yeah, I know that was stupid, but . . . that's what I let myself think. So when she kissed me in the hallway, and with me knowing that Pete definitely wasn't coming back this time . . .

I drank my coffee and tried not to be as happy as I felt, but it wasn't working. I even tried to work up some sympathy for Willis, but that wasn't happening either. *I* was the one on the hook at the moment, for murder no less, and self-preservation seemed to be the order of the day.

I leaned forward to set my cup on the coffee table and picked up the phone to call Carl. Marita answered, and after an awkward moment when I told her who I was, Carl picked up the other line.

"Where have you been? I've been trying to call you all day, and there's no answer at your apartment, either."

"Sorry, Carl. My cell phone died while I was locked up and I haven't been able to recharge it yet."

"You scared the hell out of me, you know."

"What are you talking about?"

There was silence on the line until he said, "You *are* still in Seattle, aren't you?"

I couldn't help laughing. "Is that what this is all about? You thought I was going to skip out on you?"

"Goddamn it, Ray. I don't know what the hell you're going to do anymore."

"You can't mean that."

Another silence. "No, I guess not. It's just this money thing has me a little edgy. Where *have* you been today, if you don't mind my asking? I called Dewey, but he said he hadn't seen you since eleven."

"I've, uh . . . been at Stacy's."

Carl sighed deeply. "Would it do any good if I told you that was about the stupidest thing you've done since going over there *last* night?"

"Probably not."

"Just for the record, you know how that makes it look, don't you?"

"Then you know who he was?"

"Peter Willis? He was the boyfriend, wasn't he?"

"Yeah . . . I guess he was."

Neither of us said anything for a minute, until Carl finally changed the subject. "Any ideas about who took your gun?"

"Not really. I haven't been back to my apartment in a couple of days."

"Well, don't forget, it could have been missing for a lot longer than that. Especially if you hadn't seen it in a while."

I tried to remember when I'd seen it last and couldn't. Shit. "Any word from ballistics yet?"

"Not until the end of the week. From the wound, though, they're pretty sure it's yours."

"Yeah, so am I."

"Why is that?"

"Because it makes sense. Why steal my gun and use it for a murder if you're not going to leave it near the scene afterward?"

"So you think someone's trying to frame you?"

"I'd say they already have, wouldn't you?"

"That's not what I meant."

"I know. No, I don't think anyone's out to deliberately hurt me. My hunch is that it was the easiest way for this person to divert suspicion from himself. Once he sets me up the cops spend all their time trying to make a case against me, and by the time they figure out I didn't do it, the trail leading back to him is cold."

"Well, that's one theory."

"You're not exactly instilling me with confidence here."

"Look, just find out who took your gun, okay? The last thing I want is for this thing to go to court. I don't have the time to get up for a murder trial."

"Jesus."

"I didn't mean it like that, it's just . . . Look, Ray, I'm swamped at the office. I've got more clients than I can rightfully handle but the partners are still saying I'm not pulling in enough billable hours. They'd probably fire me if they found out I was defending you on a pro bono murder case. The best thing you can do in your own defense right now is to find out who did it, and then what I can or can't do for you will be a moot point."

"Don't leave me in the lurch, Carl."

"I'm not. Trust me on this. Forget what I said before. But just find out who did it, okay?"

"Sure."

"Look, I gotta go now. Call me when you find something. Just make sure—"

"I know, I know. Call you at home."

I hung up the phone and went out to the kitchen to refill my cup. When I sat back down I stared at the wall for a while trying to figure out what to do next. Talking to Stacy would be a place to start. I certainly wasn't going to find out from the police what was on her statement. When I leaned forward to stand up I saw something that stopped me short. It suddenly dawned on me what I'd been looking at this whole time. The wall: there was nothing on it.

Well, I don't mean *literally* nothing. There was a beautiful mirror that had come off of an old vanity dresser hanging near the corner leading to the kitchen, and over by the desk she had a framed Escher print with a few pictures of friends tacked beneath. What was missing was the blood.

I suppose it was conceivable that Stacy had cleaned up everything, but when? I just couldn't see her taking the time to drag out a bucket of Mr. Clean and swabbing down the walls— between having the cops take her statement until who knew how late, trying to get some sleep before I came over, and then going to work. And with a .44 at close range like that it would have been on more than just the walls; it would have been everywhere, the "it" being Pete Willis's blood and bone and brains.

I jumped up and walked over to the wall. It looked like any other apartment wall, off-white with a few scuffs beneath a fine patina of dust. I was standing on the Oriental rug that normally would have been beneath the coffee table—it should have been bloody, too. She had obviously moved it over to cover something. I pulled up the corner and saw a brown halo of dried blood.

I let the corner fall back to the floor and went into the kitchen for another cup of coffee. I had to think. Pete Willis had been killed someplace else and brought here after he was already dead. There was no other explanation. Even if the walls had been cleaned afterward—as well as the coffee table, the desk, the rug, the couch, the ceiling . . . you get the idea—the immediate blood loss from the bullet wounds would have left fluid all over the hardwood floor of Stacy's apartment. What was there now had merely oozed out of his head once the body had been dumped on the floor.

When it hit me, I felt like an idiot. If he *had* been killed here I wouldn't have been sitting here now drinking coffee. This would be a murder scene, and the cops would have sealed it up the night before. I paced for a while and extrapolated further. Dalton must have known this as soon as he laid eyes on the scene, which was why he'd hauled me back inside to humiliate me before having me arrested. But my killing Willis couldn't possibly have jibed with Stacy's statement. So why the murder charge? The gun, sure, but what had Dalton and Haggerty been doing between the time they'd found the gun and then charged me with murder?

I had dismissed Carl's frame-up theory, but I couldn't any longer. For the first time since this whole thing had started, something like panic began to gnaw at my gut. Sitting in my car for two days on surveillance had left me without an alibi. I rinsed out my cup, put Stacy's apartment key in my pocket, and headed out the door. Knowing he hadn't been shot here, once Dalton found my gun he would have wanted to know if Willis had been shot at my apartment. And though there was no reason to think they would have tossed the place, if they did, I'd never know if someone had been there on the day of the murder. I'd have no way of knowing how long my gun had been missing.

I'd been away too long. It was time to go home.

CHAPTER SEVEN

The place had been ransacked all right, but that was just the beginning. Or was it the ending? Either way, things would never be the same again.

When I left Stacy's dusk was beginning to settle. The first thing I did was check to see if my car was still where I'd left it the night before, but I had to be careful in case the black van was waiting for me there. Once I'd walked down to the bottom of Beacon, I headed south down 8th. Poking my head around the corner of an old warehouse building I could see my car a block away in a pool of light from a street lamp. I turned and made my way back around the block to the west and circled all the way around to approach it from the south. There was still no sign of the van, though in the dark it was kind of hard to tell

After waiting nearly twenty minutes, finally sure no one was staking out my car, I made a dash for it. The old Cavalier coughed to life and, with no sign of the van, I pulled out and headed downtown. Reaching under the driver's seat I checked for my .38. It was still there, right where I'd left it.

To be perfectly honest, guns scare the shit out of me. I mean, I'm a divorce investigator, for Christ's sake. It's not like I'm taking on drug lords and biker gangs every week. In fact, if I do my job correctly, nobody should even know they're being investigated.

It was a homicide detective by the name of Ransom who convinced me I should carry a piece. He said lots of guys on the force had been able to keep weapons in their holsters for twenty years without firing them, but every one of those guys would tell you how it saved their lives at one time or another. And it turns out Detective Ransom had been right.

I'd been on a stakeout one night in the Central District near Judkins Park and had the misfortune of falling asleep at the wheel, so to speak. What brought me to was a group of high-spirited teenagers—members of some kind of "youth club" from the looks of their matching bandannas and tattoos—who had broken out the passenger window of my car and seemed intent on dragging me out to participate in one of their group activities. The .38 had, indeed, saved my life and, I'm happy to report, none of the youths lost theirs. With my piece in full view I was able to simply drive away.

All of which reminded me that I wanted to stop by and thank Dewey for saving my life, but I had other things to do first. By the time I was heading north up Alaskan Way toward home the sun had dipped below the horizon and it was full dark. My apartment is in Ballard, just off of 70th. At one time the district of Ballard had been a Scandinavian enclave, and while there were still a few businesses around that catered to Norwegian and Swedish customers the area had become one of the more diverse in Seattle. For most people the Ballard Locks—which allowed boats to travel between Puget Sound and Lake Washington—was the area's defining feature. For me it was the music, or at least it had been.

At one time Ballard was the real musical center of Seattle. Dozens of small clubs once lined the side streets off of Market and music spilled out onto the sidewalks nearly every night of the week. The Owl Tavern had, for years, been the oldest bar in Seattle and the city's premier blues club. Just up the street from the Owl was the Backstage, which sold tickets and featured mostly national acts on tour and prominent regional groups. And down a few blocks from the Backstage was the Firehouse, a popular spot for local groups on their way up, and one I'd played at on numerous occasions. The Owl and the Backstage were gone now, and the scene had pretty much shifted to Pioneer Square downtown. The change had been a good one for Dewey; the increase in traffic the last few years had helped his club considerably. But sometimes I missed Saturday night in the old Ballard.

My apartment is on 10th and after turning up 70th I made a left onto 9th—I say "apartment," but it's really the basement of a house—because I wasn't planning on driving right up to the front door. It was clear that my friends in the black van had been putting a soft tail on me: they weren't following me every minute, but they knew where I lived and where I hung out and, last night, where I had been working on my stake out. Since they hadn't been watching my car this afternoon, and they'd been foiled at Dewey's earlier, it was a good bet they were waiting for me to show up at home.

My backyard neighbor happens to be a blues singer here in town, which is how we had occasion to talk over the fence one day—he'd heard me playing Dinah Washington loud one sunny afternoon when my landlord was gone. After that, I caught his act a couple of times at the Holiday Inn down by the airport, and we always talked when we were out back at the same time. I didn't really *know* him, but it was enough for an emergency like this.

The residential street was lined with cars, but I found a spot a few houses up and walked back to Thomas Lee Wade's house, looking nervously over my shoulder as I went up the front walk. He pulled open the door almost before I'd finished knocking. T.L., as he's known to his friends, is a very dark black man, six feet tall and weighing in at probably three hundred and fifty pounds— none of it muscle. He was looking at me with solemn brown eyes, whites tinged with yellow, and shaking his head slowly.

He stepped back so I could come inside and, in his wonderfully smoky voice, said, "Wonderin' when I was gonna see you," as he closed the door.

"I need to go through your backyard, T.L. I think there might be somebody watching for me out front."

"That so?" He looked as though he were waiting for further explanation, but just as I was about to give it to him he shook his head again and turned down the hall.

I followed as he swung his bulk from one leg to the other

through a house that, under other circumstances, I would have insisted he give me a guided tour through. It was dark inside, but there was enough light to see that the walls of the hallway were almost completely covered with framed photographs of T.L. with nearly every blues great you could think of. I spied everyone from Willie Dixon, Muddy Waters, and Howlin' Wolf on up to Albert Collins, B.B. King, and Stevie Ray Vaughan. I caught a brief glimpse of what looked to be a complete recording studio through one doorway, and a living room on the other side with shelves containing thousands of LPs, CDs and tapes.

Then we entered a small laundry room in the back of the house. With my mind on what I'd just seen I almost didn't catch him reaching for the light switch.

"Wait." I put my hand on his to stop him and T.L. frowned at me. I released him immediately. "Sorry. I just . . . It'll be easier for me to see in the dark."

A tiny smile played across his mouth. "What you mixed up in, boy?"

I sighed heavily. "I wish I knew." Walking over to the back door, I pushed aside the cloth curtains that hung over the window. "Oh, Jesus."

I turned back to T.L. and he was beaming. "They were here when I come home from work. Here most of the mornin', too."

I looked out the window again in disbelief. Yellow crime scene tape had been strung across the rear entrance to my apartment. There was a sliding glass door in front that had probably been sealed, too.

"Have there been cops watching the place?"

T.L. shook his head. "Not since this mornin'. Not to notice."

I took a deep breath to calm my nerves—it didn't work— then thanked T.L. and stepped out into his backyard. Once down his back stoop the fence covered me until I reached the border between the properties. It was a fairly short wooden fence, and sturdy, and I was able to pull myself up and over in seconds.

I hit the grass and crouched down, waiting and listening. No searchlights went on, no cops came running around the house with their guns waiving, and no black van came around the corner tearing up the lawn. Standing up, I walked slowly to my back door, down the small cement steps, and could finally see what I was up against.

In the ambient glow of streetlamps filtering in through T.L.'s side of the block I could see yellow tape that designated a crime scene had been strung from a small bush on the right of the door to the downspout on the other side. That would be easy enough to duck under. It was the large sticker that went across the door and the frame that would be tricky. It was the size of a sheet of notebook paper and stated that, if broken by any unauthorized person, the violator would be subject to jail time and a healthy fine. I couldn't have cared less about the threat, but what I didn't want was for Dalton to know I'd been here.

Carefully, I tried to pry the sticker from the door. It might as well have been painted on. The part that crossed the frame was a different matter. It stuck out an inch or so, and pulled easily off of the siding of the house. Once I had a good grip on the edge I was able to gently peel it back. Of course it took off slivers of wood and chips of paint from the doorframe as it went, but that didn't matter. Once I had put it back in place, who was going to know?

Just as I had succeeded in this painstaking effort, the sticker slipped from my fingers, curling back and sticking to itself. In a moment of horror I thought I wouldn't be able to get it free, but it eventually came loose. After tacking it lightly to the door I took out my keys and let myself into my own laundry room.

Everything looked fine once my eyes adjusted to the near blackness inside. Even though I was on the back side of the house I didn't dare turn on a light. Ostensibly I shared this space with my landlord, but she spent most of her time at her boyfriend's house so I sort of considered it mine. Beneath the inner door that let into my apartment was a sliver of light. I always leave a lamp on to see by when I come home at night, and it looked like the cops had left it on, too.

After unlocking the door to my apartment, I stepped inside and closed it behind me. I could see everything except my bedroom from where I stood and it was ugly. The lamp dumped a pool of light on a complete disaster. I don't own a lot of stuff, but what I did have was everywhere. It looked as if a bomb had gone off.

Dishes and pots and pans littered the kitchen floor to my immediate right. Open food containers of every kind covered the counters. The fridge had been unplugged and was standing open. My music, several hundred jazz CDs, had all been pulled off the shelves and lay in a heap on the carpet in the living room. Bookcases were empty, their contents disgorged onto the floor, speakers were overturned, pictures had been pulled off the walls, plants had been separated from their pots, my couch was lying on its back, and papers from my file cabinet blanketed the whole thing.

The bedroom was even worse. I moved slowly, keeping the lamp that was on between me and the windows. The shades were still pulled but I didn't want anyone outside seeing movement. Every drawer of my dresser had been emptied, the sheets had been pulled off the bed and the mattress had been leaned up against the wall. The closet, where my .44 had been, was barren. Surprisingly, the bathroom looked untouched.

There was nothing left to do here. Whether or not the police had done this or found it this way, I wasn't going to learn anything from the mess. I picked up a few articles of clothes off the floor to take with me back to Stacy's, stuck my toothbrush in my pocket and was picking up my cell phone recharger when something caught my eye. The wall again.

There was a mass of smudges and streaks on the wall above where my easy chair was reclining on its side, centered by an oblong tear and two big gouges in the sheet rock. The same dark smudges appeared to be on the easy chair, and there was a dark stain on the carpet around it. What struck me most, though, was the halo of empty space in front of the chair, no CDs, no junk, nothing. I dropped what I was carrying and then went to the floor myself. Crawling beneath the level of the lamp up toward the wall I had to will myself to breathe once my suspicions had been confirmed.

I leaned back into the corner and closed my eyes for a few minutes. The pressure was becoming unbearable. I had a headache. I needed coffee. I needed to figure out why I was being set up for Pete Willis's murder. And suddenly the fear that Carl had expressed about my skipping town didn't seem so unwarranted after all. In less than twenty-four hours my life had been turned inside out, dismantled, and glued back together into something I didn't recognize anymore.

I lost track of time after that. I wracked my brain to figure out what was going on, but with little success. Other than Dalton, I couldn't think of anyone who would want to do this to me. And as far as Dalton was concerned, there were only two possibilities: either he was too good a cop to do something like that—which is what I wanted to believe—or he was too good a cop to get caught doing something like that—in which case I was fucked. Sometime later I gathered together the things I planned on taking with me and locked the place back up. After re-affixing the sticker, I made my way in a daze back toward T.L.'s fence.

The holes in the wall had come from bullets, most likely from my .44, and the smudges and streaks on the wall were blood and brain, most likely from a headshot. Which meant that there was now an answer to the question, where had Pete Willis been shot before he'd been taken to Stacy's apartment? It was my apartment.

CHAPTER EIGHT

"So, did they pay you for the door?"

Dewey smiled at me as he walked into his office. I was sitting in his chair behind the desk after Jeannine had brought me there from the kitchen.

"Compensation in the amount of three hundred dollars." His smile grew wider. "They didn't even dicker."

He had a cup of coffee in each hand and stepped into the room to hand me one. After shutting the door he sat down in a chair opposite me and we both relaxed for a moment, sipping brew from the separate pot Jeannine made exclusively for him.

Dewey broke the ice. "Are you going to divulge the identities of the gentlemen in question, or do you need an inducement?"

I followed his eyes to the shotgun, lying next to me on the corner of the desk, and grinned. "I don't know, Dew."

His eyes narrowed. "About the inducement?"

That made me laugh. "No, I mean I don't know who they are."

"Why am I not convinced?"

"I'm serious. I wish I did."

Then I told him everything I knew. The night before, I'd been staking out the Beacon Hill apartment of a young woman named Rachel Burns. She didn't have a job, as far as I could tell, and spent most of her days shopping at the Westlake Center—a fairly new shopping mall built right downtown. Lunches at upscale restaurants like McCormick's or the Four Seasons—anywhere with valet parking for her Mercedes—workouts at the Washington

Athletic Club at the Hilton four days a week, hair appointment on Wednesdays, but she was always back to her apartment by seven. She never knew when her sugar daddy was going to come calling. Which meant, neither did I.

The "daddy," in this case, was the husband of one of Carl's clients. He was a real estate developer, among other things, kept odd hours and did a lot of work from his cell phone. They didn't really make much of a secret of the affair, going out to dinner at the Sorrento or the Metropolitan Grill when they were together, occasionally taking in a play at the Fifth Avenue or a concert at the Paramount.

I was working on a circumstantial case, tracing cash flow from him to her and trying to get a good series of shots of them whenever they were together. But that didn't mean they left the curtains open and the lights on when they were in the throes of passion, either. After a week of surveillance I still hadn't been able to get a good photo of the two in anything that couldn't also be interpreted as a business relationship, so I finally resorted to simply getting a picture of him going into her building that night. Except he hadn't been to see her all weekend and by Sunday night I was getting a little weary, but I also knew the odds were in my favor. I was sure he was going to be there.

And then the light went out. Literally. There was a naked bulb outside the entry to the building, plenty of light to get a good picture by, and it burned out right in front of my eyes. In retrospect, it also probably saved my life. I'd already spent the whole weekend waiting for him, and suddenly I was in danger of not being able to get a picture. So, I took the car back into town, bought a light bulb at the Rite Aid on 3rd, and then dashed back.

I parked in the same spot and was just getting out to replace the bulb when I first saw the two guys that had stormed Dewey's halfway across the street heading toward me. When I looked at them they froze. I could tell they hadn't planned on my getting out of the car. Once they made the decision to run back to the van, I took off on foot.

"To Stacy's." Dewey took a sip of coffee, and I did the same. I wasn't getting into that.

"I figured I had a better chance of losing them that way."

"Your instincts appear to have served you well."

"I'm still alive, anyway."

"Which begs the question," he said pointedly. "Who wants you dead?"

"Right. Except for Dalton, no one that I can think of."

"What about an old case?"

"I don't see how. Most people don't even know I'm on their case. Carl's the one who shows them the pictures or information—I'm not even involved."

"Not even tangentially?"

"*Occasionally* I have to testify in court. But Christ, Dew, these are just regular people getting divorces, hardly the types to hire a hit squad."

He nodded sagely and then said, "You realize, of course, this means you've winnowed your suspects to one."

I almost laughed. "Who?"

"Stacy."

Now I didn't know whether he was being serious or not. "How do you figure?"

"At this juncture the only connection between you and Mr. Willis, is Stacy."

That came out of left field. "What connection? You can't possibly think those two guys have anything to do with Pete Willis. I mean, what about my gun? Why frame me for murder if you're trying to kill me?"

"A failed attempt to kill you, as I recall. The frame occurred afterward."

"Okay, then why keep coming after me?"

Dewey turned his palms up and shrugged. "You're no longer incarcerated. The frame appears to be a failure as well."

The two events had happened too close together to be connected, but I didn't feel like arguing the point. "Not if I can't figure out who killed Pete."

"Never hurts to have a contingency plan."

I decided to change tacks. "Even so, I still don't see how you figure Stacy's involved."

His eyes widened. "Other than the body being found at her apartment?"

"That's not what I mean."

Dewey nodded. "I'm not saying she's involved in the murder. But if someone is framing you for Willis's murder, she's the single element that connects you with him. Without her, you two would never have had occasion to meet."

I sighed heavily and leaned back in the big leather chair. "That's not the only connection anymore."

His eyebrows raised.

"I just came from my place. Dalton didn't charge me for murder because of the gun. Pete Willis was killed in my apartment."

Dewey didn't have an answer for that one, and the concern on his face only added to my own. We sat for a moment thinking our own thoughts when the door to the office opened and caused both of us to look up.

"Geoff needs to go on his break." It was Jeannine. The thrum of "Green Onions" pushed its way into the room around her and I smiled. The house band was warming up. Dewey, on the other hand, frowned. I don't think he considered R&B to be actual music.

Dewey turned to me as he was leaving. "You're welcome to stay at our house anytime, Ray. You know that."

I nodded. "Thanks, Dew. I'll be fine."

"Are you going to hang out here for a while?"

A look at my watch told me Stacy wouldn't be having her dinner break for another hour. "Just for the first set."

He motioned with his head for me to follow him and I did. We refilled our coffee cups in the kitchen and then headed out to the bar, Dewey behind it and me on the corner stool nearest the band. "Green Onions" came to a sudden halt the second he emerged from the doorway and the band immediately launched into "Yardbird Suite."

It was a good group. The organist, a skinny white kid with a perpetual scowl on his face, had been around the longest. Dewey had discovered him in a blues band playing carbon copy Booker T. solos on a synthesizer. A year later—after much tutoring by Dewey and practice in the mornings before the bar was open—he was piloting the permanent B-3 in the Low Note through Charlie Parker tunes and making real progress on the bass pedals.

The drummer was a short, stocky black kid with good jazz chops, but played a little too delicately for an organ combo. The guitar chair saw the most turnover and was presently occupied by a late-forties hippie-type who wore sunglasses and was easily the weakest link. He had apparently listened to every Freddie King album ever made and precious little else. I made a mental note to myself to burn him some Grant Green discs.

The group had only played two numbers by the time Geoff returned from his break to take over the bar, and Dewey took the opportunity to mount the stage. He hoisted his baritone sax off its stand and pulled the neck strap over his head. As soon as his lips hit the mouthpiece he began rollicking through the four-bar intro to Cecil Payne's "Man of Moods." After a two-beat break, the rest of the band hit on the downbeat and they were off.

Dewey's tone was compelling, having all the power of Pepper Adams while retaining a sentimental quality that was all his own. But it was his execution on the big horn that really impressed; it was flawless. He seemed to float effortlessly over any number of changes, the more complex the better.

Next, he slowed things down with a gorgeous rendition of "Don't Explain." I would have stayed all night if he'd played that long, but Dewey only did two or three numbers a set. He ended Kenny Dorham's "Blue Bossa" to an affectionate round of applause before climbing down off the stage.

Dewey and Jeannine had worked long and hard for many years to make the Low Note as popular as it was, and now it did good business nearly every night of the week. The crowds were attentive and always appreciative. Dewey made his way around to a few of the tables to chat with the regulars, while the band—sounding almost like Muzak now without him—played a slow blues, and then he sidled up to the bar next to me.

"Jesus Christ, Dewey. I can't believe you're not recording. This town made a cottage industry out of guys like Don Lanphere and Floyd Standifer. What the hell are you doing running a bar?"

He was beaming with pride. We'd had this conversation before. "Making a living, my friend. Making a living."

CHAPTER NINE

Shilshole Bay, west of Ballard, is little more than a mile of coastline that sits at the bottom of a towering cliff, where expensive homes overlook the strip of marinas, nautical supply shops, and seafood restaurants that sit along the water. After sneaking back out to my car and making my way north, I pulled into Sharkey's just after ten.

Sharkey's is an oddly unapologetic combination of dance club and sports bar. In the afternoons and evenings big-screen TVs and strategically placed wall-mounted sets broadcast the game de jour. The food is good—if a bit overpriced—they always have several good microbrews on tap, and the view of Puget Sound is spectacular. But when the sun goes down they fire up the lasers and disco balls, and you can hear the music thumping all the way out in the parking lot. Instead of jeans, sweatshirts and baseball caps, the place slowly gives way to stiletto heels, painted-on slacks, and gold chains. It's not exactly seventies retro, but it's definitely a meat market.

Even though Dewey paid better, Stacy said she made ten times more in tips there than she made at the Low Note. By the time I walked in the door the music had already begun. Two huge bouncers in suits that couldn't have come off the rack stood sentinel at a small table, taking money and applying a rubber stamp of a shark to the backs of people's hands. A black guy with a shaved head was taking money while an olive-skinned guy with black hair and way too much cologne blocked the entry, literally, until you paid. I told them I wasn't staying for the music, but they weren't impressed.

"Look, I'm meeting my girlfriend for dinner. She's a waitress here."

The money-taker looked at me through sleepy eyes and shrugged. "Ten dollars."

"Ten bucks? Are you kidding me?" I looked to the door-blocker for help but he just shook his head. I tried to find Stacy over his shoulder but only a small portion of the room was still visible behind his considerable bulk. Then he began to forcibly move me aside.

"I'll wait," I said, and stood back while several other men and women ponied up and went inside. When the crowd had cleared I made another attempt. "Her name is Stacy Lambert. Could you just go in and get her for me?"

For some reason that made money-taker smile. "She's your girlfriend, huh?"

I started reaching for my wallet even before the cracks began.

"Hey, Nick, Stacy's boyfriend looks taller than he did last week."

"Yeah, different hair, too."

I paid the ten dollars, forgoing the shark stamp, and waded into a sea of perfume, sweat, and cigarette smoke to find Stacy. Before the bartender was able to reach me so I could ask, I spotted her setting drinks on a table by the dance floor. She smiled when she saw me coming her way.

"What are you doing here?" she shouted over the music.

"I wanted to talk to you. When is your dinner break?"

"A half-hour ago. I haven't been able to get away."

She wanted me to wait for her outside, but I followed her back to the kitchen. After punching out, we left together. I made a show of stopping by the front table. "You know," I said to her, making sure the bouncers could hear. "I had to pay to get in."

"Oh, you don't have to do that. Franklin," she said to the bald guy. "He's with me."

I had prepared my best smug look, but never had the chance

to use it. Franklin and Nick were both engrossed in the last inning of the Mariner's game and, somehow, Franklin managed to hand my money back to me without actually taking his eyes from the TV set.

Anthony's Homeport was right next-door and we walked over. Hands in our pockets, neither of us said much until we were seated in the much more sedate atmosphere of Anthony's dining room. We each ordered soup and salad before I broached the subject of Pete's death.

"Are you going to be okay talking about this over dinner?"

"I'm all right, Ray. What do you need to know?"

"Basically, what happened when you got home and what you told the cops."

She took a roll from the basket, broke it in half and began to butter it. "I got home a little before three. I could smell the blood before I even turned on the light." She left the roll on her bread dish and took a drink of water. "When I turned on the light and saw him I wanted to run back out. The last thing I wanted to do was stay there, but I forced myself. I couldn't look at him, though. I just went to the phone and called 911. I told them someone had been killed in my apartment and waited for the police."

"And then I showed up."

Stacy looked at me as if she had forgotten. "I was expecting the police. I don't think I recognized you until after I shut the door. I never did ask you what you were doing there."

Now it was my turn to reach for a roll. When I couldn't think of anything else to say, I blurted out the truth. "I was in the area on a stakeout and I saw your light."

The look in her eyes softened. "You still have the key to the front door."

I took a deep breath. "And now I have your apartment key, too."

She lowered her eyes and smiled. When she met my gaze again, her brow was furrowed. "Pete and I hadn't been getting along for a while."

"I didn't think you ever had."

"Don't do this, Ray."

"I'm sorry. I didn't mean . . . well . . . Anyway, it doesn't matter now."

Our waiter interrupted to set salads on the table in front of us and milled some pepper over the top of each before retreating. After we'd taken a few bites I asked her if she thought the police suspected her.

She frowned. "What's that supposed to mean?"

"Nothing more than it sounds like. He was in your apartment, that's all. They must have said something."

"They asked me if he was living there."

Then I asked, too, not sure I wanted to know the answer. "Was he?"

She shook her head. "He hadn't left his place on Mercer Island yet."

Yet. I couldn't tell if she thought that was a good thing or not, so I let it go. "Was he still into gardening?"

"*Landscaping.* He cut down trees for a living."

"I didn't think there was much of a demand for loggers in Seattle anymore."

"Dead trees. That was his latest business venture. He'd cut down dead trees in people's yards before the wind knocked them down."

"Did you tell the police I'd just been there?"

She nodded and went back to her salad. As I watched Stacy eat I realized I knew very little about her. Her father had been in the Foreign Service and had died when she was young. Her bother and his family lived here in the University District, but I remember her saying that her mother had stayed in Virginia for a while after her father's death before coming out to Seattle herself. I also knew Stacy had gone to boarding school somewhere in Pennsylvania, but I couldn't remember where she'd gone to college before following everyone else out to Seattle.

I asked her how the police had identified Willis.

"I told them it was Pete."

"Did they tell you who they thought might have killed him?"

She put her hand to her mouth to hide a yawn. She looked tired, small, dark smudges beneath her eyes somehow dulling the green of her irises. "They didn't really *tell* me anything. I answered all the questions they asked and the detective said if they needed anything else they would call me."

Once the soup had been served—clam chowder—I shifted the conversation to other things. We talked about work and the Low Note, and we both ordered coffee after. Then Stacy surprised me.

"Pete wasn't killed in my apartment, was he?" Her eyes never wavered as they looked into mine.

I shook my head. "How did you know?"

"There was no blood."

I nodded.

"I mean, virtually no blood. I remembered thinking that when I first saw him."

I nodded again. Every six months or so Stacy would talk about taking the police entrance exam. She was an avid reader of true crime books, and one of her hobbies was trying to write the definitive story of the Green River Killer. To date, I believe she'd finished six pages. Still, she knew a lot more about forensic evidence than the average person.

"It looked like he was shot in the back of the head," she continued.

I realized then that we hadn't talked yet about my being arrested or what I'd found at my apartment earlier. "Stacy, Pete was killed in my apartment."

She set her coffee cup down and placed her hands on the table as if to steady herself. "Are you sure?"

"I was just there a couple of hours ago. The police have it sealed, but I took a look inside and it's pretty clear he was shot there."

"My God," she whispered. "And that's why they thought you did it?"

"That's part of the reason."

Her face took on a curious mixture of intensity and sadness.

"They found my gun outside your apartment."

The intensity suddenly went out of her eyes leaving only the sadness. "What gun?"

That was an odd question, considering she was well aware I carried a piece. "I have an old .44 I kept in the closet at home. The ballistics report won't be back until later in the week, but I'm almost sure it's mine." She was looking down at her coffee cup and I wasn't sure she'd heard me. "It wasn't there when I checked the closet—"

She pushed back her chair and stood. "I have to get back now. I'm going to the bathroom first."

As she walked away I didn't know what to think. There could be any number of reasons why she was upset. I sort of hoped it was because things looked so bad for me. After paying the check I waited by the front door for her. She didn't have to be back at Sharkey's for a while yet, but it still seemed as if it was taking her a long time.

When she finally emerged from the restroom she looked visibly upset. I walked over to meet her. "Are you okay?"

She shook her head. "Let's go."

I followed her outside and when she stopped abruptly I nearly ran into her. She turned back to me and tears were streaming down her cheeks. I reached out but she pulled away and shook her head.

"I didn't mean to do it," she nearly sobbed.

"Do what?" I took a step toward her and she fell into my arms.

"What happened to Pete. It's all my fault."

"What are you talking about?"

Her chest hitched and she looked into my eyes. The intensity was back. "I killed him."

CHAPTER TEN

Suddenly the world seemed to slip out from beneath my feet. I wanted to push her away but her eyes had me transfixed. I wanted to run away but I was clinging to her to keep from falling. In the ensuing silence I began to think I had imagined the whole thing, that she hadn't just told me she'd killed Pete.

There were a million things I wanted to ask, and just as many that I didn't want to know. Emotions mixed in me like a cauldron until I didn't know what to think about this person that I was intimately involved with. I realized then that nothing would be the same, that we would never again have—

"I told Pete where the gun was."

It took me a few seconds to process what I'd just heard. She'd told him about a gun? She didn't even know I had the .44.

"What gun?"

Stacy pulled back from me and leaned against a parked car. "I'm so sorry, Ray. If I had any idea something like this could've happen I never would have opened my big mouth—"

"Wait a minute. Wait a minute. Go back. You told him about a gun?"

She nodded.

"*My* gun?"

Another nod.

"The .44?"

And again. "How could you have known about the .44? I never told you about it. I never told anyone."

Now she averted her eyes. Looking over at Sharkey's she said, "I . . . sort of ran across it one night when you were gone."

Eyebrows raised, I said, "You ran across it?"

She ignored me.

"On the top shelf of my closet? Hidden in a shoebox? Buried behind God knows what?"

Looking back at me a tear rolled down her cheek. "Don't you think I feel bad enough about this already?

I took a step back and ran my hands through my hair, but she looked so pitiful standing there by herself that I took her in my arms again and she cried. "It's not your fault, Stacy."

She looked up at me as if she really wanted to believe it. "Even if you'd loaded the thing and left it on your coffee table, it still wouldn't be your fault."

She broke my hold and reached into her purse, for a Kleenex I assumed. I pulled out my handkerchief and gave it to her instead. She wiped her eyes and blew her nose. "That's a horrible thing to say."

"All I meant was that whoever wanted Pete dead would have found a way. It just happened to be my gun, but if it hadn't been mine it would have been someone else's. In the end, it doesn't matter what he was killed with. You couldn't have prevented it. Okay?"

She nodded and eventually she started walking toward Sharkey's, still clutching the handkerchief in her hand, and I followed. I felt awkward as I walked along beside her, as if somehow I should be more comforting. But despite the physical attraction we had for each other, I felt reluctant to risk entangling myself in its emotional counterpart. She didn't seem to be angry about it, though. In the parking lot we kissed and she promised to be home as early as she could and I promised I would wait up for her.

As I headed back to my car it dawned on me that I had a new piece of information: Pete knew where my gun had been. Unfortunately, I didn't know what that meant. And it certainly didn't answer the question of what the hell he was doing in my apartment in the first place. I couldn't tell from my brief visit how he'd been able to get in, either. I assumed that my landlord had locked up after letting the police in, but that didn't tell me how the doors had been found when the police arrived. The only way I could see to clear myself was to learn more about Pete Willis, a lot more. That would be awkward with Stacy, but I would have to try anyway. In the meantime, I thought of another person who might be able to help me.

Highway 99, also known as Aurora Avenue, was only a few blocks away, but it would take me far longer to travel through downtown than I wanted, so I made my way up the hill, headed down 85th, and turned southbound onto I-5. Traffic thickened up on the interstate as I reached the 520 interchange east of Lake Union. To my right, the light along Eastlake worked its way past high-price condos at the water's edge, down to even higher-priced houseboats floating on top of it, before it disappeared into the flickering blackness of the water itself. A few red running lights from boats were visible as they bobbed on the water, and I even glanced over in amazement as a seaplane landed in the middle of the lake with only the ambient light from the city to guide it.

Once I had passed the southern end of the lake, the Space Needle came into view but all too soon receded into the distance behind the modern skyscrapers near the freeway that dominated the Seattle skyline. After passing beneath the convention center—built over the freeway in a city that, sitting between two bodies of water, had nowhere left to sprawl—I emerged to see Safeco Field and Qwest Field just south of Pioneer Square, then took the I-90 exit heading east toward the floating bridge. Well before reaching Lake Washington, I turned off on Rainier Avenue South and drove up the hill to the Mount Baker district. A predominantly black, middle-class area twenty years ago, the area had seen an influx of young couples and new families of all ethnicities moving in over the past decade and was now a relatively diverse neighborhood.

Assistant Coroner Dr. Emily Richards still lived in the small, two-bedroom house her parents had owned and in which she had grown up. I parked behind a two-year-old Acura Integra, walked up to her front door, and knocked.

"Hi, Em—"

A second after Emily opened the door she slammed it in my face.

Great.

"Come on, Emily." I knocked on the door again. "Open up."

A few seconds later I could hear her voice from behind the door. "Get out of here, Ray. You know I can't talk to you."

"Please, Emily. You have to help me."

The door was snatched open inward with such force that it startled me.

"I don't have to do a goddamn thing for you, you son of a bitch."

"Emily, I'm desperate. Dalton thinks I killed that guy and I need to figure this thing out to get myself in the clear. Can't you do it for old times' sake?"

She actually gasped at that point. "I don't believe what I'm hearing. After all that's happened, after all that you put me through, anything I owed to you was used up a long time ago." Head shaking, she said, "Maybe they *should* lock you up. I could lose my job talking to you. Not that you'd care—"

"Please, Emily. Don't make me beg."

The tiniest of smiles played at the edge of her mouth and I suddenly knew I had her. I went down to my knees and put my hands together, preparing to supplicate her when she sighed heavily and said, "Damn it, Ray. Get off your knees already and come inside. You want some coffee?"

I followed her in and closed the door behind me. "That would be great."

While Emily went into the kitchen I took a look around the living room. It was still the same as I remembered it: two couches opposing themselves across a low-slung coffee table, a fireplace along the outside wall and an entertainment center along the other that was softly emanating what sounded like Stanley Turrentine. Along every other available space were books, in built-in cabinets alongside the fireplace and in freestanding cases everywhere else. A more eclectic mix of titles would be hard to find. African-American history, art, and literature sat side-by-side with books on chemistry, physics and biology. Civil War histories, books on jazz, and mysteries by Walter Mosley and Eleanor Taylor Bland stood shoulder to shoulder with medical and forensic science texts.

I took a seat on the plush, charcoal couch facing the front door and looked over the equally eclectic mix of magazines on her table. Issues of *The African American Review*, *Black Renaissance*, and *The Journal of the American Medical Association* were mixed in among those from *Time*, *Money*, and *Oprah*. When she emerged from the kitchen she handed me a mug of coffee and sat across from me on the other couch.

"How in the world did you get yourself mixed up in something like this, Ray?"

I took a sip of coffee. "It's complicated."

"With you," she said, "it's always complicated. I take it you're seeing that Lambert woman now?"

"I . . . I wasn't at the time."

She looked away and stared at one of the antique framed maps of Africa on the wall. Emily had her black hair pulled back tight, emphasizing her high cheek bones and smooth forehead. Her legs were crossed in well-worn khakis and she wore a simple green cotton blouse that accentuated the rich tone of her dark skin. In addition she had wonderfully expressive brown eyes and a gorgeous smile that I doubted I would get to see tonight.

Finally she turned back to me, eyes glistening with what I hoped were not tears. "It was clear from the lack of blood and tissue in the apartment that he'd been shot somewhere else and then moved. Dalton says he was killed in your apartment."

Christ. How was I supposed to answer that? "It's not what you think, Emily. I wasn't even home last weekend when it happened. I was on an assignment and . . ."

She nodded half-heartedly but the disbelief in her eyes was clear.

"Look, you know Dalton hates me. Someone is obviously

trying to frame me, and Dalton's only too eager to believe the circumstantial evidence. I need your help, Emily. I have to figure out who's doing this before I get railroaded into a prison sentence and the case gets so cold that there's no way to catch the real killer."

That seemed to help. Her nod this time was a bit more confident. "There's not much I can tell you at this point that you didn't see at the scene. Two shots fired from a .44 at close range to the back of the head, with the exit wounds obliterating probably sixty percent of the facial features."

"Did they find the slugs?"

Her expression hardened. "Not at Lambert's apartment."

I knew that meant they found them at mine. "Do you think the killer was trying to disguise the identity of the victim?"

"Possibly. We still don't have a positive ID yet. There was no identification on the victim—only what Lambert told us. I didn't think the father would be able to I.D. what was left of his face, so we ran his prints but didn't get a match."

"Is that unusual?"

"Not really. Unless someone has been arrested, or has been in the military or government service, there's no reason they would have been printed. But we sent out x-rays to his dentist and we should get a confirmation one way or the other sometime tomorrow."

"Does his father live around here?"

"Mercer Island."

Along with the Lake Washington communities of Bellevue and Medina, Mercer Island was known for its abundance of wealthy inhabitants. "That's interesting. Pete never struck me as the kind of guy with a lot of money."

She shrugged. "Not everyone who lives there is rich."

"Do you have an address for Mr. Willis?"

She shook her head. "It's Wilczek."

"What?"

"The father's name is Wilczek."

"Pete had a different last name than his father?"

57

Emily took a sip of coffee and said, "He changed it."

"You know that for sure?"

She nodded. "Yeah. I went to Dalton when we didn't get a hit on the prints, and so he did some digging just to make sure there wouldn't have been a reason for Willis to have been fingerprinted. One of the things he found when he looked in the county records was that Peter Willis had legally changed his last name from Wilczek."

"Huh. I wonder when that happened?" I thought aloud.

Emily's eyebrows raised and she said, "According to Dalton, only about a year ago."

CHAPTER ELEVEN

I thought about that for a moment. Stacy had been seeing Pete for close to a year. Did she know about the name change? And what did it mean? Was he trying to hide something? Here was another piece of information that seemed to have no obvious connection to his death. Emily and I talked about the case for a while longer but there was really little more to add—or that she was willing to tell me. We finished our coffee discussing other matters until the awkward silences became too long to bear. She called into the office to get Mr. Wilczek's address for me from someone on the night shift, then I thanked her and she promised to let me know if there was anything else she thought could help me out.

I hesitated at my car and looked back at the house. Six months ago I didn't have any idea what I was doing to Emily. The results were painfully obvious now, and I didn't like the way it made me feel. But before I became overwhelmed with guilt I climbed in and headed back over to Beacon Hill and parked a couple of blocks from Stacy's apartment. Rather than waiting up for her, I set the alarm and fell asleep. The alarm woke me up shortly after two in the morning, and I turned on the TV to keep me awake until she came home. Flipping through the channels nothing looked interesting and I finally settled for an episode of an old British sitcom on PBS.

When Stacy came home she gave me a kiss, then quickly stripped and headed for the shower. She returned wearing only a towel around her hair and slipped into bed beside me. For the next hour I forgot all about the murder investigation. I forgot all about Pete Willis, Stan Dalton, and Emily Richards. But then, as we finally settled down to sleep, I laid awake next to her for a long time, listening to her breathing, feeling the warm dampness of her hair on my face shoulder, and wondered if I was really doing the right thing.

*　　*　　*

Stacy was still asleep the next morning when I climbed out of bed and drove downtown to police headquarters. Seattle's police department is divided into five precincts. The North Precinct covers all of the area north of the ship canal up to 145th. The East Precinct takes in everything east of I-5 from the canal down to I-90. The South Precinct is responsible for everything else east of I-5 down to Renton. The Southwest Precinct takes the area west of I-5 from Roxbury Street—including West Seattle—up to Harbor Island, and the West Precinct extends north of Harbor Island through downtown, Magnolia and Queen Ann back to the canal.

Each of the precincts is responsible for assigning beat cops and patrol cars in their area and each has small departments for Robbery-Homicide. Normally for a murder in the Beacon Hill area my case would have been processed by the detectives in the South Precinct, but Seattle also has a special case squad that works out of police headquarters on Fifth Avenue. A drive-by shooting or convenience store hold-up would have been handled by the precinct. When someone calls to say they found a body in their apartment with half its face blown off, they call out the special case squad. It was just my luck that the head of homicide in the special case squad is Stanford Dalton.

I hadn't seen him since that night, and I really didn't want to see him now, but I had to try and clear the air with him. He obviously wasn't going to believe my protestations of innocence, but at least I could show him that I wasn't afraid of further investigation. In fact, that was my biggest fear: that the investigation would stop because Dalton figured I had done it.

The clouds had passed through overnight, and the morning was bright with just a hint of crispness in the air, a harbinger of the fall weather to come. I turned off of Holgate onto 4th, and as I headed downtown I checked my rearview mirror continuously— it had become second nature by now—but there was no sign of the black van. Eventually I found a parking space outside the municipal court building on James Street and walked down to police headquarters. There were already people waiting in the back of the lobby and I went to the end of the line.

When my turn came I asked for a visitors' pass to see Dalton, and the officer at the desk said, "Does the Lieutenant know you're coming?" I shook my head and he told me he would have to call upstairs first. A minute later he hung up the phone and said, "Dalton's not in but Haggerty says you can come up. You know the way?"

"Fifth floor?"

"Yeah," he said, sliding a badge across the desk.

After clipping the badge to my jacket I headed over to the elevators, of which there were two sets. One set was for the criminal justice section of the building where City Attorney Kevin Adamson and the rest of his prosecutors worked, and the other was for the police department. I went up the departmental elevators to the fifth floor and walked down the hall to Robbery-Homicide. The large room filled with metal desks and file cabinets was sparsely occupied at this time of the morning, and I spotted Haggerty's pipe immediately and walked over to him.

"You sure you want to be here, Ray?" he said as I plopped down in Dalton's chair at the desk across from his.

"I just thought I'd stop in and see how the investigation is going, because if you guys are pinning all your hopes on me you're going to be very disappointed."

Haggerty chuckled. "Speaking of disappointments, he's not going to be very happy to find you here."

"He'll get over it."

Haggerty suddenly looked up and I followed his eyes. Dalton was coming across the room with two white paper cups from Starbucks. The last thing I wanted was to piss him off further, so I quickly hopped out of his chair and into a green vinyl-covered chair next to his desk. As Dalton thought he had a visitor I could see the beginnings of a smile creep onto his face. Then he realized it was me and he looked as though he'd discovered dog shit on his shoe.

He handed a cup to Haggerty, then sat behind his desk and took a tentative sip from his own. "Out on bail, peeper?"

"The name's Neslowe."

"Fuck you . . . *Neslowe.*"

There was simply no way that I could become antagonistic with Dalton and still have anything good come out of this meeting. So I sucked it up and forged ahead.

"All right," I said, nodding. "I know I'm your prime suspect and that's fine. But I think you need to hear from me that I didn't do it. Because if you really do suspect me, then there's something else you haven't considered and that's Stacy Lambert. If I did it then she must have helped me."

Dalton looked over to Haggerty but didn't say anything. He took another sip of coffee.

"The timing isn't right," I said. "If she had walked in and caught me there like you seem to think, then when did she make the 911 call? She couldn't have. And while I know you harbor personal resentment toward me—" Dalton glared at me but I continued. "—you can't possibly believe I was stupid enough to wait until she made the call, go toss the gun into a Dumpster, and then come *back* and stick around until the patrol cars arrived before trying to get out of there."

"Don't presume to think you know what I believe. And as far as your being stupid—"

"Okay. All I'm trying to say is that I didn't do it. I don't know how he got into my apartment and found the gun, but somebody did and used it to kill Pete Willis. And I think once you get past the circumstantial evidence you'll see that it had to be someone else."

Dalton continued to sip his coffee, evidently formulating a response. "Let's cut the bullshit, peeper. The evidence is pretty compelling, and you know it. First of all we *did* catch you attempting to leave the scene, and in something of a hurry, too, I might add. And we also have your gun, found near the scene—"

"But no fingerprints."

Now he glowered at me. "If you've been talking to Emily Richards I'll throw both your asses in jail."

"Jesus Christ, Dalton. I have a lawyer, remember? Disclosure? Ring a bell?"

He waved a hand as if that were insignificant. "But even stronger than the fact that you dumped the body in Miss Lambert's apartment is the irrefutable proof that he was killed in *your* apartment. And we know from Miss Lambert herself that you had a motive, that you two were vying for her affections, so to speak."

What? Had Stacy really told him that?

"And now," he took another sip, "you're apparently shacking up with our star witness—which the jury is going to love, I might add. And while you and your lawyer might be able to come up with another plausible explanation for someone else committing the murder, it will never seem as probable to a jury as what we have on you."

I looked to Haggerty, who only raised his eyebrows, as if telling me that there was little he could—or would—do to help me.

"Listen, the only reason I'm staying with Stacy is because you guys have my house sealed off. I can't get in."

Dalton shook his head. "We've been done with the scene since we left the night of the murder."

"Well, why the hell didn't anyone tell me?"

Completely deadpan, Dalton stared at me and said, "Oops."

I wasn't sure how much more of Dalton's baiting I could stand, but there were still things I needed to know. "So that's it? No more investigation? You're not even going to try to figure what really happened, just because you don't like me. You're so blind with hatred that you can't even see beyond an obvious frame up. Have you even looked at this Pete Willis, or whatever his name is?

Do you know anything about him, what he was into, what enemies he may have had?"

Dalton sat up and set his coffee on the desk. "Again, that sounds suspiciously like you know something you shouldn't know yet."

Shit. If I gave Emily away I would be screwed, in more ways than one. "All I know is what my lawyer tells me, but I was hoping I could help you with this thing and then maybe we could all benefit."

"That's rich." Dalton looked over to Haggerty and then back to me. "You're going to help us. Let me tell you something, peeper. If I catch you sticking your nose in police business, this murder case will be the least of your problems. Understand?"

I'd had enough. I stood up and shoved the chair back. It banged against a desk and the half-dozen or so people in the room stopped to looked at me. "You're right, Dalton. Let's cut the bullshit. You might be able to impress junkies and gang-bangers with your intimidation act, but it's not going to work on me. You want to sit around here all day on your fat ass passing judgment, fine. But make any more threats against me, asshole, and you'll be the one doing time, and that's a promise."

I was standing there with my hands balled into fists and the veins sticking out on my neck, but Dalton simply picked up his coffee and leaned back in his chair.

Haggerty finally said, "It's out of our hands, Ray. Adamson has his killer and we're off the case."

"What? He told you that?" Dalton wouldn't even look at me, but Haggerty nodded. "Why the hell is Adamson even on this case?"

Like the district attorney in many larger cities, Seattle's city attorney did very little in the way of actual prosecution except for the occasional high profile case. His main function was to oversee the work of the dozen or so assistants and numerous other lawyers in the prosecutor's office. It didn't make sense that he would want to prosecute me.

For the first time that morning Dalton's face screwed up into something approximating a smile, but was really more of a sneer. "Big election coming up next year." Dalton shrugged. "I guess he wants to get in a few slam dunks before he takes his case to the voters in the fall."

Perfect. I get hung out to dry so that Kevin Adamson can beef up his conviction record before election time. I paced in a circle a couple of time and said, "So that's really it? You're off the case?"

"There *is* no more case. The case is closed."

I stared at Dalton, but his eyes bored into me with a hatred that was almost palpable and I had to turn away. I looked over to Haggerty, but he was staring at the top of his coffee cup. Finally I decided that there was nothing left to gain by staying, so I turned on my heels without another word and headed for the door.

"Peeper," Dalton yelled out after I had only gone a few steps. I turned to look at him but said nothing. "Since you're here, maybe you could pass along a little information to your lawyer." He made a show of lifting up a paper on his desk, as if to read something beneath, but it was clear he knew exactly what he was going to tell me. "Of course this is no surprise to you, but we got the ballistics report back on the slugs we dug out of your wall." Then he sneered again. "They matched your gun."

CHAPTER TWELVE

I could only shake my head as I drove across the I-90 floating bridge to Mercer Island. It didn't make sense. Dalton said they hadn't done anything else on the case, but I knew from talking with Emily that he'd discovered Willis had changed his name. Sure, it might be nothing, but it might be everything too, and Dalton hadn't even mentioned it. And then there was Stacy. I couldn't believe she had told the cops that she'd gone back and forth between me and Pete. Of course I knew it actually meant nothing, but it sounded a lot worse than it was. As far as the ballistics report, Dalton was right—but for different reasons—because that didn't surprise me either. I guess I had expected all along that the bullets would match. There was never really any doubt in my mind that it had been my gun used in the murder.

It was just after ten in the morning when I emerged from the I-90 tunnels into the sunlight and dropped down onto the floating bridge deck heading toward Mercer Island. Though the reflection off the water gave the appearance of summer, there was enough of a breeze to put a chop in the water. I could see a couple of sailboats farther north, nearer the 520 floating bridge. Had this been a weekend day there would have been many more. Interstate 90 passes across the northern shore of the island while the bulk of the island sits in the lower end of Lake Washington, across from Seward Park on the Seattle side and an unincorporated residential area between Bellevue and Renton on the east side.

While Mercer Island has the reputation of being an enclave

for the rich, it's not an exclusive community. There are plenty of neighborhoods that represent the entire continuum of society, a holdover I suppose from being an isolated community before the bridge went up. Much of its independent business has been lost to Bellevue over the years as inhabitants—especially the rich ones—choose to drive over the small span that links the island to Bellevue, with its opulent mall and boutiques, rather than shop locally.

I took the last exit on the island and turned south on East Mercer Way, looking for the home of Pete's father. Whether he could give me any answers about his son remained to be seen. And whether or not he would be *willing* to help me was another matter entirely. At a stoplight I consulted my Thomas Guide again to make sure I didn't overshoot the street. Mr. Wilczek lived along the eastern shore on Cedar Cove Road, about a third of the way down the island. I turned left toward the water when I reached the road. The area was still heavily timbered and large houses set back from the road dominated the neighborhood. At the end of the road I turned around in a driveway and began to wonder if I had the right address. On the way back, however, I spotted the mailbox, nearly buried beneath blackberry briars on the side of the road.

Peeking through the brush and trees the place looked like a shack. Most likely it had been a cabin fifty years ago, a quick getaway for a city-dweller in Seattle. Rather than attempt to drive down the overgrown ruts that led to the cabin, I found a depression in the foliage along the street and parked the Cavalier on the side of the road. The huge evergreens surrounding the property effectively blocked out the morning sun, and I proceeded cautiously on foot down the darkened driveway. The only signs that the place was inhabited were the white Ford Bronco parked alongside the house and the large tree chipper on a trailer that sat beside it. The Bronco had a magnetized sign on the front door panel that read: Willis Tree Service.

I had known for a long time that Pete cut down trees for a living because Stacy had come into the Low Note one day when she was still working there with a bandage on her head. All of us had gathered around and asked her what had happened and she told us how she had been helping Pete on a job and a tree branch had fallen and cut her head open. She'd needed twelve stitches. This had been several months before Stacy and I started dating, but I remember thinking back then—without even having met the guy—that I didn't like Pete very much.

Before I reached the front steps, something caught my eye. The trailer for the tree chipper had a flat tire. For some reason that struck me as odd. There were a few small branches lying on top of the chipper too, as well as numerous pinecones around the base. I don't know how much money Pete made cutting down dead trees, but it seemed to me that he would want to keep his equipment in better order. And it looked as if it hadn't been used in a while.

The house itself was, indeed, a cabin, with wooden plank siding and a cedar shake roof that had weathered to silver a long time ago. It had probably been beautiful at one time, but now the whole place seemed to be sinking back into the earth. Dense foliage surrounded the structure, and what passed for grass was a couple of feet high, clutching at the cabin and threatening to pull the whole place down. The roof sagged, the porch sagged, and I thought the steps leading to the porch might snap under my weight. The porch itself was littered with leaves and needles and other natural detritus. A screen door with most of the screen hanging in tatters sat askew in the frame of the front door. As I pulled it open to knock, it scraped the porch and I could see that, over time, it had worn a deep semi-circle in the wood beneath my feet.

I knocked on the door and waited a fairly long time before knocking again. Suddenly I had the embarrassing thought that I might be rudely banging on the door at some uncivil hour, but when I checked my watch it was already nearing ten thirty. That didn't seem too early. I knocked again, and finally I heard some movement in the house. I stepped back on the porch so as not to seem too threatening. When the door finally opened, I was nearly bowled over by the odors of cigarette smoke, booze, and fried food as they roiled out of captivity through the open doorway.

Holding on to the knob—as if to keep himself upright—was a grizzled old man in a flannel shirt and dirty jeans. His hair was gray, greasy, and thin on top. He had a five-day growth of gray whiskers on his face, and the skin around his eyes seemed as weathered and worn as the cabin. A cigarette burned in his free hand, and while he stared at me a length of ash fell to the floor next to gray woolen socks with holes in them.

"Well," he finally said, before I had completely finished absorbing the scene before me. "What the fuck *you* want?"

His voice sounded like Louis Armstrong with a cold and I still couldn't seem to get myself to say anything. Then he suddenly hawked up and spat past me out the open door, jarring me back to my senses. "Mr. Wilczek. My name's Neslowe. I'm an investigator and I was wondering if I could ask you a few questions about your son."

He squinted at me and said, "You a cop?"

"No, sir. I'm a private investigator."

He looked at me as if I had been speaking a foreign language and then he shook his head. "The cops already been here." He took a long drag on his cigarette and exhaled out his nose. "Twice." More ash dropped around his feet.

"Mr. Wilczek," I said, already having planned my strategy. "I'm a private investigator. I was hired by Stacy Lambert—I believe she was dating your son—to find out who was responsible for his death."

His head shook again. "The cops already caught the guy."

"The police have a *suspect*, Mr. Wilczek. Whether or not they can make a case against him . . ." I shrugged for effect, "we don't know. Miss Lambert feels that perhaps the police are not exploring all the possibilities. She feels terrible about what happened, and she just wants to make sure the right person is eventually brought to trial."

Wilczek took a final drag on his cigarette, flicked the butt out the door past me, and I wondered vaguely how dry the foliage was out there. Then he turned and headed for the interior of the cabin. "All right," is what I thought I heard his voice grate out, and I followed him inside. When I made a move to shut the door he said, "Leave it."

The interior was dark and dank, and the only light in the room—other than that now coming from the open door—was a muted TV set tuned to *The Price Is Right*. Wilczek walked over to a tired burgundy-colored couch and lowered himself onto the middle cushion. He sat with legs splayed and poured himself a drink from a forest of bottles on a coffee table in front of him that appeared to be doubling as a bar. He didn't offer me one, so I didn't have to decline. Two aged wooden Adirondack chairs without cushions sat opposite the coffee table and were the only other furniture in the place. He didn't offer me a seat, but I took one anyway.

High exposed beams with planks over them were all that existed by way of a ceiling, and the air beneath was blue with cigarette smoke. Behind the couch was a small kitchen in the corner, and opposite the kitchen a wood stove. A doorway in the back wall looked as if it led to other rooms that had been added on later. The place was no wider than a mobile home and had the same depressing feel. And there were no decorations: none. Everything in the cabin, from the dirty dishes and clothes strewn around the place, to the pile of unopened mail next to the couch, was purely functional.

Wilczek lit a fresh cigarette, leaned back in the couch, and took a deep drag. "I already told the cops everything. What do you want to know?"

"Please forgive me if I ask some simple questions, but I'm only now getting started on the investigation." Wilczek just stared at me dumbly, eyes rheumy and yellow, nose and cheeks shot through with broken blood vessels. It struck me then that Pete's father had probably been a heavy drinker for a very long time. "How old was Pete?"

"Twenty-five last February some time."

"Where did he live?"

Using his cigarette for a pointer he motioned behind him.

"In the back room." Though I had never asked Stacy, I seem to remember her mentioning that Pete lived with his father.

"Did he bring many friends over?"

He shook his head. "Stacy a couple a times, but he was mostly embarrassed of the place."

And of his father, I waited for him to add, but nothing more was forthcoming. "Is there anyone else you can remember hearing him talk about? People he might have worked with, or hung around with?"

Again with the dumb stare. He took a long pull on his drink and then said, "Why the fuck would he talk to me about that?"

Okay. I was beginning to get the picture.

"I noticed outside that Pete ran a tree service. Was that his only source of income?"

Now there was something going on behind the eyes but it quickly vanished. "Far as I ever knew. Not that the sumbitch would tell me if it wasn't." He drained his drink and then poured another. Throughout the interview Wilczek had kept one eye on me and the other on the TV, but he was starting to lose interest in the game show.

"Did he work all day?"

"He worked when he had work."

"How often was that?"

"Two, three jobs a week when he wanted to."

That was interesting. "So he didn't work every day?"

Wilczek looked disgusted. "Lazy sumbitch. We was practically starving here and he wants to go off to college. What the fuck is that? He thought he was too good for me." The last part he had said more to himself.

"So what did he do with his free time, when he wasn't working?"

"Fuck if I know. He wasn't here, that's for sure. Got hisself a goddamn dog, if you can believe that. Border collie. Take that goddamn mutt everywhere. You think he'd take me anywhere? I can't even drive. I'm stuck on this fuckin' island all day and he takes that goddamn mutt all over hell an' gone."

I hadn't noticed any evidence of a dog anywhere. "Where's the dog now?"

"Called the pound day after he died. They came and picked it up. Good riddance. Couldn't stand that little fucker." He stubbed out the butt of his cigarette on the nearly full lid of a paint can, fired up another, and said, "I wished I coulda killed him myself."

For a split second I actually thought he was talking about Pete, and my blood ran cold. "Do you own a gun?" I asked.

He set down his drink and, like a magician making a card appear out of thin air, he pulled a Colt .45 revolver from the cushions of the couch and set it on the coffee table. "Got me a shotgun out back in the bedroom, too." Further comment was evidently unnecessary and so I moved the questioning back to Pete.

"Did you see Pete at all the day he died?"

Wilczek shook his head.

"How about the night before?"

Another shake.

"Do you know where he stayed that night?"

"With Stacy, I figure. He was staying with her pretty much all the time. I hadn't seen him much all summer."

"What about when he picked up the tree chipper?"

"Pete hasn't used that thing in months. I don't know where he got the money, but I can't remember the last time he had a tree job."

Yet another interesting fact with no immediate conclusion to be drawn from it. "What are you going to do for money now, if you don't mind my asking?"

"I'm on disability. That'll get me by till my Social Security kicks in a coupla years from now." The bluster was beginning to fade. He put out his cigarette without lighting up a new one, and set down his drink with a good inch left in the bottom.

"Is there anyone else you can think of that I could talk to about Pete? Is there anyone else he would have come in contact with in his free time that you can remember?" But he was already shaking his head.

There was one more question I needed to ask, but I wasn't

quite sure how to proceed and I was afraid I would botch it. Clearly, Wilczek disliked his son, and rubbing salt in that wound might only result in getting me kicked out of his house—at gunpoint, no less. But I quickly realized there was no other way, so I asked. "Mr. Wilczek, why did your son change his last name?"

"He hated me." He wasn't looking at me. He was staring at his own hands.

"Why would you think that?"

Now his eyes looked up to mine, still weak but defiant. "He was suing me," he barked. Clumsily, Wilczek reached over to the pile of mail and knocked most of it on the floor before finding what he was looking for. He ripped the letter from an open envelope and brandished it at me. "He was suing me, the goddamn ungrateful bastard. Who took care of him when his mama died? I did. Who taught him how to drive, who taught him how to shoot a gun, who taught him how to work for a living? I did. And then the sumbitch sues me."

I wanted to get a look at those papers, but he had sagged back onto the couch, clutching them in one dirty, yellowed hand, the remainder of his drink now in the other.

"What was he suing you for?"

"I told you already. He hated me."

Wrong question. I wanted to know what Pete hoped to gain from the suit.

Wilczek downed the shot and stared at the empty glass. The expression on his face hadn't changed, but I could see tears leaking from his eyes and running down into his whiskers. That was my cue.

"Well, I appreciate your taking the time to talk with me, Mr. Wilczek. I'll get out of your way now."

The old man nodded but didn't look up.

I stood and made a move for the door, but Wilczek didn't budge. When I reached the door I turned around and said, "I'm sorry for your loss, Mr. Wilczek."

"Don't matter," he said, and something like a wheeze or a sigh came from his throat. "He was already gone."

CHAPTER THIRTEEN

Getting back into my car I smelled as if I had just played all night in smoke-filled tavern, so I rolled down the windows and stuck my elbow out as I drove back north to the freeway. Along the way I couldn't help thinking about that pistol Wilczek had pulled out of his couch. As much as he may have disliked his son, however, it was pretty clear that I wouldn't be able to run to Dalton with him as a suspect. He said himself that he never left the island, that he hadn't even seen Pete in a while, and it was obvious right from the start that he had no idea who I was or where my apartment might be located.

No names, no contacts. But there was the fact that Pete hadn't worked in a while and yet still had money. Admittedly, it wasn't much to go on, but at least it was something. East Mercer took a left just north of the freeway and I had to parallel I-90 for a few blocks before I reached the next onramp. Along the way I couldn't help running over in my mind what Mr. Wilczek had said about Pete: that he was already gone. Had he already been planning on moving out of his father's house? I suppose it was even possible that he had been planning on moving in with Stacy.

I took a look at the dashboard clock as I pulled onto the freeway heading back to Seattle. It was only eleven o'clock. As awkward as it might be, I was going to have to talk to Stacy about Pete. I needed to know everything about what he was thinking and doing just before he died. The irony of the whole thing was, it was going to be awkward for both of us because a part of me didn't really want to know. But since my life depended on it, that was just too damn bad.

Here was a guy who had grown up poor with an alcoholic father and had been cutting down dead trees for a living. What possible reason could he have for changing his name? He'd only changed it a year ago, and now he had also stopped cutting down trees. His father said he'd talked about going to college, but apparently hadn't done so. And then there was the lawsuit. Why in the world would Pete have filed suit against his own father? It was pretty clear the old man didn't have a dime. With any luck, Stacy would be able to provide a few of the answers.

Just then, movement in the rearview mirror caused me to look up. I was horrified to see a black van about a hundred yards behind me, coming up fast on my left. I had no idea if it was *the* black van, but I wasn't about to take any chances. Instantly I jammed the gas pedal to the floorboard and tried not to hyperventilate as the Cavalier gradually sped up. I had picked up a pretty good head of steam by the time I had to climb from the water up to the I-90 tunnel. Just before entering I could see that the gap between us had stopped narrowing, but I lost sight of the van in the harsh yellow glare of the tunnel lights.

I had exactly three options when I emerged from the tunnel: head north on I-5, south on I-5, or keep driving west to the stadiums. The last choice was the least attractive. The western terminus of I-90 hooked around like the end of a J and dumped its traffic out onto 4th Avenue. I didn't want to be stuck at a light or hemmed in by city traffic with a couple of hit men on my tail. The freeway provided less of an opportunity to duck-and-cover, but in the sixty seconds I had to make my decision, I went for the speed and maneuverability it offered. The second I made my decision, however, I realized it had been the wrong one.

At the place where I-90 turns into northbound I-5, what had once been a six-lane interstate narrows down to two lanes at Seneca, and there is a perpetual slowdown at the bottleneck before the freeway opens up again at Olive. Traffic gradually slowed as freeway lanes dropped off one by one. Miraculously, I couldn't see the van in my mirror. That didn't mean much, though, and I muscled the Cavalier over to the left as soon as I could, taking one of the few left-lane exits off the freeway down Seneca. If the hit men were from out of town they might stay in the right-hand lane looking for me to exit on that side.

I hit a red light, two blocks off the freeway on 5th and cursed myself. I was in exactly the place I didn't want to be: stuck in downtown traffic. There was still no sign of the van, however, and I began to wonder if it had simply been some other black van on the road. I thought about this as traffic crawled down toward the waterfront. After all, it made sense that they would have been able to pick me up on the stakeout, and then at the Low Note, but how could they have possibly known I would be out on Mercer Island? And if they *had* known it, I couldn't think of a better spot to rub me out than in the woods around Wilczek's cabin.

As I turned on 2nd toward Yesler a more frightening thought came to mind. What if they had put some kind of global positioning device on my car? Shit. Maybe they had been too far away when they figured out where I was going and couldn't make it out to Wilczek's in time. They might have made it out onto the island only in time to pick me up getting back on the freeway. With a GPS device, they could afford to be unconcerned about keeping me in view. They could follow me anywhere.

I picked up speed, ran a yellow light heading down the hill, and dumped my car in an open space near the waterfront tourist traps. Walking back up Jackson I had a good view of my car, well exposed on the street, and could see a good distance in either direction down Marginal Way. It was probably too close to Dewey's, but I wasn't up for another long walk.

The weather was holding out and the homeless in Pioneer Square were lounging in the sun as I walked past them on 1st Ave. A block away from the Low Note I ducked into the alley and knocked on the kitchen door when I reached it. Jeannine answered and held it open for me.

"Come on in, Ray. Can I get you anything?"

"No thanks. Is Dew around?"

She rolled her eyes. "He's in the office with the regional director of sales for Budweiser. You want me to tell him you're here?"

"No. I'll wait." I walked over to the industrial coffee machine near the door and pulled a white mug from a dishwasher rack nearby.

"No one's been in asking for you, so you're probably all right to go out front."

I looked out the portholes in the two swinging doors that led out to the bar and said, "If it's all the same to you, I think I'll hang out back here."

Jeannine smiled and shook her head. "Honey, why don't you get a regular job like the rest of us folks?"

Jeannine was a small woman, five-two or so, but she had a huge heart. The hairnet and apron she wore threatened to turn her into a caricature, but the effect was offset by her natural beauty. She had burnished-brown skin, tiny laugh-lines around large doe-eyes, and a small gap between her front teeth that made any smile from her that much more appealing. Dewey was a lucky guy in a lot of ways, but none more than being married to Jeannine.

I looked around and found a stool to sit on and watched as she went back to her lunchtime prep work. "Oh, the job's not all that bad," I said. "I just . . ."

She turned to me, a hand on one hip, the other with a knife dangling from it and stared at me. I couldn't help but laugh. "All right. I'm having a bad week."

She went back to her chopping and said, "You want something to eat?"

"No thanks. I'm good with coffee."

But a few minutes later she was sliding a plate with a club sandwich in front of me and I ate. I was halfway through when Dewey stuck his head in the door. He didn't seem surprised to see me. "Jeannine. I need two burgers, one with cheese, and a French dip."

"Fries?"

"All around. Hey, Ray. Grab your stuff and come out front."

I swallowed and said, "The office would be better."

"Hmm. Okay."

I hauled my plate into his office and he stood by the open door while I sat down. "I need to ask you a huge favor."

"Huge, huh? Like donating one of my kidneys?"

I smiled. "No, I'd just like to borrow your car for a while. I'm afraid those two guys might have put some kind of tracking device on my car and now I'm getting paranoid."

He nodded. "Tenacious."

"You're telling me. The only problem is I wouldn't want you driving around in my heap, in case those guys are tracking it and decide to do something stupid."

"Gail has a car." Gail was Dewey and Jeannine's nineteen-year-old daughter.

"Dewey," we both heard from the hallway. He stuck his head out and said, "I'll be there in a second." Then he turned back to me. "The car I can do. Gail can take the bus to school for a couple of days."

"Thanks, Dew."

"The kidney, I would have to ruminate on at length." He winked and said, "A couple of minutes, anyway," and disappeared out the door.

Making my way down 1st Avenue in Dewey's car a few minutes later I felt invisible. He had a late model Pontiac and driving it made my car seem like a garbage can in comparison. I had swapped parking spots first, putting my Cavalier in the lot where he usually kept his car and then drove up to Beacon Hill to catch Stacy before she went to work. Whoever those guys were, they apparently still didn't know about Stacy's apartment. And with Dewey's car to drive around in I felt as if I could go anywhere in the city undetected. Going home was still going to be tricky, but I would probably give it a try while Stacy was at work.

Muted classical music was playing on the stereo when I walked in the door, probably the Mozart piano quartets I had seen in her collection the other morning. "Is that you, Ray?" I heard from the bedroom.

"Yeah."

"There's some coffee left if you want."

"No thanks. I was just down at the Low Note."

I kicked off my shoes and took a seat on the couch. On the coffee table were Stacy's nearly empty cup and a paperback book about the Zodiac murders in California. She emerged from the bedroom then, in sweats and a thin T-shirt with no bra underneath, and immediately I felt the pull. I had planned on talking to her right away, but after giving her first one kiss and then another, it eventually led to more strenuous activity. By the time we were putting our clothes back on she announced that it was time for her to start getting ready for work.

I followed her into the bathroom and stood in the doorway while she put on her makeup. "This seems a little early for you to be going to work."

"I have to meet Michael in Wallingford for lunch."

I nodded. Michael was Stacy's brother. He had a master's degree in Russian literature, but was currently driving a bus for Metro. "What's going on with Michael?"

"He's thinking about going back to get his doctorate. We're just going to talk. I haven't seen him in a while."

Though I nodded again, it didn't make a lot of sense to me. From what I knew about their relationship, Stacy and her brother didn't really like each other all that much. I couldn't see them getting together just to chew the fat. But I had more important matters to attend to. "Stacy, we have to talk about Pete."

She had been dusting her cheeks with some type of brush when she stopped and turned to me. "I know. I guess I've been avoiding it because of what you might think about me. It doesn't seem like a fun way to spend an evening, but I will if you think it will help."

"Yeah, I thought about that too, but we can't avoid it. I'm only out on bail now. There's eventually going to be a trial unless I find out who did this, and if not I'm going to be on the hook for the murder."

She looked as if all the blood had drained from her face. She sat down on the toilet and said, "They can't do that. You didn't do anything."

"They can, and they will. Christ, Dalton acts like he actually wants to."

"Ray," she said as she stood up, and I took a step back.

"I went over to talk with Pete's father this morning, but he didn't seem to know anything about what Pete was up to."

"That bastard," she said, and walked past me into the bedroom. I went in after her and sat down on the bed while she dressed.

"Why do you say that?"

She busied herself putting on clothing and spoke without looking at me. "He didn't want Pete to do anything. He wouldn't let him go to college, wouldn't let him move out, he didn't even want him to have Sandy."

"Sandy?"

"His dog," she said, and the corners of her mouth turned up slightly. "That'll serve the old bastard right, to have to take care of him for the rest of his life. Hopefully Sandy will outlive him."

That was one of Wilczek's secrets I was not going to divulge. "Had Pete made any plans to go back to school?"

She nodded. "He was all set to start at Bellevue Community College at the end of September."

"Where was he going to get the money?"

Stacy looked at me. "What do you mean?"

"I mean, to hear his father tell it they were broke."

"Financial aid, I guess. I don't really know. He was always weird about money so I never asked."

She bustled around a few minutes more while I tried to think of what else to ask her before she left. Finally I had to come out with it. "Did you know that Pete had changed his last name?"

She stopped and looked at me. "He changed his name from Willis?"

"No. He changed it *to* Willis. His real last name was Wilczek. Do you have any idea why he would have done that?"

Stacy thought about that for a moment and I became hopeful. "Not exactly."

"Tell me."

"When did he change his name?" she asked.

"About a year ago. It looks like it was right around the time he met you . . . or maybe just before."

"I'm not sure," she said. "I didn't know he'd done that, but it might have something to do with the lawsuit."

So she knew about the lawsuit, too. "Yeah. His dad told me about that but wouldn't give me any details. Why was he suing his dad? The old man doesn't have any money does he?"

Stacy shook her head slowly and thought about it for a moment. "He wasn't suing him to get anything out of him. I think he was just trying to punish him."

"What do you mean?"

She struggled with her words before saying, "I don't know what you call it, but his father had all kinds of debts that Pete had paid off, and he didn't ever want to have to do that again. The name change might have been more symbolic than anything else, his way of telling his father that he didn't even want his name." Finally Stacy just shrugged. "It was kind of like he was getting a divorce."

CHAPTER FOURTEEN

Although I wasn't supposed to do it, I put in a call to Carl's office as soon as Stacy was out the door. He wasn't going to like it, but I needed to find out more about this lawsuit and he was the only one who could help me. I managed to make it past his secretary by claiming to be a potential client who demanded to talk to Mr. Serafin in person. When I finally got through to Carl he wasn't very happy.

"Hey," I said. "I'm the one on trial for murder here. How about a little slack?"

"All right. What do you need?"

"I'd rather meet in person."

"No way," he said. "I'm swamped. Give it to me now."

So I started in on what I knew. As it turned out, Carl had already been given the ballistics report and the information about Pete's name change from Adamson's office that morning. "That's kind of fast, isn't it?" I asked.

"Well, he thinks it's a sure thing. But we can worry about that later. Have you found anything else?"

I told him about the lawsuit and he seemed interested in that. "When did you say this was filed?"

"I don't know, but it had to be in the last two or three months. Stacy knew about it. She seemed to think it was something like a divorce."

"No, it's nothing like that."

"Why not?"

"Because, while there are certainly instances of adult children legally separating themselves from their parents, it's always for very specific reasons."

"Such as?"

"I don't know . . . abuse. Say a person was abused by their parent as a child, and now the adult child is going to have children of their own. They don't ever want the abusive parent to gain custody of the grandchild down the road, so they sue for separation in case anything ever happens to them."

"Hmm. That doesn't seem to be the case here," I said. "I'm not getting the impression that Pete had been planning on starting a family anytime soon."

"What about money? You said the father had debts?"

"Yeah, but apparently Pete paid them off. I don't know where he got the money, though. Does that tell you anything?"

"Not really. If the father still had the debts then the son might want to legally separate himself from his father's estate."

"His estate? The guy wasn't dead yet."

"Yes, but if the father were to die intestate—without a will—and assuming that Pete was his only living heir, then Pete would have become the de facto executor, as well as the sole beneficiary of his father's estate. He would inherit everything."

"Including the debts?"

"No. That's why it doesn't seem likely. Creditors take everything they can until the estate's gone, but they can't touch the son. And if the estate is insolvent the debts would die with the father anyway."

I thought about that for a second. "I don't get it. If he's not obligated after his father's death, then why pay off the debts in the first place?"

"I don't know. I admit it doesn't make much sense legally, but people sue all the time for things other than monetary gain."

"Like what?"

"Power . . . punishment . . ."

"That's what Stacy said, that he was trying to punish the old man. Pete didn't even want to have his father's name anymore.

You think he might have been suing him as payback for something that happened in his childhood?"

"Possibly, but at this point we're just guessing. I'll have to check the court records and find the lawsuit before we really know what we're talking about."

"Okay, but I'm telling you, it fits with everything I found out. I don't know what he did to Pete but, if it's even close to what I imagine, Pete might very well have wanted to hurt him that way."

". . . Any way the old man killed Pete?"

"I wish," I said. "But I just talked to him this morning and I don't think there's any way he could have."

"Too bad." After a few seconds of silence, Carl said, "Well, if there's nothing else, I gotta go."

"All right. But do you think you can find out about the lawsuit today?"

"I'll try."

"Good. What about the name change?"

"What about it? Perfectly legal."

"What if he wasn't trying to hurt his father? What if he was trying to hide something? Do you think there might be another reason why he changed it?"

Carl sighed. "Maybe he just didn't like being Polish anymore. I don't know. Look, Ray, I have to go."

"All right. Call me as soon as you know anything." But the phone on the other end had already clicked and I was talking to myself.

I hung up and went out into the kitchen for that last cup of coffee, but the machine had already been turned off. Back out in the living room I walked over to Stacy's desk. I didn't have access to court records, but I could look on the Internet to see if Pete had been up to anything noteworthy. Unfortunately, her computer had a layer of dust on it that was a pretty good indication she hadn't used it in a while. I didn't have a clue if it would log in automatically to her ISP, or if she even had one, and I didn't feel like taking the time to look. My laptop was at home, and now that I had Dewey's car I could probably get inside without being detected.

But first, there was something I had forgotten to do that demanded my immediate attention. I drove back downtown before heading to my apartment, and retrieved my car keys from Dewey. It took me a half-hour of staking out the area before I could get safely back to my car. It was a stupid risk to take, but if they did have a tracking device on it, they wouldn't necessarily be in a place where they would have to see me getting into the vehicle. Besides, there was no way I was going to leave my gun in the car with everything that was going on.

When I was absolutely sure there was no black van, or anybody else watching the car, I hustled down to where it was parked, popped the door, and retrieved my gun from beneath the front seat. Then I wrapped up the .38—along with the concealed weapons permit that was in the glove box—in a kitchen towel Jeannine had given me when I retrieved my keys, and stuffed it under my shirt for the walk back. After it was safely under the front seat of Dewey's Grand Prix, I returned my keys and finally headed home.

Even though the actual distance is shorter going up Alaskan Way, it was all city traffic with lots of lights, and it's quicker to simply get on I-5 northbound and take 80th along the north end of Green Lake, so that's what I did. Once I had made my way back through the Greenwood district and down into Ballard, I made a thorough sweep of the neighborhood, starting at 8th and working my way slowly up and down residential streets densely packed with cars. It was an old neighborhood, and many of the houses had been built before the war. Most had basements and sat high above the street. I needed to get as close as I could so that I wouldn't be spotted on foot, but still not give away the fact that I was driving a different car. Nothing looked suspicious, however, and so I finally parked at the end of the block on 69th and walked up.

The sun was still high in the west and there were no shadows to hide in. I quick-stepped without running, and as soon as I hit the property line I ducked into the yard and ran back behind the house. I stayed there a while on the back patio waiting, just in case someone had seen me and decided the time was ripe to have me share the same fate as Pete Willis. After about twenty minutes, it was pretty clear that no one was coming for me, so I stepped down to the back door and reached for the crime-scene sticker that I had peeled back two nights before. And that's when I heard it.

Someone was inside my apartment. No wonder they hadn't been tailing me: they were going to ambush me from inside. And if one of them hadn't been so careless, they'd probably be dragging me kicking and screaming into my apartment right now. But that wasn't going to happen. I hot-footed it back to Dewey's car, started it up, and prepared to take off. But I didn't.

Instead, I wound up sitting there for a minute. Something was coming to me, so I turned off the car and let it. My first instinct had been to run, but the longer I sat there in the car the angrier I became. These guys had been dogging me for nearly a week, and I had been the one running and hiding for my life. This time, however, things were different. I knew exactly where they were and I had the opportunity to end this thing once and for all. Maybe. There might still be someone after me when I was through with them, but at least I'd know who they worked for and why they wanted me snuffed. The more I thought about it, the more I became certain that they were the ones responsible for Pete Willis's murder. With any luck, the whole mess could be wrapped up in a neat package and stuffed down Dalton's throat. I'd be a free man again—provided I had the courage to go through with it. I sat there for a few more minutes, weighing my options, and finally determined I had none. So I reached beneath the seat and pulled out the .38.

I checked the cylinder to make sure the first chamber was still empty. It was an old-West technique I'd learned from Detective Ransom to make sure you didn't shoot yourself—or someone else—accidentally. Of course, if you *did* want to shoot someone, you had to fire twice to get to the next chamber, but by then things would have gone so badly that it was bound to be ugly no matter who got off the first shot.

It was quite a while before I had the opportunity to head back to the house. Cars driving up and down the block, people out for afternoon walks, and kids out of school on skateboards and bikes had the neighborhood bustling with activity. Another thing Ransom had taught me was never to stuff a gun down your pants. If you were going to use it, either keep it in a holster or hold it in your hand. Since I never really wanted to use it, I'd never bought a holster, so I was resigned to carrying the thing in my hand back to the house. It was forty minutes before the street was clear. I stepped out of the car and made my way swiftly up the block and into the backyard again.

I didn't wait this time. I slipped down to the back door, listened, and heard nothing. But I knew I wouldn't. They would be back in their hiding spots again, waiting for me. Slowly, I pulled off the crime-scene sticker the way I had before, trying to make as little noise as possible. I was sure the door would be unlocked in order to facilitate my entry, and I was right. The knob turned easily in my hand. After a deep breath, I crouched down low, to make myself a smaller target, put the barrel of the gun up against my cheek and pushed the door open.

I brought the gun down level with both hands and quickly scanned the room. Something—not a person—in my peripheral vision to the left registered in my brain, but before it could become a conscious thought I distinctly heard the squeak of a stair riser on the stairs to my right. I didn't have time to think—I had to react. The doorway I had entered was in the center of the house. To my right was the enclosed staircase that led upstairs to my landlord's house, and to my left was the doorway to my apartment. If I rushed the stairs I knew I would be exposing my rear to anyone coming out of my door, so I had to go left.

I ran over and squeezed into the small space between the wall and the door to my apartment. Now I could cover whoever was coming down the stairs as well as catch anyone coming out of my apartment. I had the gun up to my face, so that it wouldn't be exposed to the apartment door, when I heard another squeak from the stairs. Whoever was coming down the stairs was trying not to make noise, but I was ready for him.

Then, two things happened simultaneously. Just as I saw a foot emerge from the enclosure of the stairway I realized what it was I had seen when I entered the door: a laundry basket. But it was too late to catch myself. I was already leveling the gun at the stairway when the small, Asian woman emerged, and she had already seen the gun by the time I yelled, "Freeze!"

Just then the rinse cycle of the washing machine kicked in, but I could barely hear it. The noise was drowned out by the blood-curdling scream of my landlord.

CHAPTER FIFTEEN

"You know, I never really thought about dying before, until today."

"Please, don't make me feel worse than I already do. I am *so* sorry about what happened."

I was sitting with Tien Nguyen at her kitchen table, drinking the green tea she had made for us. Her hand still had a slight tremor as she picked up her cup.

Her scream had scared me nearly as badly as my gun had scared her. The instant I realized what had happened I set the .38 on the dryer and held my hands up. But she had her face buried in her own hands—her armful of towels spilled to the floor—and didn't see me. I tried not to frighten her further by telling her who I was from across the room. Once she'd dared to look at me and realized I was her tenant, she slumped down to the stairs and placed her hands over her face once more.

At that point I promptly opened my apartment door and put the gun inside, picked up the towels from the floor and set them on the washing machine, then began the first of many apologies that I would probably be imparting to her for the rest of my residence in her home. She recovered quickly—I'll give her that—and invited me upstairs to share some tea with her. I was not about to decline.

"No," she said. "I'm not trying to make you feel bad, but I never really thought about it before, you know?"

I nodded, though I wasn't sure I actually did.

Tien was a second-generation Vietnamese who spoke English

and her parent's native language with equal fluency. She was in her early thirties, with straight, black hair and a round, sunny face. She looked at me and smiled, but it didn't quite come off. I looked down into my tea. I felt horrible.

"I mean, everyone contemplates their own death on a superficial level—something that's going to happen to them sometime . . . eventually. But I've never had an experience where I thought 'This is it.'"

"You're right. That doesn't make me feel bad at all."

It didn't quite elicit a laugh, but she looked a bit more relaxed as she sipped her tea. "Does this have something to do with the crime-scene tape around the house?"

"Yeah. Sorry about that, too. But it looks like someone broke in downstairs over the weekend."

She nodded. "The police tracked me down and I had to give a statement."

"So you weren't here?"

She shook her head.

That was disappointing. I had hoped that Tien might be able to tell me if she had seen a car or heard any voices. It was maddening knowing at least two people had been in my apartment, that one of them had shot and killed the other, and that there was absolutely no evidence besides my gun to point to who the killer was. Then I made a mental note to ask Carl if the cops had interviewed any of the neighbors.

"So, now that it's over, can I take town the tape?"

I nodded without thinking and then said, "Wait a minute."

Eyebrows raised, she waited for me to explain.

"It's just . . . Well, it's not really over." And that's when I realized that Stan Dalton had inadvertently done me a favor. By trying to make me think that the crime scene was still sealed, he had also done the same for my friends in the black van. I was suddenly sure that was the reason they were no longer staking out my neighborhood. I hadn't been home in a couple of nights, the tape was still up, why bother? They probably drove by once a day to see if the tape was still there, but that was it.

Then I explained to Tien—omitting the part about Pete being killed downstairs—that the two men who had broken into my apartment were still trying to get something from me and, since I didn't know what that was, the crime-scene tape could keep me from finding out accidentally.

She nodded and sipped her tea. "The police said someone was killed downstairs."

Okay, so much for Tien's delicate constitution. When I didn't say anything right away, she continued. "Those two guys really tore the place apart."

"I thought you said you were gone that night?"

She reddened. "Oh, I'm sorry. I know I shouldn't have, but I let myself into your apartment, just to make sure there was no damage."

Yeah, and just to check out those blood stains where an honest-to-gosh murder had taken place. "And . . . ?"

She shrugged, not meeting my eye. "Just the wall, I guess."

"And the carpet."

"That should come out," she said casually.

A little surprised, I said, "I hope you're not speaking from experience."

It took her a second to understand the significance and then her eyes widened. "No. I just mean that they have things now—"

"I know. I was just teasing you." I sighed. "Well, hopefully you can understand why I had the gun. Whoever did it is trying to kill me, too."

She thought about that for a second and her forehead wrinkled. Then she said, "I thought *you* did it?"

"What?"

Now she seemed embarrassed again. "I'm sorry. I just . . ." She reached for the tea pot and poured some more into her cup. "The way the police were talking, I just thought you did it."

"Then how in the world could you invite me up here for tea—especially after I pulled a gun on you?"

Now she looked positively indignant. "You don't have any reason to kill *me*."

As ludicrous as the conversation had become, she was right. Tien had raised into relief something that I hadn't really been looking at. Someone out there must have had a genuine motive for killing Pete. Up until now I had been focusing all of my attention on who had killed him, not why. But the police had a pat answer for that one: I wanted him out of the way so that I could have Stacy for myself. Though how I was supposed to benefit from eliminating the competition while sitting in prison was a detail I don't suppose they concerned themselves with. Or maybe they were just too dumb to think about that.

"Did the police actually tell you that I did it?"

She shook her head. "No. I asked them."

I actually laughed at that point. "How did they answer you?"

"The detective said they couldn't comment on the case, but that in most murders the obvious suspect is almost always the one. Then he winked at me."

I could only shake my head. "Did this detective have a pinkie ring?"

She brightened up. "Yeah. That's the guy."

"Well, listen. Thanks for the tea, and again, please accept my apology for what happened. I'm a little on edge."

"Okay. And the police tape?"

"If you could leave it up in front, then whoever is after me will think I'm not home and I can at least get the place cleaned up without worrying about them coming back."

"Okay."

I began heading for the stairs and then stopped and turned back to her. "For what it's worth, I want you to know that I didn't kill anybody."

She shrugged. "Okay."

Great—even my landlord thought I did it.

I picked the .38 up off of the floor and stared at it. I never really liked them much before, but now I was beginning to hate guns. The apartment was still a disaster, and as I looked around it was pretty clear there was no real place to hide the .38 other than where I'd hidden the .44: the shelf in my bedroom closet. Fortunately, the Seattle Police Department had conveniently cleared everything off of it for me. I simply put the gun in the empty Magnum box and set it in the corner, then I began picking up the rest of my possessions off the floor and stacking them up around it. Whomever Pete had told about the .44 certainly wouldn't think to look in the same place for another gun, especially one he didn't know existed.

I still needed to get to my desk and take a look at the computer, but I found that I was much more content to continue cleaning the place up. I didn't have anywhere to go and I wouldn't have to think about anything for a while. I plugged the fridge back in and did my best to clean the counters in the kitchen. With nothing but clothes and books in it, the bedroom straightened up much easier. In the living room I put the stereo back together, loaded a few discs in the changer, and after Kenny Burrell's "Midnight Blue" eased out of the speakers I sat there for an hour just putting back CDs, alphabetizing as I went. Once I had righted the easy chair and the lamp near the door, I decided to put the lamp back on the floor so that the light would be in the same position in case my friends drove by this evening.

Eventually, the place was navigable and I turned on the desk lamp. My desk was in an alcove, and I didn't think it would throw too much extra light. The desk drawers had been pulled out but, miraculously, hadn't been turned over. After pushing them back in, the desk straightened up fairly quickly. I fired up the laptop, went over to the fridge and grabbed a warm Red Hook I.P.A., and then sat down to surf the 'net.

I Googled "Pete Willis," but other than the guitar player for Def Leppard found very little else. I had to go about thirty pages in before I began coming up with other matches: a police officer in Texas, some high school kids with sports stats, but there was nothing I could find about anyone in the Seattle area. Then, on a whim, I decided to put "Pete Wilczek" into the search engine and, though there was no mention of Stacy's logger from Mercer Island, what I did find was very interesting.

A computer wiz kid by the name of Piotr "Pete" Wilczek had emigrated from Poland a couple of years ago and was the owner of a small computer firm in town called Global Web Development. They designed web sites and built Internet systems interfaces for companies with their own internal networks. This was from a fairly lengthy article in the *Post-Intelligencer* about several new start-ups, including GWD. A picture of Wilczek showed a young guy with glasses in a shirt and tie, his sleeves rolled up to the elbows, smiling for the camera. He had bushy hair that needed a trim and the glint of an earring in his left ear—a diamond stud for the computer stud.

From what I could gather, Wilczek's company was a little more than a year old and had already gone from Wilczek running the show out of his house, to a staff of five with office space on Capitol Hill. The article mentioned that Wilczek still had family in Poland and was planning on moving some of them out here now that the business was taking off. In addition to the coincidence of their names, one fact about him stood out in my mind, and that was his age. He would be twenty-five years old today, the same age as Pete Willis.

Of course, it could all be coincidence, more facts that led nowhere. But what if there was a connection? It seemed implausible that the two men could somehow be related. The most logical explanation that occurred to me was that Pete had changed his name simply to avoid being confused with the computer Wilczek, sort of like having the bad luck to have grown up in Seattle with the name Bill Gates. But unless Pete had read the article in the *P.I.*, how would he even have known? He and his dad seemed pretty rustic and unlikely to have traveled in the same circles as the computer Wilczek.

I grabbed another beer—slightly cooler by now—and did some more searching, but came up with nothing else. AltaVista and some lesser search engines had other mentions of the computer Wilczek in his business context, but mostly they pointed to the same articles as Google, so I shut down the computer and went into the bedroom to gather some more clothes to take to Stacy's. It was starting to get dark and I certainly wasn't going to stay here at night until I figured out who my two friends from the black van were. I know I should have put myself up in a hotel downtown, and if I had let myself think about it for any length of time I probably would have. But then being with Stacy had never been even remotely rational.

I had a few things laid out on the bed, and was looking for something to put them in when my cell phone chirped. I checked the number and flipped it open.

"Hey, Carl."

"Ray, is there any way you can meet me tonight?"

I didn't know whether to be pleased or panicked. "What's going on?"

"I can't talk about it here at the office. Why don't you meet me for dinner."

"Sure. Where?"

"How about the Capital Grille?"

I almost laughed. "That's a little out of my price range. You buying?"

"Yeah, yeah," he said impatiently. "Just get over there. I'll meet you in a half-hour, okay?"

"Sure. But you have to tell me what this is about. It's not the cops, is it?"

"No, no. Nothing like that."

"Is it about Willis?"

"Yeah."

"Did you check up on him this afternoon?"

"I did what you asked."

". . . And?"

There was a hesitation on the other end of the line. "I'm not really sure what's going on there. But that's another reason we need to talk."

"Another? Look, just tell me what's going on with Pete."

He sighed. "I can't find any paper on him."

"What does that mean?"

"It's weird," he said. "I know you met the guy and all. And there was a person who changed his name from Pete Wilczek to Pete Willis. But on paper . . . it's as if he never existed."

95

CHAPTER SIXTEEN

The Capital Grille downtown is an upscale joint where people in two-thousand-dollar suits can come and have a hundred-dollar steak and wash it down with an eight-hundred-dollar bottle of wine before they go home in their BMWs and Porches to their Medina homes and trophy spouses. Okay, so maybe it wasn't *exactly* like that, but it's the way I always felt whenever I went there. All right . . . the *one* time I'd been there. But things didn't seem to have changed much since then. Green felt and black leather were predominant, with dark booths and fawning waiters for that special touch the executives like so much. I didn't deign to wear a tie, but I grudgingly slipped on a jacket before driving over.

Carl was at the bar when I arrived, and already on his second drink—vodka on the rocks from the looks of it. "You want a drink before we sit down?"

"Maybe just a beer."

I ordered from the bartender and walked behind Carl with my Rolling Rock toward the reservation desk. The maître d' immediately recognized Carl and waved him over as soon as he saw him. We were seated at a table that would have held four comfortably, given menus, and left to the devices of our waiter, Philip. His overly cultivated demeanor seemed better suited for a full house at the Seattle Repertory Theater than a steak house, but he still managed to go all out for his captive audience of two. As Philip waxed rhapsodic about that day's specials, his minions poured water and served us bread. Once he had finished, I didn't know whether to thank him or applaud. Carl evidently didn't have that problem: he ordered another drink.

"Are you all right?" I finally asked when Philip had gone.

He swirled the ice in his glass, no doubt wishing there was more vodka in it, and said, "The partners found out about the case."

I was waiting for him to tell me what case, when he looked up at me. Then I understood. "You mean, me?"

"Yeah. They want me to cut you loose."

Before I could respond he began looking around the room, perhaps for Philip and his next vodka.

"You want him to leave the bottle?"

He didn't even crack a smile, just upended the residue of liquor and ice cubes into his mouth and said, "Not a bad idea."

"Come on, Carl. You're beginning to worry me. We've been through this kind of thing before. What happened? Did they find out Adamson is trying the case or something?"

He was already shaking his head. "Adamson came into the office."

"What?"

"He talked to Chaney in person." Chaney was the senior partner at Carl's firm. "And then Chaney called *me* into his office and chewed my ass for twenty minutes."

At last Philip showed up. Carl downed about half his new drink in one swallow and gave him a curt, 'not yet' when asked if he was ready to order. Philip exited stage left.

"Did he say why he doesn't want you to represent me?"

Carl looked at me as if I'd just suggested he get a sex-change operation. "Your name never came up. That's not the way it works, Ray." He killed his drink, set the glass on the table, and pushed it away from him. "They talk about all the good work you've been doing, about your prospects at the firm, how great the future's going to be. He said there's a partner's meeting coming up next month, and how much the firm is counting on me to be a part of the team. They don't come right out and tell you they're going to fire you. They say how disappointing it is when someone comes in with their own agenda and how difficult private practice can be in Seattle."

I didn't know what to say, and Carl picked up his menu in the meantime. Philip suddenly appeared front and center and dazzled us by not writing down the order. Carl ordered a Porterhouse—medium rare—and a vodka chaser. I ordered the salmon.

"Listen," Carl said, after Philip had gone. "I know a couple of good people in the public defender's office—"

"Whoa, whoa. Wait a minute. You're not really going to do this?"

"I don't have much of a choice."

"Come on, Carl. You said you wouldn't leave me twisting in the wind on this one."

"I haven't. I put up fifty K for bail, remember?"

I couldn't believe this. I shook my head and then took a drink of beer. "That's not fair. Look, you know I appreciate what you did for me. Hell, everything you've done for me. You know that, but this is my life we're talking about here. I didn't kill anybody and you know that, too."

Carl simply stared.

"Are you kidding me? Because if you give me any of that crap about guilty people being entitled to a defense, I swear to God I'll skip town just to screw you out of the fifty thousand." My voice had raised and even amid the din of the restaurant, people were beginning to look at us.

He raised his hands. "All right, I'm sorry. Just take it easy, okay?"

"Well, do you really think I did it?" I asked, my voice still amplified.

"No. Jesus Christ. Will you just calm down?" Carl shrugged out of his jacket and rubbed his face in his hands. Then he leaned back with his fingers laced together over the top of his head. "I'll tell you this much. If I thought you were guilty I probably *would* risk losing my job with the firm but you're not, so I'm counting on you to clear yourself . . . for both our sakes." He let his arms fall back to his sides. "I'm making the call on this one, Ray. Irina

Vekich is a good friend of mine and a great defense attorney—better than me if this thing goes to trial—and she'll do it for me. So don't act like you're being thrown to the lions."

Despite Carl's assurances, I wasn't very happy about his abandoning me. "And what if she already has a hundred other cases? What if she doesn't have time between her hookers and crack-heads to put together a defense? Against Adamson, no less."

Carl wasn't impressed. "You'd be surprised what she can do," he said, and something like a smile appeared on his face. "She even gets off the hookers and crack-heads." Then Carl relaxed for the first time that night. "And best of all, Adamson won't go anywhere near her."

Philip chose that moment to raise the curtain on Act II, when he and his supporting cast showed up to serve the salads. He had a busboy carting the food on a tray and a cocktail waitress who handed Carl his vodka. In another first that evening, Carl set down his glass without taking a drink. Philip presented us with our salads, then produced a hand-cranked cheese grater loaded with Parmesan and we both took a hit. The next prop he unsheathed was a two-foot-long pepper mill, which Carl agreed to and I declined.

Around a forkful of salad I said, "What did you mean "Adamson won't go near her?'"

Carl nodded while chewing and then swallowed. "She's too good. He couldn't be sure he'd win. My guess is, when he finds out she's taken over he'll assign the case to one of his deputies."

"Well, that's good news, isn't it?"

"Yeah." He shrugged. "Assuming the police don't come up with any more evidence against you."

"Thanks."

"Don't mention it," he said, and took a small sip of his drink.

"When do you think she'll want to meet with me?"

"She hasn't agreed to take the case yet, but I don't think she'll meet with you right away."

"Why not?"

"She doesn't have the time, for one thing. I'll send over the file and all of the discovery documents to her in the morning. She'll read it, and if she has any questions she'll call you."

We talked for a while longer over our roughage and Philip whisked away the plates before our forks had cooled. Then I asked Carl what he had found out about Pete Willis.

"Oh, yeah," he said, taking another sip of vodka—savoring the flavor instead of salving his conscience. "I almost forgot about that. I checked out the lawsuit and there wasn't one. Not in King County anyway."

"That doesn't make sense. Unless his father lied about it."

"And that's just the beginning. I found the same name change the police did, Wilczek to Willis, but nothing else."

"What do you mean by nothing else?"

"Nothing. No birth certificate, no driver's license. That seemed odd, so I talked to one of the guys in the firm who works on Federal cases and has connections in the Justice department. I asked him to look into tax returns and social security for Willis and guess what he found?"

"Nothing?"

Carl nodded.

I thought about that while Philip moved downstage for his final production number: dinner. The same bored busboy schlepped in the food while our grinning waiter set our meals in front of us and rotated the plates just so, evidently to show off the food to its best advantage. I ordered another Rolling Rock while Carl placed his hand over the top of his glass, and with another flourish Philip headed once again for the wings.

"That doesn't make sense."

"You said that already."

"No driver's license?"

"Not in Washington State."

"What about his previous name, Wilczek? Did you look up that?"

Carl's brow wrinkled. "That's all I *did* use. You know how many Peter Willis's there must be in this country? And the info on the name change was local."

"Mercer Island?"

"Yeah. Cedar Creek Road, or something like that."

I nodded. "Cedar Cove."

Carl busily buttered his potato while I took a bite of my fish and thought about that. Finally I said, "You know, it might be just a coincidence, but there's another guy in town by the name of Pete Wilczek."

Carl had been cutting into his meat when he lifted his knife from the plate and pointed it at me. "I thought about that, but the computer guy has a different first name. It's Polish or something, with Cs and Zs and all that. Just like the last name."

"How in the world could you have possibly known about him?"

He shrugged. "I read the papers, too."

"So, basically there's no legal paperwork for Peter Wilczek, or Pete Willis in the state with the Mercer Island address on it."

"Except for the computer guy."

"Right. No birth certificate, no driver's license, no tax returns, nothing."

Carl took that as a rhetorical question and continued eating. Then I decided I'd better ruminate over my meal as well and joined him. Later on, after Philip had cleared our plates, I said, "How is that possible?"

"Hmm?" Carl squinted, then understood. "Oh, well here's one possibility. Say your guy is born somewhere else. Unless I knew where that was, I wouldn't be able to find a birth record without a Social Security number."

"What about a driver's license?"

"Same thing. Say he still has family back home, cousins, grandmother, whatever. He goes back every few years to visit and gets his license renewed. Now he's street legal in the US as long as he doesn't get stopped by the cops. And if he does he tells them he's still living back home."

I sighed. "They never recovered his wallet."

"Which is strange in and of itself. Why would his wallet be gone? Was the killer trying to hide the identity of the victim?"

"I don't think so."

Carl leaned over the table in a conspiratorial manner and said, "Do you want desert?"

"What?"

Carl motioned with his head and when I looked up I could see that Philip was headed our way with a desert tray. "No thanks," I said. Carl waved him off and pantomimed writing on his hand to indicate he would like the check. Philip nodded, winked, and about-faced.

Then Carl said, "Why don't you think the killer was trying to hide his identity?"

"Because the police knew who it was right away."

Carl smiled. "Uh huh. And how did they know that?"

I thought for a second and said, "Stacy told them."

"Exactly."

"Wait a minute. You don't think Stacy is involved in this—"

"No, no. You don't understanding what I mean. Of course she would think it was Pete. The victim was wearing Pete's clothes. If the killer is trying to hide the identity of the body then he put the body in her apartment for one reason: to *make* her identify the body as Pete. How close did she actually get to his face when she identified him for the police? Half of it was blown off. You think she really even looked at anything other than his clothes?"

I shook my head.

"Then, when the police investigate, the father says he's missing and when Pete doesn't show up for a few days it's a pretty safe bet to assume it's him. Think about it for a second. What hard evidence do the police really have other than the fact that Stacy and the father both say its Pete?"

I thought for a second. "Emily said they were going to match his dental records."

"Which I'll bet they are. But I'm also betting they're going to match them to someone who's been in one time, maybe two, and paid cash on every occasion."

Philip showed up with the check, clearly losing interest in the reviews from our table and in search of a more receptive audience.

But Carl told him to hold on while he fished out his credit card and handed it over without looking at the tab.

I wasn't quite in sync with Carl's theory yet and said, "I still don't see why that's so important."

"Because, if Willis had ever been to the dentist in his life it would have been only because it was absolutely necessary. You said yourself they didn't have two nickels to rub together. There's no way they had medical or dental insurance. What did he supposedly do for a living?"

"Tree service. He cut down dead trees."

"Okay, but I'll bet if you check with the Mercer Island city hall they won't have a business license for him. You have to figure that anyone who doesn't file a tax return is probably working under the table and not reporting it. And as long as he's not on the federal radar it won't matter how much you investigate, you're never going to turn up anything."

"So what does that prove?"

"That it could have been anyone in that dentist's office who had his teeth worked on. Just because he said his name was Pete Willis doesn't mean a damn thing. There won't be any insurance claims or cancelled checks or anything else that proves it was really Willis. It could have been a homeless bum off the street who was the same age as Willis for all anybody knows."

Philip brought back the receipt for Carl's signature, took his final bow, and brought down the curtain on another successful performance. As Carl was writing, I wondered how much he was going to tip him—probably more than I made in a day. Then the pen went down, the card went back in Carl's wallet, and he looked back up at me with a smile.

"All right," I said. "So what are you saying, exactly?"

"I'm saying that the body they found might not be Pete Willis. It literally could have been anybody. But we're supposed to *think* it's Pete Willis."

"And why are we supposed to think that?"

He actually laughed then. "Because Pete Willis is the killer."

CHAPTER SEVENTEEN

"You don't really believe that, do you?"

Carl had slid out of the booth and was shrugging on his jacket. "Hell, no," he said with a grimace, and I followed him back out onto the street.

"Then what's the point?"

Now he shook his head, as if I was a disappointing student. "It's called reasonable doubt. I'm not sure if I would have gone with that exact scenario, but all the defense has to do is provide the jury with some possible explanation that fits the evidence."

"Doesn't seem very likely."

"That's the great thing about reasonable doubt, it doesn't have to be probable, just possible. The prosecution has the burden of proof. They have to prove that all of the evidence means exactly what they say it means. The only thing the defense has to do is show that it could have happened some other way."

"And that's what you're going to do at the trial?"

He held up a finger. "What Irina's going to do at the trial."

"Okay, what she's going to do at trial?"

"If it comes to that. Like I said, I don't think anyone over at the City Attorney's office is too eager to chalk up another one in their loss column, so with any luck we'll never know." Then Carl looked at his watch for effect. "Listen, Ray—"

"I know, you have to go."

"Yeah, I do, but that's not what I was going to say. Listen, about that Burns case . . ."

Rachel Burns. With everything that had gone on the past few days, I had completely forgotten about the case I'd been working on for Carl. "Oh, man. I'm sorry, Carl—"

He held up a hand. "I know you've been busy. I just wanted to let you know that I had to reassign the case." I stared at him and he held out his hands. "I'll tell you what, turn in what you have and I'll see if I can get you something for your time."

"Great. First you abandon me, and now this. Well, thanks for dinner, anyway."

"Hey, come on, Ray. You know I didn't want it to end up like this, but I think it's the best thing for everyone."

I nodded, still not entirely sure that was true. Finally we said goodbye, and while Carl waited for the valet to bring around his car I walked back to mine. Well . . . Dewey's. So, not only was I on the hook for Pete Willis's murder, but now I was out my fees for the Burns case as well. And it wasn't as if I had a lot of money in the bank to begin with. Still, I guess I had enough to get by, and worrying about it wasn't going to change things, so as I walked I began to think more about Carl's reasonable doubt scenario. I hadn't even considered the possibility that the dead man might not be Pete. And as far-fetched as it had initially sounded, by the time I started up the car and pulled away from the curb, I realized it was the first *why* that I'd been able to come up with.

If Pete had really been that desperate to get away from his father, it might have seemed perfectly reasonable for him to kill someone else in order to escape. He would have been able to walk away, start over in a new city, and never have to see his father again. But it also occurred to me that if things were so bad as to cause someone to resort to murder that it would be a lot easier to simply kill the source of their troubles. Of course that's what the police thought about me, and it *was* the most obvious way to get caught, so I guess in Pete's case murdering someone else did make sense in some sort of whacked-out way.

The only thing that didn't make sense to me was the lawsuit. What the hell was that all about? The old man had said that Pete was suing him. If that was true, then why the need to fake his death at all? More importantly for me, however, the lawsuit would be key to any switched-identity theory at trial. Wilczek had held up something, and was clearly upset by it, so it seemed strange that Carl hadn't found a record of it. But then, if it hadn't been filed yet he wouldn't have. And there was always the possibility that the papers weren't even real. I had to find out what was in those papers he'd been holding, or at a minimum what law office they supposedly came from.

The clock on the dash read seven-thirty. Assuming he wasn't already in the bag by then, it was still plenty early enough to go over to Wilczek's house and see if I could get a look at those papers. I was already to Holgate before I made my decision, so I took a left on Airport Way, hooked back around to 4th in front of Qwest Field, and onto I-90 eastbound. On the way to Mercer Island the sun was low enough at my back that the road was mostly covered in shadow. And so, it seemed, were the answers to this case.

Despite the lawsuit, I couldn't help refining the switched-identity scenario in my mind. Pete would have had to find someone with his build and hair color and then get that person to his dentist. Correction, get him to *a* dentist. And that's where the story came unhinged for me. Carl had suggested a homeless bum. But nobody likes going to the dentist even when they have to. Besides, Pete couldn't have taken the guy in with six layers of stinking clothes on. He'd have had to clean the guy up and run the risk that he'd need a ton of work done. It would have attracted attention, the one thing Pete wouldn't have wanted. The more I thought about it, the real problem with the dentist scenario was the homeless bum.

But suppose he had found someone near his age who really needed and wanted the dental work, someone who wasn't homeless—a college student, a client, an acquaintance? It could have been anyone who matched up with Pete's description. Pete offers to be a hell of a nice guy by paying for this guy's dental work on the condition that he claims to be Pete—because of the insurance, he could say. Then, after the murder, Pete removes the guy's wallet, and as long as he's never been fingerprinted his dental records will turn out to be Pete's and they'll have successfully identified the victim. Pete doesn't show his face in Seattle again—and why would he want to—and he's home free with a new identity.

Even as I rationalized it in my mind it seemed crazy. Still, assuming it wasn't Pete, it was an explanation that accounted for why someone would have committed the murder at all. In attempting to figure out why someone would have killed *Pete*, however, I hadn't a clue. Without knowing anything else about Pete's life, the only person with a motive I could think of was the father, but the murder taking place in my apartment didn't fit with him at all. And he certainly couldn't have afforded to hire someone to do it.

Emerging from the tunnel down onto the western rise of the bridge, my attention was immediately drawn to the smoke in the sky. The wind had died down during the course of the day, and the smoke hung in the air, drifting slightly northward. A fire somewhere on the Eastside, I thought, but hard to tell exactly where. And it was almost out, too. The heaviest smoke had already dissipated high in the air and all that remained was a thin, seemingly static wisp that emerged from the trees east of the island. Once on the island itself, I lost sight of it altogether.

As I made my way off of the freeway and onto East Mercer I could smell the smoke. It must be drifting west as well as north, I thought, but then traffic slowed and I began to wonder if the fire hadn't been on the island after all. At that moment Dewey's car began to vibrate, making a horrible noise. I was about to pull over when I realized it was actually a pair of helicopters flying low overhead. They continued to circle nearby and it was then that I knew I must be close to the source of the smoke. When I finally reached Cedar Cove Road I pulled the car over on East Mercer opposite the road and just sat and watched for a while.

The last wisps of smoke rose from the trees about halfway down to the water. Two fire trucks were parked there in the middle of the street, surrounded by three or four Mercer Island police cars and an ambulance. A couple of firefighters were still struggling with the hoses, but the rest were standing and talking together, occasionally pointing at whatever had been burning. Lights rolling on all the emergency vehicles and the news helicopters overhead added more drama than the scene now warranted. Clearly, the fire was out.

One cop car was turned sideways at the head of the road, keeping traffic flowing down East Mercer and away from the scene, but I observed a knot of people across the street from the fire trucks watching. I climbed out of the car and made my way across the heavy traffic and toward the police car. The cop standing guard looked over at me.

"Looks like it's under control now, huh?"

He was young—I'd put him in his early twenties—but was still able to look at me with disdain. Did they teach them that at the academy? He didn't say anything, but did give me a grudging nod.

With the soaking we'd had earlier in the week, there wasn't much chance of the fire spreading, and as I neared the scene I could see that the firefighters had done a good job of keeping the flames from jumping to the surrounding homes. That was the only silver lining, however. At least for me. My hopes of getting those legal papers from Pete's father had vanished, and I suddenly remembered the old man flicking a cigarette butt past me out into the lawn.

The evergreens surrounding the property had been badly singed, but were basically intact. That was more than could be said for Pete's Bronco and the tree chipper: they were blackened hulks. But even they had fared better than the cabin itself. The house that I had been in just that morning was now gone, and it its place was nothing but a smoldering pile of ash.

CHAPTER EIGHTEEN

Towering hemlock and Douglass Fir above me blocked out the setting sun, darkening the road, and what blue sky I could see to the east had already deepened to navy. Streetlights hadn't turned on yet and the only illumination was the headlights of the emergency vehicles and the spotlights of the fire trucks. Frogs and crickets had begun to sing from somewhere nearby, mixing their voices with the conversation of the half-dozen people from the neighborhood who had been watching the fire.

I walked up to three cops milling around one of the patrol cars. "Does anyone know if the old man survived?"

You'd have thought I'd just asked if it was okay to bring a box-cutter onboard an airplane. One of them actually put his hand on his gun. The cop closest to me, wearing a short-sleeve blouse that showed off his well-muscled arms to good effect, put up a hand and said, "Sir, you'll have to go back across the street."

"I'm a private detective. Stan Dalton from the special case squad in Seattle knows me. He'll vouch for me if you want to give him a call," I said, and then prayed to God he wouldn't.

He frowned and said, "All right. But stay back off the property."

The tag on his uniform read "Dodson" and I nodded to him. "Did the old man survive?"

"You know who lives here?"

There was a multitude of ways I could answer that, with varying outcomes resulting from each. I could say no, and that would have been the end of it, but there was much more at stake here. For one thing, this was easily the biggest lead I'd had on the case since I started.

"Yeah," I said. "I was just here this morning, talking to him."

Suddenly all three cops were very interested in me. I knew now that I would have to give a statement to the officers and that was just fine with me, because I was absolutely convinced that whoever had killed the person in my apartment was responsible for the fire, too. "Is he dead?"

Dodson nodded. "Someone was inside. Neighbors are pretty sure it's him. They say he never left the house." Dodson gave me a hard look and said, "I'll need to get a statement from you, Mister . . ."

"Neslowe. Ray Neslowe."

Dodson leaned over to reach into the squad car and pulled out a box-shaped aluminum clipboard that held traffic citations and rooted for a statement form. He probably didn't have to use them very often. I was asked to come around to the back of the cruiser so he could set the clipboard on the trunk as he wrote. The questions began fairly straightforward: what time had I been there, was Wilczek alone, did I see anything hazardous that could have caused the fire. But quickly I began to push the statement to reflect the direction I wanted the investigation to take.

"What was your business with Wilczek?"

"I was investigating the murder of his son."

Eyebrows raised, Dodson wrote it down, but before he could ask another question I continued. "When I was here he showed me some legal papers that I have reason to believe would have shed light on the case. I think the murderer wanted those papers destroyed, and the only way he could be sure that they were was to torch the place."

Dodson was writing furiously. "What about Wilczek?" he finally asked. "Are you claiming that he was purposely killed in the fire?"

"Yes. I believe he was."

When Dodson had finished writing he scratched his face with

his free hand and said, "Do you know who's working the murder of the son?"

"Dalton and Haggerty out of the special case squad at police headquarters in Seattle."

He nodded. "All right, but I can't do anything unless the arson guys think it was deliberately set. They have to make the call."

"I understand." I pulled a business card from my wallet and handed it to Dodson. "I would appreciate if you'd let me know what the arson squad comes up with, and maybe help me get in touch with whoever winds up with the homicide investigation."

He frowned again. "Who are you working for?"

Again, there were choices to be made. I could have said Stacy, like I'd told Wilczek, but that would have led the questioning in a direction I didn't want to go. "The old man." His eyes followed mine to the smoking ruin of the cabin. Then I realized I didn't even know his first name. "Wilczek." I turned back to him and said, "The Seattle police are going to tell you that they've already charged someone for the murder of the son, but Wilczek never believed it was the man they charged. That's why he hired me." I held out my hands for effect. "And now this." Inwardly I smiled when Dodson actually nodded in agreement.

"All right," he said. "I'll see what I can do." He finally took down my address and cell phone number, and I agreed to make myself available for further questioning.

One of the fire truck crews had begun putting away its hoses as I made my way back across the street toward the spectators from the neighborhood. As I approached a man and two women, the animated conversation three of them had been having ceased. The tallest was an older man of retirement age, thin and balding with wire-frame glasses, who stood nearly six feet. Next to him was a heavy-set woman of similar age, considerably shorter, with round, fleshy features. Opposite them was a younger, dark-haired woman with a Border collie on a leash. Immediately I thought of Sandy, and realized that the old man had inadvertently saved the dog's life by giving it to the pound.

"Hi," I said. "Looks like they have everything under control."

The man agreed with me and I continued. "Did any of you see what happened?"

"No," he said. "We were watching TV and didn't hear anything until the sirens."

"Was Mr. Wilczek inside?"

The man nodded sadly. "He had to have been. Luka almost never left the house. I talked to him when I could, if I saw him out at the mailbox, but he kept to himself."

"Hmm. What about Pete?"

The man's eyes narrowed. "Are you a cop?"

I shook my head. "I was actually on my way to talk to Luka. We were trying to find Pete."

The shorter woman's hand went immediately to the man's arm and I figured them for husband and wife. "I told you something was wrong when the police showed up the other night."

He nodded but didn't look down at her. "Pete used to come and go all the time, but we haven't seen him for a week. Do the police think he's missing?"

I didn't want to get into the whole murder thing, so I said, "Something like that. You said before that you didn't hear anything until the sirens. Do you know who reported the fire?"

I looked over to the woman with the dog, but she said, "Not me. We were out for a walk and saw the engines go by." She looked over to her two neighbors. "We ran all the way home when we saw them turn in here."

"Wow. So it happened pretty fast."

The man nodded. "We didn't even smell smoke. Without any wind it just went straight up into the air. Probably saved a lot more houses around here from catching fire, too."

"That's lucky," I agreed. "Did Luka ever say if he had any other relatives beside Pete?"

The woman answered this time. "Not that we knew. Pete was an only child. I think they originally came from back East. His mother died before they moved out here."

That must have been quite a while ago, I thought. "I wonder what will happen to the property if they can't find any relatives."

The man spoke up. "They didn't own that place. They rented."

That was strange. With little to no money coming in, I had naturally assumed the place had been paid for years ago. "How long had they lived there?"

The wife and husband looked at each other. "A year?" he said. She nodded vigorously, "Come September."

Just before Pete had met Stacy. That was interesting. "Do you know who does own the property?"

"Sure." He pointed across the street. "They live right next door. There are two unimproved lots between the two places. Anyway," he said, motioning with his head, "they're right over there if you want to talk to them."

I turned, and down at the next driveway was a couple with their arms around each other, still staring at the burned out property across the street. They looked to be in their late twenties or early thirties, and were casually dressed, the man in sweat pants and a T-shirt, the woman in shorts and a windbreaker. I looked at him a little longer. Something about his face was vaguely familiar. Finally, I turned back to the man. "Can you tell me what their last name is?"

All three of them looked at each other, and I believe I even heard the woman with the dog bark out a laugh, though I suppose it could have been a cough. In any event, the man turned back to me with a grin and said, "That's Pete Wilczek."

CHAPTER NINETEEN

"Thank you. And thanks so much for inviting me in."

"You're welcome."

I was currently in the living room of computer genius Pete Wilczek's palatial Mercer Island home. Well, palatial compared to my place, anyway. His wife, Magda, had handed a cup of coffee to me and then sat down next to her husband on the couch. I took a sip from the cup and placed it back on the saucer. It was good. The two of them, on the opposite side of the coffee table from me, looked a bit worn out. Understandable, considering the likely death of their tenant—not to mention the loss of the house itself.

"I hear you say you were coming this morning?" said Wilczek. "To visit Luka?"

Pete Wilczek spoke with a thick, Eastern-European accent. I knew from the newspaper article that he'd only been in the country a couple of years, and though he no doubt spoke computer programming fluently he hadn't quite mastered all of the intricacies of English syntax. Magda didn't seem much inclined to say anything beyond "Hello" and "Thank you.'

"That's right," I said. "I don't know if you'd heard about his son."

"The police say he was killed when they question me."

I had only exchanged a few words with the two of them outside on the street when Wilczek surprised me by asking me if I'd like to come inside and get us all out of the dark night. I was happy to accept the invitation. The house was a three-story affair, looked fairly new, and while not necessarily expensively furnished, it was plenty comfortable. I was seated in a large, white, overstuffed chair, only barely able to resist the urge to kick off my shoes and lounge a leg over one of the arms.

"As I told you outside, Luka hired me to look into his son's death." Wilczek's brow wrinkled slightly and I realized that I'd slipped up. "Well, 'hired' probably isn't the most accurate word. I knew Pete Willis, and his father asked me to investigate, informally, as a favor."

That seemed to placate him for the moment. "Is there somehow we can help you?"

"I'd just like to ask a few questions, if that's all right? Probably the same things the police asked when they were over."

"Okay."

Wilczek was about five-ten and solidly built. He had brown hair, cut short and had a two-day growth of beard that made him look rugged, in a well-scrubbed way. No earring tonight, though—I guess that was only for photo ops. The tortoise-shell glasses seemed to be the only concession to his intellectualism. His wife, by comparison, appeared much more fragile. Her hair was darker, almost black, and tied up in a loose bun at the nape of her neck. She was thin, with a gaunt face and long fingers, but seemed calm and confident, despite the language difference. She sat there stolidly beside her husband, a casual hand on his leg, and made eye contact easily with me.

"I guess what I'm most curious about is how Pete and his dad came to live here with you."

Wilczek smiled. "Not exactly with us."

"Right. I mean next door."

He nodded. "After we buy house, I want to get property next door ready for renting out. So I look in phone book for a . . ." He looked to his wife, but she had nothing to offer. "Someone to cut down dead tree in front of house."

"Landscaper?"

"Yes. And when he hears my name is Wilczek, he say that used to be his name, too."

"So Pete had already changed his name to Willis when he first met you?"

He shrugged. "That was the name in phone book."

"That's kind of a bizarre coincidence, isn't it?" Wilczek just looked at me. "Kind of strange?"

Then he understood. "Yes. I ask him if he knows his family, from Poland, but he tells me his grandfather was born in America, so he doesn't know. I'm only a year here and so I don't know if we are related or not."

"Is Wilczek a common name in Poland?"

He thought for a second and nodded. "Like Willis. Not so common like Smith or Jones."

"I got it. So, how did they wind up renting from you?"

"Pete tells me about his father and that they have difficult problems with money." He shrugged, not quite with embarrassment. "I tell Pete if he work for me, cut grass, weed flowers, and fix up house next door, then he and his father can stay at house for cheap."

"Do you mind asking me how cheap?"

Again he turned to his wife, but didn't seem to expect anything this time. "Sometimes two hundred . . ." Then he turned back to me. "Sometimes nothing. My wife thinks they take advantage of me. But I feel like they are family in a strange way and so I don't mind. I make lots of money with my computer business so it doesn't matter to me. I want to help."

I tried to give him a reassuring smile. "Sure. And this was about a year ago?"

"Yes. In September."

"Do you happen to know where they were living before then?"

He shook his head. "Not exactly. Renton, I think he say."

"Okay. Can you tell me about the fire? How did you happen to spot it?"

"I was coming home from work and I see smoke coming from house . . . uh, above the trees. I drive past. I think it is just fireplace. But when I get home I think it is too warm outside for fireplace, so after I come inside I go out on back deck to look again." He motioned behind him and I could see glass doors that let out onto a second story deck. But instead of seeing the flames that he had no doubt seen, the only thing there now was the reflection of the living room. "When I see fire, I call 911."

I gave a few seconds of solemnity that the moment required, then asked, "Do you remember what time you got home tonight?"

He looked to his wife again, but this time she answered. "Six thirty."

That was about right: an hour before I arrived. Just enough time to get the thing out. "This is very important," I said. "Do you remember seeing anyone around the house, or on the property as you were driving by?"

"No. The police ask me same thing tonight."

"How about in the last few days? Anyone you didn't recognize visiting Pete's dad or hanging around the neighborhood? Even just sitting in a car?"

He gave it a few seconds of thought, but told me no again. And that was essentially it. I drank more of my coffee and we made small talk for a while, and though I asked a few more questions it was clear that the two of them had no real knowledge about Pete and his father other than what Pete had initially told them. Wilczek wasn't usually around during the day when Pete did his yard work, and Magda didn't talk to him because of the language problem. Eventually I thanked them for their hospitality, and then I left.

Driving home I felt almost despondent. Coincidences and occurrences, information and speculation were piling up, but nothing—nothing—that was leading me any closer to figuring out who was responsible for the death of Pete Willis. And now his father. I knew it had to be the same person who was responsible for both: it didn't matter to me what the arson investigation uncovered. Someone else knew about the lawsuit and was tying up loose ends. But who could it be? I was more than a little uneasy with the realization that I didn't have the first damn idea. It was pressure enough to know that I would be going to trial for murder in a few months, but that was compounded by the fact that I wasn't sure I even had the skills to find the real killer.

I took photographs of cheating spouses and served legal papers to reluctant defendants. I had no experience hunting down cold-blooded killers. And at this point I wasn't even sure of exactly who had been killed. Taking the switched-identity theory one step further would mean that Pete killed his father in the fire, a perfect crime—in addition to the sweet revenge—if everyone thinks he's already dead. In the end, however, it was still just a defense attorney's theory, and seemed more likely to lead me astray than focus me on the problem at hand. It was abundantly clear that I still didn't know enough about Pete to figure out why someone would want him dead.

The Rainier Avenue South exit was coming up and I took it so that I could hit Bayview from the north back to Stacy's apartment. Stacy had the day off tomorrow, so I decided she was going to have to bite the bullet and tell me everything she knew about Pete. Maybe if I took her out somewhere for lunch I could get her talking. Time was slipping away. I had used up an entire day and the net result was another death and still more questions. I was no closer to figuring this thing out—maybe even further away—than I had been the day before. And to top it off, Dewey was going to need his car back before long and I would be exposed to my pals in the van again.

I slowed the car as I approached 17th. There was a small parking lot in the back of Stacy's building, but it only had enough spaces for about half the residents. This time of night I would have to find a spot on the street. I didn't see anything as I drove by, so I swung around to College and approached from the other end of the block. An opening appeared next to a driveway. By pulling up until the bumper of the Grand Prix touched that of the pickup in front of me, there was still enough room for the owners of the house to get by me without having Dewey's car towed.

It was after nine o'clock by the time I walked in the front door, and I was beat. I took a look in the fridge, but I was more tired than hungry, and headed for the bedroom. Setting the alarm had been a good idea, so I did it again, stripped off my clothes, and crawled into bed. After lying there for a while, rehashing the same stale information and leads that went nowhere, I eventually drifted off.

It seemed as if I'd only been asleep a few minutes when I heard the alarm. I reached over and shut it off, but it started up again. That brought me out of my torpor. The clock said it was only twenty after eleven. When the buzzer sounded again I realized it was someone at the front door. I hopped out of bed, confused, and ran to the intercom by the door. Stacy wasn't due home for hours.

I pressed the button. "What?"

"Mr. Neslowe?" It was male voice.

"Who is this?"

"Seattle Police Department."

Great. "What do you want?"

"Is this Ray Neslowe?"

"Yeah. Come on up." I buzzed him through and opened the door a crack, then retreated back to the bedroom to put my clothes on. A knock on the door came before I had finished with my pants. "Hang on," I yelled. Pulling on a T-shirt I reached the door and opened it to reveal a pair of Seattle's finest.

"Ray Neslowe?" the short one in front asked me.

"Yeah. What's this about?"

"Lieutenant Dalton would like to see you downtown at police headquarters."

I scratched my head. "Now?"

"Yes, sir."

"Can't it wait until morning?"

"The Lieutenant says no."

"Huh," I scoffed. "What else did the Lieutenant have to say?"

Now the shorter cop turned to his slightly taller companion just behind his right shoulder, exchanged looks, and then turned back to me. "He said if you don't come with us voluntarily that I should arrest you."

CHAPTER TWENTY

"Just what the hell do you think you're doing?" It was pretty much what I figured. Dalton was none too happy about my statement to the Mercer Island Police but, frankly, at this point I was beyond caring. Fuck 'em if they can't take a joke.

"I'm trying to solve a case that you seem to have absolutely no interest in solving."

Dalton whirled around and loomed over me as I sat in the chair by his desk. "You don't know shit, peeper. You don't think like a cop, you don't act like a cop, you don't have the instincts of a cop—"

"Good," I yelled. "Because I don't want to be a cop. All I want to do is figure out who killed Pete Willis and get you off my back."

"Really? Is that right?" Uh, oh. Time for sarcasm. "Well, it's too bad we don't have any real police detectives right here in Seattle. Aren't we lucky to have you out there solving crimes for us? Oh, but wait a minute. You haven't solved shit. As a matter of fact, wasn't that your gun that killed Willis—"

"I didn't shoot—"

"Shut the fuck up, Neslowe!" he screamed. I made a move to get up and he actually pushed me back in the seat. "You keep your ass planted in that chair."

As stunned as I was, I remained defiant. "No."

I was absolutely sure he was going to hit me then, but fortunately Haggerty was there to pull him off. When I escaped from the chair I stood and backed off a couple of paces. "Look, I know you're pissed off at me. I'm sorry about what happened with your daughter, but that's not my fault."

"Ah, fuck you. Save your pop psychology for someone who gives a shit."

I stood there dumbly. I had absolutely no idea what else to say.

"You really don't get it, do you?" Dalton seethed.

"I guess not. Maybe you should clue me in."

He counted the points on his fingers as he said them aloud. "We've got your gun. We've got slugs with Willis's blood on them from your apartment that *match* your gun. We've got you running from the building where the body was dumped. *And* you had the hots for the same woman as the victim. Now do you have a fuckin' clue?"

I was more frightened at that moment than at any other time during the investigation. For a moment I thought that Dalton and Haggerty truly believed I had killed Willis. It was one thing to have a circumstantial case against a person and quite another to actually believe that evidence. My own personal experience had shown that if I had preconceptions about a case, the evidence I found would invariably support them. In other words, I tended to find what I was looking for. I knew Dalton had been happy enough to hassle me about the gun, but never dreamed he actually wanted me to be convicted. For some reason I had convinced myself that, despite his initial glee at my arrest, he was actually working to find another suspect.

"Now let's see what *you* got," he continued, the occasional fleck of spittle landing on the chair where I'd just been sitting. "You got a lush who's grieving for his dead son, passes out one night, accidentally lights his couch on fire with a cigarette and burns himself to a crisp. So where's the fuckin' murder?"

I'd never seen Dalton this upset, and that frightened me, too. But matching his anger was not going to get me anywhere, and neither was being frightened. It was then I realized that shrinking away from Dalton during the investigation had actually been keeping me from collaborating—however distantly—with the very people who could help me most.

"I'll tell you where the murder is." I took a couple of steps back and planted my backside on the desk across the aisle from Dalton's. The squad room was nearly empty at this time of night, except for a couple of detectives across the way who had apparently become inured to Dalton's histrionics. "When I talked to Luka Wilczek yesterday morning he told me about a lawsuit that Pete had filed against him. Actually, he didn't say it had been filed, only that Pete was suing him." Dalton continued to stare at me, his anger only slightly attenuated. Haggerty continued to watch Dalton, which was not a good sign. Nevertheless, I forged ahead.

"Now, I had Carl Serafin check to see who had filed the suit and what it was all about, but there's no record of it in King County. When Wilczek first waved the papers in my face, he was pretty upset, so I went back tonight to see if I could actually get a look at them. And when I got there . . . well, you know the rest."

"Who else did you tell about the lawsuit?" said Haggerty.

"Tonight? No one."

"Then who else could have known about it?"

"Tons of people. Wilczek must have told someone else besides me. Pete could have told any number of people. The people at the law office where the suit was drawn up would have known, but I don't think that's how it happened. I have no way to prove this, but if the killer had been staking out Wilczek's place he would have seen me go in there that morning, then either talked with Wilczek himself or figured out that I knew about the lawsuit, and torched the place that night to keep anyone from investigating the lawsuit further."

"That's bullshit," Dalton said, but he sat down at his desk and appeared at least to be thinking it over.

"Maybe it is," I said. "But I'm going to keep on following this thing until I can prove it doesn't have anything to do with Pete's murder."

"How'd you find the old man?" Dalton asked.

I couldn't give up Emily, but fortunately I didn't have to. "Stacy."

He nodded. "She give you any indication why Willis changed his name?"

I hesitated, more out of embarrassment than anything else. "Not yet."

Dalton turned to me as if he couldn't believe what a dumb shit I was. "Did you *ask* her?"

I sighed. "I haven't really had the chance."

The two partners looked at each other and then back at me.

"She did tell me something that I don't think you know." They waited for me. "Pete knew that the .44 was in my closet."

Dalton sat up now. "How?"

"When we were dating she found it in the closet one day and when they were back together she told him it was there. That had to be why he was killed at my place, because that's where the gun was." Dalton was about to protest and I waved him back. "I know it doesn't prove anything, but that's the only explanation. Hell, I never even knew the guy. I'd met him exactly one time, when Stacy came to the Low Note to pick up her last paycheck. I never even talked to him. I didn't know the first thing about him, where he lived, what he did for a living, nothing."

Dalton looked over and exchanged glances with Haggerty, which I took to be a good sign.

"The only thing that makes sense to me is that he took someone over there to get the gun, and somehow ended up getting himself shot instead. I mean, for all I know he was going to use it to kill someone himself, you know, and it ended up going wrong. And that's important, especially if he was intent on killing someone."

They were still listening so I decided to go for broke. "Because maybe it wasn't even Pete who was killed. His face was gone, for Christ's sake. Has the body been positively identified, other than Stacy's statement?"

Haggerty gave Dalton a look and got a nod in return. "We have a positive from the dental records."

"What records? One dentist? I'll bet the records match a Pete Willis who'd only been in once or twice," I said, finding myself parroting Carl's words, "and paid in cash. He was working under the table, not paying taxes, so I know for a fact he didn't have insurance." Haggerty was nodding slightly and I knew then that I was on the right track. "Isn't that about the size of it?"

"Yeah," he said with a slight grin, and I wondered where this was going. "But there was a little more than that at the dentist's office."

"What?"

"One of his other patients."

Now Dalton was grinning and I had a pretty good idea who they were talking about. I shook my head. "Stacy?"

"None other than. She'd been going to him for a while and brought Willis in as a referral. It's mostly like you said, but the staff identified him from a photo Lambert had given us. So it's him."

Okay, so flush the switched-identity theory. And my defense along with it. This was also the third time something Stacy had given the police had left me a step behind. Suddenly I felt as if I was going to have to start all over again, and at that moment I found myself wanting nothing more than to quit spinning my wheels and take my chances in court. I didn't know what else to do. Everything seemed to hinge on information that Stacy had, but hadn't given me. She was the only link I had to Pete and his past, and at this point I didn't care how awkward it might be. She was going to have to tell me everything.

"All right, but I still stay there's something wrong with Luka Wilczek's death, and I plan on finding out what it is. That lawsuit has to lead to something, and I think the killer torched Wilczek to keep me from getting there. Have you heard anything from the arson investigation?"

Haggerty said, "It's pretty low priority. They won't even start until tomorrow morning when it's light."

"All right." I stood. "I'm assuming I'm free to go?"

"Just one thing," Dalton said, his anger seemingly dissipated. "If you plan on making any more statements to the police, come over here and do it. I have enough on my plate without talking to some flat-foot who's creaming his shorts because he thinks he's going to get in on a murder investigation."

I nodded. "Anything else?"

Haggerty waved his arm and then I took a cab back to Stacy's and crashed. I was exhausted and crawled into bed without even turning on the alarm this time. I figured I would wake up when Stacy came home, or that I might even wait until morning to get some of my questions answered. I was more than a little surprised when I woke up the next morning and turned to find the place next to me hadn't been slept in.

I sat up and yelled out. "Stacy?"

When there was no answer I shuffled out into the front room and then on into the kitchen. She wasn't there. No coat, no purse. I had a bad feeling about this. Stacy hadn't come home last night.

CHAPTER TWENTY-ONE

"Hello," came the groggy answer from Stacy's cell phone.

"Stacy?"

"Ray? What time is it?"

"I don't know . . . eight something."

She groaned. "I've only had four hours sleep."

"Where the hell are you?"

"I'm at Karin and Lisa's"

The names were vaguely familiar. I was pretty sure they were two women who worked at Sharkey's and shared an apartment somewhere on the north end. "Why didn't you come home last night?"

"I called at midnight but there was no answer at the apartment."

"Why didn't you call my cell phone?"

"I don't have it in my phone anymore."

I tried to hide my disappointment. "All right." I also didn't want to tell her about my little run-in with Dalton. "Is everything okay?" Silence. Uh oh.

"Stacy?"

"Yeah . . . I guess." There was a tightness in her voice.

"What is it?"

"Well, it's no big deal . . . I just got kind of creeped out last night. For a minute I thought someone might have been following me."

Oh no. "Was it a black van?"

"Huh? No, not a car, a person."

"You *saw* someone? What did he look like?"

"I don't know. I saw somebody in the parking lot when I left to see Michael, and then when I showed up at work, I thought I saw the same person again. It was just weird, that's all. It's probably nothing, but it creeped me out."

"You must remember something. Was it a great big guy?"

"No. I think he was pretty average. It's probably not even the same person."

"Well, that's no good. I want you to keep an eye out for this guy and, if you see him again, try to remember everything you can."

"All right . . ."

"Listen," I said. "I've been putting this off but I can't do it any longer. I have to meet with you this morning. We need to talk."

"God, I haven't even finished sleeping yet."

"This is important, Stacy."

"I know. All right. What time?"

"How about eleven?"

"How about twelve?"

"Okay. Do you want to meet at the Blue Star and have lunch?"

"All right. I'll see you there at noon."

"And make sure—"

"I know," she said. "Look for anyone suspicious." But the tension in her voice was gone now, letting me know she wasn't worried about it and that I shouldn't either. "Now, if you don't want me to be late I'm going to go back to bed."

After we said goodbye I went out to the kitchen and made some coffee. While it brewed, I fired up Stacy's computer to see if I could get online. It probably would have made more sense to cart around my laptop, but I was in the habit of leaving it home so that it wouldn't be sitting in my car, tempting someone to break in. When the coffee was finished I filled a mug and sat down to see if I could get anywhere with it.

It didn't take long to discover that she didn't have a working Internet account—at least not one that I could find. Still, I messed around for nearly an hour before I finally gave up and fished around in her desk drawers hoping to find an AOL disc. A few minutes later I had set up a new AOL account—I had done this once before but fortunately it had been on a different credit card—and started trying to get my life back in some semblance of order.

Rather than obsess about the case that morning, I decided to relax and try doing some normal things for a while. I went to my own web-mail account, deleted a couple dozen junk e-mails, then replied to the two that actually meant anything to me. One was from Carl, asking me to attach the photos I'd taken if I wanted to get paid for the Burns investigation. The other was from a friend of mine, Kurt Wetzel, inviting me to hear some music. His e-mail said that Garry Vaughan was playing at the Central Tavern in Pioneer Square on Friday night and that I should try to meet him there if I was in the area.

If I remembered correctly, Vaughan was a distant relative of Stevie Ray Vaughan and was doing well in smaller venues trading on his cousin's name, but hadn't been able to break out nationally. I wrote back to Kurt that I would look for him if I was around, but that I couldn't be sure if I would be able to make it.

Carl's email I left unanswered. I hadn't developed the film yet, and I would probably be talking to him again before I did. After that, I surfed the 'net for a while, checking out guitar prices on eBay and eventually purchasing Jake Langley's latest disc, with Joey DeFrancesco on the B-3, on Amazon's Canadian site.

Once I had turned off the computer I looked in vain through Stacy's music collection for something to play. The only thing that was even nominally jazz was Steve Miller's *Born To Be Blue*, so I put it on, turned it up, and headed for the shower. When I emerged from the bathroom, freshly washed and shaved, Miller was romping through Horace Silver's "Filthy McNasty." I stopped for a minute to listen to his guitar solo and then nodded to myself. "Tol'able," I said, and went into the bedroom to dress. I put on some khakis and a flannel shirt, then gathered up the rest of my clothes, put them together with the few things Stacy had in her basket, and hunted for the laundry soap.

In my continuing effort to remain normal that

morning—coupled with the fact that I still had two hours to kill before lunch—I grabbed a handful of quarters from the jar on the desk and hiked down to the laundry room in the basement. The laundry room door was kept locked, but could be opened with any apartment door key in the building so that everyone could have access. Which didn't make a lot of sense to me. I wasn't as if people were going to walk in off the street to use the laundry facilities, especially considering there was a security door that needed a separate key just to get into the building. Oh well.

There were two washers and two dryers, and at this time of the morning all of them were empty. I fed coins into one of the washers and started it up, dumped in the soap and the laundry and, as I was leaving, noticed a series of storage lockers. They were basically large wooden cabinets that appeared to be about six feet deep and three feet tall, five of them on the bottom and five on top. Each individual wooden door had a padlock that was numbered. Since there weren't enough for the entire building they probably cost extra, and I wondered fleetingly if Stacy had one.

Back up in the apartment I was content to finish the pot of coffee by sitting on the couch and looking out of the large picture window. The view straight down the hill and across I-5 overlooked the industrial area south of downtown, including the ships being loaded and unloaded on Harbor Island. Off to the right, the scene encompassed the two stadiums and a slice of Elliott Bay. Overnight the clouds had moved back in and were blanketing the sky. It also looked as though the temperature had dropped a good deal, judging by the number of heavy coats I was seeing on pedestrians.

In the middle of the last song of the Miller disc I found myself actually smiling during Phil Woods' solo on "Red Top," and congratulated myself on successfully fulfilling my morning's mission. When the disc had finished I decided not to put anything else on. I leafed through Stacy's true-crime book and marveled at how she could continue read that stuff—especially after what she'd been through. Twenty minutes later I went down and put the clothes in the dryer, and an hour later hauled them back upstairs again to fold.

At eleven-thirty I drove up I-5 to 45th and took a left into Wallingford, ten blocks south of Green Lake. The Blue Star was out at the end of the district, just before the road crested Phinney Ridge and dipped down into Ballard. I arrived a few minutes before noon, ahead of Stacy, gave my name at the reservation desk and waited outside, watching the lunchtime traffic at the drive-through across the street at McDonalds.

She showed up about ten minutes later and they still hadn't called my name. After she kissed me, we went in to take a seat on the benches just inside the door.

"Did you see anyone?"

"Nope. A couple of cars drove by, but no one out walking."

In the middle of her update about the previous night's shift at Sharkey's, we were taken around the side of the kitchen to a table by the window and given ice water and silverware. The two of us looked over the menu for a minute, and then she finished with her story. When the waitress returned Stacy ordered an egg burrito, and I ordered the same. Once our coffee had been poured I dumped some cream in mine. I thought about delaying, but there was never going to be an easy way to do this, so I went ahead and launched in.

"I need to tell you what happened last night."

"What do you mean?" she said, with some apprehension.

"I went over to talk to Pete's dad again last night, and when I got there the place had burned to the ground. He was killed in the fire."

She looked appropriately shocked but stunned me by saying, "Was Sandy in the house, too?"

"Jesus, Stacy. A man died last night."

"I'm sorry," she said, and took a sip of coffee. "I know how that makes me look, but I told you he was an asshole. He wanted to control Pete. He was practically keeping him prisoner and he got what was coming to him as far as I'm concerned." Now her eyes locked on mine. "But that dog didn't do anything to anyone."

As I leaned back I ran a hand through my hair and exhaled loudly. "The dog's fine," I said, but I wasn't about to tell her why. "Look, I think somebody torched the place, and I think it's the same person who killed Pete." Though I couldn't be certain, for an instant I thought I saw something like terror flicker in her eyes. Then I leaned forward, my forearms resting on the edge of the table. "Stacy, you need to tell me everything about Pete."

The look on her face suddenly turned belligerent. "What, about our sex life and everything?"

I sighed. "No. You know that's not what I mean." She nodded, but she didn't say anything. "I'm trying not to get panicked, here, but things aren't looking good for me. I'm scratching at everything I can think of and coming up with very little. And now, it seems, every time I go to the police they have something you've given them that I didn't know about."

"Like what?"

"Like telling them about us, for starters."

"I don't believe this, Ray. I was just about catatonic that night. I hardly remember what I said. They asked me questions and I just answered them. My God, it was horrible."

"Well, what about giving them a picture of Pete? You didn't tell me about that."

"They needed something to show to witnesses, and they sure as hell weren't going to get it from Luka." The anger was coming back now. "What was I supposed to do? They asked me for a picture and I gave it to them."

"All right. I'm sorry. I'm not accusing you of anything. It just emphasizes the fact that I haven't been able to talk to you in depth, the way I've needed to, since this whole thing began."

"I understand that. What do you want to know?"

I was all set to ask her if Pete had any friends when, for no conscious reason, I heard myself changed tacks. "Why haven't you wanted to talk to me about this?"

Photos of old-time logging in Seattle covered the walls of the Blue Star, and Stacy turned to stare at a picture of a choker setter at the booth across from us. As she did, she unconsciously ran her fingers across the scarred wooden surface of the table.

"Stacy," I said gently. All of a sudden I was sure she knew something she wasn't telling me. "Please, tell me what's going on."

She turned back, but kept her eyes on her coffee. "I don't know what to do, Ray. I'm scared."

Now I was too. "Of what?"

She sighed, and I could see her lower lip quiver. "I tried to tell the police everything, but I couldn't."

I reached for her free hand and took it in mine. She squeezed back, but couldn't meet my eyes. Then her breath hitched and I saw a tear roll down her cheek. She released her coffee and wiped her face with the back of her hand.

"Stacy? What's going on? Please, tell me."

And then our food came, but not before she looked at me and blurted out, "I think I know who killed Pete."

CHAPTER TWENTY-TWO

To say I was stunned beyond belief doesn't begin to do justice to the staggering, mind-numbing shock I felt at that moment. But I'd been through this with Stacy once before. Maybe she had meant it in a different way and I tried to make my voice sound calm as I asked her for clarification. "Are you saying you actually know who the person is?" But she stayed silent for the moment, salting her potatoes and spreading salsa on her burrito. "Stacy?"

She looked out the window, as if someone might be standing close by, listening, then turned back to me. "Ray, I told you I don't know what to do about this. I think I could be in trouble."

"Then it makes even more sense that you should tell my why. If you know who killed Pete, I don't understand why you can't tell me."

Now her features contorted into something like pain. "Because." Then she lowered her voice and leaned toward me. "I don't want to wind up with a bullet in my head, too."

This was beyond belief. "Stacy. I'm going to go to prison if I don't find out who did this. You have to tell me."

"I can't."

"Then tell the police. Please."

"If I tell the police then he'll know, and he'll kill me, too."

I stared at her in disbelief. What was she really asking me to do, trade my life for hers?

She was genuinely fearful, that was obvious, but would she actually stay silent while I was convicted for murder? I didn't think it would go that far, but I was afraid she might stall for so long that it would make putting the real killer behind bars that much more difficult.

Stacy started eating and I looked down at the plate in front of me. I wasn't hungry anymore. "Stacy—"

"Please, Ray. I know how strange this seems, but you have to believe me. I don't feel comfortable talking here. Why don't we go home first, and then maybe you can help me figure out what to do? I don't want to make a mistake and have something happen . . . to either of us. Okay?"

Well, that was something. I might have to go gently, but I was fairly confident that I could get her to tell me. I went through the motions of preparing my own food. Before I could take a single bite, though, I had to know something first. "Look, just tell me one thing."

The fear surfaced again.

"I don't want a name, but I want to make sure I'm clear on this. Are you saying that you know the actual person who killed Pete?"

She visibly relaxed. "Well, I didn't see it happen, but . . ." Then she nodded.

Back home she told me the whole story, in her own way, and in her own time.

"Do you want to go somewhere else where you'd feel more comfortable," I said, trying to keep my eyes from the place on the floor where she had discovered Pete's body.

"No, this is the best. If he is out there watching me I feel safer here."

"Do you think that was him last night?"

"Oh, I have no idea. It might have been, but that's why I was so freaked out. I should have been paying more attention this whole time. I saw someone and . . . I just didn't know what else to do."

"No, that was a good instinct."

Stacy was sitting on one end of the couch, her legs folded beneath her, and she reached for the glass of water on the coffee table. I was sitting on the other end of the couch facing her. On the way home I had managed to convince her of the need to tell me what she knew. I did promise to make sure she knew what I was going to do with the information, and she made me swear that any decision to go to the police would be done together. I agreed, but I would have sworn to anything at that point.

She took a drink of water and set her glass back down. "I can't just tell you what Pete did, or it will sound stupid."

"What *he* did?"

"Yeah. I guess in some ways it might seem as if he brought it on himself, but it's more complicated than that. Pete had a difficult time growing up. He was born somewhere in Pennsylvania—I don't remember the town—and he'd lived there all his life. His dad worked in the mines until he got so sick that they had to put him on disability and then he had to retire. But instead of taking his payments monthly, he wanted it all at once. So he cashed out the amount that he paid in and wound up with only about a quarter of what he would have had by now."

"What did Pete's mom say about that?"

"Well, this was much later, just before they moved out here. Pete's mom died when he was just a few years old. I think Luka blamed Pete for her death."

"How did she die?"

"Car wreck. She was hit by a drunk driver."

My eyes widened.

"Yeah, well anyway, Pete was the only one left to take the brunt of Luka's anger about his mom's death, and so he was sort of abandoned in his own house. Luka didn't give him anything without punishing Pete for it in some way."

"How do you mean?"

"Well, food and clothing. Luka didn't want to spend anything on Pete. So he would beat him, or lock him in a closet when he had to, but when Pete was young Luka was forced to take care of him. There was nothing else he could do if he didn't want to be

135

responsible for Pete's death. You can imagine how hard it was on Pete, and as soon as he was old enough he stopped asking Luka for anything. He would go out to the Salvation Army drops and pick through the boxes for clothes. He would root through garbage cans and Dumpsters, and as often as he could he would stay over at friends' houses for dinner and breakfast the next morning.

"People in town knew what was going on, so it wasn't quite as bad as it could have been. By the time he was in junior high, he needed actual money for school supplies and things like that, so he had to go to work. He would do anything, shovel snow, collect bottles, but mowing lawns was what he liked best and people around town let him do as much of their yard work as he could. I don't know what made him do it, but he actually finished high school."

"Things must have eased up a little after that, though, after he was able to work full time?"

She shook her head. "No. That's when they got worse. Luka told him he had to pay rent."

"Really? Why didn't he move out?"

"He couldn't do it. People won't rent to someone who has their own business. They need to know they'll get their money regular, every month. And besides, Luka went around threatening anyone who even offered anything to Pete. It was no secret that he had a thing for guns, and no one wanted to get mixed up with him. During the winter Pete would nearly starve because there wasn't as much work. There was no way he could escape from Luka, at least not until he came out here."

"How did that happen?"

"Well, after Luka had to retire, he wanted to get as far away from the East Coast as he could, as far away from the mines and bad memories as he could get. So, the day after the check comes he puts the house up for sale. Once it sells he throws what he can into the back of a station wagon and makes Pete come with him."

"How could he do that? Why would Pete even go?"

"I don't know. There's a lot to the story that I never found out. All I know is that somehow Luka coerced him into coming to

Seattle with him and they got a cheap apartment in Renton to start. Only now, instead of things getting better, they were worse. Luka must have known that his money wouldn't last, and he was more dependent on Pete than ever. So Pete started in mowing lawns, saved up and bought a used chain saw, and then started going door to door in the station wagon looking for dead trees to cut down. He was on Mercer Island one day and thought he hit the jackpot when he found a guy who needed a bunch of trees cleared from an adjoining property."

"Pete Wilczek?"

She looked away and nodded. But her story didn't jibe with the one Wilczek had told me.

"Wait a minute. Did Pete ever have an ad in the phone book?"

She wrinkled her brow. "No. He could barely afford gas money. Why?"

I sat back and thought about that. "Pete Wilczek lied to me," I finally said. "He told me he found Pete's name in the phone book and called *him* to come out and cut down the trees."

Now her features hardened. "That wasn't the first lie he told you."

"What do you mean?"

"Well, Pete started spending a lot of time out there, working on the cabin they eventually moved into. This guy and his wife invited him to dinner every night and Pete said the guy talked to him about his father a lot. He was obsessed. He wanted to know everything about Pete's family, what happened to his mother, how he had grown up, if he had any cousins, everything. And then . . . I know it sounds crazy, but this guy made Pete a proposition."

"Wilczek?"

"That's not his name," she said, with a frustrated anger. "That's Pete's name."

I held out my hands, confused. "They had the same name, you mean."

She shook her head. "Pete sold him his identity."

CHAPTER TWENTY-THREE

"Jesus, Stacy, why didn't you tell me any of this before?"

She looked down at her hands. "I was hoping you'd find it out on your own, and I could stay out of it."

I could only shake my head. "So you're saying that Pete Wilczek, the computer guy, is really someone else?"

"I don't know who he is, but he's not Pete Wilczek. Pete needed the money to get away from Luka—"

"How much?"

"I don't know. He wouldn't tell me."

"Where is it now?"

Stacy's expression became pained and she just looked at me.

"Oh, shit. It wasn't still in the cabin, was it?"

"I don't know, Ray. I told Pete to put it in a safety deposit box, but I don't know if he ever did. After this guy helped him change his name to Willis, Pete didn't want to go near anything that was even remotely official. He didn't want to blow the deal."

I sat for a minute just trying to get my head around the whole thing. Pete had certainly been resourceful enough—had been since he was a kid—but he could never put together enough of a bankroll to break away from his father, so he sold his identity. But something went wrong. "Had you already met him at this point?"

"No. I didn't know him until after he had changed his name"

"Why did he tell you all of this?"

"He was making plans."

"Yeah, I'll bet he was."

Stacy stood and walked into the kitchen. I followed her and sat at the small round table that functioned in the apartment as both breakfast nook and dining room. She opened and closed the fridge and looked in a couple of cabinets, as if she didn't know what to do next. Finally she filled a kettle with water and put it on to boil. She picked up a box of lemongrass tea off the counter and held it up for me to see.

"No, thanks."

After pulling down a mug, she opened a pouch and dropped the tea bag in.

"Did he tell you how the identity switch happened?"

Leaning back against the counter, Stacy crossed her arms beneath her breasts and looked past me out the kitchen window and almost imperceptibly moved her head back and forth. "This guy already had the forms there at the house on Mercer Island. He had Pete fill them out and then took him down to the courthouse and that was all there was to it. The tricky part was getting Pete legitimate ID, so the guy arranged to take Pete back to Pennsylvania for a day. Flew him first-class early in the morning so they could get back before Luka suspected anything. Back East, in his hometown, it was easy for Pete to renew his Pennsylvania driver's license in his new name. Everyone knew him, and all he had to do was show them the legal name change. So that gave him a legitimate Pennsylvania driver's license that he could use if he ever needed identification."

I nodded. Just the way Carl had said. "How about Wilczek's ID?"

"When they were back East, he was able to get a birth certificate and a social security card with his old name for the computer guy. I don't know what he did after that."

"Okay. So now Wilczek has Pete's social security number, birth certificate, everything he would need to get a driver's license, passport, or anything else he might need. What did Pete get?"

"This guy—" She still refused to call him Wilczek "He was also able to get Pete fake Washington State ID. He had a driver's license, birth certificate, social security card—"

"But they were all phony."

"Yes. If he had used them for anything where it was going to be officially checked it wouldn't have matched up with him. It was fine for getting carded at a bar, opening an account at the video store, or registering for college . . ."

The kettle began to whistle and she took it off and filled her cup, then brought it over and sat down at the table with me.

"It seems like that would have left him in a pretty vulnerable spot."

She dunked the tea bag a few times. "For most people, it would have. But Pete wasn't thinking that way. All he wanted was the money. After what he'd been through in his life he figured that it was actually going to be pretty easy."

"You must have met him fairly soon after that."

"Right after. I think he'd gone to Pennsylvania only a few days earlier. He was still in the apartment in Renton and had cut down a tree for some friends of mine. They thought he was nice, and they knew I was single, so they invited us both to dinner." She smiled then, the first time that afternoon. "He was always accepting dinner invitations."

Trying to keep her on track I said, "When I talked to Luka he seemed pretty upset about Pete going to college."

She frowned. "Pete was starting to break away even then. When he told Luka he'd signed up for a night class, I thought he was going to kill him right on the spot."

"It wasn't his father who killed him, was it?"

"No." Emphatic. "Luka was dependent on Pete."

"Well . . ."

"Be patient." She blew on her tea and took a tiny sip—still too hot—then set it back down again. "This is where the trouble started. Last September, after he and Luka moved into the cabin on Mercer Island, Pete started hanging around with some volunteer fireman. He thought that might be a great thing to do, but when he looked into it . . ."

"Background check."

"Civil service was out because he didn't have . . ." She

shrugged. "He wasn't himself anymore. So, for a while, the classes at college were about all he could do."

"When we were together," I began as delicately as I could, "you told me that he'd slept with another woman."

She sipped her tea, not really anxious to get into that part of the story.

"I'm not sure Pete understood what loyalty was all about. He certainly never learned it from Luka. So, when the opportunity presented itself, I don't think he really knew what he was doing."

That was stretching credulity, I thought, but it wasn't something I was going to debate. On the other hand, I could remember quite vividly how badly he'd hurt her. I wanted to respond, but there seemed to be no point. He wasn't going to hurt her again, ever. "Did you know who this woman was?"

She rolled her eyes. "One of the assistants at the dental office."

I smiled. "The one you took him to?"

"How did you know that?"

Now it was my turn to be dramatic. "Are you kidding? I told you I've been working my ass off on this thing. Jesus, Stacy, I wish I would have known all of this from the start."

I hadn't meant it the way it sounded, but she looked wounded anyway.

"I'm sorry," I said. "It doesn't even matter anymore." I waved my hand to emphasize the point. "And I do appreciate your telling me everything now."

She stared into her cup of tea for a minute before beginning again. "It wasn't until we got back together again—after us—" Our eyes met briefly and she went back to her tea. "—that he became obsessed with becoming a fireman. He couldn't talk about anything else. He bought all of the test preparation books, got all of the forms from the county and the City of Mercer Island, started studying for the test."

"Wouldn't he have had to be fingerprinted?"

"Just for starters. The irony is, it finally started to dawn on him that he'd done exactly the same thing Luka had: he took a bunch of money up front, and then realized it wasn't going to last. I don't think Pete ever thought in terms of having a career his whole life, and now he suddenly realized the necessity of it.

"A little too late, I would think."

Now Stacy looked up at me, and the pain was visible in her eyes. "He wasn't convinced of that. Or maybe I should say he wound up convincing himself that it wasn't too late."

Then I understood the full import of her expression. "He didn't try to confront Wilczek, did he?"

"He talked about it." She nodded to herself. "He talked about it a lot."

I could see where all of this was heading. "And the gun?"

She pressed her lips together tightly before saying, "I never put the two together. I honestly didn't know what he was thinking. We were talking about you—" She stopped herself and something flitted behind her eyes. "No, *he* started talking about you one day, asking me all kinds of innocuous questions about your job. Most of them I didn't even know the answers to. But we got onto the subject of guns, and I knew you had the one in your closet, and . . ."

"And you told him about it."

She nodded.

"Did he actually confront Wilczek?"

"I don't know. Well . . . yes, I suppose he must have. I know he did."

"You think Wilczek killed him."

She reached out finally, to grasp my hand in hers, and I let her. "That's what happened. I'm sure of it. He knows Pete was dating me. He would have to assume Pete told me. And now with Luka being dead . . ."

"Did you ever meet him?"

"No, thank God."

"Well, that might help." To give myself time, I stood and walked over to the sink to get a glass of water. But there was nothing to think about. "We have to go to the police with this, Stacy."

"No." She twisted around in her chair facing me. "He'd know it was me."

"But if we get him behind bars, it won't matter." I had poured my water. Stacy was still staring at me. "What?"

"And if the police can't find any proof? Then he won't be arrested. I couldn't take looking over my shoulder all my life."

I brought my water back over to the table, but still hadn't taken a drink. Sitting down, I tried to reassure her. "They'll get him. If he did it, they'll get him."

"How?"

I tried to think. "Fingerprints. If Pete lured Wilczek over to my apartment, he probably wouldn't have been suspicious enough to worry about leaving prints. If he touched anything, once they find his fingerprints it'll be all over."

"He could have gone back and wiped them after he killed Pete."

All right. Forget that one. "What about the simplest thing of all? Wilczek's identification is going to match up with Pete's from Pennsylvania. Once they put them together it'll be easy to figure out that Wilczek is using Pete's ID."

"That doesn't prove he killed Pete."

I was getting exasperated. "Well it doesn't matter. The police will be watching Wilczek and he'll know it. He won't be able to make a move. It would be suicide to try anything at the restaurant with that many people around, and I'll be staying here. He can't do anything. But we have to tell the police for that to happen. If you think about it, we're probably in *more* danger now."

The visible concern on her brow had not diminished. I had thought at this point it was just a matter of convincing her, but now I wasn't so sure. There must be something else. "What is it?"

"It's not just him I'm worried about."

"What are you saying?"

She turned away, and the thought that she wouldn't tell me nearly sent me into a panic. In as calm a voice as I could manage, I pressed. "Stacy?"

"It's ridiculous. I'm almost embarrassed to say, it sound's so melodramatic."

"Well, it sounds important enough to you."

Her forehead relaxed slightly and she took my hand again.

"Tell me," I said.

"It was just a couple of weeks ago. Pete had taken me to this sports bar on the island, the place where the firemen all hung out. He wasn't even talking to me. I'd gone to the bathroom and was just coming back. They'd been talking about TV shows when I left, but when I came back, as I was nearing the table I heard him say something about Wilczek. That startled me because, why would he be telling them his real name? So I knew he could only have been talking about the computer guy."

She took a deep breath and let out a ragged sigh.

"What?" I prompted.

"Like I said, I don't know what the full context was, but as I was sitting back down, I heard Pete say that Wilczek was in the mob."

CHAPTER TWENTY-FOUR

It took a few moments for what she'd said to sink in. The mob? She was right—it did sound melodramatic. "Are you sure he wasn't still talking about a TV show?"

Stacy nodded. There was no uncertainty in her eyes.

I kept trying to figure out a way to do something with all of this new information without going to the police, but I knew in my heart I didn't really want to. What I wanted to do was to run all the way down to Dalton's office and spill the whole thing to him right now. The mob? Had she really said the mob? In a case where things hadn't made much sense to begin with, this was the most senseless information of all. Wilczek had only been in the United States a couple of years. When would he have had time to hook up with organized crime? And what mob? In Seattle?

Stacy stood and headed for the bathroom and I moved back over to the couch to sort things out. The way I saw it, the most important thing to do right now was gather evidence against Wilczek. But how to do that? First would be the documentary evidence, I supposed, but what would that really show? And the name change was going to make it incredibly difficult. Normally, a person would have changed the name on all of their legal documents, but Pete hadn't done that because Wilczek wanted his old name. Since Pete had voluntarily given up his identity, he didn't have one now. Wilczek had it, and everything was going to show that it was his . . . except the place of birth.

There were legal documents that Wilczek couldn't have

changed, however, his immigration papers, green card, visa, etc. They would still have his real name on them, whatever that was. And now with homeland security concerns, he would most likely have been fingerprinted as well. It wasn't much, but it was a place to start. Once I proved that Wilczek had acquired Pete's identity, it would be pretty easy with Stacy's testimony to show that Pete had wanted it back. And if there were any of Wilczek's fingerprints still in my apartment—

Fingerprints. The police had already finished processing the crime scene. And yet even if they had Wilczek's prints from the scene sitting in the case file, there's no way they could possibly think to connect them with Wilczek himself. They would simply show that someone from Poland, working in the US, had been in my apartment at some point in time. I told Stacy when she came back out to the living room, but she turned me down flat.

"Don't you see," I pleaded. "They could have the evidence right now. All I need to do is point them in the right direction."

Her lower lip actually quivered. "And point a gun at my head?"

"That's not fair, Stace. I'm trying to save both of us."

She hung her head and I reached out a hand to her. Then she pushed herself across the couch and snuggled in my arms, her head on my chest. A minute later I felt, more than heard, her crying against me. I held her more tightly and she suddenly let her emotions go. Tears flowed for several minutes while I smoothed back her hair, and occasionally attempted to dry her cheek. Sometime later she finally had to pull away to get some Kleenex. She blew her nose a couple of times and then brought the box over with her and set it on the coffee table in front of us, one hand still clutching a fresh tissue.

"I'm sorry, Ray."

"That's okay. I know this hasn't been easy for you."

She brushed at the wet spots on my shirt and managed a weak smile. "I got you all wet."

She put her head on my shoulder and we sat for several minutes in silence. I didn't know what Stacy was thinking, but

I could guess, and it wasn't very pleasant. Still, I needed to take some action, for her sake just as much as mine.

"Listen, Stacy. I need to tell all of this to my lawyer." She stiffened slightly in my arms, but said nothing. "You don't have to worry, because she can't say anything to the police—"

Stacy sat up. "She?"

I nodded. "Carl can't represent me, because . . . well, it's a long story. Basically the partners in his firm don't want him doing any pro bono work, especially on a case they think he'll lose."

"So, who's your lawyer now?"

"Her name is Irina Veckich. She's a public defender. I'm going to try to meet with her today, and I really need to tell her all of this. We need to get moving on gathering evidence, and the police won't have to know a thing. But I need to talk to her about all of this, figure out where to start, and get her started planning my defense in case we can't turn over Wilczek before the trial."

The worry was still on her brow, but I could see in her face that she wanted to help me. "She'll have to go to the police. It's against the law to conceal a crime like that."

"It wouldn't be concealing anything. Right now there's no evidence of a crime, so she doesn't have to say a word. That's why we have to get busy getting together what we can. When we actually have proof, then we'll go to the police. Not before."

"Promise me."

"I promise."

"If he finds out, he'll come after me."

"I know, I know. It'll be just between her and me for now. Wilczek already knows that I'm investigating Pete's death, but he has no idea that you and I are connected."

She gripped my forearm. "What if they're watching my place and see you."

I nodded. "That's what I've been trying to tell you, Stacy. The longer we just sit around and wait, the more we'll be at risk. I need to get out there now and find a way to put this guy in jail for what he did to Pete. That's the only way we'll ever be safe."

"Be careful," she said, and buried her head in my chest again. "I can't lose you, Ray."

"I'll be okay. But the sooner I get going on this, the sooner we'll both be able to put it behind us."

She surprised me then by wrapping her arms around me and hugging me for a long time.

Stacy hadn't showered before meeting me at the Blue Star, and while she was in the bathroom I took the opportunity to give my lawyer a call. The phone number Carl gave me rang a dozen times before switching over to voice mail. A confident alto voice told me that if I was hearing the message it was because she was in court. I left my name and cell phone number and was surprised to get a call back before Stacy finished her shower.

"Hello?"

"Mr. Neslowe," she began without preamble. "I have an hour open about twenty minutes from now. Think you can get down here by then?"

"Uh, sure. Where are you—"

"Central Building, 3rd and Cherry, eighth floor. Just ask for me at reception and I'll come out to get you."

"Okay. I'll be there in—" There was a clunk on the other end and I was talking to dead air. I pulled the phone away from my ear and looked at it, but the phone had no idea what that was about either.

Ten minutes later I was circling the south end of downtown in Dewey's Grand Prix, looking for a parking spot. With the Municipal Building, County Building, King County Courthouse, and the police department headquarters all located within a six-block radius, it wasn't easy. Complicating the task was the fact that all of the streets downtown were one way. You might see a spot on a cross street but you'd have to go up to the next block and come back around in order to get to it. Or a spot might open up to your left, but you were three lanes over, forcing you to circle the block again—which meant that there was no way in hell it would still be there. Of course I could also cough up ten bucks to *pay* for parking, but that was a last resort.

Time was ticking away when I finally spotted something that would work. On the corner of 2nd and James, at the entrance to Chinatown, was a fenced off section of construction with a large Dumpster full of broken sheet rock next to it. There was just enough room to squeeze in at an angle between the fence and the Dumpster. Since the fence extended onto the sidewalk, I figured I could, too, and managed to back in with one of the rear tires up on the sidewalk and the front fender sticking slightly out into traffic. Good enough. Climbing out I looked around and smiled: even better, there was no meter. Then I locked up and headed back up the hill and over to 3rd.

The Central Building is a large, squat structure with office space above and retail stores at street level: a Kinko's, Subway, and Cherry Street Coffee—all of which I frequented regularly—and the Rite Aid where I'd purchased that light bulb on the evening this whole nightmare had begun. After passing through a security check in the lobby, I rode the elevator up to the top floor. The Public Defender's office was located to the right and took up most of that wing on the eighth floor.

Just as I reached the double glass outer doors of the office, a black man in a dark blue suit carrying a leather briefcase held the door for me. I thanked him, but he walked on by without even glancing at my face. A knot of fear tightened in my stomach the second I realized it was the City Attorney, Kevin Adamson. I walked over to a receptionist at a long wooden desk, still a bit nervous, and gave my name. I told him I was there to see Irina Vekich, and he called her up to say that I was there.

I drifted over to the row of heavy wooden chairs along the wall, but there was no place to sit down. People with file folders and dejected looks populated the seats, so I paced slowly and tried to calm myself down before Vekich came out. Adamson had to be working on dozens of cases at any one time, and many of the suspects in those cases were no doubt represented by legal aid lawyers. It made perfect sense that he should be here, talking to the attorneys he would be going up against . . . or did it? Why in the hell would he come here? Wouldn't the lawyers here have to go to *his* office?

At that moment a large woman in a burgundy suit walked briskly up to the reception desk from the offices in back and met my eye.

"You must be Neslowe."

"Yeah," I said, walking over and shaking her hand. It was soft, very warm, and slightly damp.

"How did you ever wind up making enemies in such high places?"

"Excuse me?"

"Kevin Adamson never comes down here, but he was just in my office." She shook her head slowly. "He wants you to fry."

CHAPTER TWENTY-FIVE

"I didn't think Washington State used the electric chair," I said, following her through a maze of cubicles back to her office.

She shook her head. "Figure of speech. I could have said, 'He wants you at the end of the rope' but, criminy, it sounds like I'm quoting Louis L'Amour." She stopped at her door and held out a hand. I walked through and I sat down with a heavy sigh in the only available chair.

"Ah, come on," she said, rounding her desk. "It's not that bad. They have a circumstantial case, weak motive, and absolutely no physical evidence that ties you directly to the murder."

"Other than the fact he was killed at my apartment?"

Her eyes widened. "Well, that's a bad break, but it doesn't actually prove you did it."

"I don't understand this. Carl said that Adamson would probably drop the case when he heard you were on it."

She grinned, clearly pleased with her reputation. "Normally, yes. But this isn't a normal case."

"What's different?"

She leaned back in her leather chair and smiled warmly at me. "It's complicated."

Irina Vekich was not what I had expected. In my mind she had been a five-foot-two, tough as nails, chain-smoking, take no prisoners litigator. This woman appeared anything but. For one thing, she was big—and I don't mean fat. She was probably five-ten, big-boned, and had plenty of curves in all the right places. Her features were large, as well—full lips, large eyes that protruded slightly, and fleshy cheeks that dimpled when she smiled. With blond hair worn long and lush, and smooth alabaster skin, she looked more like a bombshell from the fifties than someone prosecutors feared.

"My feeling is that he's being pressured to try the case."

"*He's* being pressured? By whom?"

"Like I said, just a feeling. But Adamson's not our biggest worry anyway."

I almost laughed. "What is?"

"Your alibi. Where were you that night?"

It took me a second to orient myself. "I was on a case for Carl. I was staking out the apartment of a woman south of Chinatown. In fact, I'd been in the car for a couple of days trying to get pictures."

She took out a yellow legal pad and began casually taking notes. "Did anyone see you?"

"No."

"Did you go anywhere?"

"No—yes. I had to go get a light bulb at the drug store right downstairs."

"Okay, date and time stamp on the receipt. You still have it?"

"Sure. I think it's still in my car."

She continued writing nonchalantly. "Well, if the time matches the time of death then you couldn't have been in Ballard if you were downtown buying light bulbs."

It was then I began to understand something about Irina Vekich. She was supremely confident, and not in a supercilious way. She was just flat-out unflappable. I had the sense that nothing in the courtroom ever panicked her, that even if something did manage to take her by surprise, she wouldn't really be surprised by it and certainly wouldn't act that way.

"Listen, Ms. Vekich—"

"It's Mrs., and please, call me Irina."

"Irina. The reason I wanted to meet with you is that I think I know who the killer is."

She seemed amused. "Who?"

"Pete Wilczek."

She pursed her lips and nodded slightly. "Since you're probably not talking about the victim, I assume you're speaking of Global Web Development." It wasn't a question.

"Yeah."

"This must be based on recent information. There was nothing about him in Carl's files." Again, her tone was rhetorical. She wasn't asking for confirmation. "Why don't you tell me how he's connected to this?"

It was amazing. For the first time in a week I actually felt there was some hope. I looked into her eyes and she motioned for me to proceed. So I did. I started with the interview of Pete's dad, the fire, my meeting with Wilczek, then everything Stacy had told me. She didn't ask any clarifying questions, but was content to let me spill everything.

It took about a half-hour and she didn't look at her watch once, but when I finished she said, "Okay. We'll need to meet again because I have a motion hearing in about fifteen minutes, but there are a couple of things you can get started on. First, I don't have the time or the connections to get the information from immigration, the IRS, or the Pennsylvania documents. Get Carl to help you. Tell him I said we need it on this one. The firm doesn't have to know. It would be nice to know what this Wilczek's real name is but, frankly, that's probably an impossible task."

"How come?"

"We know he's been in Seattle a short time, but we have no idea how long he's been in the country. We don't know what port of entry he used or when. And if he's illegal . . ." She let the implication speak for itself. "The only thing we can really show is that no one named "Pete Wilczek" emigrated from Poland two years ago, and that's not much. What we need is to find some other records with Willis's social security number on it. Try the Selective Service—hopefully they'll have a record of him signing up when he turned eighteen."

She was incredible, and her confidence was infectious. "Anything else?"

"No. That should be good for the documents. The second thing is Wilczek himself. At the moment he's basically an unknown. You need to change that by investigating him. This is your specialty so you should get on it right away. Figure out what he's into. If he is involved in organized crime you should get a fairly clear picture of that after a few days. See who he's meeting with during the day, find out what he does at night, basically put together a complete surveillance that will help us come up with something that makes him look like a murderer."

Then she leaned back in her chair and thought for a second. "And finally, you'll need a way to steer Dalton in the right direction without actually telling him anything."

"Are you kidding? He hates my guts."

She shook her head. "No. He's just getting pressure from Adamson. I think that's why he's pissed off."

I took a minute to outline what I had done for Dalton in the past and told her about what had happened to his daughter.

"Okay," she said. "But that's not why cops get angry. Take it from me. Adamson has his case and he's probably ignored every reservation that Dalton's raised. I wouldn't be surprised if he went to Dalton's captain and had him order Dalton to close the case. Now every time Dalton sees you it reminds him how he's been removed from his own investigation."

"You don't think he's still upset about his daughter?"

"Sure he's still upset, but not with you."

"Then why is he taking his anger out on me?"

Vekich smiled broadly and said, "Because he doesn't think you did it."

I was feeling quite a bit of relief as I hit the street. The pressure was easing up, in spite of the possible threat still posed by Wilczek. Vekich wanted me to get started on the investigation and then meet with her on the weekend to tie up any loose ends before she began planning a strategy for the trial. I had to admit that Carl was right. I couldn't have been in better hands. My step quickened, and rounding 2nd onto James I had been practically jogging when I suddenly stopped short.

The dormant construction site I had parked next to was now fully active, with yellow-hatted workers streaming in and out through the fence and a large crane moving I-beams to the unseen accompaniment of a jackhammer. I could also see a huge garbage truck upending the Dumpster over its cab and into the truck bed, completely blocking off James Street. What I didn't see was Dewey's car.

It was gone.

CHAPTER TWENTY-SIX

"Listen, buddy, I don't care how much money you have, I can't give you the car."

After a promising turn of events, my day had gone to hell in a hurry. I had hiked all the way back up the hill to police headquarters only to be informed that I was in the wrong place and would have to talk to someone in the West Precinct at 8th and Virginia—twelve blocks north—in order to find out where Dewey's car had been towed. The desk sergeant was nice enough to give me the number, but I spent ten minutes getting a busy signal before I finally decided to walk. Along the way I pulled out a hundred dollars from my meager bank account, figuring that the towing charges had to be less than that. Hoping, actually. Yeah, I really saved a bundle by not parking in a lot.

When I had reached the construction site initially, it took me several minutes of collaring workers before I reached somebody who could give me any answers, first about what had happened to the Grand Prix. I was told curtly that they needed to empty the Dumpster and so they had it towed. My second question was who in the hell starts a construction job at three in the afternoon. The answer to that was that the crane had broken down the day before and rather than pay a crew to sit around all morning waiting to use it, they had come back in the afternoon after it had finished being repaired.

At the moment, however, I was standing at the window of a wooden shack at the police impound lot at Fairview and

Mercer—another twelve blocks north of the West Precinct—
being told by an old guy in a rent-a-cop uniform that I couldn't
have the car. Tired and hungry, I tried to be as patient as I could,
while above me loomed the Seattle landmark "Toe Truck," a giant,
fifteen-foot, pink toe mounted on the back of a matching pink
truck. I was not amused.

"Look," I said. "They told me down at the precinct that you
have my car here. I really need to get it back."

The guy in the booth looked as if he was in his late sixties,
with bad teeth, sagging skin, gray hair and an attitude to match.
"And like I told you, yeah, we have a Pontiac Grand Prix, dark blue,
personalized license plate B-A-R-I-S-A-X in the lot, registered to
a Dewey Beckley. But this," he said, holding up my license, "ain't
Dewey Beckley."

"I told you that already. He's loaning me the car and I need
to get it back to him."

"And I don't give a rat's ass if he gave it to you for a birthday
present. Like *I* told *you*, only the registered owner can get the car
out of impound. Now, get the hell outta here."

Great.

I took my license back and walked out to the street. Heavy
traffic raced by on Mercer from Queen Anne Hill down to the
freeway. The warmth I had acquired from my long walk had
seeped out during my discussion with Officer Friendly and now
I could add being cold to my list of miseries. The Space Needle
jutted up from Seattle Center off to the right while behind me on
Mercer the entrance ramps to I-5 funneled cars onto the interstate.
And in front of me? A two-mile hike down to the Low Note just
to tell Dewey I'd lost his car.

Fuck it. I walked up the hill to the next corner and started
flagging down cabs. Mercer was a good street for it and in a
few minutes a lime-green station wagon turned the corner and I
hopped in back when it stopped, giving the driver the address of
Dewey's place and trying to get comfortable in the warm stench
of the cab's back seat.

I had the driver let me off on Yesler and walked down to

Pioneer Square. The ride had cost me ten bucks, but was worth every penny. It was nearly six o'clock, and the temperature was already in the low fifties. No big deal if you're wearing a heavy overcoat, but all I had on was a canvas jacket I had slipped on that afternoon and it wasn't nearly enough to keep me warm.

The Low Note had quite a few customers for a Thursday night. I found a spot at the bar and listened to an organ trio on the sound system while Geoff worked his way down to me. "What'll it be, Ray?"

"Uh, how 'bout a Guinness?" Geoff nodded and was turning away when I asked, "Is Dewey around?"

"In the office," he said over his shoulder.

I waited until I had my beer and then walked back. The door was open and I plopped down in a chair. Dewey was busily punching out numbers on a large calculator with about three feet of tape spooled out on the desk, and when he reached the end of his computation he leaned back in his chair as another foot ratcheted out of the machine.

"Just the man I wanted to see. I need to get the car back this weekend. Gail's going out of town with some of her friends and I'm dubious as to her car's chances of successfully completing the return trip. I told her she could take the Pontiac."

I just nodded and took the hundred dollars—down to ninety now—out of my jacket and tossed it on his desk. Instead of picking it up, he frowned. "What's this?" Then I tossed the keys on top of the bills and he broke out in a grin. "Where'd you get towed?"

"Construction site down at the end of 2nd."

"Is the car okay?"

"Yeah. I'm pretty sure. If you want me to go get it, you need to sign something that says I'm acting on your behalf. They wouldn't release it to me."

"Don't worry about it. I'll cut Geoff loose as soon as I can and have him walk up to get it. Is it up on Mercer?"

I nodded and took a pull on my beer. "I just need to get the key to the Cavalier."

Dewey rubbed his chin and said, "Well, that is a conundrum, but I suppose there is a way."

"What are you talking about?"

He leaned back even further and reached up behind him to a speaker mounted on the wall behind the desk. A mono line coming from the system out in the club ran into the office so that he could listen to music without having another set-up. There was a small volume knob on the bottom and when he twisted it, out came the organ trio I had heard out at the bar.

"Ah, come on, Dew. Don't make me do this. Not now."

He stood and walked around the desk. "I'll go check on Geoff and see if he needs any assistance. You sit and listen." Then he was out the door.

I tipped up my bottle again and then settled in to listen. After a while it seemed pretty clear that I was listening to Jimmy Smith, but when I heard the baritone sax solo I was pleasantly surprised. It was a great combination, but one that I had never heard before except on George Benson's first recordings for Columbia—and I knew that wasn't what I was listening to here. The tune was a medium-slow blues and though I wanted to say it was Cecil Payne on the bari, I was familiar with most of his recordings from hanging out with Dewey, and I'd never heard anything like this before. But then, before I could even take another drink of beer, in the middle of the solo the horn player suddenly went into the head of Payne's blues "Bringing Up Father." It had to be him.

I was grinning with delight when Dewey came back in.

He said, "Well?"

"Gotta be Cecil Payne on the horn."

"Absolutely. And . . .?"

"I want to say Jimmy Smith, but I've never heard of those two recording together."

Dewey laughed and handed me the CD jewel case: *Six Views of the Blues* by Jimmy Smith on Blue Note. I turned over and looked on the back. Sure enough, a 1958 recording with Payne, Kenny Burrell and Art Blakey.

"He played the entire head of 'Bringing up Father.'"

Dewey nodded as he perched on the edge of the desk. "He loves that riff on the blues. He even plays it on another tune on that disc. I don't think he can help himself."

I gave the CD case back to him and Dewey handed me the key to my Cavalier. "Thanks," I said.

"Sure. You sticking around for the music?"

"No. Like I said, I need to get back on this case."

"How's it going?"

"Better. I have a suspect finally, and I'm pretty sure he's the guy."

"Hey, that's good news."

"Yeah."

He nodded toward the nearly empty bottle in my hand. "One for the road?"

"No thanks. But I might grab a bite to eat before I take off."

Suddenly Dewey started. "Ah, dammit. I forgot to tell you. Stacy called."

That wasn't good. "What did she say?"

He grinned. "The first thing she said to tell you was, and I'm paraphrasing here, to give her your goddamn cell phone number." Now I could relax. If it had been urgent Dewey would never have forgotten to tell me in the first place. "Then she said she was making dinner and that you should let her know what time you'd be coming home."

I didn't say anything after that and we looked at each other for a few moments. Finally Dewey said, "How's *that* going?"

I shrugged. "It's not the smartest move I've ever made, but . . ."

He could only shake his head and laugh. "But what the hell ya gonna do?"

"Something like that."

He wasn't entirely convincing, but he said, "I hope it works out this time."

"Thanks, Dew," I said and we both stood.

"I never did much like that Willis character anyway."

"Yeah, well . . . there must have been something there."

"Ah, yes," he said and clapped his hand on my shoulder as we headed out of the office. "*Some people cry and some people die by the wicked ways of love.*"

I thought about that for a second and when we reached the bar I said, "Neil Young?"

Dewey laughed again. "Led Zeppelin. Now go call your girlfriend. I have a bar to run."

"Is everything okay?" Stacy asked, after I told her it was me. "When I didn't hear from you I started to get worried."

"I'm sorry. I had some problems after I got done at the lawyer's. I'm down at the Low Note now."

"Hang on a second." I waited and when she came back she said, "I looked around the apartment all morning for your cell phone number, but I couldn't find it. Give it to me now."

I chuckled and gave it to her. Then I had to break the bad news. "Look, I have to go on a stake-out tonight." When she didn't respond I continued. "I have to watch Wilczek to see if I can learn anything."

"Does it have to be tonight?"

"My lawyer said as soon as I can."

"We haven't really seen each other all week. I thought I could make us dinner." This time I stayed silent. "Come home, Ray. You can start first thing in the morning. You don't even know if he's home from work yet, and if he is he may not go out again. And what if he doesn't even show up at home until late? You won't know where he's been, and I'll have just been sitting here alone."

"That's a lot of ifs."

"One night, Ray. It's my night off. Please?"

I looked at my watch; it was closing in on seven. She was probably right. It was far more likely that he would go somewhere or meet with someone on Friday night, and if I tailed him first thing in the morning I'd have his whole workday schedule down. Finally I sighed and said, "All right. I'll be there in a few minutes."

"Thank you."

"Do you need anything from the store?"

She was silent for a second. "No. But we only have a couple of beers in the fridge, so if you want any more you might want to get some."

"Okay, I'll do that. See you in a few."

I stopped on the way out to tell Dewey I wasn't staying and braved the cold yet again. The Cavalier was in a small pay lot at the foot of Washington. Dewey paid by the year so he would always had a spot when he came to work. There was no attendant at the lot, just a couple of malevolent looking barrels with chains and padlocks around them waiting for someone to accidentally stick their money in the wrong slot.

There was nothing that you could really call a grocery store downtown, so I cut over to Jackson and up the hill to 4th, planning to stop at the Safeway on Beacon Ave. I had just reached the northeast corner of Qwest Field when I looked up to my rearview mirror in preparation for a lane change. My gaze had just gone back to the road when I did a double take and said, "Shit."

I changed lanes anyway, and looked behind me to see another vehicle move in behind me two cars back. There was no doubt in my mind now. It was the black van.

CHAPTER TWENTY-SEVEN

At the moment we were both buried in rush hour traffic so there was nothing to panic about yet. What I couldn't be sure of, though, was how patient my friends would be. I would have to stay on main thoroughfares for a while, where there was plenty of traffic, but I also couldn't be sure they wouldn't simply blow out my window with a shotgun if they got the chance, so I couldn't let them come up beside me either.

It was when I pulled up to the stoplight at Airport Way, however, that I realized what I would have to do. If I hadn't had that scare coming back from Mercer Island I probably wouldn't have had the presence of mind to consider it, but looking to my right I realized I was approaching the onramp to eastbound I-90 one block further up. Fortunately, I was in the front of the line. Unfortunately, I was also three lanes over to the left. I took a deep breath and revved up the engine, watching for the light to change. If I didn't wind up plowing into someone, it might actually turn out to be to my advantage.

A steady stream of traffic was still flowing through the yellow light onto 4th from Airport Way when the light changed to green. I knew there was no way to outrun the van, so I was going to have to be strategic instead. I jetted into the intersection well ahead of the car to my right. The minivan two lanes to my right, however, kept pace with me for the first ten yards but they had to slow for the traffic still going through the yellow. I gunned ahead, pulling over quickly through two lanes. I had one to go and was rapidly approaching the light but had to stop for the knot of cars that had come from Airport Way heading for the onramp.

I took a quick look behind me and saw that the van was just as stuck, a good four or five cars back. I was completely surrounded by a protective crush of cars and since it was now clear that I was heading for the freeway, the guys in the van couldn't risk losing their place behind me for fear of not getting on the onramp themselves. A middle-aged woman in a VW bug let me cut in front of her as I gradually eased forward. Turning right onto the onramp I kept looking at the light, hoping it would turn yellow and allow me to escape, but it stayed solid green and I went back to concentrating on how to execute my original plan.

The onramp turned one hundred and eighty degrees while also climbing upward in order to pass back across 4th and over the top of Brougham Way out to I-5. I crossed all of the lanes to the left in order to get as much speed as I could before climbing the hill, but my old Chevy gradually began to slow. And I still had to get back over to the right to get on I-5 south. The elevated freeway kept rising all the way to the exit and, to my horror, I realized that a sixteen-wheeler was going to reach it at the same moment I would. Frantically, I looked over my shoulder to the right, braked heavily, and was able to get in just behind the semi and make the exit. Horns blared behind me, but I couldn't spare the time to check the rearview to see if they were for me or the black van.

Once on the freeway, the grade headed downhill, but I knew that would only be for a few hundred yards before it climbed again toward the West Seattle Freeway. Because of the late hour, traffic was moving at a good clip, and as I passed beneath Beacon Avenue I shook my head at the irony. I should have been up there heading home instead of down here trying to shake a tail. After racing the car past a white furniture truck on the left, I could see an open space of about fifty yards over to the right. I headed for it and was able to take a peek in the rearview behind me. They were still there, just moving up beside the truck and gaining on me.

Passing a brown sedan on the right, I took a chance and headed for the left lane again, gained several car lengths on the van—which had been boxed in—and slalomed between cars to get back in the right lane as we passed the Forest Street exit. Only one more to go, and I didn't dare miss it. There was only one place in Seattle that I could think of where I might be able to lose a tail, and that was West Seattle. I hadn't thought of it until it was too late last time when I turned north on I-5 instead of south.

Although West Seattle isn't an island, it might as well be. The freeway is elevated nearly the entire way from I-5 across the southern tip of Harbor Island until it touches down again at Alki. Best of all, there are only two exits before Alki, the first at Marginal Way, which I was planning on taking. The next was Harbor Island itself, which would require the van to completely exit the freeway, turn around on the island, and enter the freeway westbound in order to get off the island. And by then I'd be long gone. If they missed that exit they wouldn't be able to turn around until they hit West Seattle, and I could be on Capitol Hill before they reached I-5 again.

I made the exit to West Seattle, took a look behind me and spotted the van only a single car back. This was going to be tricky. I slowed way down as the freeway passed over 4th Avenue again, and traffic began shooting by me on the left. The van wasn't budging, so I took a chance. I put on my left turn signal and eased left between cars, but didn't completely leave the right lane. The black Mustang behind me laid on the horn, but I ignored it, praying that he wouldn't try to pass me on the right. There wasn't really any room, but still . . . I kept my speed slow and a gap began to open up in front of me. Then I pushed the gas pedal to the floor, moving all the way to the left, and was pleased to see the van do the same.

But just before the Mustang could blow by me on the right I wrenched the wheel over, cutting him off and hitting the Marginal Way exit amid a chorus of honking horns and screeching tires. A quick look in the rearview revealed that the van was trying desperately to stop and exit, but traffic would not permit it. The continuing wail of horns caused me to grin as I jetted down the off-ramp. I turned right as soon as I could, and then up to 1st and back toward town.

My heart was racing and I was panting as though I had held my breath the entire time. I didn't stop the car until I reached Stacy's apartment, and then I drove past it. They were just a little too close now to feel safe, and so there was no way I was going to park anywhere near her place. I took the car all the way over to 18th and Walker and parked in front of a church. With darkness beginning to close in around me I felt a modicum of safety as I walked back, and it helped somewhat to calm my frayed nerves.

By the time I reached the building, I was hunched over against the cold and my hands trembled slightly as I unlocked the door and walked inside. What I had to decide now was whether or not to tell Stacy about my friends. They were probably working for Wilczek and, just like Dewey had said, were trying to make sure I took the fall for Pete's murder. Being dead was a good way to ensure that. Wilczek wouldn't care how hard the police looked into my murder because they wouldn't find anything. He just didn't want them looking any harder into Pete's. It also gave a little more credence to what Stacy had said about Wilczek being in the mob.

As I ascended the stairs the heat couldn't penetrate my cold exterior fast enough, and my mood darkened. I hadn't wanted to believe the two were related, Pete's murder and the black van, and if they were it could complicate things further. If it really had been Wilczek who killed Pete in the attempt to wrestle the .44 away from him—or even executed him after a heated argument—then I might have a chance at uncovering some evidence to that effect. But if it had been Wilczek's goons who had killed Pete, I had a sinking feeling that there wouldn't be any evidence to uncover.

I could hear music leaking out from the front door of the apartment. Taking hold of the knob, I was glad to discover it was locked. I unlocked it and pushed inside to the sounds of Bonnie Raitt. Stacy came around the corner of the kitchen with a glass of wine in hand, set it down on the coffee table, then came over and wrapped her arms around me. We stayed that way for a long minute and I buried my face in her hair, wondering how much I should tell her about what had happened that afternoon. I could taste the wine on her lips when we kissed and thought a glass of my own would be good right about now.

When I released her she looked around and said, "You didn't stop at the store?"

"No. I just came straight here."

She gave me a sad smile, and I realized she'd been pretty good to me through all of this. Whatever happened down the road, it was nice not to be alone now, and I was kind of glad that I hadn't gone to Mercer Island. As far as I was concerned Wilczek could wait. I wanted to kiss her again, but then I didn't know if we would even make it to dinner.

Finally, I tossed my coat over the arm of the couch and said, "What are we drinking?"

Stacy had new potatoes, halved and brushed with olive oil, already in the oven. Two salmon steaks with lemon and dill were waiting to go in next to the potatoes, and the asparagus was still in the fridge. I poured myself a glass of the French rosé that was on the counter and then put some water in a pan for the steamer while Stacy set the table. At the sink I had cut away the bottom ends of the asparagus and was taking off the outer skin at the base of the stalks with a potato peeler when I felt her arms around me. She wouldn't let me turn around, but held me close and said, "I love you."

I tried my best not to unconsciously say something that could be construed as negative, but I'd waited too long to say anything.

"It's okay," she said, and I could feel her head pressed against my back. "I'm not going to propose."

I turned around, prepared to protest, but she cut me off. "I'm sorry, Ray. I know I shouldn't have said that. It just slipped out."

I searched in her eyes for some sign of hurt, and couldn't find any. "I don't know what to say, Stace—"

"Don't say anything. I mean it. Let's pretend it never happened."

It was a perfect dinner. Stacy brought out candles and lit them, exchanged Bonnie Raitt for James Taylor, and dimmed the lights in the rest of the apartment so that we could enjoy the view out the kitchen windows. We talked about people we knew, about the Low Note and Sharkey's, and mercifully avoided the case and her declaration of love. When dinner was over we left the dishes in the sink, left the lights down low, and finished what was left of the wine at the couch. When the music ended, neither of us made a move to put anything else on.

I was against one arm of the couch, my legs stretched out at an angle beneath the coffee table and my free arm over Stacy's shoulder. She was leaning with her back against me, lying the length of the couch, and had pulled my hand into her lap. Finally, I realized I had nothing to fear and brought the conversation around to the inevitable. "How are you doing?"

"Pretty good, I think. How did things go with the lawyer?"

"Carl was right—she's terrific."

"Did you tell her . . . everything?"

"Yes. And she understands completely. We're not going to the police at all. She wants me to start investigating Wilczek, find a connection to Pete, and any possible links to organized crime."

She squeezed my hand in approval.

"There is one thing, though."

That caused her to sit up and turn toward me. "What?"

"Well, I haven't figured out exactly how to do this, but if Wilczek's fingerprints were in my apartment then the police already have them. And, if he was fingerprinted to get into the country they'll match up with his real identity."

She nodded, a look of concentration on her face.

"What that means is that the police might already have his real name just sitting in their files as someone who was in my place once, but have no reason to suspect him. So, I may have to get some help from someone inside the police department to get me a list of those names. It might be the only way to tie him to the murder."

"Do you know someone who could do that?"

"Yeah. I think I do."

"As long as no one knows that it's on your behalf, Ray. That's the main thing."

"I know. Don't worry. I'll make that point absolutely clear."

She relaxed back into my arm and we stayed that way for a while. "This is nice," she said. "We should do this more often."

"Kind of tough, with you working nights."

Stacy set her cheek on my arm, then brought my hand up and kissed it. "I won't be working nights again, at least until this thing is over."

"Really? How'd you swing that?"

Finishing off her wine, she set the glass on the table and then pulled her legs up beneath her to talk to me. "I quit today. I called in and said I wasn't coming back."

"Wow. Whatever prompted that?"

"I did a lot of thinking this afternoon while you were gone, and I realized that I can't just go on pretending that nothing's happened. Pete's dead, and the same thing could happen to me."

"Stacy—"

"I'm not being fatalistic. I'm just saying that I can't keep going in to work like nothing's changed. I don't know who's following me, or who might be hoping to kill me when I least expect it, and I just decided that if it is going to happen it's not going to be while I'm waiting tables. I'm not going to continue walking through my daily life like a drone while all of this is going on. I can't do it."

I put my hand on her back. "So is this just for a while, or permanent?"

Her head seemed to nod slightly, almost unconsciously. "I'm not sure. But I am going to look into taking the police exam again."

I smiled. "Good for you. You've always wanted that. What's this going to do to you financially?"

She took a breath and sighed. "It's not like I spend a lot of money going out or anything. I've been saving my tips for a year so I should be okay for a while, at least until this thing's over. But I'm not going to be afraid anymore, Ray."

"Well, I think it's great."

She took my glass and set it on the table, then held my hand in both of hers. "Along those lines, I wanted to ask you something."

"Sure."

"I know you have a lot to do the next few days and you probably won't be here much . . ."

"Yeah?"

"Do you think it would make sense for you to bring your .38 up here so that I could have something to protect myself?"

I tried not to let the surprise show on my face. "Hmm. I guess that is something to think about."

"If there is someone watching me, it won't take long to figure out that I'm here all by myself."

"Oh, I know that. It's just . . . Well, for one thing I don't have the gun in the car anymore."

"Where is it?"

"I left it back at the apartment."

"Could you get it?"

"Look, Stacy. Before we get into that, I want to tell you about some thinking I've been doing. If what we think happened to Pete really did happen, then it's a powerful argument for *not* having a gun up here. In fact, that's why I took it into the house in the first place. I don't want someone taking it away and using it on me, like what happened to Pete. And I really don't want to be worried that it could happen to you."

She let out a breath she'd been holding and said, "I hadn't thought of that."

"Yeah. Look, if anything weird happens just call 911. Even if it turns out to be a false alarm. That's why you pay taxes. Use it."

"All right," she said, then leaned in to kiss me.

I kissed her back this time and before long she was leading me to the bedroom. When we had undressed and climbed under the covers she said, "Ray, I want to ask you another question."

I wrapped her in my arms. "Sure."

"And I don't want you to think I'm trying to force you to do something."

Oh, Christ. Where was this going?

She pushed a strand of hair back from her forehead. "I know you've been in your apartment a while, and I completely understand that you don't want to give it up. But with all that happened there, and with what's happened between us . . ."

"Yeah?"

"I'm not asking you to move in with me."

I smiled.

"But I know you're going through a tough time with your work, and if you stayed here while you're dealing with it I might be able to help." She put her hands on my face. "I just want to be with you, Ray. Nothing more. I just want to be with you right now."

I nodded in relief. For a second I thought she was going to press me about the gun again. "Okay," I said, before I could talk myself out of it. I looked into her eyes, now brimming with tears, and then kissed her gently on the forehead.

"We'll figure it out," I said, and she pulled herself up on top of me. I was going to say something else, but she put a finger over my lips to stop me. After that, we didn't need to talk.

CHAPTER TWENTY-EIGHT

The alarm went off at four-thirty. I figured if Wilczek was a type-A who went into work at six, I would need to be in place by five or so in order to tail him. I took a shower, dressed, and headed out to the car at about ten minutes to. Stacy didn't budge. It would have been nice to stop for a cup of coffee or something before heading over to Mercer Island, but I didn't want to have to take a leak and not be able to. Stakeouts are not my favorite thing.

I rarely try to take surveillance photos during the daytime. Most people with something to hide are pretty circumspect in the daylight. At night they feel safer and tend to expose themselves more often. That's usually when I get my best pictures. Tailing Wilczek like this was a rarity for me, not to mention the fact that I had absolutely no idea what I was hoping to see.

And that was the thing that was really jamming me up. My theory that Pete had been killed because he wanted his identity back was just that, a theory. There was absolutely nothing that Wilczek could do in front of me, other than walking around with a sandwich board saying *I did it,* that would get me off the hook. Still, there was little else to do if I wanted to make something happen. Even if I discovered that he couldn't have been the shooter, at least that would be progress of a sort. So, off I went.

There was little traffic at this time of the morning, and it only took a few minutes to get to Wilczek's neighborhood. Another advantage of starting out this early was that I had the cover of darkness to conceal some of my movements. I drove slowly, making as little noise with the car as possible, and went to the end of the road. First rule of surveillance: never let the suspect drive by you on a stakeout. So, unless Wilczek went in for early-morning swims on Lake Washington, I was safe. I positioned the car on the south side of the road, opposite from his house and on the property line between the two houses on my side of the street—which causes a lot less suspicion than parking right in front of someone's house.

On the front seat next to me were my cameras. Even when I know who the suspect is, I like to have something to reference later, in case they meet up with someone I don't know. It's been my experience that even a bad photo of the unknown person is infinitely better than a description in attempting to identify who they are. When I'm on foot I like to use a digital Minolta DiMage with a built-in telephoto lens. Hidden within the confines of my car, however, I have a Canon 35-millimeter with a 28-300 millimeter auto-focus zoom lens.

I set up the Canon and then waited . . . and waited . . . and waited. The longer my wait went on, the more frequently I began to check my watch. The waiting, however, was the least of it. I began to get cold just sitting there, even through my down jacket. Of course, it didn't help that I had to have my window down to prevent the rest of my windows from fogging up. I had set up by quarter after five, and two hours later Wilczek still hadn't emerged from his house. I was thinking it would be just my luck that the guy worked banker's hours and I'd be sitting out here another hour when the garage door slowly rolled open at twenty minutes to eight.

I snapped a couple of shots of the car backing out, but had to hunch down in the seat when the rear end of the car turned toward me. I peeked up just in time to see him pulling past the remnants of the cabin in a black Lexus and fired up the car to follow. Initially I figured that Wilczek must have set an eight o'clock start time for himself, but I quickly realized that wasn't going to happen. We spent nearly forty minutes on I-90 just going the three miles from Mercer Island to the exit at Boren.

This late in the morning, rush-hour traffic was at its worst. I tried to stay a couple of cars behind but it wasn't easy. And I don't mean that I was too far away. At one point the two cars in front of me both pulled into a gap in the other lane to gain a few seconds advantage in their commute and left me right behind my subject. I maintained the gap, however, and it wasn't long before other cars moved in to take their place.

Finally, we turned off on Boren and paralleled I-5 north for a mile toward Capitol Hill, then Wilczek surprised me by turning before we had even reached Swedish Medical Center. He went two blocks east and pulled into a parking lot behind a gray-brick office building south of Seattle University in the First Hill area. I pulled to the curb just beyond the entrance to the lot and in the rearview mirror watched him take his briefcase into the building. Now what?

After about twenty minutes, when I was sure he wasn't going to come back out to the car because he'd forgotten something, I climbed out of the car and walked around to the front of the building. It was an older, two-story affair, probably built sometime in the sixties, with ground-floor entrances along East Terrace Court and access to the upper floors through a lobby on the side of the building. Inside, there was a small elevator on the left that went up to the second floor and a set of well-worn stairs on the right. I didn't want to get caught on the stairs, so I checked the directory to see where he was located. Global Web Development was in Suite C-1, whatever the hell that meant.

Eventually I decided it didn't matter if he saw me. I'd just tell him I was on my way to ask him a few more questions. I hiked up the stairs and the last door at the end of the hall on the right was Wilczek's. His offices overlooked the street, not the parking lot, so I was in the perfect spot; I could cover the car and the entrance to the building from any number of locations in back and still couldn't be seen from his windows. Then I went back to my car to wait. But this time it was going to be a lot more pleasant. In addition to discovering Wilczek's offices, I had also seen a restroom on the ground floor.

When I reached my car I drove back down to Swedish and found a spot near Starbuck's just as someone was pulling out. Before going inside I walked down toward the hospital looking for a pay phone. The streets surrounding the hospital were packed with restaurants and fast-food places, and I made note of a bagel shop that I wanted to hit on the way back. Eventually I located a phone at an entrance to the hospital located between a Baskin-Robbins and a drugstore. I looked up the number to Wilczek's office, punched the number into my cell phone and dialed.

I wanted to nail down when he went to lunch, and I was going to do it by posing as a potential client who could only meet with him during his lunch hour. A young male voice answered the phone and when I asked for Wilczek he said he was on the phone. Even better. I said I'd try back again and hung up, secure in the knowledge that Wilczek was busily working in his office.

I walked back to the bagel shop, bought four with cream cheese, and then stopped at Starbucks for a Grande Americano with four shots and plenty of room for cream. It didn't make the time go by any faster once I was back in place behind the office building, but it certainly made me more content while I waited. Unfortunately, the longer the morning dragged on the more certain I became that this was not the way to go. There was little else to do, though. I tried getting in touch with Carl, but he was in a meeting. The search for the lawsuit Pete had been planning had reached a dead end, and until I discovered Wilczek's real name Carl was the only person who could help me.

I still needed to devise a way to figure out if the police had discovered any fingerprints at my apartment, and I had a couple of ideas there. The first, obviously, was Emily. She could probably get a look at the fingerprint evidence fairly easily. Whether or not she would be willing to do it for me was a very different matter. But there was another possibility. My detective friend, Jack Ransom, from the North Precinct might be willing to look into it for me. After all, my apartment was in their territory, and it was conceivable that he could be working with Dalton on the case. Hell, he might even have a copy of the file on his desk and could tell me without Dalton ever knowing. It was worth a shot.

I also had to get back to Officer Dodson about the fire, and I dialed information to get the number for the Mercer Island Police Department. I talked to someone who confirmed that Dodson was out on his beat and was transferred to the dispatcher's office where someone said they would get a message to Dodson to call me. A half-hour later the phone rang.

"Ray Neslowe?"

"Yeah?"

"Hey, Neslowe. Next time you get a bright idea about somebody being murdered, go find an officer whose career is already in the toilet."

"Dodson, sorry about that. If it makes you feel any better, Dalton chewed my ass, too."

"It doesn't."

I took a breath and started over. "I'm sorry for not telling you who I was, but I still believe the old man was murdered. He was in the house, wasn't he?"

There was no answer, and for a moment I thought he might have hung up on me. "Why should I tell you anything?"

"Because I have a client who's going to rot in prison if I don't find out who killed the old man and his son."

"What if your client did it?"

"Then I'll be able to stop begging guys like you for information."

There was another pause while he apparently thought it over. Then he said, "What do you want to know?"

"Was it arson?"

"The arson guys say there's no way to tell."

"Where did the fire start?"

"On the floor by the corner of the couch. It was probably a cigarette."

"Or someone could have lit the couch with their cigarette lighter."

"Like the arson guys said," Dodson repeated. "There's no way to tell."

"Okay. What about the stuff in the bedrooms? Was it all destroyed?"

"What stuff?"

"You know, clothes, books, whatever, in the bedrooms."

"There was nothing there."

"What," I said, "you mean there was nothing left?"

"No, nothing at all. There were two bedrooms and a bathroom in the back end of the house and the arson guy says that, other than two beds which had been stripped down, the rooms were empty."

That was the strangest thing I had ever heard. "The bedrooms were empty?"

"That's what the report says."

"Why would they be empty?"

"Hey, you're the detective. You figure it out. Now, if there's nothing else . . ."

"No, I guess that's it. Thanks, Dodson, I owe you one."

"Let's just say I'll be happy if I never have to talk to you in an official capacity again."

"Well, thanks anyway."

He laughed and then said, "Goodbye, Neslowe."

For the next hour I sat in my car and tried to figure out why the bedrooms in Wilczek's house would have been empty. If Pete had been secretly moving his things out I could understand his room being empty, but why Luka's? Beyond Pete moving out, the only thing that made sense was the money. But Luka wouldn't have had it, and if the murderer had looked for it and found it, why empty the bedroom at that point? It was yet another puzzle piece that I couldn't get to match with anything else. The information was piling up, but none of it was fitting together. Meanwhile, the surveillance continued.

I watched as the occasional person went into Wilczek's building. Other than parking myself in the lobby and following everyone who came in, however, I had no way to know if they were going in to see Wilczek. A couple of men in chinos and oxford shirts left and then returned a half-hour later, and I figured them for employees. Of which business, again, I was clueless. About eleven I thought about calling back, but decided to hold off and save that call for when I might need it later. It was twelve thirty-five when Wilczek emerged from his office and climbed into his car.

Instead of driving out to Boren, though, he hooked around to Jefferson, and I tailed him up to 14th. He drove toward Capitol Hill and eventually made his way to a Thai restaurant on 16th. It must have been a regular haunt because he drove straight into the tiny parking strip on the side and walked in without even looking around. For a moment I wondered why he would choose a place so out of the way when there were plenty of places to eat near his office. But the reason soon became apparent. Even in this neighborhood there was no place on the street to park. The streets around Swedish were probably a zoo at lunchtime. I circled the block twice and, figuring he would be at lunch for a while, finally gave up and made my way back out to Broadway. I dumped the car in the parking lot of a QFC, walked up a block to a Subway housed in a mock-adobe structure that had once belonged to a Mexican restaurant, and bought some lunch of my own.

I decided to bring my sandwich and Coke back to Wilczek's building to wait for him, but I was astonished to find his car already there. Then I nodded to myself. He had probably ordered his food to go and just driven over to pick it up. This was a pathetic stakeout. Not that it mattered. He couldn't have had time to meet with anyone of significance and still make it back before I did. And now I was back staring at the building and bored out of my mind.

At least the weather had begun to warm up that afternoon. There was still a solid cover of clouds, but they were very light in color and appeared to be at a high altitude. After lunch I decided to walk up to Boren and get a newspaper. Wilczek's car hadn't budged in the ten minutes it took. Not that I was worried. Not a single wiseguy or mafia don had come to meet with him, and except for lunch Wilczek had been in his office—presumably working—all day. The only thing of note that happened that afternoon was that the two guys in oxfords disappeared for a half-hour again. What made it in any way out of the ordinary was that they hadn't returned either time with food or coffee. It must have been business. I hopped out and followed them on foot, and when I entered the lobby they had just reached the top of the stairs. One of them looked at me but I had already turned toward the elevators. When they were out of sight I made my way up the stairs just in time to see them turn into Wilczek's office. While not significant in terms of getting me off the murder charge, it was something, which was more than I had seen all day. I decided the next time the boys took off I would follow them.

For now, though, it was back to the car. Three hours later, at six-thirty, Wilczek finally emerged from the office and I tailed him back up Boren to I-90 and home. I gave him plenty of time to park and get inside the house before I headed down Cedar Cove Road. I was much more exposed in the daylight, but at least the sun had already begun to set and it wouldn't be light for long.

Then something extraordinary happened. I hadn't even had time to bemoan the fact that I was missing dinner when the garage door began rolling up again. I had learned nothing at Wilczek's work, but that wasn't surprising, especially if his work was legitimate. This evening trip would, with any luck, be much more educational.

CHAPTER TWENTY-NINE

I had to be careful not to let him see me this time. If my car became too familiar he'd begin to get suspicious. As it turned out, I needn't have worried. I almost lost him a couple of times. There was far less traffic than there had been in the morning, and I had to race through a yellow at the end of Mercer Way. Then I found myself stuck behind a slow-moving pickup while he raced down the onramp to the freeway. I didn't catch up to a comfortable distance again until we had almost reached the tunnel.

When the Lexus emerged from the other end, however, I did notice something interesting. There was a passenger in the car. Magda, no doubt. And there went my hopes for a high-level mafia meeting. It didn't take much of a detective to figure this one out. Seven-thirty on a Friday night with your wife? Must be taking her out for dinner. Now *there* would be an exciting stakeout. I decided to call it a day, but first I wanted to make absolutely sure that was the plan and continued my tail.

Wilczek stayed on I-90 all the way to 4th and then he surprised me by turning right. I had expected him to head toward downtown. But when he turned right again at Royal Brougham and drove between the stadiums, I realized he was simply going around the back way down 1st. Traffic slowed to a crawl through Pioneer Square, especially with the rain holding off. People milled about in front of the numerous bars and clubs and streamed out into the street in packs going from one to the next. In order to encourage more patronage, most of the clubs with music had gone in together to offer a joint cover charge that would get you into all of the clubs. You paid at the first place you went to, and could bar hop the rest of the night without paying an additional cover. It was a busy night.

As we went through the square I stayed right on Wilczek's tail to avoid getting separated by a red light. All of my attention had been focused on the traffic—pedestrian and otherwise—in front of me, and I figured Wilczek's would be as well. But when I saw the Central Tavern I suddenly remembered that this was the night Kurt had wanted me to meet him to see Gary Vaughan. That was an idea. Kurt had been a computer programmer with Microsoft for years and was now an independent contractor. He might know something about Wilczek.

We passed Yesler and angled left up 1st toward the Pike Place Market but never made it there. Wilczek stopped halfway down, looked for a place to park, and when he couldn't find one, pulled into a pay lot. I figured I had time and circled the block to get myself in position behind them. I had a pretty good idea where they were heading and they didn't disappoint. On the corner of 1st and Spring was McCormick & Schmick's, one of an upscale chain of seafood restaurants around the country. The couple made their way up Spring Street arm in arm, Wilczek held the door for Magda, and they disappeared inside.

I disappeared, too. Continuing on up to 2nd, I headed back toward Pioneer Square. An open parking spot on Cherry—even though it was several blocks from my destination—was a gift on a Friday night, and I parked, gave thanks, and hurried down to meet Kurt. On the way I put in a call to Stacy.

"How'd it go?" she asked.

"It was a bust. He and his wife are downtown having dinner so I'm knocking off."

"So, what's next?"

"I have to meet with someone, but I was wondering if you wanted to come down and see some music with me. Maybe we could grab something to eat."

She thought about it for a long second and I almost thought

something might be wrong. Then she said, "Do you think everything will be okay?"

I knew what she was asking. "Yeah. He's not going to do anything tonight, and I haven't seen anything to lead me to believe we're in any immediate danger. Come on. You must be tired of sitting around the apartment all day."

"I can't argue with that, but I already ate, and plus I'm sitting here in sweat pants and a T-shirt so I'll need some time to get ready. Where did you want to go?"

I told her about Gary Vaughan, that I thought the music started about nine so she had plenty of time, and that I was meeting someone there. We said goodbye and I made my way down to 1st and over to the Central.

The Central Tavern has backed into the distinction of being Seattle's oldest continuously run bar. That title used to belong to the Owl Tavern in Ballard, but a few years ago the owners closed the doors. It has since reopened as an Irish pub, but with none of the regulars there and no live music it just isn't the same. I went in once to see what it was like and haven't been back. The Central is a great old place. It's a narrow, high-ceilinged room that seems as long a football field. The bar runs the length of the room on the left-hand side of the place, a good-sized dance floor abuts the stage at the far end of the room, and tables fill the rest of the space.

I was way too early to catch Kurt so, after paying my cover charge, I pushed my way through the crowd and found a single seat at the bar. I ordered a Guinness on tap and a burger and fries to go with it. Early Allman Brothers from the sound system competed with conversation in the club, but people weren't yelling at each other to be heard yet. That would come later.

The stage was packed with Vaughan's equipment. There was a Hammond B-3 on the far side of the stage with a Leslie speaker next to it and a couple of synths on top. A drum kit with half a dozen toms and almost as many cymbals dominated the left side, and Fender bass and guitar amps were squeezed in around them against the back wall. Overhead was a large rectangular grid with Par lights mounted the entire way around. Mic stands, monitors, and cables seemed to cover what little floor space remained and a column of speakers stood along each side of the stage guarding the mass of electronic gear. It looked to be a four-piece group with Vaughan as the only guitarist. I sipped my Guinness and was pleased that circumstances had allowed me to be here.

Vaughan wasn't due to begin for another hour so I took my time eating, ordered another beer, and shortly before eight thirty I felt a hand clap my shoulder. I turned, expecting Stacy, but it was Kurt, grinning ear to ear. "Ray. I didn't think you'd come."

I hopped off my stool and shook his hand. Even though I'm almost six-two, Kurt is easily six-seven in his socks and a good head taller than me. "I didn't think I'd be able to," I said, "but I really need to talk to you about something, and I since I was downtown anyway . . ."

He was nodding, but the grin had melted away. "What is it? Is it serious?"

"Sort of, but we can talk about it later."

"Okay. Come on," he said, in his light but distinctive German accent. "We have a table over here."

I grabbed my glass and followed him with ease, his head and shoulders cutting through the crowd like a shark fin above the water. He must have had someone here early in the night to have nabbed a table this late. I sat down next to a tall blond with a hawk nose and rather large breasts, conspicuous even under the bulky cable-knit sweater she was wearing. A small, thin-lipped man with a determined look sat next to her holding her hand, and Kurt's girlfriend, Janis—pronounced Ja-nees, accent on the last syllable—an exotic-looking massage therapist originally from France sat on the other side of the table with Kurt.

Kurt himself had been born in East Germany and had emigrated after the Wall had come down. He was part of a generation of computer programmers who had grown up behind the iron curtain—with very few computers, writing code by hand on paper. I thought he was a genius, although he would always shake his head at the suggestion. He had continued working for Microsoft as a contractor even after leaving the company as an employee, and I had a feeling it was because he could do things for them that few others—from any country—could do. After German unification he began spending almost as much time in Berlin as in Seattle, and it was only after he figured out a way to maintain dual citizenship that he had become a U.S. citizen a couple of years ago.

He was tall and gangly, with a gaunt face and a thin, patchy beard that ran along his jaw line. His hair was long and pulled back in a small pony tail and he wore a small gold hoop in his left ear. Two ashtrays and two pitchers of beer sat on the table—one pitcher nearly empty and one ashtray nearly full—and everyone had a glass. Kurt made the introductions. Carrie was the woman in the sweater and Jerome was her boyfriend. They were friends of Kurt's, though I had never met them before. But that wasn't surprising. Sometimes it seemed to me that there were very few people in Seattle that Kurt didn't know.

I caught up with Kurt while Janis talked to Carrie and Jerome, and eventually Kurt and I headed up to the bar to refill the pitchers. As it neared nine o'clock I began to check my watch more frequently, but Stacy finally appeared just as Vaughan's group was climbing onstage, and I introduced her around the table. It took Kurt and me a few minutes to secure another chair, and the six of us managed to crowd around the table just as the lights came up. We turned our chairs and looked through the haze of cigarette smoke as the band launched into their first number and immediately drowned out all but the most determined of conversationalists.

As the dance floor began to fill I thought I recognized the opening riff and grinned with delight when it was, in fact, David Lindley's cover of the Isley Brother's "Your Old Lady" from his first album. Vaughan didn't quite have Lindley's guitar chops, although he was a decent slide player. He also had a deeper voice than Lindley, but there the comparisons ended. The group had really made the song their own, speeding up the tempo slightly and changing the minor feel of Lindley's version to something a little brighter, a little livelier. The middle solo was also a revelation.

Vaughn dropped the slide and performed some blistering runs on his Telecaster that actually made me wonder if I didn't prefer his version more.

Vaughan had a great look in jeans and a T-shirt, with long, wavy blond hair and John Lennon glasses that made him look like Waddy Wachtel from the seventies, but the rest of the band was just as interesting. His bass player had short black hair, spiked on top, and wore black, peg-leg jeans and a pink jacket and tie. The drummer was fox-faced, wore his brown hair in a long mullet, and was fluid motion. And on the organ, a large black man in camouflage parachute pants, a black T-shirt and sunglasses, alternated between a Malcolm X scowl and a Louis Armstrong grin. They were excellent musicians, and they played well together.

Stacy sat beside me and took an occasional sip of my beer. Behind us Jerome had his arm around Carrie, but Kurt hadn't even made it through the first number before he and Janis pushed their way onto the dance floor. Watching his head and shoulders bob above the crowd was an added pleasure in a night of terrific music. Vaughan's group finished the set with what I assumed were original numbers, all of them well done.

When Kurt returned with Janis his face was shiny with perspiration and bright with joy. Santana came up on the sound system, and Kurt leaned down to speak in my ear. "I'm going out to have a cigarette. Let's talk."

I nodded. "I'm going outside to talk with Kurt," I told Stacy.

"I'll come, too," she said, and joined us out on the sidewalk.

Kurt lit up and leaned back against the wall of a darkened coffee shop next door. "What did you want to talk about?"

Stacy was wearing a jean jacket and had her arm around mine, holding tight against me for warmth. Foot traffic streamed by us in both directions, and the faint sounds of music from other clubs filtered through the noise of the traffic on 1st. "I'm in a little trouble with the police and I'm trying to clear myself." His expression darkened with concern, but I waved him off. "Anyway,

I have reason to suspect that Pete Wilczek of GWD is involved, and I wondered if you knew him."

Kurt exhaled a plume of smoke, made even thicker from the cold air, and smiled like the Cheshire Cat. "I know Wilczek. What did he do?"

I looked to Stacy and her grip tightened even more. "Nothing that I can prove yet, but I need some background on him and anything you might be able to tell me would help. For instance, I don't think Wilczek is his real name."

Kurt nodded. "That's obvious."

From the corner of my eye I saw Stacy turn toward me, but my eyes stayed with Kurt. "How do you know that?"

"Because Wilczek is a Polish name."

"Are you saying that he isn't Polish?"

Kurt laughed. "If Pete Wilczek is Polish then I'm the Pope." He took a last drag on his cigarette and dropped it on the pavement. Then he ground out the butt with the toe of one of his size-fifteen Romeos and said, "I'm pretty sure he's Romanian."

CHAPTER THIRTY

"What I'm saying," Kurt continued, "is that it would be like living in Texas all of your life. You would be able to tell the difference between a Texas accent and an Oklahoma accent very easily, where someone up here wouldn't think there's a difference at all." Kurt hadn't wanted to discuss specifics out on the street, so the three of us were walking up 1st Ave. toward the Low Note to see if there was an open booth. If nothing else, I'm sure Dewey would let us use his office. "Where I grew up, in Guben, it was a divided town. On one side of the Oder was East Germany and on the other side was Poland—like Kansas City or St. Louis here—so I became very conscious of Polish accents."

"Even in English?" I asked.

He smiled. "Not at first. I mean, not consciously, because I hadn't met that many Poles over here. But after a while I found it was very easy to hear the accents in English, especially Romanian."

"And you think Wilczek is Romanian?"

"Absolutely."

"Why would he lie about that?"

Kurt looked over my head as if he expected someone to step out of the shadows. I was not comforted. "Let's go inside first."

By the time we were half a block away we could see a line outside the Low Note.

"Uh oh," Stacy said.

"It's okay." I nodded my head to the left as we were crossing the street. "Let's go down the alley."

When Jeannine answered the door she didn't bother saying hi, and left it open to run back to the kitchen. "This way," I said, and led the two of them through the kitchen and into Dewey's office. Then I left them there and went back to the kitchen. One thing about Jeannine, although she might be working her ass off she didn't look harried.

"Looks like a busy night."

She was flipping burgers on the grill and didn't look at me, but she did smile. "New couch for the living room, that's what we have out there tonight."

I laughed and said I needed to use the office for a few minutes.

"You should tell him you're in there first."

"Will do."

I headed back out into the club and waited at the end of the bar. The place was packed, and it looked as if he had hired a couple of extra waitresses. The trio was playing a swinging version of what sounded like Wayne Shorter's "Adam's Apple." Very nice. The kid on the B-3 was doing a tremendous job. There were even several couples dancing. Dewey was at the bar alone, and when he finally saw me he finished pulling a couple of beers and then wiped his hands as he made his way over. "Ray," was all he said.

"Dew. I just wanted to let you know that Stacy and I are in your office with a friend. We just need a place to talk."

He nodded and started heading back.

"We'll be out of there in a few minutes."

He raised a hand with his back to me and I thought I heard him yell, "No rush."

Back in Dewey's office Kurt was sitting behind the desk, fiddling with the speaker and Stacy was leafing through a restaurant supply catalog. "It's only for the stereo system," I said.

Kurt nodded and turned around, disappointment on his face. We could hear the thrum of the band through the walls but not the actual music itself. I closed the door, Stacy set down the catalog, and Kurt started back in. "All I can really do is tell you what I know is going on in Romania. Whether or not Wilczek is part of it, there's no way to know."

"That's okay. I just need a place to start. I sat and watched him all day today and didn't learn a thing."

Kurt nodded. "Right now, the biggest center of Internet crime in the world is in Romania. And it makes sense. Under Communism there was a flourishing black market and now that the Russian money is gone, the police only have the ability to fight conventional crime. They do *nothing* about computer crime, and don't have the money or the tools to do anything even if they wanted to."

"What about in Russia?" Stacy asked and I nodded, remembering. Her father had been part of the American Consulate when she was young.

Kurt held out his hands. "Not as much as in Romania. They have bigger problems. Their population is shrinking to the point where soon there will only be half the people they had at the time of the breakup of the Soviet Union. Young people are getting out of Russia, not trying to figure out how to stay and survive."

Stacy's brow wrinkled. "I didn't know that."

Kurt nodded. "It's very bad right now. In Romania the conditions are somewhat different. There are still a lot of young people. They are just as interested in computers as kids are over here, probably more so. There is less to do there, so the Internet is the world where most of them spend their time.

"They are highly trained but there is no legitimate business to pursue. They fix up old Dell and Compaq computers that have been discarded in Germany, France, even Great Britain. At first, when Internet crime was fairly simple, people would occasionally work together but there was no real organization. Now there are countrywide organizations that specialize in this crime. People can learn how to acquire passwords, how to hijack Internet accounts, steal identities, any kind of Internet crime."

"Like the computer viruses?" I asked.

"No. That's a completely different crime. The viruses out of Germany and elsewhere are designed to actually shut down the

Internet, crash the system. It's more like computer vandalism—they don't actually get anything out of it other than the satisfaction of seeing something destroyed. The crime out of Romania is more like burglary. They're out to steal your money."

"How do they do that?"

"It's developed over time, but the most effective way they have now is called phishing. The idea is to get you to come to their web site on your own and give them your passwords."

Stacy frowned. "Why would anyone do that?"

He nodded. "That's where the deception comes in. A phony e-mail is the easiest way. Millions of e-mails are sent out that look like legitimate requests from banks or any site where you would use a credit card, asking you to go to the site and update your information by clicking on the provided link. The link takes you to a site that looks just like the legitimate sites, but is really theirs. When you enter your account information and passwords on their site, now they have them too. Then they immediately go out and use that access you've just given them to find out your credit card numbers or bank accounts and clean you out as fast as they can before you figure out what happened."

"Jesus," I said. "How the hell are you supposed to know if it's legit or not?"

Kurt was already shaking his head. "These days most legitimate e-mails won't put a link in for you to click. They will ask you to go the site first, logon there, and then update your information there if that's what they want you to do. If there's a link in the e-mail, there's a good possibility that it's fake. Even if you're not sure, all you have to do is look at the URL. If you roll over the link it won't be the site you think you're going to, but people generally don't pay attention to the address."

Stacy looked at me with wide eyes. "Oh, my god. I think I may have done that once."

Kurt laughed. "You would have known by now if they were going to do something. But you might want to change your passwords the next time you get a chance, just to be on the safe side."

"That still seems like such a long shot," I said. "You'd have to send a lot of those, and it seems like word would get around fairly soon."

"Yes, it does. That's why they are continually changing tactics. They will send messages saying your e-mail account will be stopped if you don't respond, or that your account needs to be paid. But that's just the start. They have far more sophisticated ways of getting what they want."

"Like what?"

"Trojan horse programs that load onto your computer once you go to their site. You don't even have to enter any information. Once the browser opens at their site it inserts a program on your computer while you're waiting for the page to load. The program records keystrokes."

"I've heard of that," I said. "Aren't there also programs that can allow someone to control your computer from a remote location?"

Kurt nodded. "But usually they take too long to load and people get suspicious and kill the new window. The keystroke programs are quicker. They simply record everything you press on your keyboard, and the next time you go online they send the information back to the criminal. Once the criminals have separated out the individual words they can see what sites you've visited, and any passwords you've entered."

"And if you do your banking online . . ." I said.

"They clean out your account and move on to the next victim."

I thought for a moment, and then said, "So, you think Wilczek might be involved in this?"

"I have no idea," Kurt said. "Only the fact that he's Romanian makes me think he might. And that he is somehow trying to hide the fact.

"Assuming he is, why would Wilczek want to be here? Aren't there pretty stiff penalties for Internet crime in this country?"

Kurt shook his head. "I don't think he would worry about getting caught."

"Why not?"

"Anyone doing this would have programs on their computers to re-format the hard drive with one click, or keep all the important information on a thumb drive so they could always keep it with them. Being here, they would also have access to English speaking employees. One of the easiest ways to spot a phony e-mail is when the language is incorrect."

"I've seen that," I said. "It's obvious. I've also noticed that some seem like they have random characters in the subject line."

"Yes. In Europe they usually run programs to generate the characters they need for their particular language. And the programs change all the letters, even the ones that are the same in English. So, when the e-mail goes out and is read by someone without the transposing program it looks like garbage. There is also the benefit of his legitimate business and US address getting their e-mail through spam filters, or simply as a cover for any illegal activity. That might be another reason for being here."

He had stopped and looked as if he was trying to figure out how to say something. "What?" I prompted.

"It's just a rumor, but I've heard that Wilczek's company is working on security issues for online retail companies."

"What kind of security?"

"Exactly what we've been talking about. I've heard that he's been helping to combat the Romanian organization."

That made sense to me. "So he would be pretending to help, but could actually be providing the Romanians with back doors and all kinds of ways into the user accounts."

"Yes," Kurt said. "And being Polish would lessen any suspicions that people might have if they knew he was Romanian." Then he smiled. "It's funny. I didn't make the connection when I heard the rumor, but it was in the back of my mind. Now, I see it."

"How do we find out if that's what he's really doing?"

Kurt held out hands. "It's just a rumor. I don't know if it's true. It could all be bullshit."

"I know. But if we prove that he's not doing anything illegal I can at least stop looking at him."

He grinned. "I could go undercover, see if he'll hire me and find out from the inside."

"Not that I would let you do it anyway, but I don't have that kind of time. I have a murder rap hanging over my head."

"Ray . . ." Stacy was probably worried about saying too much to Kurt.

Kurt frowned. "Is that what this is about?"

I nodded. "If this is what's going on, I think Wilczek might have killed a couple of people to keep his secret."

Stacy said, "You think Pete knew about the Internet stuff?"

"If he did, the whole thing would make a lot more sense. Pete would have had more leverage against Wilczek to get his name back and there would also be more of a motive for Wilczek to kill Pete to keep him quiet."

"How does that involve you?" Kurt was still worried.

I gave him the short version and he said he would try to help any way he could. At that moment the three of us turned as the door swung open and Dewey entered the room. Embarrassed, Kurt began to remove himself from behind the desk, but Dewey waved him down. "Sit. I'm just here to see my girl."

Stacy grinned and stood to give Dewey a hug.

"I could use you out there tonight. You still working at Sharkey's?"

"Nope. I'm done with waitressing for a while. I think I'm going to finally try to take the police exam."

Dewey beamed, as though she was his own daughter. "Good for you. Well, I need to get back. I just wanted to take my chance to get back here and say hi. I don't think I'll get another one tonight."

Just then we heard Jeannine yell "Dew!" from the kitchen.

"See . . ." And with that he left us.

I turned around to see Kurt deep in thought. Stacy was still smiling from seeing Dewey as we sat down, but my attention was focused on Kurt. "What's up?"

He looked at us and nodded. "There might be a way."

"To do what?"

"If you can figure out how to get into his office, I could give you a keystroke program to put on his computer. Use the same thing on him that he's using on others."

"Why not do it the safe way and send an e-mail? Load the program the same way he does."

"No," said Kurt. "He would have all kinds of firewalls and filters, and it might even lead him back to us."

I thought about it for a few seconds. "There are a couple of problems with getting inside. First, I'm not at all sure I could do it alone. I don't break into places, never have, so it would mean walking into the office during the day and posing as a client. But he's seen me, so I wouldn't even want him to be in the building. Plus, I don't know enough computer jargon to pass myself off as a potential client." Then I smiled at Kurt. "You, on the other hand . . ."

He actually laughed and held his hands up. "I'm no spy."

"Which leads us to the second problem. I could do it during lunch, but there would have to be someone on the outside to tail Wilczek. Once he started back to the office I would have to get out of the building in a hurry. Maybe you could just go in with me to talk to one of his employees, and if we find an empty office we might be able to get the program on their computers."

He nodded. "I could do that."

"But it still leaves us with the problem of watching Wilczek."

"No it doesn't," Stacy said, and both of us looked at her. "I'll do it."

CHAPTER THIRTY-ONE

"Stacy—"

"No," she said. "Just listen, Ray. When you guys go inside you put your cell phone on vibrate and when I see him come back I'll call you and you'll know to get out."

I looked over to Kurt and his eyes widened. He clearly had no opinion on the matter.

"That's not enough time," I said to her. "This afternoon he picked up Thai food on Capitol Hill and drove right back to work. He was only gone for ten minutes. If we're still inside when he pulls into the parking lot it'll be too late for us to get out."

"Then I'll follow him," she said excitedly.

I didn't say anything, but I wasn't happy about the idea.

She put a hand on my arm and said, "This is just like what I'll be doing in the police department."

"Yeah, in a few years, after going through the police academy—and with a partner."

"Come on, Ray. I'll make sure he doesn't see me. I can even use your car."

I rubbed the back of my neck and sighed. When I looked up at Karl he shrugged and said, "It might be the only way."

Now I had to stand up, so I could pace in the tiny spot of empty floor available in the office. "There's one thing we have to realize in doing this, and that's that we're only going to get one shot. If we blow it we're never going to get another opportunity to get back into his office. But more importantly, we don't even know that he's done anything yet, certainly nothing that we can prove. And at the same time, if he *did* kill Pete we're talking about a man who put two—not one, but two—bullets into the back of Pete's head and blew his face off."

Stacy turned and looked at the wall. Shit.

"I'm sorry," I continued, "but that's the reality. And because he *could* be a cold-blooded killer we would absolutely have to take this to the cops if we blow it. Unfortunately, at this point they won't have any more evidence than we have. We'll have to go to the cops to protect ourselves, but he'll also be tipped off that we're looking at him and he'll be able to hide any illegal activity he's up to. And at the end of the day I'll still be on trial for murder."

Kurt was staring down at the papers on Dewey's desk, not meeting my eyes. Stacy, on the other hand, turned back to me and stared me down. "And who do you think he's going to come after first? You think he's going to believe that Pete didn't tell me everything? What if he's the one who's been following me?"

Now Kurt was beginning to look panicked. "It's okay," I told him. "I don't want any of us to do anything risky. I promise. I wouldn't even ask you if it was." I went back and sat down next to Stacy. "But what you just said has me even more convinced that you shouldn't be involved."

"I need to do something, Ray. Please. He won't even know I'm there."

The right thing to do would have been to say no, and leave it at that. There were other considerations, though, and time was one of them. "Okay, here's what we'll do. Tomorrow is Saturday. I'll stake out Wilczek's place on my own. If he doesn't go in to work I'll head over to his office and see if anyone is there. That would be the best time to go in, if he's not even at work. If he does show up for work Stacy can follow him when he leaves for lunch and if, and only if, he sits down to eat will she give us a call and we'll go in."

She nodded in agreement.

I asked Kurt, "Can you have that program ready by tomorrow?"

"I have a copy of the program now, but I'll need some time

to make a few modifications. I'd also like to put an expiration date on it."

"What's that?"

He said, "It's a line of code that deletes the program from the system it's on at a set date."

"Like a self-destruct?"

"Yes. I don't want to leave anything behind that can be connected to me."

I hesitated before asking, but finally said, "Are you sure you want to do this?"

Kurt nodded vigorously. "Oh, yes. If he's doing illegal things like this on the Internet he's ruining it for everyone. They have to be stopped. I just want to know how long you'll need the program to be on his machine."

"I'd like to say it will only be a couple of days, but I have no idea how long it will take. Is a month too long?"

"No. That's fine."

"Do you have any idea what you'll talk to those guys about?"

He nodded. "I actually had an idea for a start-up when I was with Microsoft. I drew up a business plan and wrote out a prospectus but didn't really have the motivation to go forward with it. I'll just bring all of that and hint around that I'm worried about security. See where it leads."

"Great. I'll pretend to be your financing, going along for the ride to see if it's going to pan out before giving you the money. Sound reasonable?" They both nodded and I said, "So, let's plan on tomorrow. I'll give you both a call by ten if it's on, and we can meet south of Seattle University. There's an I-HOP up on 14th and Jefferson. We can meet there at eleven."

With that settled, Kurt unfolded himself from behind the desk and the three of us walked back out to 1st Avenue, through the front door this time. I wanted to say goodbye to Dewey and listen to the combo for a minute. The organist was into a wild solo that had everyone hooting and urging him on. Dewey was frowning, but I could also see his head slightly bobbing to the rhythm. When the group finally came back around to the head the crowd erupted in applause for the organist, but it also told me why Dewey had been frowning: Ray Charles' "I Got A Woman." Oh well, if it was good enough for Jimmy Smith, I guess Dewey had decided there wasn't much he could do about it. After a final wave to Dewey at the bar we pushed through the crowd that was still waiting out in the street, and headed back down to the Central.

Gary Vaughan's group was well into their next set when we arrived and I was surprised to see a sax player on the stand blowing an alto. He had a buzz cut that was going gray, wore a red shirt under a black jacket, and had a silver earring in his left ear. We had missed the introductions so I never caught his name, but toward the end of the set Vaughan made a comment about his being the official dentist for the group, and everyone laughed. I had no idea what they were talking about, but he played some tremendous solos.

It had been a long day and I had to get up early in the morning, so when the set ended Stacy and I stood to leave. After telling Kurt I would give him a call in the morning I walked Stacy to her car. She had a silver Stanza going gray with age that was parked in a lot down on Washington. Before she opened the door she said, "Thanks for letting me do this with you."

I nodded. "The only reason I hesitated is for your safety. You know that, don't you?"

"I know. It makes sense. But thanks anyway." Then she put her arms around me and I rested my cheek on her forehead while we hugged. In my mind, however, I couldn't stop thinking about Wilczek. Sure, we had a plan to get inside and find out what he was up to, but this wasn't the movies. We had no idea what we would find when we went in. There were a million things that could go wrong, from a receptionist simply telling us that we couldn't talk to anyone other than Wilczek himself, to being turned over to the police for attempting to get into Wiczek's computer. I didn't believe that we were in any actual physical danger or I wouldn't have involved anyone else. Still, I could do without another arrest.

I watched Stacy get into her car and get underway before going back up to my own. When I reached Cherry I walked up a block further and came back to my car from the east, just to make sure I didn't see anyone watching for my return. Other than a few people out walking with purpose, heads down toward their destinations, I saw no one. The drive back was thankfully just as uneventful and I was almost convinced that there was no GPS device on my car. Even so, I parked in front of the same church I had the night before.

When I walked into the apartment, Stacy was already in bed. I turned out the lamp on her desk and headed into the bedroom.

"What time are you going tomorrow?"

"Same as today."

She groaned and I lay down next to her, her face the only thing peaking out from beneath the covers. I yawned and said, "What do you care? You slept through the whole thing this morning."

Her arms emerged and pulled me toward her, nuzzling her face in my neck. "I know," she said. "But I missed you when I woke up."

We kissed and soon she began pulling at my clothes. I sat up. "Let me go brush my teeth real quick."

Another groan, but I ignored it. I stripped down to my boxers and T-shirt and padded into the bathroom. The toothpaste was nearly empty. I squeezed the last bit out onto my toothbrush and tossed the flattened tube into the wastebasket. I hadn't realized how full the basket was, however, and half a dozen slips of paper puffed out onto the floor. Continuing my brushing I stooped down to pick them up. Receipts mostly; Stacy had probably cleaned out her purse. The last one I picked up caught my eye and I stood slowly, quickly finished brushing, and rinsed out my mouth.

I looked over toward the bedroom door and then back to the piece of paper in my hand. I'd always been under the impression that Stacy's family had been well off back when her dad was alive. Both she and her older brother had gone to boarding schools and Stacy had owned several expensive horses and continued to ride equestrian after college. I suppose it could have been given to her by her mother, or that she could have come into an inheritance, but it seemed strange that she wouldn't have mentioned it. It sure as hell wasn't a year's worth of tips. But I also realized I was a long way from knowing everything there was to know about Stacy and, as far as her personal finances were concerned, it was probably none of my business.

In the end, there could be a million explanations, none of which I felt like mulling over tonight. Hell, I didn't have any way of knowing if the money was even hers. But I looked at it hard for another minute, then wadded it up and threw it in the wastebasket with the rest of the trash. Back in the bedroom, I climbed underneath the covers and tried to put out of my mind what I had seen: a deposit slip for nine thousand dollars.

CHAPTER THIRTY-TWO

I had been sitting in my car across the street from Wilczek's house for almost an hour before it finally began to get light, and I checked over my cameras in the filmy, gray light of dawn. The sky was overcast, a solid lid of cloud cover above the tree line. I had my window cracked and was leaning against the door, hands in my pockets, watching the house. Every couple of minutes I would yawn, then try to readjust myself on the seat. For a while I was distracted by the thin, barely visible plume of my own respiration, and eventually I became mesmerized by the steady rise and fall of my chest as I breathed in and out.

It must have been sometime after seven when the door to Wilczeks' place opened and he stepped out onto his front stoop without shutting the door behind him. A light fog had rolled up the street from the water and, although I could make him out, it was enough to keep me from seeing exactly what he was doing. He stood for what seemed like several minutes at the door, then made a movement with his hands, bringing them up to his chest. It was then I saw the gun. He looked up the street in both directions, the gun now hanging down loose at his side, before descending the steps toward the street.

My breathing quickened, but I couldn't move. I should have fired up the car and spun out, surveillance be damned, but I stayed frozen in place. He was halfway across the street when he made eye contact with me. What the hell was he doing? His head seemed to be shaking almost imperceptibly and the look on his face was one of utter disappointment. I wanted to reach under the seat for my .38, but then I remembered I had left it at my apartment.

Fog swirled around his legs as Wilczek closed the distance to my car. I tried turning away, but every time I looked back his eyes were locked on mine. It was maddening. I needed to move. I needed to get the hell out of here. Wilczek reached the front end of the car and went past it. Maybe he hadn't seen me. But then I heard a noise behind me. Footsteps. My heart was racing and I shut my eyes, praying that it wasn't him behind me. I heard a tapping on the window, and I knew it was the barrel of the pistol in his hand. I wasn't going to give him the satisfaction of killing me face to face, though, and stayed with my back to the window. When I heard him chamber a round I changed my mind.

"Wait!" I yelled, trying to turn.

I didn't have a chance. The window exploded in a shower of glass, blood and brains as I felt myself rocked forward by the blast.

It wasn't until I heard myself scream that I woke up. I jerked around quickly, my heart pounding against my ribs, and looked out the window to see the woman I had talked to the other day recoiling in fear. Confused, I turned back to Wilczek's house. No mist, no open door, and no killer. It was lighter out than I had remembered. I'd been sleeping. Shit. I rolled down the window.

"I'm sorry," she said. "I didn't know you were sleeping."

"What are you doing?"

Now she looked embarrassed. "I knocked on the window but you didn't move. I just wanted to make sure you were okay."

"What?" I was still having trouble putting it all together.

"Yesterday you were taking pictures of Mr. Wilczek's house, but today you were just lying there." She shrugged. "I got worried."

Ah. "No, I'm fine."

She smiled. "Would you like to come inside and get warm, have a cup of coffee?"

"Uh . . ."

"Jim's just reading the paper. Besides, Mr. Wilczek won't be out of the house until this afternoon."

"He doesn't work today?"

"I don't know about that," she said. "But he never leaves the house before noon on Saturday."

I had to think about it for a second. With all the adrenaline that had been dumped into my system from the scare I didn't need any coffee to stay awake, but my stomach was empty as a football. Finally I rolled up the window and popped the door. When I stepped out I looked back at Wilczek's. "You're sure?"

"Not in the year he's been living across the street from us."

I nodded. "Coffee would be great."

She led me up a walkway alongside the house and to a door that opened directly onto the kitchen. As promised, Jim was reading the *Times* Saturday edition at the kitchen table. The woman said, "I'm Brenda Garvey and this is Jim."

"My name's Ray Neslowe."

"And you're not a cop?" Jim said, looking over the paper.

"No."

The paper came down and both Jim and Brenda Garvey stared at me, as if they were suddenly sorry they'd invited me in.

"I'm a private detective. I'm working on a case."

They looked at each other and I guess they decided that was okay, because Brenda walked over and poured me some coffee and Jim went back to his paper. "So," Jim said. "What's he done this time?"

"*This* time?"

Brenda handed me a steaming mug and motioned toward a chair at the table. I sat down while she refilled her husband's cup and he folded the paper and laid it in front of him. "There were a couple of cop cars out front right after he moved in. That must have been, what . . ."

When he hesitated, Brenda jumped in, "Last September."

"Do you remember what it was about?" I asked.

Jim smiled. "Why have you been watching his house?"

I had a lot of choices here, but elected to go with something resembling the truth. "My client suspects Mr. Wilczek of stealing from him, through his work on the Internet. He thinks Wilczek might not even be his real name, and that he's been working with other hackers in Europe to gain control of people's access codes and rip off their bank accounts."

Brenda's eyes widened, but Jim only frowned. "We don't know what the trouble was last year, only that a sheriff's car and an unmarked police car stopped by one night. They stayed about a half-hour and then took off. No trouble since then until the other night."

"What happened the other night?"

"The police were at the cabin talking to Luka. They went over to Wilczek's before they left."

This was a new development, but I didn't have the chance to pursue it when Brenda said, "Have they found Pete Willis yet?"

"I'm afraid the reason the police were over the other night is because Pete had been killed."

Brenda put a hand on Jim's shoulder and then walked over to busy herself at the kitchen sink. Jim said, "And now his father, too. I assume he died in the fire?"

"Yes."

"Did they have any family?" Brenda asked, still not facing us.

"The police are handling that. I'm not really sure. I would like to get some more information about the police who were here last year. Are you sure it wasn't a Mercer Island police car?"

"Yep. It was a green and white county car. I remember that."

"Were the officers in the unmarked car in uniform?"

He thought for a second. "No. I'm pretty sure they were wearing suits."

So it wasn't local, then, it was Federal. Immigration, most likely. If Wilczek actually bought the house across the street it meant he'd had to fill out all kinds of paperwork and, not being a citizen yet, Immigration might have wanted to check on his resident status. I'd been thinking that the only way to find him was through his name, but if Wilczek had bought the place before he'd met Pete, then I might be able to find his real name from his real estate title.

"Listen," I said. "Thanks for the coffee, but I really need to get going. I would like to ask you one favor, though."

Jim nodded and Brenda turned to face me from the sink.

"If you happen to see Mr. Wilczek leave before noon, could you give me a call?"

I fished out a business card from my wallet and handed it to Jim. He looked at his wife, and then smiled at me and said, "Sure."

It was just after eight as I headed back to First Hill and, though not nearly as brutal as the morning before, the going was anything but brisk. Gradually I made my way across the bridge with only a couple of slowdowns. Everyone had their lights on and I expected the dark clouds to cut loose and rain on us any second. When I finally made it off of I-90 and was driving up Boren a few drops hit my windshield, but they stopped by the time I had reached Wilczek's office. I left the car running in the parking lot and ran into the building to see if GWD was even open today.

There were no hours listed in the lobby, so I made my way upstairs and back to the corner. I twisted the knob and it turned in my hand, but I didn't open the door. Back in the car I pulled out my cell phone and punched in Kurt's number. He said he was ready with the program and could meet me at the I-HOP at nine. Stacy, on the other hand, was clearly disappointed.

"But what if he shows up while you're inside? Shouldn't I at least be watching his house?"

"I just came from there," I said. "The neighbors promised to call me if he leaves before noon." Long silence. "Look, I know you wanted to help, and that's great. I really appreciate it. But you have to see that this is a much easier situation for us. As far as I'm concerned the less you're involved in this the better."

"Are you going to be gone all day again?"

"I'm not sure. After we finish with this I need to get together with Irina Vekich. And I may have to talk with some other people. I'll call you."

"Okay . . . Ray?"

"Yeah."

"Please be careful."

I assured her I would, then we said goodbye and I drove up to the International House of Pancakes to meet Kurt. By the time he arrived I had long since finished my breakfast and was beginning to get dirty looks from my waitress. Then I paid my check, over-tipped her, and we headed out to my car. Since I didn't want Kurt involved any more than necessary we left his VW Microbus on the curb and would come back for it when we were finished. He retrieved a heavy, black notebook from the bus and then folded his gangly frame into my passenger seat.

"Do you have the disc?"

Kurt smiled and grabbed a chain around his neck, pulling something out from his shirt and holding it between his fingers.

"What the hell is that?"

He looked hurt. "It's a memory chip."

"I thought we were going to use a floppy disc? Jesus, we don't have time to crack open a hard drive and stick in a chip—"

When Kurt laughed I realized I had been missing something. "What?"

"I have a thumb drive." He dug something out of his jacket that was about the size of a disposable lighter, and proceeded to place the chip inside of it. "I don't use floppies anymore. No moving parts," he said, holding out the thumb drive. "It holds a lot more data and it's a *lot* more reliable."

"Okay."

"And I thought, if I get in there and there's something interesting I have plenty of room to copy it to the thumb drive—"

"No way. Absolutely not."

Now he frowned.

"I'm sorry. But all I want to do is put the program on the computer and that's it. If we start taking too much time in there, we could get caught."

After a second he said, "Okay, so what's the plan?"

"Well, we don't have business cards or anything so I think we need to approach this as though we're making a very informal visit. We say we want to talk with Wilczek, and when he's not there we say it doesn't really matter, we're just gathering general information from various companies before deciding which ones to talk specifics with. You have your business plan and stuff?"

He held up the folder.

"All right. I don't know how many people are in the office, but I do know that Wilczek's not there. My phone is on vibrate and if I get a call it will be because he's just leaving his house on Mercer Island. So that should give us tons of time to get out."

"What do you want me to do?"

"I wish I knew. We're going to have to improvise. Basically, you're the technical guy. Let them know—in very general terms— what kind of security we're looking for. If they won't talk about that or don't know, fall back to the Internet design stuff. What we're looking for is a window of opportunity when we can be alone with the computer. And we should be prepared for a situation where we don't get the opportunity. I think you just need to keep them talking. Keep asking to see stuff. Keep the meeting going until we see a chance. I'll be monitoring the time and I'll try to get us out of there before we become too obvious. How long does that take to install?"

Kurt put his hands out, thought, then said, "Thirty seconds."

It barely took longer than that to drive back to Wilczek's building. The two of us casually walked inside and then I took the lead up the stairs to the end of the hall and stopped when I took hold of the knob.

"Let's not make a big entrance," I whispered. "I'll talk to the receptionist."

But when I opened the door there was no receptionist. On the left was a small waiting area with a TV set and a table full of magazines. On the right were four office cubicles separated by five-foot partitions. Straight ahead, at the back of the room, was an actual office door with large glass panels on each side. Through the glass I could see the front end of a desk to the right of the door and bookcases to the left.

We stood there for a few moments but no one came out to

greet us, so I began walking toward the office, looking into the cubicles as I went: typical workspaces with darkened computers and piles of papers, files, and correspondence. I had just reached the third cubicle when I heard a voice say, "Hello?" Before I could answer a young man came around the corner of the fourth cubicle and nearly ran into me.

"Ah," he yelled, and took a step back, clearly startled. "You scare hell out of me. What are you doing here? We closed."

I looked back at Kurt and he nodded. This kid was Romanian, too. "Pete told me to meet him here at . . ." I made a show of looking at my watch. "Nine-fifteen. Isn't he here?"

Now he looked confused. He was wearing a blue-striped oxford shirt, open at the collar and rolled up at the sleeves, khakis, and tassled loafers. "Pete does not work on Saturday. Are you sure you have right day?" The kid was young, maybe twenty-five, and was acting strangely, moving ever so slightly from foot to foot.

I took one of my own business cards out of my wallet and looked at the blank back. "Nine-fifteen a.m., on the 8th. That's today isn't it?"

But he wasn't paying attention to me. He was looking over my shoulder toward the door. Was someone coming in? Had I interrupted something?

"Look," I said. "I'm supposed to meet here with Pete and discuss a possible business deal. I'm sure your boss doesn't want you—"

"Excuse me," he interrupted, and walked quickly over toward the waiting area. "If you just wait here for minute . . ." he glanced back at the office quickly and then to us. We followed him over and stood next to the chairs. "Please, wait," he said, then put his hands out motioning us to stay put.

I nodded.

"Good. I be right back." And with that he disappeared out the door.

Still in shock I looked over at Kurt, and he grinned at me. He had his thumb drive out and nodded toward the kid's computer. "Would now be a good time?"

CHAPTER THIRTY-THREE

"Get busy," I said. "I'll stay by the door and let you know when he's coming back. Kurt took off and I eased open the door just in time to see the back of the kid's head disappear down the stairs. Going to the restroom, I figured.

"I think he's going to the can," I shouted and looked over to the cubicle, but Kurt was already leaving it and heading for the office door. "What are you doing?"

"I'm going to see if I can get into Wilczek's computer."

"Kurt, we don't have time for that." But he ignored me and went inside anyway. I checked the hall again, but there was no sign of the kid. When Kurt emerged from the office and headed back to the cubicle I said, "What are you doing now?"

He appeared a second later with the thumb drive in hand and went back into Wilczek's office. I just about had a heart attack when I looked out the door again and saw that the kid had not only left the restroom but was halfway up the stairs, and hustling to get back. I eased the door closed and yelled, "Kurt! He's almost here. Get the hell out of there. Now."

"Just a second," I heard.

Shit. We didn't have a second, so I took a chance and opened the door myself. It nearly hit the kid and he startled again. "Hey," I said, casually, closing the door behind me and ignoring the pained expression on his face. "You have a restroom around here?"

He pointed down the stairs and tried to get past me, but I stepped in front of him. "I'm sorry, is it downstairs?"

"Yes," he said, "downstairs," and made another attempt. This time I had to grab him by the arm to stop him and I thought he might take a swing at me after he had recoiled from my touch. I feigned ignorance again and said, "Where exactly? Near the elevator?"

"Yes. Just past elevator."

"Hey, thanks. I'll be right back." And then I hustled down the stairs myself, hoping like hell that Kurt was out of Wilczek's office. I didn't think the kid could hurt him, but that didn't mean he didn't have a gun stashed in his desk for just this sort of occasion. I was more than a little nervous as I waited downstairs for the minimum necessary time and then raced back up to the office.

As it turned out, I needn't have worried. When I entered the office I would have thought it was empty, except for the voices coming from the cubicle. I headed over there and as I round the corner I could see the two of them talking animatedly at the kid's desk. He looked up at me briefly—just long enough to scowl—and then went back to Kurt, who had pulled up a chair behind the desk and was pointing out something on the computer screen. Oh, well. I was just the financing. What the hell did I know?

I looked around for a chair and pulled one over to the entrance to the cubicle. We sat there for a good half an hour. I checked my phone at least a dozen times to make sure it was turned on and prayed that Brenda Garvey would spot Wilczek if he left the house. The two of them talked about interfaces, gigabytes, and microprocessors for a while, and while I knew enough about computers to follow along I certainly couldn't have joined the discussion in any intelligent way. But when Kurt began talking about his project I perked up and paid attention.

His idea was a retail platform for small businesses that combined the best features of Amazon and eBay. It would allow businesses that either did not have the time or the funds to devote to their own web sites a place to do business on the Internet. Similar in theory to the way larger firms like Toys R Us and CD Now used Amazon, it would be tailored to regional brick-and-mortar businesses who were interested in expanding into mail-order. But it would also allow consumers to comparison shop, similar to their experience on eBay, promoting competition among online vendors.

The kid, whose name I never did learn, seemed excited about the possibilities of designing the site. I could tell, however, even as a phony investor, that it would take a ton of money and the commitment of dozens of retailers to even get started. It also seemed a little clearer now why Kurt hadn't been eager to devote all of his energies to this thing, especially with the amount of capital it would take to launch. I waited patiently until the subject of the payment platform came up.

"What kind of help can your firm give us with security?" I said.

The kid shook his head. "We are not security firm."

"Well, that's not what I heard."

Now the kid looked worried. "What do you hear?"

I shrugged. "I talked to some of the companies you do business with and it came up in conversation. Look, we know a lot of computer crime is coming out of Europe and we want to be protected. We don't want our consumers' bank accounts cleaned out by hackers and leaving us responsible. We want to be proactive in stopping this stuff before we even begin to assemble vendors for the site."

The kid looked over at Kurt, who shrugged and said, "He's the money."

For a fraction of a second I thought he was going to repeat that they didn't deal in security, when he suddenly said, "You have to talk to Mr. Wilczek for that. I don't know. You should come back Monday."

"Sure," I said, standing. "I guess I must have had my days mixed up after all."

As enthused as the kid had been about Kurt's project, he was clearly glad to see us go. I'm pretty sure I even heard him lock the door after us. Out in the car I asked Kurt how it went.

He smiled. "I was able to get it on both computers."

"Yeah, and you just about gave me a heart attack in the process."

"Sorry. I wasn't sure how much information we would get from Anton's computer."

"That's his name?"

"Yes. I wouldn't have even bothered with his computer except it was already on. I didn't think we would get another chance like that to access Wilczek's computer."

"Yeah, you're probably right. Still . . ."

Kurt smiled again.

"All right. How long till we learn something?"

He thought for a moment. "If they're doing what we think, they'll definitely have someone like Anton there tomorrow to work through the key-stroke files and put together possible account takeovers—that's probably what he's doing today. But I don't think we'll be able to get anything you're looking for until Wilczek comes back on Monday. So, Monday night, maybe Tuesday."

"Okay."

I wasn't going to be greedy. At least I wouldn't have to sit on Wilczek's house anymore. I dropped Kurt off at his van and told him I'd give him a call Monday night to see if he'd learned anything. As I watched his van pull away I dialed up Irina Vekich on the cell phone and got her answering machine. I told her to give me a call and let me know when we could meet, then drove out to the freeway to see Detective Jack Ransom.

Ransom was fifty-one years old, had a wife named Marian, and a 6-year old son named Joe. The reason I know all of this is because I get a Christmas card from Marian every year. It was a little embarrassing that I had yet to return the courtesy. The Ransoms had a house on the bluff overlooking Shilshole Bay, and if you looked up Seaview Avenue from their front deck you could just catch a glimpse of Sharkey's. I pulled into the driveway and was not surprised to see Jack up on a ladder cleaning the gutters in preparation for the fall rains.

As I stepped out of my car Jack nodded to me, then he went back to the gutter he'd been working on. Jack was about as tall as I was, just over six feet, but was thicker around the chest and limbs. His hair was cut short and showed plenty of gray. It took him another five minutes before he climbed down to greet me.

"Ray," he said, offering his hand. "What brings you out this way?"

As I took his hand, the other grabbed my shoulder and steered me toward the front door. "Not much, Jack. Just thought I'd ask you about a case you may have seen at work."

His face clouded over. Cop mask. This was more promising than I had expected. It meant he probably knew something about it. "Hey, Marian," he yelled once we were inside. "Ray Neslowe's here."

It wasn't Marian who appeared first, but Joe. He had run all the way down the hall to see who was there, stopped when I said hello, then retreated as fast as he had come. Jack just laughed and we continued on through their gorgeous home. Marian was an obstetrician at Harborview Medical Center. She'd bought the place cheap back in the late seventies and hadn't done much to it because she'd been so busy at the hospital. But after marrying Jack six years ago he'd transformed it into a showplace, beginning with the exterior and then remodeling the interior, room by room.

We traveled to the kitchen across polished wood floors, and although the furnishings weren't necessarily expensive, it was obvious they had been chosen with great care. The interior glowed from the soft lighting, and the roaring fireplace contrasted sharply with the gray, overcast view from the picture window that looked out onto the choppy water of Puget Sound and the temporarily obscured the peaks of the Olympic Mountains beyond.

Marian Ransom had short blond hair that framed her round face, and she always seemed to be wearing a smile. She was wiping her hands off on a towel when we reached the kitchen and came over to me with arms extended. After hugging and giving me a kiss on the cheek she asked me if I'd had lunch yet. "I was just fixing something for the boys. It's no trouble."

Though I couldn't see it, I could smell some kind of seafood soup simmering on the stove, and spied the ham sandwiches she was fixing on the cutting board. She didn't exactly have to twist my arm. "Sure."

Her smile was radiant. "Jack, could you go and get Joseph. And make sure he washes his hands."

"Will do."

When Jack had gone she went back to building sandwiches. "It's so good to see you, but I'm sure you didn't come over just for a visit."

"I wish I could say I did, but it's about a case at the precinct that I thought Jack might be able to help me with."

She looked up quickly from the cutting board. "Then you haven't heard?"

"Heard what?"

"Jack retired last year." She shrugged, almost embarrassed that I didn't know.

I gave a short laugh. "Serves me right for not coming around more often."

"I wanted to get in touch with you when it happened, but everything was so busy with Joe and work. And then when it got to be later in the year I figured you'd probably already heard, and I knew I'd be sending you a card for Christmas . . ." Marian brought the sandwiches to the table and then went to the cupboard, pulled down bowls, and began ladling up what looked like seafood bisque.

Well, one good thing about Jack's retiring was that they probably hadn't heard about my arrest. When the last bowl had reached the table Marian walked over to me and put a hand on my arm, her expression one of serious concern. "Is this about you're being arrested for murder?"

CHAPTER THIRTY-FOUR

After I had regained my composure I said, "I guess Jack isn't as out of the loop as I would have assumed."

As if on cue, Jack and Joe came into the kitchen. "Out of the loop about what?" Jack asked.

"For a retired guy," I said, "you seem to know a lot about ongoing murder investigations."

Jack nodded as he pulled out a chair and sat down. "Yeah, when I saw you pull up I figured that's what it was about."

The rest of us joined Jack at the table, with Joe avoiding any eye contact with me at all. "Maybe we should save this discussion for later," I offered.

Jack shook his head. "Not much to tell."

Marian gave me a grin and she and Joe began eating.

"Jim Razor gave me a call when he heard about it."

I nodded. I knew Jim Razor as a homicide detective out of Jack's squad at the north precinct who had worked with Jack and me on a missing person case. It must have been ten years ago now that Dewey's younger sister had disappeared from her University District apartment, and although Dewey had already gone to the police, I agreed to help if I could. Jack and I had hit it off right from the start and he had let me help in the investigation. Unfortunately we weren't able to locate Sondra Beckley in time to save her. She and her boyfriend had overdosed on heroine and, while the boyfriend had lived, he was now doing time in Walla Walla for involuntary manslaughter. Dewey had always credited me for the boyfriend's conviction, even though we both knew I couldn't have done it without the police. And Jack and I both knew we couldn't have done it without Jim Razor.

"Jim didn't give me any details, but he did say that Adamson was prosecuting. I hope you have a good attorney."

"Irina Veckich."

Jack had picked up his sandwich in preparation to take a bite, but stopped short. "And Adamson's still going ahead with it?"

"Apparently."

Jack set his sandwich back down. "What's going on, Ray?"

Eventually both Jack and I did finish our meals, and in the process I was able to relay the details of my current difficulties with the police. Joe finished his lunch first, asked to be excused, was told by Marian that he had to at least acknowledge me. He did as he was ordered, and then vanished to parts unknown. With the three of us still sitting around the table, Marian made the first comment on the case, "Doesn't your involvement with Stacy complicate things?" while Jack tried unsuccessfully not to smirk at me.

"It's not the ideal situation, but if there's even the slightest possibility that Wilczek is watching her I think it's good for him to know that she's not alone."

Jack stood and began clearing the table. "*If* she's being tailed."

"I know. But I really think we might have something on this computer tap."

"*Illegal* computer tap," Jack said from the sink.

"Hey, I thought you were retired."

"I just want you to make sure you know what you're getting into. I don't know anything about the Romanian mob, but if the Russian mob is any indication of what you can expect, I'd be watching my back if I were you."

"I'll be careful. Do you think Razor will tell me anything?"

"You'd have to ask him. But I can give him a call before you go over there."

"Monday?"

"Yeah. He'll be off this weekend."

216

We talked more while Jack did the dishes. I asked if there was anything else he thought I should be doing, but neither he nor Marian could think of another course to pursue unless Kurt came up with something from the computer tap. Marian and I hugged again before I left, I complimented the food, and I made an earnest promise about doing more to keep in touch. As Jack and I were walking out he said, "You know, Stan Dalton's the best investigator in King County, probably in the whole state."

"Well, I don't think Stan's in a position to help me, even if he wanted to."

"I know. That's not what I mean. But if you get anything on this computer scam, anything at all, you need to take it to him right away. Don't sit around trying to figure out how it helps you with your case."

"All right."

He grabbed my upper arm and stopped me at the front door. "I mean it, Ray. If Wilczek is involved in the murder then Dalton's the guy to find it out. You don't want to give Wilczek the opportunity to cover his tracks if he discovers you're on to him. I know there's some bad blood between you two, but Dalton isn't going to stop investigating this thing just because Adamson's living in his shorts. Give him whatever you get and let him clear you."

This time I took his admonition more seriously. "Okay, Jack. If you really think that's the way to play it, I'll go to Dalton with whatever I get."

"Good."

Jack nodded and then opened the door and walked me outside. "If you get into any real trouble, Ray, don't call me here. Give Razor a call and he'll find me."

I almost smiled. "What? You mean, come out of retirement?"

"You know damn well what I mean. If you get your ass in a sling, I want to know."

"But you don't want Marian to know."

He held out his hands in a shrug. "Just keep me posted."

*   *   *

217

On the way back toward downtown I put in another call to Irina and finally reached her. She gave me directions to her house and I wound up having to turn around and head back north, this time up to Lake City. Her house was just off of Sand Point Way on the northwest side of Lake Washington. I turned in at a bank of mailboxes and wound my way down to her place, a ranch-style home on the water. At the sound of the doorbell a barrage of barking erupted from the other side of the door. It took a few minutes for someone to wrangle the dogs away and the barking became more distant. Finally the door opened and Irina invited me in. She had her hair pulled back today and looked casual in blowsy pants and a heavy wool sweater as she led me through the house.

I didn't ask, but it became clear that she lived alone with her dogs. She brought me to a den that contained a large white table she was using for a desk. White walls and a light colored carpet kept the east-facing room nice and bright, even in the current gloomy weather conditions. She showed me to a couch that looked out large bay windows and a sliding door onto a small strip of grass abutting an L-shaped dock that extended out into the water. From somewhere in the house, the garage maybe, the dogs were still barking.

I accepted her offer of coffee and after bringing back a mug for each of us Irina took a legal pad and pen from her desk and sat across the coffee table from me in a floral-patterned wing chair. "So," she said. "Any new developments?"

I gave her the basic outline of my stakeout on Friday and then the computer tap while she took notes. When I had finished she said, "I have a little something for you, too."

"What's that?"

She had me come over to her desk and took the tops off of two file boxes. "These are the files from Adamson. The police evidence from your place takes up an entire box."

"You're kidding."

"If I had to guess I'd say they found something and want to hide it by burying it among a hundred other items from the scene."

"Have you looked through them?"

She shook her head. "It'd take a week. You're going to have to come to the office and spend a few days going through them to weed out the crap."

Dejected at the thought of having to wade through a mountain of evidence files, I walked back to the couch and sat down heavily.

"Now, don't get like that. I still need to go over everything with you from the top. I've looked through Adamson's paperwork, and between Carl's notes and what you've given me, I think I have a pretty good idea of where we're heading with the defense. Okay?"

"Sure," I said, but inwardly I felt the pressure ratcheting up again. Having to deal with Irina, despite her confidence, brought the trial that much closer to reality.

"All right. Pete Willis was shot to death last Monday night. The body is found by his girlfriend in her apartment and the murder weapon in a Dumpster down the street. Later that night it's discovered that Willis was actually killed in your apartment—we need to find out how the police figured that out."

"Other than my being arrested at Stacy's?"

She grinned. "It was still too fast. The timeline doesn't make sense."

"I think I have a line on that," I said. "A detective in the north precinct. I'm going to talk to him on Monday."

"Okay. So, not only is the victim killed in your apartment, but ballistics shows that the gun was owned by you and that Willis's girlfriend is now seeing you."

"Geez, when you say it like that . . ."

She shook me off as if she couldn't be less concerned with appearances. "Perfectly reasonable deduction, given the circumstantial evidence, which results in your initial arrest."

"Initial?"

She ignored me. "Now let's look at what we know for sure about Willis's death before we get into the speculation. First, there were no prints on the gun and both Willis and Lambert knew about the weapon in your apartment. The second thing is the identification of the body. There was no ID on the victim when he was found, and with the damage to his face there was no way for a visual ID. Forensic identification had to be used and turned up that the victim's real name was actually Pete Wilczek. Are we good so far?"

I nodded.

"All right. Why?"

"What do you mean?"

"I mean, usually when someone's face is blown off it's because the murderer doesn't want the victim to be identified, and given that scenario it makes sense that the killer takes the victim's ID. But why take Willis's ID? The killer had to know that the M.E.'s office was going to figure out who the victim was. What's the point?"

I sipped my coffee and thought about that for a minute. "I would say that whoever killed Pete *wanted* the police to figure out the name change right away."

"That's my thought, too. Which means I think we're on the right track by focusing on the name change. Unfortunately, that would tend to eliminate our computer wiz as a suspect?"

"Why?"

"Because, if he really did obtain Willis's identity for himself, the last thing Wilczek would want would be to have that discovered right away. He would have shot Willis in the chest so that both the girlfriend and the father could identify him as Willis. And he would have left the Pennsylvania license on the body in order to confirm the Willis ID and keep himself from suspicion as long as possible."

I leaned back into the couch and sighed. "Jesus. This guy's all I have."

"Don't worry. I just want you to be aware of the problems. Like I said, I still think this is the best line of investigation. We have a record from King County of his legal name change, and I was able to make a couple of calls back East on Friday and determined that Pete Willis had a valid Pennsylvania driver's license. So, it appears that after he changed his name he renewed his license back East, just like Lambert said. In Washington State, however, there is no record of him at all. He has no Social Security number that we can find, no bank accounts, no tax records, nothing. We know he changed his name, what we don't know is why."

"He did it for the money."

"Allegedly. Almost all of our evidence on Wilczek is hearsay from Lambert.

"She wouldn't lie—"

She stopped me with a raised hand. "Ray, that's not what I'm saying. But what we need to do is prove some of it. Get Carl to check into this real estate angle and find out who owns the title to the house on Mercer Island. Remember, though, that even if we find out Wilczek is an alias, it doesn't prove any of the rest of this. Keep on it, but we're still a ways away from connecting him to the murder. Until we do that, all we have to work with is speculation—but that's good for us. For one thing, the prosecution doesn't have a good motive. The girlfriend angle is, frankly, pretty weak. There's no evidence that you ever had any dealings with Willis, and you also have an alibi for that night. By the way, do you have that receipt?"

"Oh, I forgot. But I'm sure it's still in my car. I haven't cleaned it out."

"Why don't you get it for me right now. I'll warm up the coffee while you're gone."

I walked back outside and was met by a light but insistent drizzle, mirroring the wet blanket Irina was throwing on my investigation. It took only a minute to find the wadded paper sack from the drug store and liberate the receipt. Back inside, she examined it for a moment and then slipped it into an open accordion file on her desk

"Okay," she said, when we had returned to our seats. "Here's the theory we're working with at the moment. Willis apparently sold his identity to Wilczek for an unknown amount of money. The money hasn't been discovered, so we can't really prove that transaction took place."

I thought again about the deposit slip in Stacy's wastebasket and I knew I was going to have to confront her about it. Not that

I was necessarily worried. I may not have known Pete, but I sure as hell knew he wouldn't have sold his identity for a measly nine thousand bucks.

"Once Wilczek has his new identity," Irina continued, "he arranges for Willis to renew his license and possibly provide him with fake Washington ID. Though again, none was ever found."

"Yeah, because he covered it up with the fire."

"Okay, I'm getting to that, but first things first. Based on Lambert's recollection we believe that at some point Willis regretted his decision to sell his identity. Since he knew about the gun in your apartment he was able to get Wilczek over there on some pretense, with the object of coercing him into giving his identity back. Now, assuming Wilczek is involved in illegal activity, and may even be a known criminal under his real name, we believe he will do anything to keep from being discovered and that he would naturally refuse. We further assume that there was a struggle and that Willis was finally the one killed."

"Except that the shots were in the back of the head."

"Doesn't matter. The shots didn't have to be the result of the struggle. Willis could have been knocked unconscious before being shot. In fact, the shots to the head might be a good way to eliminate any forensic evidence of that."

"Which still leads us to the problem of why he took Pete's identity."

"Sure, but since were already out at the end of the gangplank of speculation, why not go further. Let's say Willis didn't have his ID on him at the time. What would you, as the killer, do at that point?"

I sat up and put my coffee mug on the table. "I guess I would try to find it at his father's place."

"And if you couldn't?"

A smile slowly formed on my face. "Torch the place so that no one else could either."

She nodded, the expression on her face saying that it was unconvincing but it was what we had. "Where we can get into trouble with all this, is that if the prosecution comes up with anything that disproves even part of our scenario it unravels the whole thing. And we're still left with the fact that all of these things could be random, unrelated acts. We have the father telling you about a lawsuit for which we can't find any evidence. For all we know, Wilczek could have recovered the money and Willis's ID and torched the place anyway. Or it might have been someone completely different who murdered Willis."

Irina pushed a loose strand of hair back behind her ear. "Even if Wilczek is using Willis's ID, we don't have any way of proving it. Even if we eventually find Willis's original birth certificate and social security number, Wilczek may not be using them, especially if he's Romanian." She set the pad and pen on the coffee table and picked up her mug. "The upside is that the prosecution can't prove he isn't, but that's not something I would want to bet my life on."

We sat for a moment in silence, each with our own thoughts. After a while I said, "So, where does that leave us?"

"First, find out who owns Wilczek's house and hopefully get a line on his real identity. Second, find out if there's really any illegal activity going on at Wilczek's business and get some proof of it." I nodded while she took another sip of coffee. "And you might want to consider putting a tail on Stacy Lambert."

That last one came out of the blue. "What?"

"Well, you said she's afraid someone is following her. Since she's the only direct link back to Willis, if someone is following her who isn't related to Wilczek, it might be the only way to open up a new line of investigation."

CHAPTER THIRTY-FIVE

"You want me to do *what*?"

"Irina says it might be the only way to figure out who's been following you."

The amusement registering on her face made me think for a moment that she was going to laugh. "And what exactly am I supposed to be doing around town while you're watching me? Shopping for shoes?"

"I'm serious. This might be the only way to be sure it's Wilczek. If we're completely wrong about him then finding out who's actually following you might be the only way to find the real killer."

Stacy left the couch and went into the kitchen. I didn't follow. She rummaged around for a minute and then reappeared next to the table. "I don't think I can do this anymore, Ray."

Damn it. "Why not?"

She pulled out a chair and sat at the table. "I know I said I wanted to help, but being a human decoy wasn't really what I had in mind. I'd be worried the whole time that something bad was going to happen, and I feel like that's where this is headed."

Great. "Stacy, I wouldn't even ask you if I didn't think it was important. I'm trying to clear myself of a murder charge."

Her face contorted into something like pain. "Don't you think I know that? There's not a minute goes by when I don't think about it."

I shifted on the couch, not knowing what to say. "Stacy—"

"Ray, I know what you're going through, and I know it seems selfish of me, but I can't help the way I feel. It's getting to the point where I don't even want to walk in front of a window anymore."

"These aren't assassins, Stacey. We still don't know what we're dealing with."

"That's what makes it so hard for me to take."

"And if we find out who's following you, then we'll know."

I made a move to stand up and go to her. "No, please. Stay there. There's something I have to say and I don't know if you're going to like it."

I didn't know how to respond to that and so I waited for her to continue.

"Pete and I had been growing apart ever since we got back together. I don't think I ever got over his cheating on me. I guess I felt like I owed it to him to give him another chance to show me that it was really a mistake, but things were never the way they had been before. And then when you showed up . . ." She just shook her head. "When you came back I realized I'd made the wrong decision before."

"I understand. But even if it was, it doesn't matter now, does it?"

"I don't know. Does it?"

When I didn't answer, she said, "You know, I never expected to . . . to feel this way about you—not the way I have. But I also know that you have you own way of looking at what we're doing together. I just feel I'm at a time in my life where I need certain things, and to get them I don't think I can stay here anymore."

"Stay where?"

"In Seattle."

That was something I hadn't anticipated. What a mess. She was right that I had my own thoughts about our relationship, and getting married and settling down wasn't one of them, but I also couldn't help feeling that I didn't want to lose her. "You really think you want to leave?"

She sighed and said, "I think so. I just feel like everything about this place is starting to close in on me. Everywhere I go I see things that remind me of something that didn't work out for me. Every time I see a police car I kick my self for not taking that test. Every time I go out to a restaurant I think of Sharkey's and how much I hate being a waitress. I think I'd be gone already if it wasn't for you."

"Look, Stacy, I know this has been hard. We've both been thrown into this thing by whoever killed Pete. I feel just as helpless as you do, which is why I'm working so hard. We can't run away from it now. At least I can't."

She nodded and came over next to me on the couch. "I'm sorry, Ray. It didn't come out the way I meant it. I know how hard you're working, and I love you for that. But I need for it to be over. I can't keep sitting in this apartment not doing anything. And I especially can't go traipsing all over town as bait."

I wanted to be reassuring but, quite frankly, I thought I might go a little stir crazy myself if I didn't have something proactive to do this weekend, and I had been counting on using that time to find out who was tailing Stacy.

"Did you enjoy last night?" she asked.

"Huh?"

"Being together last night. Did you enjoy that?"

"Sure."

"So did I. Let's take off, Ray," she said, as we sat together on the couch. "Right now. Let's just get in the car and go."

"What are you talking about?"

"Let's get out of here. Let's be together like we were last night, without murders and police and investigations."

I'll give Stacy one thing: she's persuasive. We talked for a while longer and I finally asked, "Where to?"

"Anywhere. Down to Portland, out to the coast, across the mountains, I don't care. Let's just take a break from this nightmare and try to forget about it for a while. We need some time . . . I need some time to be normal again, even if it's just for a day."

The bottom line was, if she wasn't going to let me tail her then there really wasn't much for me to do on Sunday. I wouldn't be able to talk with Jim Razor until Monday morning. Kurt wouldn't have anything until late Monday or possibly Tuesday. Still . . . "I understand what you're saying. But I think we should give Irina's idea some more consideration. It could be important."

"Maybe. But what if you don't see anyone while you're following me? We'll have wasted the day, and for what? And what if they wind up following *you* all day instead of the other way around? You'd be so focused on watching me that you might miss them. But if we're out on the freeway I'll be able to watch behind us. They'll have to stay close enough to keep us in sight, and we can stop along the way so that we'll be able to see if the same car is behind us when we start driving again."

I looked at her for what seemed the longest time.

"Let's pack a bag and leave right now," she said again. "We'll get dinner on the road, stay in a hotel somewhere away from everything."

Finally I nodded. "Okay."

*   *   *

Shortly after five that night we were heading south on I-5 toward Olympia. We had packed a bag, thrown it in the back seat of her Stanza, and decided to head for the coast. We stopped in Olympia the first night, had a terrific meal at the Bud Bay Cafe on the waterfront, then stayed the night at the Evergreen Inn on the bluffs overlooking the state capital building. The one flaw in her plan, we quickly realized, was that we weren't going to spot anyone behind us in the dark, but by then I was into the spirit of the thing and really didn't care anymore. She'd been right. It *was* good to get away from it all.

The next morning we grabbed some Starbucks on the way out of town and had a late breakfast at Duffy's in Aberdeen. The drive through Aberdeen and Hoquiam only took a few minutes, and a half-hour later we were walking along the beach at Ocean Shores. There were only a few other hardy souls like us who were willing to brave the icy wind coming off the pounding waves of the Pacific, but it was certainly invigorating.

After an hour on the beach we shook off as much sand as we could and decided to backtrack to Hoquiam in order to continue north up the coast. We were fortunate to have only run into a couple of patches of rain along the way. The solid mass of cloud cover overhead was a light gray, almost white, its uniformity only occasionally broken up by darker individual rain clouds beneath it. While we drove Stacy kept an eye out for familiar cars behind us, but saw nothing. Every once in a while we pulled into a turnout and sat for a few minutes just to make sure.

About halfway up the Olympic Peninsula, after detouring around the Quinault Indian reservation, we hit the last twenty-mile stretch of road along the water that isn't Indian land before Highway 101 veers off toward the Olympic National Park. It was almost three by the time we reached Forks, and we stopped for burgers and then kept driving. The Peninsula foliage was still a thick and healthy green. The relatively small percentage of deciduous trees mixed among the evergreens had only just started to turn yellow and gold. Along the north end of the peninsula we wound around the edge of Lake Crescent just as it was getting dark. I thought we should stop at Port Angeles, but Stacy wanted to push on and stay in Port Townsend.

After a day's worth of active cornering along the winding road of the Olympic Peninsula, 101 from Port Angeles to Discovery Bay seemed almost straight by comparison. Eventually we had to turn off of 101 and head north a few miles to get to Port Townsend. When we reached the town it was almost seven-thirty, but there were actually patches of stars visible in the sky. Stacy wrinkled her nose when I suggesting staying at The Tides on the edge of town and had me drive up on the bluff to the residential section of town to find a nice bed and breakfast. Unfortunately, all of them seemed to be full up for the weekend, but we eventually managed to find a place called the Inn Dearing, which had a small apartment available over the garage that someone had backed out of that morning. It was perfect.

Once we had settled in we walked down the hill to find a place to eat. Just past the movie theater there was a small Italian restaurant with checkered tablecloths and candles in Chianti bottles. Instead of a tenor singing Italian songs, however, they had a couple in the back corner of the room singing Celtic ballads. They were both dressed in black. He sat on a stool and played acoustic guitar with a serviceable but confident finger picking style. She stood next to him and sang in a high, clear, mezzo-soprano. They didn't have any amplification but the acoustics of the room were such that they didn't need it. I thought they were quite good.

Despite all the driving, it had been relaxing to spend the day circling the Peninsula, but I still hadn't asked Stacy about the money. She'd paid for our room in cash, and if there was ever going to be a good time to bring it up, I felt it had to be now. After dinner we ordered decaf coffee and cannoli.

As the waiter was leaving I said, "There's something I've been meaning to ask you."

"What's that?" She leaned back into the booth and looked at me with her clear, green eyes. For a moment I thought about not even asking her, but instead I went forward.

"I want you to know that I didn't go looking for this. It was a complete accident."

Now her eyes concentrated on me, as if she was working out a difficult math problem. "Go ahead."

I shook my head, not really sure how to proceed. "The other night, in the bathroom some stuff accidentally fell out of the wastebasket and when I was putting everything back I came across a deposit slip for nine-thousand dollars. Now, I know your finances are none of my business, but it seemed like a lot of money for you not to have even mentioned it and . . ."

She sat up, already nodding, and expressed my suspicions so exactly that it almost startled me. "With the money Pete had, you thought he might have given some to me?"

"Not really. Honestly, I didn't know what to think. It just seemed strange and I wanted to ask you about it."

She smiled as the waiter set our desert and coffee in front of us. We each had taken a bite of cannoli before she explained, "The money came from my mother."

Now it was my turn to look perplexed. The last I knew, her mother was living on Social Security.

"My mother's another reason I'd like to get away from Seattle. You know she always wanted to be rich, and when she met my father he seemed like the perfect answer. He was in the Foreign Service, had traveled all over the world, and seemed to have everything she needed. When we lived in Moscow we had servants and maids, and she thought she was the queen of something. But it wasn't real, you know? I mean, they weren't our servants, and the embassy wasn't our house. When he died so suddenly she was horrified to find out he had almost nothing. There was a couple hundred thousand dollars in life insurance but that wasn't going to last her. So, she became this bitter recluse who wound up putting all of her hopes on Michael and me. And you know how that turned out."

"Pretty much."

"But one thing she kept from me is the fact that Father had taken out two other life insurance policies, ten-thousand dollars each, with Michael and me as the beneficiaries. We were supposed to get the equity when we turned twenty-one, but since he died we wound up getting the whole ten-thousand. Except she never told me about it. It's been in the bank for the last fifteen years."

"Did she ever tell Michael?"

"He knew the whole time, but she swore him to secrecy. He got his when he went to graduate school. Evidently Mom had decided that she wouldn't give us the money until we finished college and decided what we were going to do with our lives. I supposed she thought if we didn't do something worthy enough, she might not give it to us at all."

"And you only found out about this recently?"

She nodded. "Last week, if you can believe that. Right after I told her I was chucking waitressing and taking the police exam again she gave it to me. Just like that."

"Huh. I know it probably wasn't the best way for your mom to handle it, but I think it's terrific that you have it now."

She smiled. "I used a thousand to pay off my credit cards, kept the interest in cash, and put the rest in the bank."

"I guess that also explains why you've been thinking about moving."

"It's a fresh start, Ray. It means getting away from my mom and Michael, and from the memories of Pete. I've never had a chance like this before. It's important for me."

I took a deep breath and let it out. "I know. It's just a lot for me to think about right now."

She reached over and took my hand again. I could see the pain in her eyes. "I'm sorry about this, Ray. The last thing I want to do is pressure you."

"I know that. It's just something I've never even remotely considered."

"I know this is a lot to throw at you, honestly I do. But I do want you to give it some thought, when you can." She let go of my hand and took a sip of her coffee. Her eyes were glistening in the candlelight and I thought she might be on the verge of tears. "Because even if you won't go with me . . . there's no way I can stay."

CHAPTER THIRTY-SIX

The next morning I was pleasantly surprised to find sunlight streaming into the apartment. A shaft of light had reached the bed and lay across Stacy's shoulder and the back of her neck. It illuminated her dark hair and captivated my attention as her subtle movements changed its reflection. I watched her for as long as I dared before forcing myself out of bed and over to the window that overlooked the harbor. Patchy clouds moved quickly across the sky, and when they did obscure the sun it wasn't for long.

I wanted to get back to Seattle before the morning was over. It wasn't quite seven yet, so there was plenty of time—as long as we didn't spend it in bed. At seven-thirty our hosts brought up hot coffee, eggs, and scones with homemade jam right to our door, and we luxuriated in our last few hours of freedom before heading back to Seattle and the case. After breakfast we packed up and drove down to Kingston to catch the ferry over to Edmonds.

It was a gorgeous day, though the heavy winds one always encountered out on the water kept us inside during the trip. We sat together watching the Seattle skyline to the south as the ferry made its way across Puget Sound. She didn't say another word about the previous night's discussion, but I couldn't help thinking about what it would mean to leave Seattle. The thought of moving somewhere else had never crossed my mind before, especially with my work and the contacts I had in the community. But I didn't have family here, either. Maybe she wasn't actually thinking about a radical move. If she just went to Olympia, or

Bellingham, I could still see her and wouldn't be forced into making a decision for a while.

By the time we reached Edmonds, the cloud cover had overtaken us and I knew it would be raining soon. During the trip I told Stacy everything I could about the case and by the time we were heading south on I-5 I was filling her in on my plans for the day. First I wanted to meet with Jim Razor, which she agreed I should do alone, and then hang out at Kurt's to see what he had come up with on Wilczek. She said to give her a call and she would meet me at his Capitol Hill apartment house later.

On Beacon Hill we made a cursory pass around the block before I dropped off Stacy. No one had been tailing her car and I was beginning to wonder if anyone ever had. We said goodbye and then I headed off to my own car. On the way I gave Carl a call at his office and his secretary informed me that she'd been instructed not to put my calls through. I told her to tell Carl it was an emergency and after a significant pause she put me on hold.

As I stood on College Street, waiting for the light to change, a few drops began falling from the sky. They were fat and heavy and I pulled the hood of my jacket over my head hoping it would keep the phone dry. Carl came on just as the light changed.

"Damn it, Ray. I told you—"

"Not to call you at the office. I know. Look, just tell them it's about the Burns case if they ask."

"You're not on the Burns case anymore."

"All right," I said, reaching the far side of the street and continuing to jog in the heavy rain. "But I need your help with something."

"Why doesn't that surprise me?"

"Come on, Carl. I need you to do this for me."

"Why should I? Irina's your lawyer now."

Jesus, I didn't have time for this. "Because I'm your friend and I'm going to be tried for murder. Come on, Carl. Please."

"Okay. What do you need?"

"I need you to look up the ownership on Wilczek's house. I'm thinking there's a possibility that he might have bought it under his own name—"

"Or his company's name, or a holding company—"

"I know, I know. But just check, will you?"

"I don't suppose I have a choice, do I?" I gave him Wilczek's address on Cedar Cove Road and waited while he wrote it down. Then he said, "When do you need this?"

"Yesterday."

"You don't ask for much, do you?"

"Come on, Carl."

"No promises. I'll call you as soon as I find anything."

I reached the car just as I hung up with Carl. The rain had been increasing the entire way and was now beginning to bounce off the pavement. By the time I climbed in the front seat I was soaked. I shucked off my wet jacket and turned over the engine, waiting impatiently for the heater to warm up. After two seconds in the car, the windows inside were thick with condensation.

I didn't want to call Razor, preferring to talk to him at the precinct. If he had the file there—and I was there with him—he might be inclined to let me take a peek. I found a wadded up McDonald's sack in the backseat and began wiping down the windows as best I could. Spare napkins in the glove box worked a little better. Finally I couldn't wait any longer and pulled out of the church parking lot and headed up to Northgate.

It took longer than I expected. One thing about rain in Seattle that has always mystified me is the seeming inability of Seattleites to drive in the stuff. I'm sure people in Minnesota are prepared for the snow and have little trouble driving in it. You'd think that people in Seattle would be similarly prepared to drive in the rain. But you'd be wrong. I couldn't even get to the onramp at Dearborn because traffic was so backed up. Rain was beating off the hood of my car and the windshield wipers were barely keeping up. I eventually managed to turn around and make it back to Boren, where at least the traffic was moving. But it still took me an hour to get to Northgate.

The Seattle Police Department's North Precinct is located across the freeway from the Northgate shopping center, next to North Seattle Community College. Razor ran the small Robbery-Homicide department there. After crawling down Broadway through Capitol Hill I decided to make a break for it and was able to get on the freeway at the 520 interchange. Traffic wasn't moving any faster on the freeway, but at least there weren't any lights. When I eased off at the Northgate Way exit I stayed to the right and looped back around to the south and across the overpass at 92nd and then up College Way.

The North Precinct is a low-slung concrete and glass structure that blends in well with the college campus next door. I dumped my car in a visitor spot, tented my jacket over my head as I ran for the lobby, and shook the water off before I went inside. It's a relatively new structure, which is to say it's newer than most of the other precincts. The old north precinct used to be in the University Disctrict, but there was no room to expand there and the department eventually outgrew building—at least that's what Jack had told me at the time of construction. This one was nice inside, with white walls and padded chairs in the waiting area, the desk sergeant comfortably ensconced behind bullet-proof glass, and a security door into the squad room that would take a surface-to-air missile to get through if you weren't buzzed in.

I gave my name to the desk sergeant and she gave Razor a call. I didn't even have a chance to sit down before he emerged from the security door. "Neslowe," he said with typical verbosity, and tossed me a visitor's badge. "In here."

I followed Razor through the squad room, presumably to his office. He was only about five-eight, with sandy-hair in a brush cut. He'd been a high-school athlete who'd taken his natural physical ability and combined it with martial arts training to compensate for his small stature. And it worked. On the one case I'd worked with him I'd seen him take down a guy twice his size—and with little apparent effort. Back then he had worn a letterman's jacket and, with his youthful face, could have gone undercover as a student. But he had traded that in for a leather bomber jacket, which went better with the more weathered look his face had now.

The squad room sported new desks with computers, occupied by detectives taking statements and uniformed officers coming and going. Around the outer perimeter of the room were glass-enclosed offices, and Razor led me to one now. He sat behind his desk and I took a chair in front. A couple large file cabinets sat in the corner, drawers not quite closed, with files heaped on top. He had a small hoop and backboard over his wastebasket in the other corner and Bobble-head sports figures and miniature football helmets poking out from the clutter on his desk. Behind him, where most cops had their commendations framed, Razor had shelves of trophies, most from high school, a few from college, and the rest from recreational leagues or police intramural events.

I looked at the nameplate on his desk. "Lieutenant, now. It's been a long time."

"Yeah. Somebody had to take over when Jack left. He called. Said you wanted to talk about the major case investigation against you."

Not a lot of beating around the bush with Razor. "I was just curious if your squad handled the crime scene or if it was all Dalton."

Razor picked up a tennis ball off his desk and began to squeeze it. "Dalton called and asked our guys to go over to your place that night and secure the scene. He showed up probably an hour later."

"How did you get in?"

"Door was open."

"So it was unlocked?"

He nodded.

"Did Dalton take over when he got there?"

"No. He and Haggerty were the only ones who came over from downtown. They asked our guys to process the crime scene."

I hesitated for a moment and said, "So you'd have a file here, wouldn't you?"

He nodded warily. "Sure."

"Any way I could take a look at it?"

Razor grinned. "Not if I want to keep my pension. Besides, doesn't your lawyer have all of this already?"

"Yeah, but it's in this huge box of files, every single thing they took out of my apartment is in there, and there's no way to know what might be important. I don't have a week to plow through the files and hope I'll figure out what I'm looking for. Besides, I have my own suspect and I need to get some proof before he figures out I'm on to him."

"So Adamson buried you in paper." It wasn't a question.

I nodded, trying to think of what to ask him next. He stood up then, walked to the door and closed it before resuming his position behind his desk, squeezing the ball in the other hand this time. "I'd like to help you, Ray," he began. "Unfortunately you've been charged with murder in an ongoing investigation. I shouldn't even be talking to you now."

"Then why are you?"

He shrugged, and thought about it for a second. "I saw the way you worked on that Beckley case, and I can usually get a pretty good read on a guy when I work with him. Plus, Jack says you didn't do it. That's good enough for me."

I just looked at him for a second and said, "Good enough to do what?"

The grin again. "I'll tell you anything you want to know, but it can't come from me. You'll have to go back to the files and find whatever I tell you here for yourself before you tell anyone. And if it's not there, you can't use it."

"Sure."

"I mean it. If you fuck me on this, Ray, I'll throw away the key for them when they lock you up."

I held up my hands. "Fair enough."

He set the tennis ball down and said, "Fire away."

"Fingerpints?"

237

Razor actually laughed then, a throaty sort of giggle, and his eyes squinted when he smiled. "Are you kidding? The place was lousy with fingerprints, every person who's ever been in your apartment, and then some. Dalton didn't even want to run them there were so many, but we have them if we need to."

"Okay." That wasn't good. "So . . . hair and fiber?"

"Uh, don't take this the wrong way, but you're not exactly Suzy Homemaker. The place was a pit. When was the last time you vacuumed?"

"All right, I get the picture. How about all the junk that Dalton took from my apartment. Did any of that turn out to be important?"

"I don't know."

"What does that mean?"

"It means I don't know if it's going to be important to you. It seemed pretty important to Dalton."

"Jesus, what is it?"

Razor sat up and looked over me out to the squad room, then he braced his forearms on his desk and lowered his voice. "Dalton wanted every single thing that had blood or tissue on it bagged and tagged. Everything. But first, he took a look around and bagged one item himself. After that he stood over and watched my guys collect the rest of the stuff. I think he'd have taken the sheet rock with the bullet hole if he could have. Finally, when he was satisfied he had enough, he told them to tear the place apart to look for evidence."

"Evidence? What evidence?"

The grin again. "Exactly. But my guys got the point and wrecked the place pretty good."

"I'll say. So, what was it Dalton found?"

"Like I said, everything else we took from your place had blood on it, but all of it had been spattered from the shots. I was watching Dalton working the scene, though. What he found not only had blood on it, but was sitting in blood, too."

"So it got there during the shooting. It could have come from the killer—"

"Or the victim, but in all likelihood one of them."

"So what was it?"

"An earring."

"An *earring*?"

Razor frowned. "Well, not like one that dangles."

Now I frowned.

"You know," he said, hands upturned. "Like something a guy would wear."

CHAPTER THIRTY-SEVEN

I couldn't believe it. "He did it."

"What?"

"What did it look like? Was it a diamond stud?"

"It was a small earring with a stone. I don't know if it was a diamond. I suppose it could have been a woman's."

"No. I know who did it."

Razor was already shaking his head. "You *think* you know who did it." But he was intrigued. "You really have an idea whose earring it might be?"

"Yeah. I need to—"

"You need to call Dalton."

I looked up at him and he pushed the phone toward me, reciting the number from memory. Doing as I was told, I asked for Dalton when the phone picked up but was told he was at lunch. I looked at my watch. Sure enough, the morning was gone. It was almost one. I thanked Razor and told him I was heading downtown to talk to Dalton immediately, but before I did I pointed to his computer. "Can you get the Internet on that thing?"

He actually laughed. "Yeah, why?"

"Could you print something out for me?"

"What?"

I grinned. "A picture of the guy who shot Pete Willis."

Outside, the downpour had tapered off to a steady rain. I

drove up to Northgate way and merged into the crawling freeway traffic going south. Things bogged down to a standstill a couple of times, once at 45th and again at the 520 interchange. Finally I bailed at Mercer and took Westlake down past the Monorail terminus into downtown. This time it only took forty minutes.

Along the way I put in a call to Irina's office and was told she was in court. Damn. I told the receptionist to get a message to her as soon as possible and gave her my cell number. Then I drove around downtown for a while looking for a place to park. Spotting an old man climbing into a big Lincoln Town Car I eased to a stop behind him and had to endure a lot of horn honking and middle fingers from angry drivers as I waited for him to see-saw his way out of the spot. But in the end I wound up only a block from police headquarters and the grief was well worth it.

I jogged up to the Criminal Justice Building and tried not to slip on the marble floor as I entered the lobby. I stood in line to get my pass, checking the inside pocket of my coat to make sure I had the picture with me, and was eventually able to head up the elevators to Robbery-Homicide. I could see Dalton shrugging on his coat when I arrived, but Haggerty was nowhere in sight. Dalton saw me and waited until I'd reached his desk before saying, "What do you want?"

"I want to put you on to a real suspect."

"I told you, the case is over."

Ignoring him, I took out the picture, unfolded it, and handed it to Dalton. He looked around first, as if we were conducting some sort of illegal activity. Or maybe he was just looking for Haggerty.

"Pete Wilczek," he said. "So what?"

"So, you must know by now that's Pete Willis's real name, and that it's not Wilczek's. He's not Polish, either. He's Romanian, and in spite of his little publicity stunt here, he's not exactly a model citizen."

Dalton stared at me, hard. "How do you know all this?"

"Because I know how to investigate."

"Hmpf." Dalton looked over my shoulder and then sat down with a look of resignation. I turned around and could see Haggerty

241

had just entered the squad room. When he reached us Dalton tossed the picture on his desk. "The peeper thinks he found a suspect."

Haggerty picked up the photo and looked at it. "Wilczek, huh? What makes you think he did it?"

"I read the files," I said, hoping like hell that the information I had was actually there. "I'm pretty sure that Wilczek left something at the scene."

Dalton and Haggerty exchanged looks, then Dalton said, "I repeat, so what?"

"So, if he left something at the scene then there's a pretty good chance he was there. And with what Wilczek's been doing it's not a big stretch to think that he was trying to keep Willis quiet."

"What exactly is Wilczek supposed to have done?"

Not knowing, *exactly*, there was no real way to bluff. "There's a lot I don't know yet—"

Dalton snorted. "What a shock."

"But I'm looking into Wilczek hard, and I'm convinced that he left something at the scene. I think there's an important connection between him and Willis, and when I get it all sorted out maybe my lawyer won't want me to go to you guys—"

Dalton shifted in his chair.

"Maybe she'll want me to sit on it and save it for the trial."

"That's obstruction of justice," Dalton said, but he wasn't smiling. "You'll do real jail time for that."

"Well, it might just be worth it to see the look on Adamson's face when we blow him out of the courtroom. So, you might just want to give your boss the heads up so he doesn't get his ass kicked right before the big election." I waited for a response, but both of them seemed much more interested in their shoes at the moment. I waited a little longer and then finally turned to leave. "You can keep the picture for your files, because there's damn sure going to be one in ours."

Well, I'd done what I could. And though it wasn't a lot, at least not yet, I knew that Wilczek had to be the guy. The earring

I'd seen in the picture had to be the one found at the crime scene. He hadn't been wearing it the other night because he'd lost it when he was killing Pete. Of course, there was no way to prove that in court; he could simply produce the mate and claim it's the only one he'd ever had. But I was confident that we could build a case against him. I still had a couple of months yet until the trial. We could canvas the neighborhood again, looking for witnesses from that night, and there was still the possibility that Wilczek's people were following Stacy and could lead us back to him. If I rolled up my sleeves and really got busy, I could probably scare up the same information that the police had—local phone records, credit history, immigration records if I could find out Wilczek's real name, as well as further information about Pete from Pennsylvania.

The rain had let up slightly by the time I neared my car. My cell phone rang in my pocket and, thinking it was Irina, I made a mad dash to get inside so I could give my full attention to the call. Once in the driver's seat I pulled out the phone and could see it was Kurt.

"Hello?"

"Ray, you have to get over here right now."

"What is it?"

"Wilczek did his payroll this morning, and you'll never guess who's on it."

"Who?"

"Pete Willis."

CHAPTER THIRTY-EIGHT

I called Stacy on the way over to Kurt's but there was no answer. It tried her cell phone, but she was either talking on it or had it turned off because it bounced me over to voice mail after one ring. Fortunately, my car hadn't had too much of an opportunity to cool down and was able to take care of the condensation on the inside of the windows and get me back on the road in short order. I called Stacy's cell phone at every stoplight, but still couldn't get through.

Kurt lived on the backside of Capitol Hill in a detached apartment behind a two-story Victorian house on 19th. I parked beneath a large oak tree that was shielding much of the rain and shedding many of its leaves, and made my way through the side garden of the house. When I reached the top of Kurt's stoop I knocked once and went inside without waiting for a response, opening the door right onto his bedroom.

After complaining for years that he didn't have enough room with his office and bedroom sharing the same space, he finally got rid of the bedroom. Instead, the bedroom was now a full office, with a large desk, two computers, and a host of other hardware, scanners, external hard drives, and printers. He had given away his bed and now unfolded the futon, in what was once the living room, to sleep on. With no bed taking up space during his waking hours, and enough room in his office to work efficiently, Kurt was a much happier man.

I took off my coat and slipped off my shoes, leaving them by the door, and padded into the office.

"Ray, you have to see this." I was standing behind him at his desk. Both computers were up and running. On the older Gateway laptop to his right he pulled up some HTML files for me to look at. "These are the phishing files that were on Anton's computer."

Kurt showed me HTML e-mail files from nearly every US bank in the country, all of them asking for the recipient to update their personal information by clicking on a link that would take them not to the bank's web site but to a Romanian site where the user IDs and passwords of anyone unfortunate enough to be fooled would be harvested. Next he showed me similar files from eBay, Amazon, PayPal, and a couple of banks.

"These are the newest ones," he said, showing me a PayPal email. "They send out this e-mail that looks like a site-generated notification of a payment, and in the customer comments it thanks them, saying that money has been transferred into the victim's account. Then, down here, it has a response button."

"Geez," I said. "Someone who's just trying to be nice and let the person know they made a mistake might click on that before they realized what it was."

Kurt nodded.

"What does it do then?"

"I tried it on an infected computer I have. It sent me to a login page."

"And if you fall for it they get your user ID and password."

"Exactly. There are a couple of other e-mails that simply send a keystroke program to the victim's computer as soon as the new browser launches, and installs it while they're waiting for the browser to load."

That reminded me of something. "Wait a minute. Where did you get all of this? I thought you only put a keystroke file on when we were there."

He grinned. "I did. Then, once Anton's computer made contact with mine, I installed a page view program that sends me a copy of everything he looks at. I did the same thing to Wilczek's, only I couldn't get it on until this morning."

"Wouldn't that slow their computer's down?"

"An ordinary program like that would." His grin widened. "Mine waits until the computer has been inactive for at least 3 minutes before sending me anything. If the computer becomes active at any time during the send, the program stops sending immediately. It means we lose a few pages on occasion, but it's worth it to avoid detection."

"This is fantastic, Kurt. So they're really into it?"

"Oh, yes. And this is just the start. Wilczek's computer is where all the financial information is kept. I had to wait until he went to lunch before I could get anything to look at. But when I saw this, I had to call you."

On his larger HP laptop Kurt pulled up a copy of an Excel spreadsheet that contained a list of a dozen names. At the bottom of the list was Pete Willis. "And this is payroll?" I said.

Kurt began pointing to columns on the screen. "These are the dates. Every two weeks the amounts are identical for each person, and you have columns here for income tax, Social Security—" Kurt laughed. "They even have a medical plan."

But all of the boxes to the right of Pete's salary were empty. He was definitely being paid under the table. Just then a big gust of wind hit the side of the house. The whole building seemed to shudder and the lights flickered. I looked to Kurt, expecting him to be uneasy about the power surge. "Aren't you afraid of losing power."

He shook his head while he worked. "I have battery-powered surge protectors—state of the art. Even if the power goes out completely I still have fifteen minutes to power down my systems. About the only thing that could put me out of commission is a bolt of lightning, and we have so little here it's not really a concern."

He continued tapping on the keys as I paced the room and thought about this new information. "I tell you, Kurt, I've been thinking about this thing for so long I'm not even sure what it means anymore."

"What's that?" he asked, without turning around.

"Well, all along I thought the reason Pete was killed was because of the threat, or implied threat, that he would expose Wilczek. But now we find out he was working for the guy. If Pete exposed Wilczek he would have exposed himself as well. It doesn't make sense."

"Okay," Kurt said. "Here's the money." I walked back to look over his shoulder. "These are the dollar amounts," he said, pointing to more numbers on a spreadsheet.

I looked for a minute and said, "There's nothing over five hundred."

"Yes, that's the way they keep from being tracked down. If they cleaned out every account, no matter how much was in it, they would start attracting the attention of the FBI. There have already been several court cases in the US won against phishers, and they've gone to jail. By taking out smaller amounts it becomes more of a nuisance. The victim can make complaints to the bank, but there's really little they can do. And as long as their life savings aren't wiped out they can move on and eventually forget about it.

"What makes these guys so successful is that any investigation into their work would only lead to Romania. The ISP they use is there, the e-mails are sent from there. It looks like the design work on the e-mails is done here, then sent to Romania. From there they send out the bulk e-mails back to the US, and when they withdraw the money they have it sent through Western Union to different spots around King County."

"That must be what those guys are doing when they leave every day."

"Sure. They go as far north as Lynwood and as far south as Auburn. That way the clerks at Western Union aren't going to remember specific people making numerous pickups. They probably put all the money into a legitimate bank here, in a deposit-only account. Then they would have money from Romania deposited in a separate account for the expenses of the business, payroll, rent, office supplies . . ."

"And all of this is on Wilczek's computer?"

"On a thumb drive, most of it. But I still have a lot of pages to look through. When he went out for lunch, I received a huge dump and just started going through it when I called you."

I shook my head. "So he doesn't have any of the financial information on his computer?"

"Not so far. He's invulnerable," Kurt said. "At least from the type of investigation he would be expecting. The e-mails, the account takeovers, the Western Union transfers, all of that takes place from Romania. Except for picking up the money, there's nothing to lead anyone to Wilczek's company. It's a perfect front."

Kurt went back to work and my stomach growled. "You mind if I raid your refrigerator? I haven't had anything to eat since breakfast." In a cozy little bed and breakfast in Port Townsend, I thought, and suddenly this morning seemed like a long time ago.

"Help yourself."

But before I could reach the kitchen my phone went off. It was Carl.

"I think I may have it," he said, as soon as I answered.

"What?"

"Wilczek's real name. It's Toma Vladescu. He's from Romania."

"That's fantastic, Carl. How'd you find it?"

"Well, the house on Mercer Island was purchased by the corporation, Global Web Development. So I looked up the incorporation papers to find the officers of the company and they're all Romanian. I had a friend of mine with the INS in Seattle run the names, and the only one that came up with a hit in the time-frame you were looking for was Vladescu."

"Where did he enter the country?"

"Seattle."

"And how long has he been here?"

I could almost see Carl grinning. "A little over a year and a half. I already faxed the information to Irina."

"That's fantastic, Carl. I really appreciate this."

"How's it going, anyway? Are you making any progress?"

"It's him. I'm almost positive. I just have to put a few more pieces together and with any luck I'll be able to prove it."

"I hope so, Ray. Keep in touch."

"All right. And thanks again, Carl."

"Any time. I just wish I could be there when Adamson has to drop the charges." I could still hear Carl chuckling as he hung up the phone.

"Good news?" Kurt yelled from the other room, and I went in and filled him in on what Carl had told me. He just nodded. "I knew he was Romanian."

I tried both the numbers for Stacy again with no luck. This time her cell phone rang a dozen times before bumping me to her voice message.

"Hey, Karl. Did Stacy call here this morning?"

"No."

"She was supposed to meet me over here but I can't seem to reach her." As I was saying the words the phone rang in my hand. It was Stacy.

"Where have you been? I've been calling you all afternoon."

"Ray," she said, almost breathlessly. "You have to get over here."

"Are you at the apartment?"

"No. I'm at Karin and Lisa's."

"What are you doing over there?"

"I felt trapped in the apartment. I had to get out. And now I'm glad I did."

"Why? What's going on?"

"I was right about being followed."

"What do you mean?"

"I'm looking out the window of Lisa's bedroom," she said. "And I can see them."

"Who?"

"The people following me. They're in a car right across the street."

249

CHAPTER THIRTY-NINE

The first thing I asked Stacy, while I put my shoes back on, was if the vehicle was a black van.

"No. It's dark blue sedan, four-door."

"How do you know the person inside is watching you?"

"There are two of them," she said. "And I remember seeing them at the apartment. The woman was driving and that's why I noticed them. Not that it was weird, but it stuck in my mind. Now they're just sitting across the street outside the entrance to the apartment complex. It's the same car."

"Can you see them?"

"Yes."

"Did you get the license plate?"

"No."

"All right. Well, just stay put until I get there. Is there a back way into the complex?"

"No. Just the front entrance."

"All right. I'll see if I can find out who they are. If I have to, I'll call the police and get them off your tail."

". . . Are you sure you want to do that?"

"Yeah. Things are breaking on the case. The police found an earring at the scene that I'm sure is Wilczek's, and Kurt is coming up with all kinds of illegal activity going on at his business. Besides, I've already talked to Dalton and he knows what's going on."

"You talked to the police already?"

"Yeah, but they already knew about it. I have the feeling they were stalling on Wilczek but I can't figure out why."

There was only silence on the other end as I slipped on my coat.

"Stacy?"

"Oh, I'm sorry. I was just watching the car."

"Look, why don't you get away from the window. I'll be there as soon as I can and we'll figure out what to do next, okay?"

"Okay."

She gave me directions to the apartment, in the Greenwood area, and I headed out into the storm. I'd left Kurt with instructions to search the Internet for anything he could find on Toma Vladescu, and left his apartment with my stomach still empty.

It was three-thirty in the afternoon but it looked like night in Seattle. The rain clouds had darkened to nearly black, and the wind had kicked up and was shaking loose anything that wasn't nailed down. Everywhere streetlights were coming on, their electronic eyes tricked into thinking it was dusk. Tree branches and leaves littered the ground and covered storm drains, pooling water out into the streets. The rain slashed down at an angle, carried on winds that felt as if they were going to lift up my car at times. And to top everything off, it was now officially rush hour. It was miserable outside.

Bad as the freeway might be, there was no way that I wanted to drive on flooded side streets, so I inched my way down Madison and sat in line to get on I-5. I tried Irina again, but she was still in court. I noticed the battery on my phone was running low so I was forced to turn it off. As the minutes crawled by, the intensity of the storm only seemed to increase.

Traffic moved slowly but steadily once I was out on the interstate, and I wound up going all the way back up to Northgate and snaking my way over to Holman Road. The apartment complex was on 3rd Avenue NW with its back abutting Carkeek Park. Trying to see through wipers that were smearing the rain more than clearing it, I was almost on top of the blue car before I saw it. I made an immediate right and circled the block, but as

I turned left, paralleling 3rd, there was another small street that turned down into the middle of the block. I parked between two houses and sat there for a minute listening to the rain pound on the roof of my car.

There was no good way to sneak up on the car. I would be exposed from the sidewalk in either direction, and from what I could see of the houses around me, almost all had fenced yards that wouldn't allow me access from the middle of the block. Finally I rooted behind the driver's seat for a folding umbrella that I rarely used and decided to risk it. I drove back around the block and parked as close as I could to the corner, behind a pickup truck, facing 3rd.

The one thing I had going for me was the rain. It would be difficult for those in the car to keep all of the windows clear unless they kept the car running the whole time—something you couldn't really do on a stakeout. Also, with the wind, I could pull the umbrella down around my face to keep it from turning inside out without looking suspicious. I figured I could get the license plate and call Razor to see if he could give me the owner. Then I was going to have to figure out some way of getting into the apartment complex without being spotted.

Rain assaulted me and the wind nearly pulled the door from my hand as I stepped out of the car. Trees in the neighborhood shook violently in the gusts, while the huge evergreens in the park beyond seemed to sway farther than they ought to be able. I couldn't raise the umbrella all the way for fear of losing it, and my pant legs below my coat were wet before I even reached the corner. 3rd Avenue was a wide, two-lane street with plenty of parking on both sides. Since all of the commercial property was out on Holman and Greenwood, it was mostly residential traffic, minivans and compact commuter cars.

I rounded the corner, and as I approached the vehicle I could see that the back window was, indeed, fogged up. There was another car parked behind it, though, so I knew I would have to get fairly close to see the plate. I slowed my pace, to give myself time to commit the number to memory before turning around. Just as my line of sight cleared the hood of the car behind, I saw the taillights come on and the car engine fire up. It startled me, and I should have turned and run, but I was even more stunned by what I saw on the license plate.

Instead of three letters and three numerals, the standard configuration for license plate numbers in Washington State, the plate was a jumble of numbers and letters, and only five at that. But it was the three tiny letters on the plate that had captivated my attention—the letters X, M, and T, running vertically along the left-hand side where the registration sticker would normally be. They meant that the car was a government-owned vehicle, exempt from registration. And that meant that it was most likely a cop car.

CHAPTER FORTY

I stared dumbly as both doors popped open and the detectives climbed out of the car. Both wore hooded raincoats, but the woman on the driver's side moved back toward the trunk of the car, holding her coat slightly open so that I could see the badge on her shirt and the shoulder holster under her arm. The male detective opened the rear door and motioned with his head.

"Get in."

I did as ordered.

Neither of them said anything to me as we all climbed inside. The folded umbrella was leaking water into my hands and I felt my pant legs clinging to my skin. The heater in the car was going full blast and between that and the wind outside it was difficult to make out the discussion in the front seat.

". . . turn to call him," the woman said to her partner. "I had to do it last time. You got some ID?" she said to me.

I handed over my wallet. She looked at my driver's license before giving it to her partner.

The man mumbled something, then thumbed his radio and mumbled some more. ". . . the Lieutenant there . . . he's here . . . then put him on . . ." While he was waiting he noticed the woman watching him and said, "Hey, Wells. Keep your eyes on the job, would ya?" She frowned at him and then looked back toward the apartment complex.

"What's going on?" I finally asked, but I was ignored again.

The man said yeah a couple more times into the radio, then

thumbed it off and turned around to face me. "The Lieu' says you need to meet him at Lambert's apartment, right now."

"What are you talking about? Why are you tailing her? What's going on?"

The woman looked at her partner and gave him a smile that was just short of a sneer, then turned back to her lookout.

The man tossed my wallet back to me. "The Lieutenant wants you there right now."

"What lieutenant?"

Still wearing the the deadpan expression he had maintained from the start, he said, "Dalton."

"Can't you at least tell me what this is all about? Why are you following her?"

The only answer I received was a heavy sigh. "Dalton says if you don't go over there now—"

"I know, I know, you'll have to arrest me."

"No, we'll get a patrol car to come over," I heard Wells say, "and *they* can arrest you."

"Yeah. We still got a job to do."

"So I'm free to go?"

"As long as it's to meet with Dalton."

I opened the door and stepped out without saying goodbye. Looking over at the apartments, I had no idea which one belonged to Stacy's friends. I could waste time trying to work my way there from the park, or I could get to Dalton and find out what the hell was going on. It only took a few seconds for me to race to my car and pull out the cell phone. When it powered up the message ring came on and I listened to a panicked call from Stacy, saying that she could see me getting into the car. I hung up in the middle of the message and called her back.

"Ray, what happened?"

"They're police detectives, Stacy."

"Oh my god. What do they want?"

"They wouldn't tell me. Why do you have the police watching you?"

"How should I know?"

The silence on the phone was deafening.

"Look," I finally said, "I'm supposed to meet Dalton over at your apartment."

"My apartment?"

"That's what he said."

More silence.

"I'm going to go over there now and find out what this is all about. Why don't you just stay put for now? I don't think those cops are going to do anything more than watch you, but the weather's a bitch and it's not going to make them very happy having to follow you around in it. Okay?"

"Okay."

More silence.

"Stacy, are you sure you don't know what this is all about?"

"Call me the minute you know, Ray. Promise me."

The dying phone beeped in my ear. "All right," I said. "Look, I gotta go. My battery's almost gone." Then I hung up without waiting for an answer.

*   *   *

Traffic was madness. As I neared the overpass across I-5 the freeway looked like a parking lot of red taillights. I skipped the onramp and went straight down Northgate Way. I was almost swamped by a bus in front of the mall, but eventually made it to 35th Avenue and was able to make good time south through Sand Point and Ravenna. Everything bogged down at 45th Street, though, and it took me a good half an hour to get across the Montlake Bridge and onto 24th toward Capitol Hill.

I tried not to think about what was happening, because my thoughts were frightening me. Why were the police following Stacy? I wanted to believe that it was because she knew too much about Wilczek and they were protecting her. And I might have been able to convince myself of that if Dalton hadn't wanted to meet me at her apartment. Maybe he thought she knew more than she had told him—which was true—but if that was the case why not just haul her in for questioning? I didn't even want to think about any other possibilities.

It was full dark now, just after five. Water was everywhere, pounding down on the pavement and running in mighty torrents along the curbs, splashing up around car tires, and sometimes rising above the curbs and flowing into parking lots that now looked like lakes with cars stranded in the center. The rain would occasionally let up in one part of town, only to resume again in another, with streetlights swinging wildly in the wind, tugging on their wires in a vein attempt to break free. And still I went on.

I felt as if I had done as much driving today as I had done circling the peninsula the day before. But this was ten times worse. Traffic sluggishly ebbed and flowed from light to light, and before long I stopped counting the times I nearly rear-ended the car in front of me. My shoulders were tense, and my neck felt so tight I thought the tendons might freeze that way. No matter—I still refused to let myself think. The thoughts were there, a nebulous mass somewhere deep in the back of my mind, but I wouldn't let them form. Eventually 24th merged into 23rd as I drove through Madrona, then I passed Judkins Park and finally made it across I-90 into Beacon Hill. I went through College and took a right on Bayview, and I could see the flashing lights before I turned onto 17th and parked.

Pushing hard on the car door against the wind, I climbed out and walked toward the building. Cops had the chinstraps of their hats down to keep them on, and clear plastic covers over the top to keep them dry. The unfortunate patrolmen standing in the rain wore blue ponchos. I walked up to one of the ponchos, gave my name, and waited while he radioed inside. When I was given the go ahead, I walked up the stairs and into the building.

Instead of going right up to the third floor I stopped on the landing, surprised to find a knot of police officers down a flight in the basement hallway. I descended the stairs and a uniformed officer met me before I had even taken a step down the hall.

"I'm sorry, sir. You'll have to go back upstairs."

"Let him through," I heard from behind the officer, and I

looked over his shoulder to see Haggerty waving me over with his pipe.

Detectives carrying boxes were spilling out of the laundry room and I became even more confused, until Haggerty put a hand on my shoulder and led me into the room. They had what must have been Stacy's locker open, and what I assumed were the contents piled on the washers and dryers. Two detectives were going through the boxes taking some sort of inventory. I looked over to Haggerty and asked him what was going on.

"Pete Willis's possessions," he said, pointing the tip of his pipe stem toward the boxes. "Everything he owned."

CHAPTER FORTY-ONE

"That doesn't prove shit, Stan, and you know it."

"We're not talking about a box of scrapbooks and high school dance pictures, Ray. She has everything down there, his socks, his underwear, the goddamned sheets off his bed, for Christ's sake, so don't tell me it doesn't prove anything."

I'd gone upstairs after talking with Haggerty and found Dalton in the middle of our apartment directing his people. He was immaculate, as always, in a black, knee-length overcoat and freshly shined shoes, and gave the appearance of a man just beginning his workday. I felt like a wrung out dishrag. We were standing over by the couch while two detectives and two patrolmen tore the place apart. Even my stuff was fair game.

"They were practically living together. What do you expect? You talked to the father—he hated Pete. Pete was moving out. You must have known that."

The sad expression on Dalton's face told me I was missing something. "Did you look into his room when you were over there that morning?"

Shit. "No."

"We did. All of this stuff was there. She took it before she torched the place."

I took a few steps away, trying to clear my head. Even after walking up three flights of carpeted stairs, my shoes still squeaked on the hardwood floor from all the water. Dalton had his eyes on his team, but he wasn't moving.

"What possible reason could she have for taking all of his stuff, or torching the house?"

"Come on, Ray. The money."

"That doesn't make sense, Stan. If she'd found the money she would have just taken it. There's no reason to take all of his stuff." But even as I said it I knew it wasn't true. There was no money to find, only a safety deposit box key. And that could have been hidden anywhere.

Dalton walked over to me and lowered his voice. "She found the money." He reached inside his coat pocket and pulled out a folded sheet of paper and handed it to me. I took it and read. It was a photocopy of a bank printout showing nine separate deposits of nine thousand dollars and three other deposits for smaller amounts, all of them made in the three days before we'd left town, each at different branches. The total was just under a hundred thousand dollars. It was Stacy's account.

"The bank has to report any deposits of over ten-thousand. She was trying to fly under the radar."

I handed the sheet back to him. "How did you find out about the money?"

"We didn't. But it's standard operating procedure on a murder case. We monitor everyone's bank accounts—even yours—and when we started getting these hits I decided to wait until they stopped before we picked her up. It's been two days since the last one and so I decided to move before she skipped town."

"How long has the tail been on her?"

"Since the first deposit."

"Were you tailing us yesterday?"

"For a while. But since you were with her, I knew she wasn't going to skip. We picked her up back here this morning when you dropped her off."

"So what the hell do you think you're going to find up here?"

"The other earring, I hope."

I walked past Dalton and sat on the couch while he went back into the bedroom to talk to one of his detectives.

Stacy. There had to be an explanation, though. It couldn't be as cold-blooded as it sounded. And now she was trapped in that apartment complex in Greenwood and I didn't know when I would be able to talk to her after the police picked her up. I couldn't stay here any longer and pushed myself up off the couch. I was heading to the door when Dalton caught me.

"Don't go up there, Ray."

"Have you picked her up yet?"

"Not yet."

"Then you'd better arrest me now because I'm going up there to talk to her."

The uniform guarding the door moved in front of me so I couldn't leave. I just stared at him until I heard Dalton's voice behind me. "Let him go."

My hands were shaking and I gripped the steering wheel hard to keep them still. The stress and the lack of food had given me a terrific headache. Could I really have been that stupid, that blind not to see it? There had to be some other reason, but I couldn't get my brain to come up with anything, so I focused all my attention on fighting through traffic with something like panic working up from inside me as I wondered what I was going to say to Stacy.

I drove down Beacon all the way to Occidental, the rain coming in sheets now, blotting out everything from view between the impotent beats of the wiper blades. Eventually I made my way onto the Alaskan Way Viaduct, staying on 99 to get to Greenwood. The red of brake lights and stoplights alternated with the blinding glare of headlights and my head began to pound. Wind shook the car, pushing against it, trying to keep me away, but I would not be denied.

It took me all the way to Green Lake before I worked up the nerve to call her. My phone was nearly dead and I had no idea what I was going to say, but I had to let her know I was coming.

"Ray, where are you?" she said, her voice so cheerful I almost thought I had punched in the wrong number.

"I'm coming up to see you."

"I'm not there. I escaped!"

"What?"

"Lisa and I crawled out the back window and sneaked over to her car. I hid in the back seat and she drove right out. I got away!"

I suddenly had the most fleeting of irrational thoughts—that she could be halfway to Canada by the time Dalton finally figured it out—before being plunged into despair. "Stacy, the police are at your apartment. They think you killed Pete. They think you killed his father."

There was silence on the line. Then she said, "I have to get out of here, Ray. I need your car. Why don't we meet at your apartment?"

The pain was throbbing behind my eyes, a bus to my right nearly buried me in a wave of water, and the phone began beeping in my hand. "Don't, Stacy. You can't get in, anyway."

"I still have your key." More beeping.

"That's not what I mean. It's—"

But there was no answer. The phone was dead, and I threw it onto the passenger seat floorboard.

I took a left on 80th, then cut back south toward Ballard on 15th. I was driving on autopilot now, trying not to think about anything. My thoughts would only torture me. I drove straight into the driveway. Tien's car was gone so I pulled all the way under the carport, even though it wasn't providing much cover with the wind driving the rain beneath it. Water had pooled on the lawn and was spilling out onto the driveway and racing down to the sidewalk. I walked around to the back door—it was unlocked—and to the inside apartment door, also unlocked, and went inside.

A single lamp was on in the corner—the one that had been on the night Pete had died—turned upright now. I could see Stacy sitting on the couch, but she didn't turn when I walked in. I went to her and as I rounded the couch I could see she was slumped over, her arms hanging down between her knees. The first thing I noticed was that she was crying. The second thing I noticed was the gun in her hands.

CHAPTER FORTY-TWO

"Stacy—"

"Get back, Ray," she said, swinging the barrel of the .38 up to chest level. "I'm not ready to do this yet."

"Do what, for Christ's sake?"

Thankfully, she didn't answer. We were frozen in tableau for several seconds before I tried again.

"Don't," she said, choking back a sob.

So I turned and sat in the chair and she lowered the gun. Her eyes were red and puffy and her mouth was set in a frown. Damp hair hung limp around her cheeks and clung to her green raincoat.

Leaning forward I said, "Stacy, please tell me what's going on."

She turned to me and wiped her face with her arm, leaving a glistening trail of snot on the sleeve of her coat. "He cheated on me . . . again. Can you believe it?" she asked, her voice raising. "I give him another chance and he fucks around on me again!"

"I don't understand—"

"That lying son of a bitch," she screamed, "cheated on me!"

I made a move toward her and she stood in an instant, the gun trained on me again. I froze.

"I'm sorry I had to involve you, Ray. But I had to find out what was going on in the investigation."

My head was pounding so hard I could barely keep my eyes open. I felt light-headed from lack of food, and I sat back in the chair feeling almost like an observer, outside of my body, wondering what was going to happen to the poor sap sitting here.

"So you killed him?"

She sniffed and wiped her nose again. "It was the most satisfying thing I've ever done in my life."

"You found the key to the safety deposit box, obviously."

"It took a while after I got his shit back to the apartment, but yeah."

"And Wilczek?"

She grunted her displeasure at the name. "Pete was working for him."

I nodded.

"Wilczek was using Pete's name in exchange for a hundred grand up front, and a job. As soon as he had all this money, he suddenly thought he could do anything he wanted, that the rules didn't apply to him anymore."

"So break up with him—"

"God damn it, Ray!" she yelled at me. Then she lowered her voice and said, "I'm pregnant."

There wasn't much I could say to that. But suddenly all the vows of love and the desire to start a new life with me suddenly made sense. I tossed the keys onto the couch where she'd been sitting. "Go ahead. There's nothing else I can do for you."

"What did you tell them?"

I closed my eyes and tried to rub out the pain. "Who?"

"The police?"

I just wanted her to go. "Nothing."

"Did you tell them about the key?"

I couldn't figure out why she was asking these stupid questions, and began to get irritated. "No . . ."

But as soon as the word was out of my mouth I realized I had fucked up. She still thought she had a chance. "Look, Stacy, they know everything, all right? They have your bank statements, all of the stuff down in the locker in the basement, everything."

"But they don't know about the key. I could have gotten that money from anyone."

I couldn't believe this. "They have your earring."

She pulled the mate out of her pocket and flashed it at me. "But they don't have this one."

It wasn't until that moment that I realized she was going to kill me. "Jesus, Stacy, please don't do this."

"I can't risk it, Ray."

"Come on, Stacy. What possible reason do I have to tell them anything? There's nothing in it for me. Christ, I'm giving you my car to escape in. You don't have anything to fear from me."

I was starting to become sick to my stomach and thought I might become physically ill. A heavy gust of wind hit the window behind her and I could see her start. But she maintained her composure and turned her attention back to me.

"Don't do this, Stacy. Please, just take the car and go. I won't even tell them I saw you here."

She was thinking—about what I would never know, because at that moment the world began to spin itself apart. The apartment door exploded in a shower of splintered wood and the two guys from the black van filled the space where it had once been. I didn't even have time to recover from being startled when I saw her bring the .38 up and fire.

I pushed myself up from the chair too late. She had hit the first man coming in the door but by then the second already had his gun out and was shouting for her to stop. I screamed, "No!" but she fired again and when it went wide he put a bullet into her chest. She hit the floor before I had even taken a step.

I knew as soon as she'd gone down that she was dead. The gunman came charging over immediately so I let my momentum carry me past Stacy and around the couch to keep him away from her. "Forget it," I shouted. "It's over."

He was a good six inches taller than me—my nose barely reaching his chin—and he had to weigh three hundred pounds easy, none of it fat. He had the same wide, flat face and short red hair I'd seen at Dewey's. This close, I could see the skin on his cheeks was freckled and looked puffy from steroids.

"Aw, fuck me!" he yelled, clearly angry that he'd had to kill someone. "That fuckin' bitch! What the fuck was she doin'?" He was still moving forward and I put a hand out to stop him. He slapped it aside, and I thought he might toss all of me aside, when we both heard a moan from across the room.

"You'd better call 911," I said. "Get someone here for your partner."

He glared at me for a moment, holstered his weapon, then pulled a cell phone from his coat pocket and dialed as he turned away.

I went back to Stacy. Her head was heavy in my hands as I checked for a pulse and found none. The gun was still in her hand and, although I knew I should leave it for the police, I couldn't stand to see her that way and picked it up and set it on the desk. As I did, I looked over to see the gunman tightening a belt around his partner's leg. When he had finished he glanced up at me. "You got a pillow?"

His partner was lying on the floor grimacing in pain and trying to hold together what was left of his thigh. I went and got a pillow from the bedroom and handed it to him. When the gunman had put it beneath his partner's head, he stood up and reached into his jacket pocket.

After what had just happened I knew he wasn't going for the gun, but now I had no idea what he was doing here. Then he brought forth a sheaf of folded paper and handed it to me. "Ray Neslowe?"

"Yeah?"

"These papers are to notify you that divorce proceedings have been initiated on behalf of your wife, Emily Richards. You hereby have thirty days in which to obtain legal council or respond to this notification and express your desire to participate in the proceedings, or forfeit any and all rights in the final decree."

I could only stare at him in disbelief.

As he turned back to his partner he said, "You've been served."

CHAPTER FORTY-THREE

It was well after midnight before Dalton and Haggerty had finished with me down at police headquarters. We stayed at my apartment first for a couple of hours going over the events of that night, then we moved downtown to discuss the previous week in detail. I gave up everything on Wilczek, everything Kurt and I had done, and what we had learned. Dalton wasn't too happy, but he decided not to bust me for it. Evidently, even he felt I'd been through enough.

It had been Dalton's idea to have me arrested the night of Pete's murder. He'd called in a favor to Adamson and had me arraigned the next day. In Seattle, the City Attorney doesn't need to go before the grand jury to go get a murder indictment. Dalton had liked Stacy for the murder from the start—and hoped that, if she thought the police suspected me, she might let her guard down and they could get some hard evidence against her.

As far as Wilczek was concerned, the police hadn't suspected anything about his illegal activities until they put him together with Willis. I had to call up Kurt that night and have him destroy everything he had pulled off of Wilczek's computers and delete the programs he had loaded on them. The police were going to need to begin their own investigation from scratch, and with something this big they didn't want any evidentiary problems when it came time to take Wilczek to trial.

When they finally cut me loose I emerged from the Criminal Justice Building not knowing what to do. I couldn't stay at either apartment even if I'd wanted to—which I didn't—and I didn't feel like hanging out at the Low Note all night waiting for Dewey and Jeannine to put me up. So I did the only sensible thing I could think of.

The rain had finally stopped. Black clouds were still moving across the sky with alarming speed, powered by a strong and steady wind that gusted only occasionally, but for the moment the rain had stopped. I stepped out of the car and pulled my coat tight against the cold. I never hesitated, though. It took a couple of minutes after I'd knocked before the door opened.

"Ray? What is it?"

"I'm sorry to wake you up like this, but I didn't know where else to go."

She stared at me for a minute, but then Emily finally opened the door and let me inside. I took off my coat and handed it to her, then removed my shoes and socks and made my way out to the kitchen. Emily put on some water for tea and sat at the table while I made myself a sandwich. Between bites of sandwich and sips of tea I gave her the short version, which still took an hour.

When I came to part about the process servers she sucked in her breath. "Oh, no. I'm so sorry, Ray. I had no idea what they were doing. I asked the lawyers if they wanted me to have you sign the papers, but they said they would take care of it. They didn't tell me anything about hiring those guys."

"Forget it," I said, and nearly laughed. "They probably saved my life."

Later on I took a pillow from the bedroom and tossed it on the couch, but Emily shook her head and took me into the bedroom with her. She held me until I fell asleep and I didn't wake up until she kissed me on the forehead as she was leaving for work the next morning.

I don't know what I would have done without Emily that first week. Most days I would get up about noon, make some tea, and sit at the kitchen table looking out into the back yard at the fruit trees. Mostly it rained. But there were hours at a stretch when the clouds would break up and permit the sun to make a futile attempt to dry things out. Once in a while I would wander out to the front window and stare at my car, but there was no place to go. Eventually I would wind up on the couch and Emily would usually find me napping there when she came home.

I didn't mope around when she was home, and she didn't try to give me a pep talk. One night, though, in the middle of the week, she said that Dewey had been up to the coroner's office to talk to her. She said he wanted me to come by some night, that he had something he wanted to give me. I nodded and answered noncommittally, but she kept pressing me until I understood that this was something I probably ought to do.

By the weekend I felt well enough to call Tien and tell her I was moving out of the apartment downstairs, although I still didn't have a place to stay yet. There wasn't much there—as Dalton would have put it, a few boxes of scrapbooks and high school dance pictures—but there were also my clothes, my computer, my business files, and my music.

On Saturday night Emily surprised me by saying that since I was already staying in the spare bedroom there was probably enough space to keep my stuff there too, just until I found a place. That inspired me to finally leave the house. Sunday afternoon I drove up to Ballard and piled my things into the backseat of the car. I left a note to Tien telling her to keep the security deposit, and giving her Emily's address so she could forward my mail.

When I was bringing in the few boxes that represented the sum total of my life, I noticed an LP that made me smile for the first time in a week. Monday I actually went to the post office for a change of address form and looked in the paper for an apartment. I did take time out, though, to put the LP on the turntable and make a tape. That night Emily called to say she was going to have to work late. I told her that was fine, that I would probably go down to the Low Note, and if she wanted to stop by we could go home together. She said she would try to make it.

CHAPTER FORTY-FOUR

The band was on a break when I walked into Dewey's place. He spotted me immediately from behind the bar and motioned with his head toward the back room. I shook him off and ordered a beer when I reached the bar.

"How are you, Ray?"

I took a pull of my beer and said, "Better. Kind of took the wind out of my sails, but I'll be fine."

He nodded. "Emily didn't have much time when I talked with her." Dewey picked up a rack of glasses and began to put them away. "She couldn't really tell me very much . . . you know, about what happened."

When Dewey looked back at me I grinned. "You want me to fill you in?"

He held out his hands, but it was obvious from the look on his face that his curiosity was killing him. "All right," I said. "But you'll have to do one thing first."

His eyebrows furrowed. "What?"

I reached in my coat pocket and tossed him the tape. His eyes lit up before it even reached him, and after he caught it he wasted no time in shutting off the tape currently playing in the deck. A few patrons at the tables—a good crowd for a Monday—stopped and looked around, but Dewey had it playing again in no time.

As soon as the first notes of the piano introduction came out of the speakers he said, "Oh, yeah," and I felt a little disappointed that he was going to get it so quick. "West Coast," he said, nodding.

"But not the guys from Hermosa Beach. Central Avenue. Sounds like Hampton and Red, maybe Larry Marable on the drums. Fifty-seven, fifty-eight, before Hamp was arrested, anyway." He seemed genuinely surprised, however, when the bari sax came in. "What?"

He looked at me and I broke into a big smile.

"Will you listen to that," he said, and started to laugh. "I haven't heard that since we were sitting around the control room with Les listening to the playback."

"Are you serious?"

He waved me off with what I knew was embarrassment. "Ah, what the hell do I want to listen to my own records for?"

I looked over at Geoff. He nodded and walked over to the tape deck and turned up the volume and the whole room was treated to the distinctive baritone sax of the seventeen-year-old Dewey Beckley. When the song was over Dewey let the tape continue to play, and after he brought over my second beer I suggested we go into the back room to talk.

"You know," Dewey said when I had finished with my story. "If it wasn't you telling me this I would have believed it."

"Well, no one wishes it wasn't true more than I do. I just couldn't see what was going on because I was working so hard trying to clear myself. Killing Pete was bad enough, but what she did to the father seems almost evil."

"She wasn't evil."

We both looked up. It was Jeannine. She'd been standing in the doorway with her arms folded, a cup of coffee in one hand.

"What do you mean?" I asked.

"Sondra," Dewey said, and I had an inkling of what Jeannine meant.

"She was never evil inside. It had to be something else. And if I go around believing that people can be evil inside then I'd have to believe the same for Sondra. And I just can't do that."

I nodded, but I guess I wasn't quite as sure.

We were silent for a moment and I heard a couple bleats of the organ's bass pedals through the wall as the band was returning to the stage. Dewey stood and said, "Come on, Ray. There's something I want to give you."

We made our way out to the bar and then he led me over to the stage. As we neared it Dewey waved a hand in front of his throat, indicating for to the band to stop. But there was only the organist and a drummer. The guitarist's equipment was covered with a sheet.

"Where's the guitarist?"

"Moved on. But I think I've found a replacement."

We had just reached the stage, and as he said this he gently pulled the sheet away to reveal my Epiphone Casino. It was blonde 1961 model with a fixed bridge and the original P-90 pickups. I could tell it was mine at once from the chip in the headstock and the wear pattern on the pick guard.

I looked at Dewey. "What's that doing here?" I had hawked it almost six months earlier to pay the rent and never managed to find the time or the money to buy it back.

But he didn't say anything. Instead he handed me a pick and climbed onstage, motioning me to follow. Sitting on the stool I picked up my guitar and plugged into a Fender Twin Reverb while Dewey warmed up his mouthpiece. I played a few chords, pleased that someone had already tuned it, and after a few minor adjustments I waited for the band to begin.

Dewey looked back at the organist but didn't call out a tune. He hit three ascending staccato notes and by the time he and the group had finished the first phrase of the song I knew we were into Horace Silver's "Peace." I played Jr. Cook's harmony line with Dewey through the rest of the head, and then comped along with the organist and drummer while he took a chorus. When he was finished he set his horn down and made me play the next five.

For nearly ten minutes I worked my way through the changes of the slow ballad, and in doing so seemed to work my way out of everything that had happened over the last two weeks. By the time the tune had finished I felt almost whole again.

Dewey came and went as the night progressed, playing a couple of songs here and there, but I continued to play, searching for that place that would make the pain go away, that place where the outside world couldn't intrude. I remember seeing Jeannine watching at one point from the back doorway, and another time I saw Emily at the bar. She just smiled at me as I went back inside the music.

It wouldn't last forever, I knew. Eventually the set would end. The musicians would stop playing, the customers would all go home, and the bar would close. But I also knew something else. No matter what happened when this night was finished, the music would always begin again.

E.B.O. / December 17, 2004, Campbell, CA.
/ June 11, 2005, Campbell, CA

It seems to me that "The Olympia Riff" began as little more than an exercise. After finishing the Steve Raymond short story "Lying Through Your Teeth," I still wasn't ready to dive right into a novel. I remember being so impressed then by my newfound ability to write fiction that I wanted to get to know my new protagonist, Ray Neslowe, by writing a short story about him first. The structure is the same as the earlier story, with sections divided by Roman numerals, ten in all, but it also sets a pattern for the novel to come by not having Neslowe actually play the guitar. Instead, he goes to see another guitarist and mentions playing, and I felt that was enough. Looking back in order to figure out the reason for this I think that, even though he was patterned after Steve Raymond, I didn't want him just to be a clone. I wanted there to be differences between the two, especially since I was attempting to move out of the realm of the amateur sleuth and write about a legitimate private investigator. So while his love of the music is very present in the stories about him, I didn't necessarily want his being a musician to play as much of a role as it did in the dental mysteries. Finally, in going back and editing the story I made the pleasant discovery that all of the characters, with the exception of the antagonist and his wife, had been named after the colleagues I worked with in my first three years of teaching. Despite the challenge of embarking on a new career—and a highly demanding one at that—the collegial atmosphere created by my colleagues is something I would never experience again. They were the best teachers I ever worked with, and honoring them in this way by making them part of another challenging and unsung profession still seems fitting, and I'm glad I did it.

THE
OLYMPIA RIFF

A Ray Neslowe Story

I

I came charging across 4th Avenue as fast as I could, grabbed the front door of the Oyster House before it shut, and ran straight into Art Prentice. The greasy musician had evidently changed his mind about going inside and turned around in the foyer. I was moving so fast that I nearly knocked him down.

"Sorry," he said.

I tried to hide my face, but our eyes met as we bumped and I mumbled my own apology. Then he left.

Son of a bitch. The guy I'm tailing runs smack into me. Good luck continuing the surveillance now. The next time he saw me it probably wouldn't take him thirty seconds to put me together with the clod who'd run into him at the restaurant. Oh, well, as long as my investigation was completely hosed, I might as well have a drink. I continued on into the Oyster House lobby and took a right into the bar, ordered a Fish Tale Ale from the bartender and decided to take a load off.

The bar was in the front end of one of the nicer restaurants along the waterfront in downtown Olympia. I was here on a case for my employer, Carl Serafin. Well, he wasn't really my employer—I'm a freelance investigator—it's just that Carl happens to get me all of my clients. He works for a big law firm in Seattle that uses a couple of larger agencies in town for their primary investigative work. But for their *pro bono* stuff they let Carl handle it with instructions to keep the expenses down, and he throws as much work my way as the firm will let him. They don't like me very much. They think I'm a screw-up, but I suppose my performance tonight wouldn't lead them to think otherwise.

The subject of my current case was one Arthur Prentice, sometime musician, full-time scam artist. His latest escapade, unfortunately for him, happened to involve the driver of an Olympia diaper service that was based in Seattle. Prentice had pulled the old swoop and squat—the how-to ads by insurance companies have been all over TV—cutting in front of the van, then stopping suddenly in order to make a few bucks on a fender bender. Prentice was going all out on this one though, claiming whiplash as well. Carl's law firm represented the diaper service and I had been hired to get solid evidence on Prentice that would expose the scam.

Now, normally the insurance company investigator would have handled this kind of case, but the diaper service was hoping to avoid making an actual claim to their insurance company by exposing Prentice first. Since it was basically a nuisance case that wasn't going to net Carl's firm a dime, he was able to farm out the investigative work to me on two conditions. The first is that I could get it done over the weekend—the claim had to be filed Monday—and the second was that I didn't get paid unless I was able to forestall the claim. From the looks of things, I would be footing my own bills for my weekend in the state capital.

I took a sip of beer and stared out past the bar across the open expanse of The Oyster House. The place was basically an open room with lots of columns and a full wall of windows that looked out onto the water of Puget Sound—the southernmost tip of it anyway—and hadn't really decided what it wanted to be: upscale seafood joint or sports bar. There were TVs mounted in nearly every corner, tuned tonight to the NBA playoffs. I thought for a second about watching the game, but eventually settled on devoting my full attention to drinking. I'm glad I did. When I saw Art Prentice being seated in the dining room I almost spilled my beer.

As soon as he sat down he craned his neck around to look at the game going on behind him, and I couldn't believe what I was missing. That picture alone would have ended the investigation. I threw down a tip and ran out of the place as fast as I could without attracting attention. When I'd run into him earlier he looked as if he had turned around because he forgot something, and now I knew what it was. Actually, he forgot to leave something behind. At the time he'd been wearing one of those white, foam braces around his neck from the "accident." Now it was gone.

II

It took a lot more time than I would have liked, waiting for traffic, in order to get across the street and retrieve the camera from my car. When I finally reached it I took out my Minolta DiMage with the built-in telephoto lens. I like to use a digital camera for doing surveillance when I'm out of town. It's often difficult to find a one-hour photo place when I need one, but there's usually a Kinko's around that's open 24 hours. Besides, a regular 35-millimeter is not only obvious but bulky, and while the digital isn't great for really long distances, it's incredibly compact and I can slip it into a shirt or pants pocket in no time. From a block away it would be perfect. I walked quickly down to Water Street and across 4th Ave to a wooden boardwalk proclaiming itself to be Percival Landing.

It was perfect. There were a dozen or so boats tied up at the slips, and the long wooden walkway of the landing looked directly across the marina into the Oyster House. Plenty of people were out walking, taking in the night air, and so my camouflage was almost unnecessary. It was a warm night in May—warm for the Pacific Northwest anyway, which means anything over sixty—so I didn't need a topcoat, and it was already beginning to get dark. I had on black jeans, a royal-blue T-shirt, and a navy sport coat. The blue sport coat and dark-colored shirt look a lot less suspicious in the beam of a headlight or if I'm seen lurking around. Wearing all black practically screams, "Hey, I'm doing something illegal here!"

I walked past a couple doing some serious necking and found a spot about ten yards away from them on the railing, directly across from the dining room. At first I pretended to take some shots of the boats in the marina, and actually snapped a couple of a gorgeous 30-foot varnished wooden ketch. Quickly adjusting the camera for telephoto I then took a look in the restaurant and searched the tables for what seemed longer than necessary. I took the camera away from my eye in disbelief and then looked again. He was gone.

It seemed impossible that I could have screwed up twice in the space of fifteen minutes. After a few more seconds I eventually located his table, but just as I did a waitress began seating a woman there. She had a walking cast on one foot and a wrist brace. She wasn't exactly fat, but she was only about five foot four, and probably went one seventy-five or one eighty. When the waitress didn't clear Prentice's beer from the table, I suddenly felt a little more hopeful. The restrooms were near the front entrance and I moved my view over toward the reservation desk.

Bingo. He strolled out from behind a knot of people and as he made his way to the table and I clicked off a couple of shots. He was about five ten, skinny, with black hair that was worn long in the back and—as I'd noticed in the foyer—hadn't been washed in a while. When he arrived at his table he bent over to kiss the woman on the cheek. Another click. Come on, I thought, wait until you're in your seat to check out the game. But he looked up for a few seconds at the TV before sitting down. I clicked another one anyway, then pulled down the camera and looked around to see if anyone was watching me.

The couple next to me had moved on to some serious groping by now. An older woman walked by with her dog and scowled at the couple, and then a group of young people, dressed in black with black lipstick, black nail polish, and spiked hair came by in the other direction. Even their hoots and hollers hadn't disturbed the couple, which was just fine. With this pair around no one was going to pay the slightest attention to me. I brought my camera back up and waited patiently. In less than two minutes he did it again. Full profile, head turned almost ninety degrees at a forty-five degree angle looking at the game. You didn't need to be an orthopedic surgeon to tell there was nothing wrong with his neck.

With my money-shot in the bank, I headed back to the car to get some establishing shots of him coming out of the restaurant without the neck brace. The photos from the landing were fine, but they weren't exactly close-ups. Together with some full-face ones as he left, however, it would be all I'd need to get paid. As I was driving around the block to reposition the car, I saw a KFC and stopped in to grab a bite to eat. Prentice and his date would be another half-hour at least, so I wasn't worried about missing him. Provisioned with wings, rolls, and a can of Coke, I managed to find a spot just up the street from the entrance. It wasn't ideal, but it would do.

So I started in with my chicken and a wad of napkins, took fifteen minutes to polish off my meal, and after wiping as much grease as I could manage off my hands, settled down to wait. After half an hour I began to wonder if I'd missed them. Fifteen more minutes went by and I had to take a leak, but by then it was too late to go into the restaurant. Besides, with my luck I'd run into him again as he was going out. Another quarter of an hour went by and my back teeth were floating. Now I was becoming seriously concerned—and not just about my bladder. It wasn't too much longer, however, before I began to hear sirens. Then, to my utter amazement, an ambulance pulled up in front of the Oyster House.

I was lucky in one respect. Had I found a spot directly across from the front door, my view would have been completely blocked. As it was, I could clearly see the paramedics hop out of the vehicle, pull a gurney from the back, and go into the restaurant as two waiters held the door. All I could think of was that this would slow down Prentice even more, sticking around to gawk at the choking victim, or heart attack, or whatever had happened.

Ah, but I had forgotten with whom I was dealing. It wasn't long before the doors opened again and out came the paramedics with their stretcher—and Art Prentice.

III

He wasn't actually on the gurney. His date was. But he was holding her hand and talking to her as they wheeled her around the back of the ambulance. No doubt comforting her with reassuring words like, "Gee, honey, we sure know how to dine and dash in style," or, "Thanks so much for holding off on your fake heart attack until I finished my coffee and desert." Of course I was snapping pictures like crazy. Once the ambulance doors were closed and the driver headed up front, Prentice ran in the opposite direction—sprinted was more like it—but by then I was out of disc space. Damn, that would have made a nice shot.

I popped the door as soon as traffic would allow and ran myself, but not after Prentice. I knew where he was going. I made a beeline for the restroom of the Oyster House. Feeling much relieved afterward, I made my way to the reservation desk and asked the gal standing guard where the closest hospital was. The only thing I received in return was a wrinkled nose.

"The woman in the ambulance," I said, assuming an

appropriately concerned expression, "I think I might know her and I wanted to see if she was all right."

This time I received and eye roll. Finally she spoke, but not to me. "Lindsey, this guy knows the two who left in the ambulance."

The woman walking up to the counter said, "Good, you can give me their names. They left here owing us hundred and fifty bucks."

Whoa. "I'm sorry, I didn't say that I *knew* them, I only said that I thought I might have recognized them. I just want to go to the hospital to make sure they're not the people I know."

The two women looked at each other and finally Lindsey consented to give me directions. "Just head uptown on 4th till you get to the top of the hill. Stay to the left and after about a mile take a left down Lilly Road."

"Thanks—"

"You can tell them I called the cops, too. They're not going to get away with this."

I was curious to know why she suspected them of anything, but I didn't have long to wait. To my left, a couple of uniformed police officers walked up to the desk and asked for a Ms. Scharmach. Lindsey said, "That's me. We had a couple of people leave without paying."

One of the officers took out a notebook and began filling out information. "What time was this?"

"About ten minutes ago. An ambulance came and picked them up."

The officer stopped writing and looked up at Lindsey. Just then a couple came up to be seated and the woman I had first talked to led them into the dining room.

Lindsey stepped closer to the officers to explain. "The woman said she couldn't breathe, that she was allergic to shellfish and she must have eaten some by accident. The guy who was with her said her throat could close up and she could die if she didn't take her medication, but she'd accidentally left it at home. Well, we took her into my office but she just kept getting worse. It was really creepy. Finally we had to call 911."

"Uh, what makes you think there's something suspicious going on?"

"First of all, the husband, or boyfriend, or whatever he was, was telling us to call 911 the whole time. And he didn't even seem that worried. And all of this happened *after* they finished desert. I mean, come on. If she was allergic to something it would have happened right away, not at the end of the meal, just before the check comes."

"Hmm." More writing by the officer. "Do you know their names."

Lindsey shook her head in obvious disgust. Then our eyes met and she brightened up, pointing to me.

Uh oh.

"But he does."

Great.

IV

"You're a real *dick*."

"What?"

The officer in charge—his name was Booth—was in his thirties with sandy hair cut short and a rugged, outdoorsy face. He was about five-eight but had a tough, wiry frame. He was looking at the business card I'd just handed him. Then he glanced at his partner and said, "This guy's a private *dick*."

"No kidding," said the partner, and he looked over at the card. He had the name Johnstone on his uniform. Johnstone was slightly taller than Booth, but thicker and softer, and showed the beginnings of a gut. His wore his hair longer and squinted through a pair of wire-frame glasses. "Sure enough. Ray Neslowe, private *dick*."

Great. I was sensitive enough about my chosen profession

around cops, but I absolutely hated it when they tried to be cute. I reached for the card but officer Booth pulled it away and stuck it in his uniform pocket.

"Listen—officers—like I told you before, I'm a licensed private investigator working on a case and I really can't give you any information without compromising my investigation."

Johnstone actually laughed at that, a tittering giggle that was kind of scary. Booth just grinned at me, which I eventually decided I liked even less.

"Get this guy," Booth said. "We're compromising his *investigation*."

But Johnstone was bored already, looking over at a full glass of beer on the bar as if he'd like to drink it and then sit down and order another. We had moved over to the end of the bar, out of sight of the dining room but fully visible to anyone coming into the restaurant. I just wanted to get outside and get the hell out of there.

"Why did the hostess say you knew those people?"

I decided to lie. "I don't know them. I'm here on a case that has absolutely nothing to do with those people who left in the ambulance—"

"Then why would it *compromise* your investigation to tell us?"

Okay, that was stupid. I shook my head. "That's not what I meant before. It doesn't have anything to do with my investigation. I just thought I might have recognized the man, is all, but now I'm pretty sure it's not him."

"That's not what he *meant*," Booth said to Johnstone. "Then what's the name of the man you *might* have recognized?"

I hesitated.

"You know, seeing as how it doesn't have anything to do with your *investigation*."

Screw it. I made something up. "Sean Phillips. We went to high school together. But he lives in California now so I really don't think it's him."

Booth smiled. "The dick doesn't *think*."

Johnstone finished writing and said, "So I hear."

"Well, then is your *investigation* just about finished . . . *dick*?"

I gritted my teeth and said, "Yes."

"Good," he said, "because we're just about finished with you, too." Booth hitched up his gun belt while Johnstone put away his pad, and the two of them left without saying goodbye.

I sat on a barstool, trying to keep my anger under control. I would have loved to punch that smug little smile off of Booth's face, but since I'd never hit anybody in my life—least of all a cop—it wasn't a very realistic fantasy. The bartender raised his eyebrows at me and I shook him off. I went into the restroom again, just to give the cops more time to leave, and then headed out to my car.

I wanted to make a quick stop by the hospital to check if Prentice's car was still there. I needed to show him the photos tomorrow morning and then get back to Seattle, so I wanted to make sure that he didn't go out of town or stay the night somewhere else. My plan was to simply tail him until he went to sleep, get my pictures printed up, then get some sleep myself. I pulled out of my parking spot and hadn't even made it to the next intersection when I saw them behind me: the Olympia cops.

V

I dropped the needle on the speedometer to thirty and held it there while we crawled together through downtown. We had to wait for a long light on Plum Street, and as we headed up the hill past the offices of the *Daily Olympian* I was sure that any second they were going to flip on the lights and pull me over, but they simply stayed on my tail. Because 4th Ave. was a one-way street, I could see why Lindsey had told me to stay left when I reached the Ralph's grocery store at the top of the hill. Pacific Avenue intersected 4th at a crazy angle and veered off toward the right. I kept going straight after the light turned green and found that the street I was on had changed its name to Martin Way. My escort was still right behind me, though, and I swear I could see Booth smiling in my rearview mirror.

The speed limit went up to thirty-five, but I stayed at thirty hoping that Booth would pass me. No such luck. This stretch of road had no sidewalks, a commercial district with businesses that operated on a larger scale. Landscaping supply, equipment rental, a veterinary hospital and a few hotels dotted the way. I was so busy looking behind me that I only just glimpsed a hospital sign as I passed a stoplight that seemed to be in the middle of nowhere.

Damn it. Should I turn around? The road went up a hill and crested onto another dense commercial district. I was almost to Lacey, I realized, and could see the sign for Lilly Road just up ahead. I pulled into the left turn lane with my tail right behind me. I had half a mind to get out and ask them what the hell they were following me for, but that was about as plausible as my belting Booth in the mouth. The light finally changed, I turned left, and two blocks later I could see the main entrance to Saint Peter's Hospital. The cops were still behind me and I was damned if I was going to lead them to Prentice's car, so I went straight.

The cops turned left into the hospital.

Of course. They knew where Prentice was and had gone the same way I did. And I'd made the bone-head play of letting them know that's where I was going too. They still couldn't be certain that Prentice had anything to do with my case, but I'd probably removed a lot of doubt. Well, there was nothing I could do about it now. I pulled over to let some cars pass, made a U-turn and went back to a 7-11 on Martin Way to take a look at a phone book. The nearest Kinko's, it turned out, was only two blocks away on Pacific.

All told, I spent an hour at Kinko's. One of the things I like about the Minolta is that it uses standard jpeg files for the photos so I can upload them to any computer, without software, just like it was an external drive. This late in the evening I had no trouble getting on one of the Kinko's PCs and had the image files uploaded and cropped with Photoshop in about a half-hour. I picked six of the best shots, and it took another half-hour to print out three photo-quality sets: one for Carl, one for my files, and one for Prentice. While I was waiting I logged on to my e-mail service and sent the image files in an attachment to Carl. Ah, the wonders of technology.

At about ten o'clock, pictures in hand, I headed back to the hospital. I circled the lot three times but saw no sign of Prentice's beat-up Honda—or Booth and Johnstone, thankfully. The address Carl had given me was in West Olympia and that's where I had tailed Prentice from earlier that evening, so I drove back through town and up the hill overlooking the Sound to go back there. The place was in a run-down residential neighborhood just north of Capital High School. I drove by, but his car wasn't there either. There were two ways I could go now. One was to simply wait for him to come home, and he would either show up eventually or not. But I could just as easily check back in a couple of hours, and with the same results. Opting for the latter, I drove back downtown.

The few times I had been in Olympia before, were usually to see Tor Petersen, a friend of mine who plays guitar. He has a group with a regular gig at The Spar, a working-class restaurant, bar, and smoke shop named after a logging term for a tall, de-branched tree that was used for hooking lines and cables. The restaurant was in the front of the place and was decked out with vintage photos of the area's long-gone timber industry. I wasn't sure if they would be playing tonight, but I stopped in anyway and felt hopeful when I heard music coming from the rear of the building. I walked on back to the bar and peeked inside. Tor was just beginning a solo. I smiled, ordered a Red Hook, and sat down at the bar to watch.

They were only nominally a jazz band; most of the changes they played over were 12- or 8-bar blues, but their song list was almost exclusively jazz. "Work Song," by Nat Adderley, Clifford Brown's "Blues Walk," and any number of soul-jazz tunes by Horace Silver and Bobby Timmons were played with tremendous enthusiasm and swing. When I walked in they were into an extended 24-bar blues that sounded a lot like Lee Morgan's "Sidewinder."

There were four musicians on the small bandstand at the back of the room. In addition to Tor on guitar was a drummer with a small Gretch kit, a bass guitar player with a Fender P. bass, and an organist. The organist was playing a C-3, smaller brother of the Hammond B-3. Though it has a significantly lighter sound than the B-3, he was playing through a Leslie speaker and must have had all the lower stops pulled out, which prevented the thin, Ray Charles organ tone and had him sounding more like Sonny Phillips.

Tor was working the middle of the neck on his Gibson ES 175. It was a 1975 sunburst design with humbucker pickups and a Venetian cutaway and, although I prefer a blonde finish myself, I knew from playing it over at his house that it was set up well and played beautifully. Tor had a dark tone, largely a result of his choice of a Polytone amplifier with a fifteen-inch speaker rather than the single or double twelve-inch speakers of most guitar amps. But he still had plenty of presence and sounded great out in front of this particular instrumentation. To break up his single-note lines, he usually threw in a few two- or three-note chords that gave him a style somewhat reminiscent of Billy Butler.

When Tor finished I applauded loudly, and he looked up as the organist began his solo. He smiled and acknowledged my presence with a quick nod. The head came around again after the organ solo and it turned out it was "Sidewinder." I don't know how long they had been playing, but Tor took off his guitar as soon as the song had ended, and the band went on break as he walked over to the bar to greet me. "Hey, Ray. What brings you down here?"

"Just doing some work and I thought I'd stop in and see if you were playing tonight."

"I'm always here," he said, grinning. "You want to sit in? Did you bring your axe?"

I waved a hand and said, "No thanks. I think I'll just watch tonight. You guys sound good."

Tor was of Norwegian ancestry, with blond hair and a slightly darker goatee that he wore around an engaging smile. He stood about six-four, and though he was in his early fifties he still looked as in shape as he had during his days of playing college football. I shook his rather large hand, and as he ordered a beer I marveled again at how he could play so well with those huge fingers.

"You need another one, Ray?"

"No. I'm good."

He received a pint of beer from the bartender, drained about half of it, then turned to me. "How's business?"

"Carl's keeping me solvent. I actually finished my case down here earlier than I thought I would."

"Where are you staying? Do you want to come out to the house?"

"Thanks, man, but I already have a room here in town. I need to do a couple of things in the morning and then I have to split. How's Kellie?"

"Good," he said, and proceeded to update me about his family.

His wife owned a nursery in town and from his account was doing all the business she could handle without expanding—which she was trying to talk him into. They also had a son who had just started college and a daughter, recently married the summer before. Then he proceeded to tell me what was new with all the local jazz musicians in town, Steve Luceno, Travis Shook, Bert Wilson, and about the passing of Bob Nixon, which I hadn't heard about. In the interim he finished his beer, ordered another, and still beat me to the bottom of my first. Eventually the talk came back around to his group. "I wish you could have seen us last week. We have this sax player in the band now and it sounds great."

"I don't know, Tor. It sounds pretty good right now, seriously. So where's your sax man?"

"He should be here, though he still can't play his horn yet."

"What do you mean?"

"Oh, he was in a car accident a few days ago. Some asshole rear-ended him."

My scalp began to tingle, but I ignored it. It had to be a coincidence.

"So, how long is he going to be laid up?"

"Oh, it's just his neck. He has to wear a neck brace for a couple of weeks, until his doctor tells him he's okay."

The tingling wasn't going away.

"Speak of the devil," Tor said, standing. "Here he is."

I finished my beer and prepared for the inevitable. When I turned it was to see a man with greasy hair and a white, foam neck brace standing in front of me.

"This is Ray Neslowe." Tor said. "Ray, this is our new sax player, Art Prentice."

VI

Of course I shook hands with him. What the hell else was I going to do? He smiled at me for about two seconds, his brow wrinkled, and then he said, "Didn't I see you . . ."

"The Oyster House. Yeah, that was me."

"Late for a hot date, huh?" He wiggled his eyebrows like Groucho Marx and it was all I could do not to sneer at him.

"Something like that." Fortunately I had finished my beer and I could leave.

"You gonna stick around for the next set?" Tor asked me.

"Nah. I gotta get going. It was good to see you again."

We said goodbye and Tor said a few words to Prentice before heading back up to the bandstand. The bartender wouldn't take my money when I first ordered my beer—probably hoping I'd run a tab—so I had to get his attention and wait for him to get down to my end of the bar. In the meantime, the band started up and I was pleasantly surprised by what I was hearing. It was the intro to "Full House" by Wes Montgomery. I gave the bartender a five and while he was getting my change I sat down to wait. When the group broke into the 6/8 section of the tune I decided to stay for the rest of it.

Tor took the first solo, but as good as it was I kept being drawn back to the solid comping of the rhythm section. For a minute I almost wished I had taken him up on his offer to sit in. Out of the corner of my eye I could see that Prentice had worked his way down to the end of the bar and was huddled there with a couple of rough looking characters I hadn't noticed before. When all three of them raised their heads in unison to look at me I picked up my change from the bar and left, exchanging nods with Tor on the way out. If I ever wanted to work in Olympia again, I was going to have to keep a lower profile.

It was only a few blocks to my hotel. Carl had done me a favor and booked me into the Phoenix Inn on the waterfront with the firm's credit card—but only for the one night. The room was clean and had a big TV, and when I crawled into bed just after midnight I flipped through the channels looking for the Jimmy Kimmel show before I realized it was Saturday, turned off the TV, and went to sleep.

My wake-up call came at five-thirty and I was out the door by six. Whenever I have to serve legal papers or deliver pictures on an assignment like the one today, I always like to get to the person's house while they're still in bed. Something about standing at the front door in boxers and a T-shirt and rubbing the sleep out of their eyes tends to make people a lot less belligerent when they get the bad news. And if I'm lucky, they don't even fully comprehend the situation until I've left.

I drove up to Legion Way first, to a little breakfast joint called Jake's for some eggs and coffee. Shorty before seven I rolled up to Prentice's house and parked behind his Honda. I took the envelope of pictures and headed up the walk, only to find the door ajar when I arrived. I turned and looked around, but didn't see any movement on the street. The sky was overcast and the temp was probably in the fifties. I was wearing a jacket and was still a little cold, which meant there was no reason for the front door to be open. I rang the bell a couple of times, laid on it for about fifteen seconds, then went inside.

"Mr. Prentice," I yelled.

Nothing.

"Hello? Anybody home?"

It had probably been a fairly nice home when it was first built, but now it was run-down and seedy. A worn, stained, pink carpet covered the front room floor and led up to a pair of broken French doors that opened into a dining room at the far end opposite the front door. Mismatched furniture, some with stuffing poking out of holes in the arms had been arranged around a small TV with rabbit ears and a low coffee table. The table was littered with beer cans, junk mail and, like a centerpiece arising from the detritus, a rather conspicuous bong.

"Mr. Prentice," I yelled again.

His car was out front, though that didn't mean much, but it still bothered me that the front door was open. I took a quick look back outside, then decided to simply leave the pictures on the table. I cleared a space for the envelope, placed the pile of photos on top, and prepared to leave. But I didn't. The most striking feature of the front room was the cardboard boxes, piles of them, stacked neatly into every corner of the place. I had to know what was in them.

After another quick peek outside, I opened one and found floor cleaner. Another had bath soap, another was full of face cream, and still another contained toothpaste. The first thought that came to mind was Amway, but the name on all of the boxes was Quixtar. There was no paperwork in the room, but through the French doors it looked as if they used the table in there for a desk so I went to take a look. The perimeter of the dining room was also lined with boxes, but the table top was completely covered with papers, invoices, sales receipts—and something that drew my immediate attention: medical bills and insurance claims.

These papers were at the end of the table where someone had left the remnants of a ham sandwich and a pile of potato salad on a paper plate. It was astounding: strained knees, lower back pain, sprained wrists, tendonitis, carpal tunnel syndrome, chronic fatigue syndrome, allergies, and a host of other maladies that could easily be faked. What was most fascinating, however, was that the majority of the claims were for a Leanne Prentice, Art's wife, and no doubt the woman I had seen loaded into the ambulance at the Oyster House last night.

Then the doorbell rang and my heart just about stopped. I threw the papers back down on the table, my hands shaking, and looked over to see the front door opening inward. I bolted out of the room, through the kitchen, looking for any other way out of the house. My heart was now racing, adrenaline pumping and in a few steps I reached a short hallway. To one side was a sliding door that let out onto the back yard. I should have gone out and never looked back, but it was too late for that now. In the other direction down the hallway was a series of doors—one of which had a foot sticking out of it.

Suddenly I was a lot more concerned about that foot than about what was going to happen to me as a result of getting caught in the house, and headed in that direction. Before I had even reached the doorway, I could see it was the bathroom. The foot itself belonged to a body, a body lying in such a way that it was obviously dead.

"Freeze," came the shout from two uniformed police officers at the end of the hall. I raised my hands, but couldn't take my eyes away from the body on the floor, the lifeless form of Art Prentice.

VII

"God dammit, Neslowe," Booth said as he cuffed me behind my back. "What the hell are you doing here?"

"Look, I'm was just dropping pictures off, that's all. The door was already open. Go look at the coffee table if you don't believe me. When you guys came in I'd already found Prentice in the bathroom."

"Prentice?"

"Yeah. This is his house. Isn't that why you're here?"

Booth shook his head. "Lady next door called 911 and said a man was breaking into the neighbor's house." We were back in the kitchen and Booth called out to Johnstone, who was still in back in the hall. "C.J., did you call homicide yet?"

"Yeah. They'll be here in a couple of minutes."

"Okay. I'm going to take this guy out and put him in the car."

"Wait a minute," I said. "I didn't do anything."

"Get this, C.J., the *dick* didn't do anything." But there were no smiles and laughs this time as Booth pushed me through the living room and out the front door. At the squad car he reached in the front, popped the back door, and started to push me inside.

"Wait a minute. Why are you calling homicide? You don't know it's a murder."

"It doesn't matter what I think."

"Check the body. I mean, how long ago did that woman call? Prentice has been dead a hell of a lot longer than five minutes."

A pained expression contorted Booth's face. "You don't get it, do you? If I find a dead body and you're standing over it, I have to arrest you. I don't get to cut you loose. The homicide detectives will have to do that later. So just sit in the car until they get here."

"What about the cuffs?"

He just shook his head as he put a hand over mine and pushed me into the back seat. Booth then disappeared into the house and, as promised, a few minutes later an unmarked car, another patrol car, and an ambulance showed up. The coroner arrived a little later. By now there was a crowd gathering on the opposite side of the street. Caged in the back of the car, the only thing I could hear was a barely audible garble from the radio in the front seat as I watched law enforcement personnel going in and out of the house. After about twenty minutes Prentice came out in a body bag and headed off to the hospital, most likely to be pronounced dead on arrival by an emergency room physician. Another twenty minutes later Booth finally came out to retrieve me.

"You're in luck," he said, hauling me out of the car.

"Why?"

"You'll see."

Inside the front room two detectives were huddled with Johnstone, going over his notebook. The tall, thick-chested one with dark, curly hair and a matching beard turned as we came in. "Is this the guy?"

"Ray Neslowe," Booth said. "Private detective out of Seattle."

The detective frowned at Booth. "Take the cuffs off. Then I want you and Johnstone to get out and start canvassing the neighborhood. Find out if anyone was seen going into the house other than this guy."

Booth did as he was told, and though I couldn't see his face I could definitely feel the heat coming off him. It was clear he didn't enjoy taking orders. But the detective ignored him as he made introductions. "Detectives Krupp," he said, pointing to himself, "and Berg," thumbing toward another man, taller, with thinning hair and glasses. "What were you doing in here this morning?"

As I explained to Krupp, his partner took notes, and I gave them the whole thing, from the baby diaper van right on up to getting cuffed by Booth. As I spoke, however, I realized that I didn't have an alibi for last night once I'd checked into my room. Prentice had still been at The Spar when I left, and so he must have been murdered during the night at some point. And after being caught in the house with him this morning I was obviously going to be the prime suspect. They probably figured we had argued about the pictures, and that Prentice said he was still going through with the insurance claim in spite of them. Naturally I would have become angry with him because I knew I wouldn't get paid if he did that, even though the pictures proved it was a bogus claim. And so that left me with no choice. The only way I was going to be able to collect a fee for my time and keep Prentice from making the claim would have been to—

"Okay, you're free to go."

VIII

Something didn't add up. As I sat in my car, staring at the back of Prentice's Honda, I still couldn't figure it out. Why had I assumed he had been murdered? Because that's what always happened to guys like Art Prentice. Eventually they scammed the wrong person and ended up with a bullet in the head, or a knife in the back, but they didn't end up on the bathroom floor from a heart attack, or whatever the hell they thought had happened to him.

And whatever it was, Krupp wasn't saying. I'd tried to pump him for information but he wasn't having any of it. When I asked for my pictures back he just shook his head and told me I could put in a request at the police station and get them back after the case had closed. Finally he made me give him my card and promise to make myself available if they needed any further questioning, then he dismissed me. I had to admit, I didn't like it any better than Booth had. On the other hand, what was the point? My case was finished and I was free to head back home. But the whole thing still bothered me, and was going to keep on bothering me until I found out what had happened to Prentice. That didn't seem very likely at this point, however. Short of becoming a cop myself, I had a feeling I was never going to get anything from Krupp. And then I had an idea. Why not get a cop who could?

Booth and Johnstone's car was long gone, but since they had been on last night at the Oyster House they must be working overtime and were probably due to be off soon. I drove back downtown at a good clip and took a right on Plum, where I knew the city hall was located. I didn't know precisely where the police station was, but I was pretty sure it would be close by. Eventually I found it out near I-5. It was a low-slung brick building with a fenced parking lot, and the only thing that distinguished it from any other government building were the few police cruisers parked among the other vehicles there.

Inside the front entrance was a modern-looking raised desk along the side, and I asked the desk sergeant there if Booth and Johnstone were still on duty.

"Why do you want to know?"

"I was a witness last night to a medical emergency at the Oyster House. They asked me to meet them after their shift because they had a few more questions to ask me."

Sergeant Underhill was a heavy-set woman who looked to be in her late forties with dark hair already beginning to go gray. And she wasn't buying it. "I can't give out that information. If you like, I can give you their number. You can leave a message and the officers will get back to you."

"Gee, that would be great."

She actually stared at me for a few seconds, as if trying to determine whether or not to believe me, before finally giving me the number. To my credit, I didn't run out the door when I left.

So I parked across the street near the pay phones at the back of a Chevron station and waited for Booth and Johnstone to show up. An hour later I was having déjà vu, wondering if I was in completely the wrong spot or if the two officers were already home in bed sleeping. They showed up, however, a little after ten, and I instantly wished I had parked farther away. After tailing me last night, they could hardly help but recognize my Cavalier. Fortunately they drove straight into the parking lot and didn't look around as they walked into the building. I had to wait another half-hour for them to emerge in their civilian clothes, and when they did the two of them climbed into the cab of a green Toyota pickup with Booth doing the driving.

I was even more exposed as I tailed them back out to Plum and then up to 4th Ave. Because of the long lights, I couldn't afford to have more than one car between us, and for most of the trip I was directly behind them. But either they didn't notice or didn't care as we took the same path I'd been on last night, down Martin Way and on into Lacey. The truck eventually made a right in between a Red Lobster and an Olympia Pizza, but drove past the restaurants to a small parking lot next to the movie theater in front of an Irish pub called O'Blarney's. Again, the two cops went up to the door without looking around, knocked, and after a minute or so were let inside. I went up to the door a few minutes later, but it was locked. The sign said it opened at eleven, and a glance at my watch told me I still had ten minutes to go. So I sat in my car like a kid waiting to go on his first job interview. It wasn't exactly that I was nervous so much as apprehensive about their reaction to my intruding on their personal time.

When I saw the waitress unlock the door I walked up and went inside. To my right was a small dining room and to the left were bar tables and pool tables. The bar itself connected the two rooms. Other than employees, the officers and myself were the only other people in the place. I walked over toward them and could see they had already started on a couple of beers.

Booth looked disappointed to see me. "I thought that was you at the gas station." Then to Johnstone, "They really ought to keep the doors locked a little longer around here."

Johnstone nodded. "Keep out the riff-raff."

"The undesirable element."

"The low lifes—"

"All right," I finally said. "I didn't come here to be insulted."

Booth just looked at me, took a drink of his beer and said, "What do you want, Neslowe?"

"I want your help."

Johnstone tittered and Booth grinned. Leave it to me to lighten the mood. It had been a morning of surprises, but none more than when Booth said, "Have a seat."

As I pulled out a chair and sat down, the waitress came over to take our order. I hadn't planned on it, but decided to get some lunch to go with the Moss Bay ale they had on tap. Johnstone drained his glass and ordered one as well. Once she had gone, Booth sighed and said, "So, what do you want?"

"Just one thing—how did Prentice die?"

The two men smiled at each other and Booth said, "I told you it was your lucky day." Then his grin widened. "Didn't Krupp tell you?"

"He just ordered me out of the house. I was never so annoyed to be cut loose in all my life."

Heads nodded all around, then Booth's expression turned serious. "Give me one good reason why I should tell you?"

I thought for a second, but the only thing I could come up with was, "Professional courtesy?" They both laughed at that. Yeah, I was a regular comedian.

"Look," I finally said. "The reason I was tailing Prentice in the first place was because of an insurance scam. When I was in the house I saw paperwork for all kinds of things that could have made people pissed off at him. I just doesn't make sense that if this guy slipped in the bathroom and hit his head on the toilet, or whatever happened, that someone else didn't help him along—someone who was the wrong person to piss off. I don't know. It just didn't make sense that Krupp let me go like that. He didn't even want to hold me on the B and E."

"Now *that*," Booth said, pointing at me, "was professional courtesy."

"What?"

"If it had been me, I'd have thrown your ass in jail for being in that house, no matter what had happened to Prentice. But Krupp doesn't work that way. He looks at the big picture. And in the big picture of this case, you weren't important."

"Tell me why not."

Booth looked over at his partner. "C.J.?"

Johnstone said, "I was with Krupp and Berg when the ME was making his examination. He said that the victim's throat had involuntarily closed due to an allergic reaction. The most likely cause, he said, was from shellfish of some kind."

IX

The food and the beer came at that moment, giving me a minute to digest what Johnstone had said about Prentice being allergic to shellfish.

"You know," I said, around a bite of club sandwich, "that's why they went to the hospital last night. The Oyster House?"

"Right," said Johnstone. "But it was the woman, not him. And besides, by the time they got to the hospital she had been miraculously cured."

I smiled. "You guys checked out the hospital?"

Booth shrugged. "That's what we do. The two of them wouldn't sign a consent form or give the hospital any personal information, so they had no choice but to release them against medical advice."

"Then who gets stuck for the ambulance bill?"

"The restaurant, I guess," Johnstone said.

"But isn't that illegal?"

"It's a case for small claims court, not the police."

For the next few minutes the three of us concentrated on our food. But after a while I thought of something else. "Where was the wife, anyway?"

"Huh?"

"This morning. Where was Prentice's wife, Leanne?"

Booth nodded. "We found out from the neighbor that she works as telemarketer at a boiler room down in Tumwater. Evidently she'd stayed with her sister the night before. Krupp wanted her to come back up to the house so he sent us to pick her up."

"After our shift was already over," grumbled Johnstone. He had finished his second beer and was waving the empty glass at the waitress.

"Isn't that a little early for telemarketers, to be calling people on a Sunday morning?"

Booth shrugged, "Maybe they're calling back East. Who knows?"

"I thought Congress was trying to stop that that stuff."

"Again, not our jurisdiction."

I nodded. "So, how'd she take the news?"

"Well, she wasn't in very good shape to begin with."

"I know."

The two of them exchanged glances, and my scalp suddenly began to itch. Booth had been wiping his mouth with a napkin and set it down very slowly. "What exactly do you know?"

I was a little confused now and held out my hands. "You know, the walking cast on her foot, the wrist brace . . ."

Johnstone said, "I don't think we're talking about the same woman."

I described her to the best of my ability but, though they admitted it could be her, they were obviously not convinced. Then I remembered the pictures. I went out to my car and retrieved them and when I showed them my photo of Leanne Prentice they agreed it was the same woman they had picked up that morning.

"And you say you took these last night at the restaurant?"

"Yeah."

Johnstone frowned. "The miracles continue."

"What do you mean?"

"He means," Booth said, "that she didn't have a cast on her foot or her wrist this morning when we brought her back to the house."

"But I thought you said she was in bad shape?"

Booth was already nodding, but didn't say anything right away. Johnstone was still staring at the photo. "Yeah," Booth said, finally. "She'd been beaten up pretty good—black eye, fat lip, bruises on her arms."

I took the photo from Johnstone and looked at it again. "But last night she was fine. That means—"

"He knocked her around last night," said Booth. "So what?" But he was challenging me with his eyes. He wanted me to say what he already suspected.

"Well, it's just that when I was in the house, looking over all of the insurance claims, I noticed that most of them were for her. She had the cast and the wrist brace. She went to the hospital last night. What if she told him she'd had enough, that she didn't want to work his scams anymore? He gets mad and knocks her around, so she decides to cut out to her sister's, but not before slipping him a Shrimp Louie for a nightcap. He croaks while she's at her sister's and when she comes home the next day her problems are over."

Booth took a noncommittal bite of his hamburger while Johnstone drained another beer.

"Well?" I prodded.

"It's a theory."

"It's more than a theory. The pictures don't lie. We should go over there right now before she has the chance to destroy evidence."

Johnstone laughed, but Booth was not happy. "In the first place, Neslowe, there is no 'we.' And in the second place, this is not our case. I couldn't do that even if I did buy into your murder theory."

"You don't think it's possible?"

"You're missing the point. The homicide detectives already have the case. If somehow she managed to slip him some Oysters Rockefeller along with his Hamburger Helper last night, they'll figure it out."

I fumed for a minute and then said, "Come on. Wouldn't you like to put one over on Krupp, solve the case and get credit for the collar?"

Several more customers had drifted in during our conversation and our waitress began spending more time over on the dining room side. Johnstone had evidently had enough and headed to the bar himself for a refill.

"Thirsty," I said, when he was out of earshot.

"We pulled two double-shifts in a row the last two days. We have twenty-four hours off before we report back again. I'll probably have to pour him into bed this afternoon."

"So, what do you think? If it doesn't pan out, Krupp never has to know that we were even there."

Booth had finished his burger and shoved the plate out of the way. "I don't know how they do things on re-runs of *The Rockford Files*, but in the real world we have a chain of command. Now that might sound stupid to civilians, but in police work—just like the military—it works. And while I don't necessarily get along with Krupp, he's my superior. He's the one trained to deal with this kind of stuff," Booth nodded at the photo on the table, "not me. The only thing I would ever do in a situation like this is go to him with the information. But that's it. I would never go behind his back, and neither would anyone on the force, for two reasons. First off, Krupp is good, very good, and I don't have any doubt in my mind that he's already figured out this angle and has either written it off or pursued it. Second, not only is it career suicide, but when I eventually get promoted up the chain I want my subordinates to show me the same respect." He took a sip of his beer and leaned back. "At the end of the day, Neslowe, it's not about me and Krupp, it's about serving the people of this community. That might sound corny to you, but then I really don't give a shit what you think about it."

I could only nod in agreement. "Fair enough."

Johnstone came back, his beer already at half-mast, and said to Booth, "You wanna shoot some pool?"

"Just a second," I interrupted. "When I first came in I asked you guys if you'd do me a favor."

Johnstone's eyes widened. "This wasn't it?"

"What?" said Booth.

"Get me in to see Krupp so that I can show him the picture."

Booth just stared, apparently disinclined to help me, and so I gave him what I could.

"I'm just a civilian but I have a conscience, too. I have to go back to Seattle today and I'll never know if this picture might have been important to the case. Maybe Prentice did die by accident. Fine. But at least I can go home with the knowledge that I did everything I could to figure out what really did happen. I realize there's absolutely no reason why you should do this for me, but I'm asking anyway."

Booth looked over to Johnstone, who had a pained expression on his face. "We could stop at the store," Booth suggested. "Pick up a half-rack before I take you home."

With that Johnstone relented and the three of us stood up to leave. I flagged down the waitress, but she must have assumed I was a police officer as well and didn't have a ticket made out. I paid for my meal anyway and in the parking lot Booth told me to meet them in the lot behind the station.

Booth and Johnstone led the way into the rear entrance of the building, took some good-natured ribbing from other officers for showing up back at work soon, then took me up the stairs to the detective squad room. It looked just like any other modern office building, with chest-high partitions dividing the space into cubicles. As we rounded the end of a corner cubicle I heard one of the loudest eruptions of laughter in my life and a second later could see that it was Detective Berg standing outside one of the cubicles. He stopped laughing when he saw the three of us and I heard him say, "Lester," and nod his head toward us. Detective Krupp's head emerged from the center of the cubicle as he stood to see who it was.

Berg was chuckling again as Booth approached, but Krupp simply said, "What's up?"

"Neslowe here has something he thinks you should see."

I showed Krupp the photo and laid out my theory about what might have happened. He looked up at Booth when I was finished, but Booth didn't apologize. Then Krupp looked at his watch and said, "Well, we were just about to head down there. You might as well come along and see this."

Booth and Johnstone looked at each other as Krupp and Berg led the way. Nobody seemed to notice me as I tailed along behind. At the bottom of the stairs we turned in the opposite direction from the back door and walked down a hallway lined with rooms along the perimeter of the building. Krupp and Berg stopped at a door, nodded toward the one next to it, and then stepped inside.

I followed Booth and Johnstone into the other room, dimly lit with a large window opening onto an adjoining room. I quickly realized it was one-way glass and that I was behind the mirror of an interrogation room. I was introduced to Lieutenant Karr and an assistant district attorney whose last name was Albert, who were also in the room, but what was most fascinating was what I could see through the mirror.

Berg was standing off in the corner with his arms crossed, while Krupp sat at a Formica covered table with his back to us. Across from him was a man dressed in a suit and tie—the defense lawyer, no doubt—and next to him was a slumped and battered Leanne Prentice.

X

Booth was right: Krupp was good. Very good.

For nearly an hour Krupp sat and talked without asking Leanne Prentice a single question. He simply laid out the case as he had uncovered it, point by point, beginning with the medical records he had obtained of her husband's allergic reaction to shellfish. He moved on to explain the discovery in the house of prescription slips for epinephrine in various forms to counteract the allergic reaction. They had been made out for her husband and verified as legitimate by his doctor. Krupp had also located the pharmacy where they had been filled, with dates and amounts, but said that there was no sign of the drugs anywhere in the house, including the bathroom. All of this in less than twenty-four hours, I realized.

Next he moved on to the cause of death itself. Finely shredded pieces of crabmeat had been found throughout the potato salad that her husband had been eating and would eventually, upon autopsy, be confirmed as the reason for the allergic reaction. He went on to state that the larger bowl of salad in the refrigerator indicated that it had been homemade and therefore her husband would have had no reason to be suspicious of the ingredients. After the allergic reaction began, he had headed straight for the bathroom. Most of the contents of the medicine chest had been found in the sink, indicating the victim had been looking for epinephrine to stop the attack. Not finding the drugs, the victim suffocated before he could leave the bathroom to reach a telephone.

Now Krupp moved on to Leanne herself. He went over one by one the multiple insurance claims for various illnesses and injuries found in her name and then brought out the copy of my photo from last night. By this time, however, the shock had worn off. Her lawyer had made a couple of attempts to end the interview, but since she hadn't been expected to comment he'd been persuaded to stay. After the photo Krupp explained that she had even gone to the emergency room the night before claiming to have the same allergy that her husband had, but that there were no supporting documents among her medical records to show this. He also brought up that she had obviously been beaten the night before by her husband, and that fact, along with being found the next day without the walking cast and the wrist brace, clearly indicated a desire to end the medical fraud that was going on. He also added that the removal of the cast and brace before she had apparently known of her husband's death could also indicate prior knowledge of his death. That was something I hadn't thought of.

It was a masterful performance, one that might not have worked on every suspect, but was clearly having the desired effect on Leanne Prentice. At one point I even caught her lawyer shaking his head. Krupp finished up by outlining the probable chronology of events the previous night, explaining how the investigation would proceed—interviews with friend and co-workers—and outlining the trial process. By the end of it she was blubbering, the handkerchief she had been using to wipe her eyes wadded into a tight ball in her fist. The lawyer put an arm around her, attempting to stand her up, encouraging her that she had nothing to fear, but in the end it wasn't enough.

"I'm sorry," she said through the tears.

"Leanne! Don't say any more."

"It's not like you planned it out," Krupp said calmly.

She nodded, staring at the table. "I just couldn't do it anymore."

The lawyer stood and shouted, "This interview is over. Right now."

Mrs. Prentice looked up at him as if she didn't know who he was or why he was there, then lowered her eyes again. "After he beat me up I knew it was never going to stop."

"Leanne! Stop this. Please."

"He was going to keep making you do it," Krupp added.

"I had to do it."

The lawyer threw up his hands and walked in circles.

"Tell us what you had to do, Leanne."

"This is all inadmissible," the lawyer shouted. "This is against my direct council."

Now she looked almost annoyed with him, before turning her attention back to the handkerchief in her palm. I expected her to tell Krupp about the medical fraud, but instead she said, "I put the crab in his salad."

"That's enough," shouted the lawyer.

"But you had to do something else, too," said Krupp.

She nodded, as if realizing she had left something out. "I had to take his medicine."

At that point Krupp stood and turned to the lawyer while Berg stepped over to take Leanne Prentice by the arm. "You're right, counselor. I think we're finished here."

I looked over to Booth and Johnstone. Both had smiles on their faces, shaking their heads as if they had just witnessed an incredible performance by a professional athlete. Johnstone even said, "Now *that* was worth coming back for."

Out in the hall I saw Detective Berg taking Leanne Prentice away, and then I shook Booth's hand. "Thanks. For everything."

He shrugged and then grinned. "I guess you're not such a bad dick after all. Chalk it up to professional courtesy."

"Well, I appreciate it." Then I turned to Krupp. "I want to thank you, too. I know you didn't have to let me in there. That was terrific work."

"You're welcome. Having your photos helped. We'd have had the information eventually, but it would have taken a few days to interview all of the witnesses. In a case like this, if the witness thinks you know everything right away they figure they don't stand a chance."

"Will she be charged with murder?"

"Initially, but the D.A. will have to decide on what to indict her."

"Anyway, I appreciated seeing you in action."

He smiled, but then looked at his watch, clearly ready to move on. Booth said he and Johnstone had to be going and we were just about to take off when my cell phone rang. I looked at the number. It was Carl.

"Down the hallway and to the right," Booth said before taking off with Johnstone. By this time Krupp was long gone.

I nodded and answered the phone. "Carl."

"Ray. I just got the pictures. Fantastic. What did Prentice say when you showed them to him?"

"Uh . . . well, what could he say, really?"

Carl laughed. "So, I take it he's not going to be filing a claim?"

Before I could answer I suddenly had a horrible thought. Would the firm refuse to let Carl pay me if they knew Prentice was dead? And then I realized just as suddenly that I wasn't about to take that chance.

"Nope," I said. "I think we've seen the last of Art Prentice."

ABOUT THE AUTHOR

Eric B. Olsen is the author of six works of fiction in three different genres. He has written a medical thriller entitled *Death's Head*, as well as the horror novel *Dark Imaginings*. He is also the author of three mystery novels, *Proximal to Murder* and *Death in the Dentist's Chair* featuring amateur sleuth Steve Raymond, D.D.S., and *The Seattle Changes* featuring private detective Ray Neslowe. In addition, he is the author of *If I Should Wake Before I Die*, a collection of short horror fiction.

Today Mr. Olsen writes primarily non-fiction, including *The Death of Education*, an exposé of the public school system in America, *The Films of Jon Garcia: 2009-2013*, an analysis of the work of the acclaimed Portland independent filmmaker, and a collection of essays entitled *The Intellectual American*. His most recent book is *Ethan Frome: Analysis in Context*, a contextual close reading of Edith Wharton's classic novel. Mr. Olsen lives in the Pacific Northwest with his wife.

Please visit the author's web site at https://sites.google.com/site/ericbolsenauthor/home or contact by email at neslowepublishing@gmail.com.

Printed in the United States
By Bookmasters